PERCHANCE TO DREAM
Fairytale Anthology Book 3

www.YeOldeDragonBooks.com

Ye Olde Dragon Books
P.O. Box 30802
Middleburg Hts., OH 44130

www.YeOldeDragonBooks.com

2OldeDragons@gmail.com

Copyright © 2023 by the included authors

ISBN 13: 978-1-952345-96-8

Published in the United States of America
Publication Date: May 1, 2023

Cover Art © Copyright 2023 by Kaitlyn Emery

All rights reserved. No portion of this book may be reproduced or transmitted in any form or by any electronic or mechanical means, including photocopying, recording or by any information retrieval and storage system without permission of the publisher.

Ebooks, audiobooks, and print books are *not* transferrable, either in whole or in part. As the purchaser or otherwise *lawful* recipient of this book, you have the right to enjoy the novel on your own computer or other device. Further distribution, copying, sharing, gifting or uploading is illegal and violates United States Copyright laws.
Pirating of books is illegal. Criminal Copyright Infringement, *including* infringement without monetary gain, may be investigated by the Federal Bureau of Investigation and is punishable by up to five years in federal prison and a fine of up to $250,000.

Names, characters and incidents depicted in this book are products of the author's imagination, or are used in a fictitious situation. Any resemblances to actual events, locations, organizations, incidents or persons – living or dead – are coincidental and beyond the intent of the author.

TABLE OF CONTENTS

FOREWORD

Wow! This is our third year. We are so excited! Three years of bringing you amazing new stories so far outside the box they are practically in another galaxy.

This year, we had a record number of submissions and it was terribly difficult to say no to any of them. They were all *so good*. You are holding our largest volume ever! Our returning authors allowed us to revisit familiar places, like Stoney Setzer's bizarre Sardis County, Tennessee. We saw this phenomenal little town in our very first anthology, *When Your Beauty IS the Beast*. And Meaghan Elizabeth Ward introduced us to Callanway Broch in *Tales from the Tower*. We're so pleased to see their sagas continue in our volumes. But many other returning authors like Pam Halter, Beka Gremikova, Kathleen Bird, Kaitlyn Emery, Michelle Houston, and Lindsi McIntyre brought us brand new landscapes and characters to charm and delight you, our readers. We're so grateful to each and every one of them for their creativity, for their stories. They raise the bar with every anthology!

Then we have another group—our new writers. And we have several this time! Hailey Huntington, Laurie Lucking, Angela Watts, Rosemarie DiCristo, Jessica Noelle, and Allison Tebo are new to Ye Olde Dragon Books, and we are so pleased to add them to our happy family. They have added such dimension and creativity to our world, and we are excited to see what they'll do next. We have everything from a princess who can't seem to get a good night's sleep to a space-faring community willing to sacrifice one young woman to a cryofreezing experiment in the name of science. Now that's a huge leap, isn't it? We have humor, horror, fantasy, and science fiction—a little bit of 'something for everyone'!

I love all our writers, but if there is one thing I live for—one thing that truly warms this old dragon's heart: getting a new writer into print for the very first time. I live for those moments because I remember the thrill of my first time in print so long ago. It doesn't happen often, but once in a while, we do have that honor. So I'm happy to say that we are honored to present Christy Eberling's debut story *Frozen Beauty*. She did such a superb job and we were thrilled to offer her first contract.

You are holding a labor of love. This book was pulled together despite a lot of health issues, family issues, and crisis after crisis from *all* parties involved. Yet, despite it all, you are holding the fruit of our labors.

And we will continue to do this work as long as God gives us the strength and grace, for it is what we love to do.

You, the readers, make it all worthwhile. We are grateful for your continuing support, and we love you all! We hope you enjoy the journey.

Deborah Cullins Smith
April 2023

Part 2:

Ditto to what Deb said. Joys and crises, discoveries and moments of "Remind me again why we're doing this?"

You, the readers, combined with our authors, returnees and new friends, make this all worthwhile.

Keep an eye on the **Realm Awards** this year. Nearly twenty stories from last year's two anthologies have been entered in the competition. I'm looking forward to seeing several of our authors walk up onto the platform to accept an award.

And do try to visit the **Ye Olde Dragon's Library storytelling podcast**. As we move into Season 2 at the end of May, we're adding author interviews to the mix, and we're giving our Ye Olde Dragon authors first dibs on claiming time and dates to chat – about their stories in our anthologies, other books they've written or are working on, their writing journey and their plans and hopes for the future.

And keep an eye out this fall, where our theme for the third **Classic Monsters anthology** will be *Creature from the Black Lagoon*. Tentatively titled: ***Don't Go In the Water!***

Keep up on all our shenanigans at *YeOldeDragonBooks.com*.

Michelle L. Levigne
April 2023

SLEEP
Rosemarie DiCristo

They lied to you.

The true story is like nothing you've been led to believe.

But I suppose a story about a dewy-eyed fifteen-year-old princess awakened by her true love's kiss is heaps better than the reality: that the princess is thirty-eight years old, with middle age spread and varicose veins caused by her thirteen kids.

Yeah.

Thirteen.

Obviously, the prince has already kissed me. And not while I was sleeping.

Oh, relax, it's all on the up-and-up. We're married. But have you noticed how almost every chronicle of the so-called adventures of people like me (you know, "fairy tale characters") ends at the marriage and is silent about the happily ever after?

Don't misunderstand.

I love my man.

I love my children.

I also (ahem!) love that thing you do to get children. All thirteen of them are "love children." But there are thirteen of them.

Thirteen!

Anyway, here's the real story, recounted in my own words, as I spoke and thought them on the day that it happened. Or, as close to those words as I can remember. After all, it's been one hundred years.

~~~~~

Something, anything has to change.

I mean, look at what my life has become.

I've spent nearly two decades pregnant, and without fail, get pregnant again just a few months after giving birth.

I have thirteen kids, names and ages as follows: Paxton, fourteen; Dunstan, thirteen; Celia, twelve; Amalia, ten; Thorston, nine; Phyllia, eight; Grixton, seven; Veelia, six; Elston, five; Lillia, four; Julia, three; Auston, eighteen months; and Thalia, seven months.

I know what people think: "You're a princess; you have servants; how bad can things be? You probably don't even see your kids except maybe at mealtimes, when you all sit around a super-huge table eating rich and royal food cooked and served by a bevy of servants."
~~~~~

Wrong.

We're a progressive kingdom. No servants. Workers, yes, but they have rights, and jobs, with salaries. And to prove we-the-elite are *not* so elite, we have jobs, too. Just no salaries.

Prince Michael's job (he's my hubby) is going out on quests. That basically involves him riding around the countryside on his glorious white steed with all his friends on their somewhat-less-glorious steeds. They hunt and fish. They have archery contests. They swim and hike and take part in all sorts of athletic exploits.

My job, if you haven't already guessed, is bearing, raising, caring for, and feeding… thirteen children. And while, technically, I can employ my subjects to help with all that, it's thirteen, *thirteen*, **thirteen** bloody blasted children, and after about one week of helping, each and every one of my employees, invariably, quits.

Do you know how much food we consume? This month it was twenty-five pounds of pork chops, thirty-five pounds of ground beef, and forty pounds of chicken wings, all packaged and portioned and ready to cook because, yes, we have supermarkets here. But we've also discovered that keeping cows and laying hens saves lots of money where fresh milk and eggs are concerned. Time, not so much, since I do the milking, the gathering, and the cooking.

Do you know how many diapers I go through? Fifty a week. I wash them all. And that's cloth diapers, since we don't want the plastic ones ending up in landfills. (But what, exactly, will all that soap and excess water do to the environment? We've got no idea).

Then there's the hundreds of other clothes I wash, plus the five hours of folding and sorting, and, oh! do *not* get me started on the ironing.

Paxton, Dunstan, and Celia, my three oldest children, help a little with all the work, but they're still kids after all and want to play. And in any case, the others make so much of a mess that it's impossible to keep up even with the oldest kids helping. And of course, the youngest three (that's Julia, Auston, and Thalia) are still in diapers and there's a polka-dotted unicorn doing backflips in the palace moat…

Huh? What? Oh, sorry. This has become a several-times-a-day thing for me: dropping off to sleep, mid-sentence. In a "mid-sentence" that often makes no sense. But that's because, well, heck, I'd give anything for a real night's sleep because sometimes (no, often) I hallucinate like I just did because there are really no unicorns anywhere in our kingdom. At least not anymore, but there's a red light burning on the patio…

Crud. I just did it again.

It's the youngest two who are driving me crazy. Oh, they're sweethearts, don't get me wrong, but they are still in… diapers. Oh, drat! I said that already. Yeah, well, it's something that bears repeating.

They're in diapers.

Here's the deal with those youngest two.

Auston and Thalia need feeding. (And not to be too-much-information, but that's not bottle feeding).

Plus, Auston and Thalia wake and cry every night. Every. Night. Whether I feed them or not. Man, you can almost set your clock by them. They cry at 9 p.m. At 11:30. At 2:15. Then at 3 a.m., at 5 a.m., and one last time as dawn breaks.

They usually start with urgent, rasping grunts that mean they'll soon be yelling non-stop. Auston roars with rage if he's not propped up in his crib. Thalia lets out an unending squealing wail if she's not lying down in hers. And through it all, my hubby the prince, if he's home at all, bangs on the walls, bellowing, "For goodness' sake, shut them up. I can't bear it any longer. Shut them up!"

You might think Prince Michael's a beast, or at least an awful example of a husband, but I'm afraid his parents and mine, plus all those servants we call employees, as well as the palace guards and everyone else within earshot of my babies' wails, feel the same. Because they all live in the castle with us, and they're sick of the crying.

They think I can't cope, that I'm a failure, that I'm doing something wrong. Mom says I'm doing nothing wrong besides worrying too much, therefore my anxiety is being communicated to Auston and Thalia and that's why they cry. Michael's mom says I'm too lax with the older kids; why don't I *demand* they help me? Yes, well, why don't you demand Michael stick around and help you with your stuff instead of expecting me to do it for him and you?

Sorry. Sore point with me.

Even the employees and palace guards are quick to offer advice. No one is quick to offer help. And absolutely no one has been sleeping well.

It's an awful lot of pressure on me and it builds onto the gnawing, relentless weariness I already feel that sucks every bit of joy I should have toward my family clear out of my mind. I'm out of my mind. I really think I'm totally and completely out of…

Sorry.

Lately, I've been trying a new routine that I hope will not only prevent darling hubby from banging on the walls, but also keep everyone else in the palace from hearing Auston and Thalia's shrieks. Each night, placing Auston on my left hip and Thalia on my right, I carry them down-down-down to our former dungeon (in our enlightened palace we no longer use dungeons), where I sit on the floor, babies on my lap, back propped against a damp stone wall (that way, there's less danger of my hurting myself or Auston or Thalia if I topple over when I slip into sleep) and let them yowl away.

I jig them up and down. I murmur sweet nothings. I sing them lullabies. But they stay restless, sometimes actually turning aggressive. Biting, for instance. Not wanting a feeding when I think they do or wanting one when I think they don't. And always, always bawling their sweet little heads off, until the dawn.

That's when the other eleven kiddies leap from their bedrooms, and it's time for my day to begin. Again. When it never really ended.

But it has to end, or, at least, the craziness and utter exhaustion do.

Maybe it's me. Maybe I *am* a failure as a mom. But what can I do differently? Well, with thirteen kids (it's summer, and none of them are in school) I can't leave the palace, so I summoned Pansy to give me advice. She's the oldest and wisest of the seven fairies in our kingdom.

"How do I care for a large family without going out of my mind?" The words burst from my lips the second she was ushered into my antechamber. "What do I do? How do I do it? How can I find a servant — er, no, sorry, *employee* — who won't go out of her mind, too, and quit on me? Dang, *are* there any servants left in this kingdom, or serfs, or prisoners, or even one of my own passel of kids who I can force to do my bidding? Why are Auston and Thalia so much more colicky than any of the others were, and how can I stop it so I can get some peace?"

Wise, beneficent Pansy leaned forward and intoned, "When the children are home, try to limit the distractions."

"My children are always home," I protested. "And they are the distractions."

"Seek out quiet times of contemplation," she advised with a beatific smile.

"I don't remember what 'quiet time' means," I wailed.

"And always remember, Eleanore Dawn..."

I leaned closer to hear Pansy's sage words of advice.

"Sit-down family dinners are supremely important."

"Our dinners are a madhouse because there's multiple 'sit-down' tables for the kids, me, Michael, our folks, his friends, visitors like the King of Darvinia..." My sigh rose up-up-up from my shoe-tops as, regretfully, I dismissed Pansy.

Next, I summoned Daisy, who's a little less old and slightly less wise than Pansy. I begged her for "Just a little respite. Really. A teeny-tiny break. Then I'll gladly take care of my kids again, because I truly adore them, and adore being a mom."

Daisy smiled encouragingly, so I rushed on. "Or — this is much better — give Michael a taste of what my days are like. Just a smidgeon of an inkling. Because then I'm sure he'd gladly share the work with me. He's a good man, really. He's a prince. Ha! I'm talking right now about the dictionary definition, meaning *a good fellow*. Am I rambling too much? I guess exhaustion makes me ramble too much..."

Daisy's smile was patient and understanding as she pronounced, "Organization is the key to keeping your clutter at bay."

Clutter? Wait, did I mention clutter? Or had she seen past my anteroom into my bedroom? I snuck a quick look back. No, impossible, the doors were tightly shut. I said kindly, because Daisy is my second-favorite godmother, "But if thirteen kids, one prince, plus all his friends *create* the clutter..."

Her smile grew more patient and twice as understanding. "Then everyone needs to pitch in to help."

"But if thirteen kids, one prince, plus all his friends *are creating* the clutter..."

"Then make some quiet time for yourself, Eleanore Dawn," Daisy interrupted, gently. "Don't neglect *you*."

Again, with the quiet time. I dismissed Daisy, too.

Alas, that was oh-so-typical of Pansy and Daisy. Really. When you consider that, at my christening feast, all my fairy godmothers gave me gifts like *let her have a temper as sweet as molasses* or *let her sing like a nightingale and dance like a hollyhock in the wind*, it's clear that none of them are equipped to live in the real world.

"If only Nightshade were here to offer advice," I carelessly muttered. Despite Nightshade's reputation as the most evil fairy on the continent, I'd heard she'd lived well after leaving our kingdom. She'd married a handsome, rugged man and had more kids than I did. Of course, rumor is that she turned hubby into a toad when he refused to share in the housework...

Hmm. *What a useful gift that would've been,* I mused, then shook my head and summoned Aster, the most worldly of the good fairies.

"Godmother Aster, please. You're my last best hope," I cried out as she entered my antechamber. "How do I take care of a family of eighteen people? That's counting the kids and the folks, you know, but not counting me. No one counts me. I'm the crazy worker-bee, yes, crazy, I'm going crazy here—"

"Eleanore Dawn—" Aster began, but I overrode her.

"Is it because I've got thirteen kids that I can't cope? I love my kiddies, but—"

"Eleanore—"

"—there are thirteen of them and two can't sleep the night—"

"Eleanore—"

"—and the other eleven need me to pick out their clothes and find their lost baseballs or sew up their torn rag dollies or—"

"Eleanore Dawn!!!!"

I gulped and shut up, but then, in a small, meek voice whispered, "I mean, I love them, I do, and Michael can be a sweetheart when he's around and the babies aren't crying —"

Aster twirled one hand and suddenly my lips were zipped shut.

I mean that literally. Aster has that power. I couldn't speak if I wanted to.

I scowled at her. Even if Aster's a fairy, I'm a princess, and what she did is a punishable offense, even in our enlightened kingdom. But she's Aster, my favorite godmother, so my brows unclenched as I nodded once to let her know I'd keep quiet this time, and she twirled a hand again.

She spoke before I could. "Face facts. You've got thirteen kids, Eleanore Dawn. You ain't gonna have peace until —"

"When?" I interrupted, my voice agonized.

She eyeballed me like she might twirl that hand again, but instead said, "When your youngest turns fifteen or so, you'll be lucky if she wants to get within one hundred yards of you. Teenagers, right? And by then, the rest of your lot will be grown and gone."

"So…" My words came haltingly. "You're telling me I've got to put up with this for…?"

"About fifteen years. Unless…"

"Unless what?" I was afraid to ask but the words burst forth anyway.

"You're only thirty-eight." Aster smiled a cheeky smile. "I didn't go through my changes until I was fifty-six. I think you know what I'm implying."

I did and screamed a low but piercing scream.

That night, I tried bringing my two howling offspring to the attic. I'd grown tired of damp, drafty dungeons. And there, inside the doorway, as if waiting for me, was Nightshade.

People have warned me for years that Nightshade is dangerous. Well, that's kinda-sorta true.

But only kinda-sorta.

Danger is sometimes in the eye of the beholder.

I've always found Nightshade fascinating. And not only because of the toad thing.

Like, even though she must be over four hundred years old, she looks younger than I do. She dresses in black, clingy gowns, has sleek jet-black hair, full pouty lips painted a dark, blood red. A real fashionista, you know? While Pansy, Daisy, and Aster are plump podgy little matrons who dress only in pale, safe, pasty pastels and yards and yards of tulle sewn into fluffy puffy wide-skirted ball gowns that went out of style eons ago and when did it get to be such a long slog of a walk to my attic because gloriosky, my feet feel like…

Oh, crud, I sleep-slipped in front of Nightshade. I peered at her anxiously.

"Tired, my pet?" she asked, and smiled a slinky, sly smile. Then she stepped aside to show me what her body had been blocking.

It was a spindle. Probably the only one left in our kingdom, because of the great danger spindles present to me. I'd been warned of this my entire life, along with other nuggets of wisdom, like "look both ways for horses before crossing the road."

Involuntarily, I backed away a few steps. The movement sent Auston and Thalia wailing.

Nightshade gestured to the spindle. "Just reach out. Touch it. And all will be well."

"Well?" I twisted my lips and informed her, "Yeah, right, I don't think so. My folks told me exactly what that does."

Yeah.

Right.

They told me what *exactly* that does.

I cocked my head at Nightshade.

Her smile was serene. "A curse is a curse only if it harms you."

I thought back to what the last fairy had gifted me with on that long-ago christening day. "It'd just be sleep, right? Not death?" My voice was almost shrill with the need to know.

"Sleep," Nightshade promised. "Not death. For one hundred years."

A century of sleep. For me, and the kingdom. "And no one ages in all that time?" I questioned.

Her nod oozed compassion as she gestured to the spindle, so I gently placed my babies in Nightshade's arms, scrunched my face, shut my eyes, and started to thrust a fingertip forward. But first...

"Don't put the entire palace to sleep," I implored.

"I'm a mom, too, and a wife," she murmured knowingly. "I'll leave fourteen people awake. Prince Michael..."

"...And all our children. So he can know what it's been like."

"Agreed." She grinned at me.

That's when I rammed my fingertip into the spindle.

END

THE SPINDLE TRAP
Beka Gremikova

Today, Theryn would curse her family.

And today, she would save them.

She closed the door of the tower room and slid the bolt in place—more out of habit than any real fear she'd be interrupted. The only people left in the palace were her parents, herself, and her loyal maid, Hylda. In celebration of her momentous sixteenth birthday—also the anniversary of the day she'd been faery-cursed as a baby—she'd suggested the servants be given the entire week off from their duties to spend time with their families.

Her parents had complied, little suspecting it was all part of Theryn's plan. While a wicked faery had cursed her to die by spindle-touch on her sixteenth birthday, Lady Luce, a family friend and faery, had altered the spell into a century-long sleep for Theryn and those within the castle.

Now, she intended to make great use of that sleeping spell. But there was no need to sweep the innocent servants into her insanity against their will. She swiped her fingers across her skirts and sucked in a deep breath before turning to survey the spacious chamber.

Over the past six months, she'd slowly accrued everything she'd need for her hundred-year sleep. Against one wall sat a four-poster bed complete with the softest mattress she could find, full of large, fluffy pillows. Not far from the bed nestled a cot for Hylda.

And, most importantly, in the middle of the room—

"You got the spinning wheel!" Theryn breathed.

Hylda, her unwilling yet loyal accomplice, grunted in response from her seat at the wheel. She frowned at Theryn from behind her glasses. "Do you know what it took to smuggle this in here?" She traced her fingers across the dark wooden spokes. "If the ministers find us—"

"They won't." Theryn had prepared for that, too. She strode over to the window and gazed out at the fields of golden wheat that stretched far off into the distance. "I sent them on a witch-hunt for spinning wheels all the way to Ildebar." From this vantage point, far-away Ildebar—the floating city ruled by faeries and known for its giant, magical swans—glimmered like diamond-spangled clouds.

"Every last minister went?" Hylda snorted. "How did you convince them to do that?"

Theryn leaned her elbows on the window ledge. "You know how they are. I told them I was getting more and more paranoid the closer we got to my birthday. They ate it up with a spoon and rushed off to save the day."

She wasn't sure who she disliked more—the ministers or the faery who had started all this trouble to begin with. At least with the faery curse, there seemed to be a positive side: Years ago, Theryn's estranged uncle had been turned into a beast—and had been showered with riches, honour, and sympathetic attention because of it. He'd even been gifted a kingdom of his own from a dying king.

No wonder her parents didn't talk to him anymore. Not that they talked to each other much, either.

"Those ministers would scale mountains to get on your good side, I think." Hylda shook her head.

"There's only one way to get on my good side right now," Theryn muttered. "And none of them are willing to do *that*."

No, the ministers were not backing down from their endorsement of her father's decision to break away from his marriage to Theryn's mother. And Theryn suspected they may have planted the terrible idea in her father's mind, though she couldn't fathom *why* they would do such a thing. All she knew was that six months ago, she overheard her parents arguing between themselves—and arguing with the ministers. Then the parade of paperwork and divorce proceedings had begun.

When she'd broached the subject with the Head Minister of Castle Affairs, he'd merely given her a pitying glance and told her not to worry about anything, that she'd be taken care of.

Theryn gritted her teeth. This was about far more than just her.

Her mother had always said to do what was best for the kingdom— and indeed, their land had flourished under her parents' care. Now it was Theryn's turn.

She could picture all too well the strife that her parents' divorce might cause in the kingdom: nobles would take sides; currency would have to be altered; and who knew what would happen to foreign relations with other nations.

No, the ministers had to be got out of the way. And since Theryn found violence distasteful, she figured the distance of a century would work just as well. It could be her family's new start.

A chill breeze swept off the fields and blasted her in the face. With a shiver, she turned away from the window and wrapped her shawl tighter around her shoulders.

Hylda tilted her head. "Are you nervous?" she asked softly.

Theryn studied the spinning wheel with its mass of spokes and shining spindle. She reached out...and yanked her hand back. She was confident in her plan to distance her family from the ministers, but there was one aspect that terrified her. The other side of the curse—waking up from a kiss. "Did you get my notes to Lady Luce?" she asked as she plucked at the frayed hem of her shawl.

Hylda nodded, rising and fluffing the pillows on the bed. "She'll make sure to find a nice prince and ask him those questions you wrote before she sends him to wake you."

Some of the tension eased from Theryn's limbs. If the prince couldn't pass Theryn's interview, she didn't want him anywhere close to her lips. But she'd written other things in her letter to Lady Luce. Most importantly, she'd entrusted their kingdom—and all its inhabitants—to Ildebar's care while she and her parents slept. "Thank you. You—are *you* certain you wish to come, Hylda? Your children are out there—"

Hylda's eyes watered. "And my grandchildren," she murmured. She sighed. "But they understand why I have chosen to accompany you. A maid must serve her mistress—and a mother longs to protect *all* her children. Including those bound by soul and not by blood."

Theryn's lips wobbled.

Then Hylda scowled, and within a few blinks she'd turned from a doting mother to an irate one. "But I still don't think you should be doing this at all, my child—you shouldn't be trying to solve your parents' problems for them."

Not this conversation *again*. Theryn's nerves faded under a wave of prickling heat. She resisted rolling her eyes and swept closer to the spindle, the heels of her shoes rapping against the cobblestones. "I must *try*, Hylda. Mother and Father are too close to the situation to understand the consequences."

Hylda squinted at her. "And perhaps *you* are too far from the situation to understand the context."

"They're *my* parents! Surely there's nothing more to understand?" Her parents loved her, she loved them, and once they were far away from the ministers, everything would be all right.

Hylda shook her head with a sigh. "There's always more to understand, my dear."

Theryn bristled at her maid's patronizing tone. "Well, perhaps *you* would like to ask them, then."

Hylda sucked in her cheeks. She knew as well as Theryn that such a thing would not go smoothly.

"That's what I thought." Theryn rubbed her hands together and nibbled on her bottom lip.

This was the best course. At the end of the century, Lady Luce would find a nice prince, ask him a few questions, and, if he passed the test, give him a nudge to the abandoned castle, where he'd kiss Theryn awake. Then her parents would snap out of whatever insanity the ministers had suggested and make up.

There was no way her plan could go wrong.

She took a deep breath. "I know you don't entirely agree with my methods, Hylda, but thank you for your help." She leaned over the spinning wheel. "I—I think I'm ready now." She didn't want to think about Hylda's words, didn't want to let the maid's doubt leech into her confidence.

Hylda hurried over, her arms outstretched to catch Theryn when she fell. At least, that was the hope; Lady Luce hadn't been quite sure how quickly the sleeping spell would set in for the others in the palace.

Theryn stretched out her hand, her fingers trembling slightly. She shook out her limbs.

When she woke up, she'd be on the other side of a century. She would forge a better future for those she loved—away from prying eyes and meddlesome mouths.

She settled her finger against the spindle. The point didn't even break her skin. Still, the hazy fog of magic crept over her, and she yawned. Her eyelids fluttered. Hylda helped her to the bed, where Theryn crawled under the blankets and hugged a pillow to her chest.

Hylda sank onto the cot, covering a yawn with her hand. Another breeze snuck through the window, and Theryn caught the crisp scent of autumn air before sleep took her over completely.

~~~~~

She woke to the young, startled face of a prince very close to hers. Freckles spotted his nose and cheeks. His dark eyes widened.

"It worked!" His voice came out slightly higher-pitched than she'd expected—he couldn't have been much older than her, then. He cleared his throat. Spots of color made his freckles pop.

He was…rather *adorable*.

Theryn pushed aside the surprising notion and instead said calmly, "Of course it did," before she sat up to rub her eyes and shake out her hair. She didn't want to meet her parents looking sloppy.

"You…seem rather calm about being kissed by…a stranger," he stammered.

She tossed back the blankets and speared him with a questioning look. "You *did* receive my note from Lady Luce, didn't you?"

The poor boy stared down at his hands, his face going redder. "Yes. The fairy…she asked me questions…and…gave me a note. It—it said I had your p-permission to…" He swallowed and waved at her. "To kiss you."

His discomfort with the whole situation eased her. At least this part of her plan was going smoothly so far. If this was a portent of what was to
~~~~~

come...

"Yes, that's all fine," she said. "I decided that if I had to be kissed by a stranger, it must be someone *I* found worthy."

Better a prince with a sense of propriety and manners than one who thought he could take whatever he wanted without consequences.

The prince scratched at his neck, then adjusted his well-worn tunic and cleared his throat once more. "Well, please excuse my forwardness anyways. My name is Prince Edvyn of Ildebar."

"Ildebar?" Her heart quickened. "So you and your family have been looking after our kingdom for us, then?"

Edvyn wandered over to the window, brushing off the thick layer of dust from the ledge. Theryn followed him and grimaced as pain stabbed at her joints. She peeked over his shoulder. Not much seemed to have changed in a century, except Ildebar looked much closer now. It hovered over the wheat fields while giant swans carried people back and forth from the sky.

"We've tried our best," he said with a sigh. "I suppose you and your parents will take over again?"

"That is the hope," Theryn murmured, riveted to the scene before her. She'd never visited Ildebar herself—had never seen it so close...

How much else could change in a hundred years?

Edvyn sidled away from the window, fidgeting with the colourful tassels on his sleeves. "Umm... Forgive me, but I don't really know the proper next step. I've never rescued a princess before. Am I supposed to pro—" He seemed to choke on the word. "*Propose* now?"

"Not so fast, little sir," a groggy voice muttered from nearby.

Edvyn started and whirled around.

"Good morning, Hylda dear." Theryn wandered over and kissed her maid on the cheek.

Hylda stretched out her arms and cracked her knuckles. "Have you seen your parents yet?"

"I'm on my way right now." Theryn turned to Edvyn with an encouraging smile. "Hylda just wants to make sure she approves of you before we continue with any official betrothal business. We can discuss the next steps later on." Once they could sit down with her parents and she could get their opinions. She bit back a giddy grin. She couldn't wait to see them without the ministers there to poke their noses in business that was none of their concern.

Hylda grabbed the back of Edvyn's collar and towed him over to the spinning wheel's stool. She forced him to sit and stood in front of him, arms crossed. "You go on, Theryn."

Theryn patted the prince's shoulder on her way to the door. "She won't bite you, I promise. Meet me at the throne room when you're done.

And maybe get him something to eat, Hylda?" Theryn slipped out into the hallway, down the curving staircase, and into the silent castle.

It felt strange to walk the halls knowing that everyone who once worked within them had died. They'd stayed with their families, worked the fields, grown old, had a new generation take their place...

She blinked back a wave of awed dizziness. If she thought too long on it, she'd muddle her mind. She had to focus on the reason why she'd done this in the first place.

Her parents were in the throne room, slumped sleeping at a paper-strewn desk. Theryn's heart leapt at the sight of them, and she quickened her pace.

As she approached, her mother sat up first, blinking and yawning. She stared at Theryn, brow furrowed. "Theryn? Wha—what day is it? It's—it's still your birthday? We didn't miss it?"

Theryn swallowed a laugh. "Well, maybe by a hundred years...but it's all right."

Her mother's face paled, and she shot to her feet. "The—the curse? It came to pass?"

But Theryn was staring down at the papers on the table. A chill curled down her spine as she read the official legal headings. "You were discussing your divorce on my *birthday*?"

Her mother bit her lip. "The ministers were rather—rather insistent..." She trailed off as, beside her, Theryn's father shifted and stretched.

"Oh, bother the ministers!" Theryn wrapped her arms around her mother's shoulders. "They can't hurt you now." It made her queasy to see her calm, controlled mother so nervous.

"Hurt *her*?" Her father's voice, slightly groggy yet still sharp, broke in. "You needn't worry about *that*."

Theryn bristled. "Well, I *did* worry!" she snapped. "You can't just put away the queen because the ministers say so! They don't run this country!"

Her mother flinched, and she stepped away from her daughter.

The king stared blankly back at Theryn, his gaze reticent. "You don't understand, Theryn." His eyes flicked to the queen, and his lips curled slightly. "Let us handle this. Don't concern yourself."

Don't concern herself? Over matters of her own family? As if she were some stranger with no stakes in how this played out? Theryn choked down her vitriolic reply.

"You don't understand! *I* handled this! Who do you think invoked the curse?"

Her mother wobbled. "*You* brought the curse down on us—*on purpose*?" She stumbled a few steps and braced herself against the table.

The inkwells rattled.

The king started to laugh. He doubled over, clutching his stomach.

What was going on? Theryn backed away, glancing at her mother for answers, but the queen stood stone-faced, her shoulders hunched. Gone was the sure, regal woman Theryn had always known. Her mother looked…guilty.

"She's just like you," the king gasped as he wiped his eyes. "Can't leave a curse alone." He grew sombre, and his voice went cold. "Go on, Theryn, ask your mother the truth behind your curse."

Chills skittered up Theryn's arms. She tugged her shawl tighter as her mind raced. What truth? What had she missed? What had been kept from her?

What element had she completely missed in her careful planning?

She turned to the queen. Her mother didn't flinch, though her eyes gleamed softly. "I suppose if I don't tell you, he will."

"She wants answers so badly, might as well give her the real ones." The king's voice broke on the last word. He stared at the queen as though he were assessing an enemy he'd once loved and trusted.

The queen sucked in a breath. "I…I asked the faery to curse you."

Words strangled in Theryn's throat. She swallowed them down and tried again. Her voice came out as a croak. *"What?"*

"Oh, it wasn't supposed to be a *killing* curse—"

"But she hired the wrong witch," her father said flatly.

This was all too much even for Theryn's brain. Her knees buckled, and she crumpled—

A pair of unfamiliar arms caught her, and she found herself pressed against someone's chest.

"Pardon me," Edvyn's voice murmured in her ear.

She could only lift her head and nod. She turned her attention back to her parents, desperate for answers, *anything* to explain the pain tearing into her soul. The room seemed to spin, and she shook her head to clear the fog.

"Why?" she asked finally.

How could this be happening? She'd had everything planned so perfectly—

And perhaps you are too far from the situation to understand the context. Hylda's voice slid through her thoughts. Theryn didn't think her maid had known—but perhaps she'd suspected the truth would be far darker than Theryn was prepared to accept.

"Even…even before his curse, your uncle always outshone your father—even though he'd done nothing to deserve it! He wasn't even the Crown Prince! When he turned into a beast and had that ridiculous sob story, everyone ate it up. Riches, honor, fame—all for a prince who spent more time arguing about politics than doing anything to fix problems.... If *I* had magic, I'd have cursed him, too!" The queen paced, her face flushed. "Because of his curse, his new kingdom *flourished*. I just wanted to give our nation the same attention and honor. I wanted a king who *deserved it* to bask in those rewards." She turned to Theryn, her arms outstretched, her eyes wide and pleading. "Surely you understand? Haven't I always taught you to do what's best for the kingdom?"

Was *this* why their land had always been so well cared for? Not because her parents had done good work, but because their coffers had been filled with sympathy gifts for having a cursed daughter? Not because they'd truly been better than her uncle, but because they had *believed* themselves to be?

Not because they'd used their talents for the benefit of their citizens, but because they'd used *her*?

"So...you...asked the faery to curse *me*?" The family she'd fought for, the family she'd longed to protect...had they even been worth saving? Hylda had given up time with her children and grandchildren—for *this*?

"Can you blame me for being angry?" The king's nostrils flared. "I *just* found out six months ago—I mean, six months before your sixteenth birthday." He glared down at the papers in front of him. "The ministers were only putting *my orders* into motion!"

Theryn's vision blurred. She'd had it all wrong the entire time.

Edvyn shifted his stance behind her, sucked in a breath as though he were about to say something. She grabbed his arm, which was still wrapped around her waist in support, and squeezed. She gave the slightest shake of her head and hoped he understood the message.

He sighed, but the tension did not ease from him.

Her parents seemed to notice the prince for the first time.

"Who's this?" her father demanded.

"The prince who woke me," Theryn said when she could speak without letting a sob escape. "Edvyn of Ildebar."

Her mother's eyes narrowed. "I don't think he should be privy to any more of this discussion."

"Fresh air sounds lovely," Edvyn said coldly. Theryn stiffened in surprise at his tone. "If she'd join me," the prince continued, "I would like to invite the princess for a turn around the gardens. We can leave you to discuss your proceedings in the...*secrecy* you desire."

"I'll go with him," she blurted before her parents could answer.

Her parents exchanged a glance and, in unison, nodded.

Theryn barely felt Edvyn half-carry, half-drag her outdoors, where a crisp autumn breeze chilled the tears on her cheeks. He helped her sit on a stone bench just outside the palace gates.

"I—I'm so sorry," he whispered.

She wiped her eyes. She felt like a court jester, an absolute fool. For once, she had no answers, no confident reply. She leaned over, gripping the edge of the bench. "I...I don't know what to do. What to say." This world felt strange to her, menacing. It wasn't the future she'd concocted.

"I hope I didn't step out of line back there." He edged a bit closer on the bench—near enough to comfort without invading her space.

She choked on a laugh. "I think that's the least of my worries at the moment. Etiquette is apparently not my family's strong suit." After all, what could be crueller than cursing one's own child for the sake of power and money?

And *both* of her parents had treated their divorce as though it were something that didn't affect her—something that she was too childish to understand.

Which, perhaps she was. But only because they hadn't sat her down to explain what was truly going on. Because they hadn't given her the chance to make an adult, informed decision about how their actions would shape hers.

She was glad her back was to the castle. Right now, she didn't want to acknowledge it. She could understand why her father couldn't bear to live with her mother any longer—Theryn was grappling with similar feelings. Fiery wrath toward her mother for everything she'd done—and a sputtering resentment and sadness that her father had barred her from understanding the truth until it was too late.

Edvyn stared into the distance, his hands clasped between his knees. His mouth was turned down, his brow furrowed deeply. He sighed again and tore his fingers through his hair.

Talk about etiquette—Theryn hadn't even thanked him for his assistance. "Thank you for helping me," she whispered. "You've been very kind."

He scratched his cheek, lips pursed. A tinge of red returned to his skin. "I...I wish I could do more." He swallowed. "I...I know we hardly know each other, but... If you wish, if you need it, my castle is open to you. Our countries have been allies for so long, I'm sure my parents would be happy to help you until you can decide what to do next."

Despite her wretchedness, she couldn't help asking, "Are you inviting me to elope?"

His entire face turned scarlet. "N-not *yet*! I—I mean—of course not—my mother would *kill me*!" He coughed and rubbed his face, which only drew her attention to his freckles.

His scattered reply helped alleviate some of her gnawing anger—reminded her that not all was quite lost in this future. "Your mother...is she like you?" she asked.

Edvyn dug the toe of his riding boot into the dirt. "Somewhat.

More…confident, I suppose, but that's what ruling Ildebar for the last fifteen years will do to you. You have to have confidence to keep all those faeries in order." He smiled ruefully. "I think she'd be thrilled to have another princess in the castle. She had all boys. It can be very…chaotic."

"She seems to have raised you well, at least." Better than Theryn's parents had raised her. A loud, boisterous castle sounded soothing in comparison to the suffocating secrets behind them. "I'd love to accompany you."

His eyes lit up — and then he chewed at his bottom lip. "Oh. Will that be all right? You're the heir —"

"I…I think my parents will understand why I might want to leave. At least for a time." Until she could look at them again without thorns of rage piercing her heart. Until she could look at them again and remember they were her parents and not her enemies.

She stood, smoothing out her skirts. "Might I bring Hylda along?" Theryn winced to think of what Hylda might say once she learned what had happened in the throne room. She didn't know what she could say to the loyal maid who'd given up so much to be with her. How to explain that the future they'd sacrificed for wasn't meant to be.

"Of course. Is there anything else you'll need?" He tapped his boot against the path. "I…I'd rather not linger *too* long here." He shuddered.

Theryn couldn't blame him. She didn't really want to be around her parents anymore, either. She stepped toward the castle. "I'll go pack a few clothes and find Hylda." She hesitated. "Thank you again. This couldn't be what you expected to find."

He shrugged. "It's the least I could do."

Her eyes stung. What would everyone say when they reached Ildebar? Would the faery court call her a fool for going to all this trouble for nothing?

Edvyn touched her arm. "Would you like me to come with you?"

She blinked at him a few times before she realized he thought she was nervous to return to her castle. What a dear. At least, no matter what she faced next, she had Edvyn there with her as a friend and ally.

"It's all right," she whispered. "I'll meet you back out here."

And then she'd face the future she hadn't planned — a future that couldn't be controlled by a spindle trap.

But, she supposed, picturing her parents at each other's throats in the throne room, there were worse fates than that.

END

WAXING AND WAITING
Allison Tebo

I threw open the tower windows and chucked the contents of my dustpan over the sill. Today marked the tenth cycle that my fellow fairies and I had spent in confinement—one hundred human years safeguarding the royal palace and the sleeping princess. One hundred years of sweeping, dusting, and mopping, as well as fixing the occasional plumbing problems or bricklaying a new wall in the kitchen when Verity blew up the oven.

It would have been easier work with our wands, but we had agreed not to use magic within the barrier—it caused a bubbling effect in our spell dome that could be detected by magic users outside the castle walls. We had kept Rosalina safe from Bastaba for a hundred years, and we weren't going to blow it by using our wands to sweep. So we had put our magic away and accepted a life of strained backs. Being a fairy godmother was certainly not as glamorous as stories made it out to be.

"This was never in my job description," I grumbled as I closed the windows and turned to help my friend, Lorella, heave a freshly beaten carpet into the room and unroll it with a thump of heavy velvet. "I wasn't made for heavy labor."

Verity skated down the hall and grabbed onto the doorframe as she slid by so that she jerked to a stop. She poked her head in, a little breathlessly, and beamed at us.

"Today's the day!"

We had all taken turns saying that to one another since dawn. We could hardly believe that our exile was nearly over. Before midnight, a handsome prince would hack his way through the castle hedge, plant a kiss on Rosalina, and break the curse forever.

And free us from cleaning. Never in our immortal lives had we so anticipated the appearance of a human.

"I've got a great idea," I muttered as I tried to rub a sore spot between my shoulder blades. "In just a few hours everyone will be waking up anyway, including the staff. Why don't we leave all this for them?"

"That wouldn't be very nice, Araminta," Lorella objected.

I sighed and walked by a gargoyle, cracking the end of my towel at his ear to remove a stray dust bunny as I passed. Safeguarding a castle-full of innocents—and keeping them clean—was a lot of work. It was a wonder we hadn't gone mad. Fortunately, fairies told time differently.

Every ten years only felt like one year to us.

Still, ten years was a long time.

I finished gathering the cobwebs from the ceiling, then went out to the balcony and dumped the dustbins' contents over the side.

Pausing for a rest, I slipped the locket out of my pocket and took a quick peek at the portrait inside. I touched Mickle's likeness with a thumb. I wished that my last memory of him had not been of us fighting.

I gave myself a shake and called down into the courtyard where my friend was wiping the prime minister's dirty face. "Verity, it's just Rosalina's room left."

We assembled a moment later in the tower room, pausing in the doorway to gaze at the sleeping princess.

More than likely, she was dreaming of her prince. Somewhere out beyond the palace hedge, the Grand Fairymaster who had countered Bastaba's curse with a sleeping spell had also vowed to find a proper match for Rosalina in due course. He and his council had promised that once the spell took effect, they would wait eighty years into the enchantment, then would select a promising baby and groom him into a man worthy of Rosalina's affections. To ensure that their feelings were reciprocated, the two young minds and hearts had been connected through magically induced dreams.

Verity took Rosalina's legs and I took her head. Rosalina's glorious golden hair—the very stuff I had, ironically, blessed her with—got in my way considerably.

"Don't drop her!" Verity gasped as we lurched drunkenly toward the trundle bed.

"In the two thousand six hundred and eight times we've moved her, have I ever dropped her?" I snapped at Verity.

"Now, now, dears," Lorella reproved as she stripped the bed. "It's almost over. Just hold your tempers a few hours longer."

Verity and I didn't have the breath to continue arguing anyway. Rosalina was a lot heavier than she looked. The last time I had seen her awake, she had been hammering away at a buffet table and I suspected that she must have put on a few pounds before she went to sleep.

I silently chided myself for my disrespectful thoughts. But familiarity bred contempt, and hundred years was more than enough time to develop plenty of familiarity.

At least I was never bored. But I was lonely. Even with Verity and Lorella always near, they couldn't ease my heartsickness.

It had been only the three of us present at Rosalina's eighteenth birthday party when she had pricked her finger on a spindle. In consequence, we had taken on the responsibility of staying at the castle to cast a spell bubble to shield the princess and her court until the enchantment was over.

Mickle should have been with us. He should have been there to watch over her for the last hundred years. He should have been with me—and he would have been, if only we hadn't argued.

In all honesty, Mickle and I were always bickering, so much so that others had doubted our deep friendship. But this had been different. It had begun with an argument about birthday gifts. Mickle had insulted my very existence by implying that if I had given princesses useful gifts instead of something as useless as golden hair, our lives might not revolve around protecting mortals from sleeping curses. I had immediately responded that at least I wasn't so selfish that I spent weeks gallivanting around the country instead of keeping a close eye on Rosalina—unlike certain people who were always absent when they were needed most. Mickle had been offended by this and had indicated that he found me weak and clingy. Things had deteriorated from there.

At least, that was how I thought I remembered it. What I remembered most was that the argument had begun over who gave better gifts—a topic that felt distressingly infantile in retrospect. Wounded pride no longer felt comparable to the hurt of having lost Mickle.

"No more cleaning *ever*!" Verity exclaimed, dumping a dustbin over the balustrade as we gathered on the balcony. "I'm going to sleep for a hundred years after all this is over."

"Don't say that," Lorella admonished, with a glance back at the slumbering princess. "We mustn't joke about such things."

I nodded. It would be terrible if we jinxed ourselves when we were so close to the finish line.

"I'm not joking," Verity insisted. "I'm exhausted. I'm going to take a bubble bath that lasts half a century and then I'm going to sleep twice as long."

There was a brief silence as we considered such a delicious possibility.

Verity looked over at me and Lorella. "So what are you going to do when you get out?"

"Read," Lorella said promptly. "I've fallen so far behind on my personal reading challenges."

I wasn't about to admit what my first thought had been that I would try to find Mickle. "Uh, travel, I suppose."

But I didn't fool my friends. They could be depended upon to see through me just as surely as they could be relied upon to make me feel awkward.

Verity trailed a finger across the balustrade, a study of casualness. "What about Mickle?"

My heart squeezed in my chest at the sound of his name.

"He left, Verity," I said flatly. "It's over."

"You don't know that," she protested. "After all, you've been in hiding all this time."

My jaw tightened. "I'm sure he's forgotten all about me."

Verity opened her mouth to push the issue, but Lorella stepped on her foot to shut her up.

I straightened abruptly, avoiding their looks. "Come on, let's finish up this room."

We threw ourselves into the final thirty minutes it took to set Rosalina's room in perfect order, then stepped back to admire our work. When the prince showed up, he would be greeted not only by an enchantment that needed to be broken, but a spick-and-span castle. Everything was perfect, except for the crick in my back and the hollow place in my heart.

We gathered on the balcony with bowls of popped corn and a telescope so we could watch for the prince.

We waited.

And waited some more.

"What is taking him so long?" Verity complained. "It's nearly teatime."

"Speaking of which," Lorella said, eyeing the popcorn bowls that we had emptied over an hour ago, "it's time one of us was making it."

We drew straws and Verity lost.

"I'll stay here a bit longer," said Lorella, peering through the telescope once again as Verity wandered away to brew the tea.

I was too restless to linger any longer on the balcony. I drifted inside and stood for a moment by Rosalina's bed, with one finger touching the fresh roses we had placed on her nightstand. It was as if saying Mickle's name aloud had laid its own spell on me.

I looked at Rosalina, noticing that she was smiling in her sleep. Was she dreaming of her true love, courtesy of her fairy godparents?

I frowned. Only the Grand Fairymaster could send dreams, but a normal fairy could receive dreams. It was entirely within the realm of possibility for a fairy to ask the Master to contact someone important to them—say, their true love.

But there had been no contact from Mickle in all these years. Every time I dreamed of him, the dreams were only memories, not messages.

If he still cared, he could have asked the Grand Fairymaster to contact me. But he hadn't.

I went over to the mirror to give it a brief rub and paused to examine my reflection. Short, plump, with brown hair that was beginning to show traces of premature silver. I sighed and measured my waist with my hands. There had been an awful lot of stress eating for all of us during this enforced exile, but the evidence showed a little more clearly on me than it did on the others. Even if Mickle came walking through this door right now, I didn't look like quite the same fairy he had once fancied.

I scowled and turned away. As soon as I got out of this place, I was going overseas to try to forget what I hadn't been able to forget in the last hundred years.

I looked toward the princess's bed. The freshly laundered pillows and quilts looked so inviting. My gaze fell on the trundle bed beside the four poster and found myself yawning. I wasn't a superhuman, after all. Even a fairy got tired sometimes. What could a few winks hurt?

I collapsed onto the trundle bed, flopping around a few minutes until I was good and comfortable and then pulled the coverlet over my head and nodded off.

~~~~~

One minute I was in a heavy stupor—vaguely aware that I was snorting and drooling. I thought I felt and heard movement in the room, and the thought swept over my sleepy mind that it was probably Verity coming to rouse me.

The covers were suddenly yanked back from my face, allowing the full force of the sun to slam into my eyelids. I opened my mouth to yowl. But before I could, someone kissed me on the lips.

Definitely not Verity or Lorella.

My eyes flew open, but I couldn't see much besides eyebrows and the bridge of a nose.

"Blahhh!" I managed to shout, swinging away with my fists until I hit throat. The kisser receded, choking.

I sat up in bed, goggling at the man in front of me.

My old lover beamed at me with adoration. "Hello, gorgeous! How is my darling Minty?"

Minty. Mickle was the only person on earth to ever call me by that nickname.

My eyes flicked wildly over his familiar form, a tall, gangly frame that looked as if it had been created by a slapdash puppeteer. The same noble brow was there, with the piercing and jolly gaze, the same flyaway hair now touched with white and the salt and pepper mustache.

It was my Mickle.

"What are you doing here?" I gasped, gazing up at him.

Mickle smiled at me happily. "I came to break the spell, of course!"

I blinked. "But you can't. Only greeting Rosalina with true love's kiss will break it."

"I know," Mickle said complacently. "That's why I kissed her."

All of the old melty feelings were snuffed out like a candle. "Excuse me?" I said coldly.
~~~~~

"I got my hands on a love potion and kissed Rosalina to break the spell." Mickle grabbed me close, swept me to my feet, and began stampeding me back and forth in a breathless tango.

I shoved him away. "Just wait one minute, mister. You have some explaining to do!"

He was still capering around the room. "You're free! Isn't it wonderful?"

I merely glared. The man who claimed to love me had just created a love spell so that someone would fall in love with him.

Someone who wasn't me.

Mickle seized my hands. "The spell is broken!"

I focused on the last part of his sentence. "It is?"

We both looked down at noticeably silent Rosalina.

She was still prone, but I thought her breathing was a bit shallower. Despite my frustration with Mickle, my heart leapt.

"Rosalina?" I called.

The princess sighed and started to roll over.

"Oh no you don't," I said, reaching down and giving her a light slap. "Wake up!" I pulled her into a sitting position. "You are going to get off that bed by yourself today or, so help me, you will be in trouble with more fairies than just Bastaba." I shook the girl so hard her head lolled back and forth. "**Wake up.**"

"Araminta, be gentle!" Mickle reproved, reaching out to pull the girl toward him.

The moment he touched her, Rosalina's eyes fluttered open.

I threw my hands up in the air. "Hoor—" I began.

"Oh!" she gasped, gazing up at Mickle. "You woke me up."

"—ay?" My cheered died awkwardly in my throat. "Um, actually, I woke you."

But Rosalina wasn't paying any attention to me. She slipped her hand into Mickle's, gazing up at him adoringly.

"Hey," I protested weakly.

Rosalina tilted her head as she examined the surprised Mickle. "You're not quite like the boy I've been dreaming of."

"I should say he isn't," I interjected sourly. "He's no boy."

Mickle shot me a haughty look.

Rosalina squeezed Mickle's hand and smiled up at him. "But looks aren't everything, are they?"

Mickle's frozen smile was starting to crack a little, and I had the feeling he was trying to ascertain whether he had just been insulted.

I grabbed Rosalina's hand and tried to respectfully pry it free from Mickle's arm as an utterly unfamiliar feeling surged through my stomach like an undigested meal: jealousy.

"You can't love him, Rosalina. Look—he has wrinkles and everything."

"Oh, I don't know," she said with a thoughtful yawn. "He's attractive in a mature sort of way."

Mickle shot me an awkward smile. "We can probably reverse this."

"You mean you're not sure?" It was just the sort of cockamamie scheme that Mickle would dream up. "You had better reverse it, buster."

He smiled slowly at me. "Why, Minty! You do still care."

I did, and that made me glower at him all the harder and deny it as hard as I could. "I mean her parents wouldn't approve of Rosalina marrying an old fairy, you numptygawk!"

Rosalina fluffed her hair. "I'm eighteen and I can marry whoever I like." She smiled at Mickle. "Isn't that right, lovey-dovey?"

I gawked at her. I didn't remember the princess as being quite such a dodo.

"What kind of cut-rate love potion did you use, anyway?" I asked Mickle out of the side of my mouth.

"I was in a hurry," he muttered.

"Of course you were," I grumbled. "You're always in a hurry. If you had just stuck around and been available for the last hundred years, you might have learned something about patience!"

I had barely got the words out before I got a mouthful of pillow.

"You leave my true love alone!" Rosalina snarled. "No one talks bad about my . . . um . . . what was your name again, lambkins?"

I pried the pillow from my face and considered smothering her with it. I liked her better when she was asleep.

I jumped as Verity and Lorella suddenly burst into the room.

"We were downstairs and heard—" Verity stopped talking as she gaped at Mickle.

"Mickle!" Lorella scurried forward and hugged Mickle joyfully. "Dear old friend. It's so good to see you!"

Verity grabbed him from the other side. "We've missed you so much!"

They huddled together in a tangle of happiness and I folded my arms, trying not to show how pleased I was that we were all back together again.

There was a swish of silk as Rosalina rose majestically from her bed and fixed our happy group with a look of royal censure.

"Excuse me, midgets," she said coldly. "I would appreciate it if you would get your hands off my true love." She yawned again but followed it up with a glare.

Verity and Lorella goggled at her.

"Midgets?" Verity repeated, looking wounded.

I vaguely remembered that Rosalina had possessed a streak of naughtiness, but this outright sauce was something I had never seen from her before. Either this was some latent personal development or a result of the love potion, it was impossible to tell.

"Princess!" Lorella exclaimed. "How can you be awake?"

I threw Mickle a glare. "Why don't you ask our friend here?"

Mickle straightened his tunic with an aggrieved air. "Yes, I just saved you all. You're welcome. I woke Rosalina with a love potion to free all of you from your imprisonment."

Verity and Lorella exchanged confused glances.

"I've missed you all," said Mickle tenderly. He looked at me. "I've especially missed *you*, Minty."

Verity, the sentimental little gossip, decided to stick her oar in.

"She missed you too. She talks to your picture in her locket."

I nearly died, right then and there.

"I do not."

I had thought I hid that habit so well from the others.

Lorella shoved Verity. "Hush! This is Mickle and Araminta's affair."

Verity threw up her hands in exasperation. "I'm just trying to help!" She turned toward me and the grinning Mickle. "I mean, you are in love with one another, aren't you?"

"Yes!" he said, just as I yelled, "No!"

He shot me a look of sorrowful judgment. "It's not like you to lie."

The nerve of the man! As if I would really declare my affection while a love-crazy snippet hung on his arm and every word. I had some pride.

"You never came back! You never even sent me a message."

"I never came back because I couldn't come back. After we . . . after I left . . . I went searching for the best gift in the world. I decided to retrieve a genie lamp. You know, the gift that keeps on giving? Sadly, I was the unfortunate victim of a magical cave-in so powerful I've been trapped inside a cavern with nothing but a genie to keep me company all this time."

Unbidden sympathy washed over me. "You've been caught in an enchantment too," I said softly.

Mickle, noticing my tone, reached for my hand. But I wasn't quite ready to forgive him. I folded my arms and waited.

He sighed. "As you know, genies can't grant wishes to other magical beings. It took some doing to find a spell to break through that block, but I finally did it. As soon as I got out of the cave, I went to the Fairy Council and heard all about the enchantment that was put into effect a hundred years ago. But even they couldn't remember where the castle was; your protection spell was too strong. So I began searching for you on my own. Something led me straight here. I could see the castle clear as day, though no one else could."

Verity beamed. "Why, this proves you're in love! Only true love could see through our blocking spell—"

"Verity!" I snapped, my face burning with sudden heat.

"True love?" Rosalina gasped. "What are you talking about? Micklepoo is in love with me—not that fat old fairy."

I had spent a hundred years guarding this brat and this was the thanks I got? All those feelings that had plagued me over the years washed over me in an ugly rush. Mickle had left me because I was too bad-tempered, too fat, too argumentative.

Mickle managed to pry himself free of Rosalina again and turned me toward him. "What do I have to do to prove myself?"

Before I could make some tart response about throwing himself into a bed of thorns, Mickle dropped impulsively to one knee, so hard that I heard his knee-cap pop.

"Ow!" he roared.

"Are you all right?" I asked automatically. I was angry, but I didn't want him to break a leg right in front of me.

Mickle brushed my concern aside and captured my hand. "I love you, Minty, and only you. I always have."

Verity shrieked into her hands and Lorella elbowed her into silence.

Mickle smiled up at me. "Will you marry me?"

My mouth dropped open. It wasn't exactly the kind of proposal a woman dreamed of. After all, my lover had just kissed another girl and caused her to fall in love with him due to a love potion, before immediately pivoting to propose to me. But still...

Rosalina, who had been watching all these proceedings with confusion, glares, and a variety of yawns, let forth a piercing shriek and darted forward to throw her arms around Mickle's neck, nearly choking him. "No one is marrying my Mickle!"

Again, it was not the kind of proposal that women dreamed of.

It took all my control not to slap Rosalina in the face. "Stop that! He's old enough to be your father—or your grandfather!"

Mickle bristled. Despite Rosalina's headlock he managed to squeeze out a protestation. "I wouldn't go that far."

"Ugh." I rubbed my eyes. "This is just our luck. Rosalina's prince was supposed to be coming today. He would have fixed everything." I glared at Mickle. "Instead, we got you and your love potions."

Mickle looked suddenly uncomfortable. "Um . . . a prince?"

"What do you know about it?" I demanded suspiciously.

He coughed. "Well, as I said, I was in a frightful hurry to find you. A few miles back down the road I came upon some callow youth. His horse was quite surprised when I jumped out from behind a tree, giving me time to catch the reins. Since I couldn't spare the time to explain, I yanked the joker off his horse and bunged him into the bushes and . . . I stole his horse."

Verity and Lorella sucked in their breath and clutched at one another for support.

"That was Rosalina's prince, Mickle!" I shouted.

He shuffled his feet awkwardly. "I did shout an apology as I rode off."

I lowered my face into my hands and tried very hard not to scream. "That was the prince coming to break the spell—and you ruined it. How could you be so stupid?"

"My intentions were pure," Mickle said feebly.

I opened my mouth to lambaste him further, but Lorella moved forward a little and gazed into Rosalina's glazed eyes with a worried look.

"You know, I'm no expert, but I don't think she's fully awake. I don't think that love potion can replace true love's kiss." Lorella chewed on her lip. "But a love potion is a fairly powerful magic. Great enough to create . . ."

"A bubbling effect," I interrupted, my heart pinching.

Verity clapped her hands to her mouth, muffling a gasp.

Mickle's love potion had acted like a signal beacon. Any being on the watch for it would have surely spotted the outline of our spell.

And, deep down, we knew that Bastaba was always watching—today more than ever, because this was her last chance.

"Oh dear," Lorella murmured.

A roar of thunder caused everyone but Rosalina to race to the window.

A cloud was gathering on the horizon, thick and dark and tinged with a greenish glow.

Bastaba was coming.

"This is all my fault," Mickle murmured. His ubiquitous twinkle was gone. He looked more sober than I had ever seen him—utterly crushed.

As I looked at him, I noticed the sad wrinkles at the corners of his eyes, thought of the time he had spent alone in that cave, wild and restless, and all my frustration fell away as I finally found the answer I had been looking for all this time.

Mickle did love me, and he always had, and everything he had done today—however foolish—had only been because he was trying to find and free me so that we could be together.

I took his hand, and when Mickle met my gaze, I saw some of the light returning to his face. Hope bloomed inside of me too.

"We can still fix this," I announced, interrupting Lorella and Verity's concerned murmurs. I looked to Mickle. "Where exactly did you leave the doofus—I mean the prince?"

Mickle chewed the tip of his moustache. "About a mile down the road."

"Oh!" Verity clapped her hands over her eyes.

Lorella tugged at her hair. "Was he in any condition to walk after you left him?"

"I don't know," he said doubtfully. "He looked awfully spindly."

"The prince?" Rosalina said thoughtfully from behind us, making us all turn to look at her. She was tottering uncertainly and I lunged forward.

"Rosalina — no!"

Despite my efforts, she was slipping toward the floor. I tried to prop her up, but the princess was much taller than me and my muscles were weak after a day of cleaning. I ended up underneath as a kind of humanoid cushion as she sank to the ground.

"Not again," I groaned, struggling out from under her. "Wake up, Rosalina!"

Lorella shook her head. "It's no good. The love potion couldn't work because the love you and Mickle have is too powerful and cancels out the spell. Your love is its own kind of magic."

Mickle looked up and our eyes met across Rosalina.

Everything was falling apart, but I was suddenly inexpressibly happy.

Verity broke into my ecstatic revelation. "What are we going to do? Without the prince, we're doomed!"

I dragged my attention back to the problem at hand and looked out the window again. "If the prince is out there, there's no way he can get here without our help." I looked at Mickle. "You go get the prince."

He grabbed my arm. "I won't leave you again."

My heart performed a little somersault as I reached up to squeeze his fingers. "You're the one with the most dangerous job — and the only one I would trust to fight your way through that mob twice. We'll hold the castle until you get back."

"We have a castle full of helpless courtiers and an invasion force outside our doors," Verity protested. "We can't protect them all."

"We still have some time," I assured her. "And we can use our wands now — that will help."

"Let's do it," Lorella agreed. The four of us clasped hands briefly, together again, and exchanged smiles of varying confidence.

Mickle blew me a kiss and climbed out the window and down a trellis, dropping into the courtyard with a jaunty salute before disappearing through the hedge.

"Come on," I said to the girls, tearing my eyes away from his retreating back. "We have to get our wands!"

We ran out the door.

"Come on, ladies, let's move it!" I yelled, mounting the banister and sliding down it. But I forgot to lean back to slow myself and slammed into the newel post at the end of the banister a second before Verity crashed into my back, sending us both tumbling down the last few steps in a flurry of flying skirts and curses.

Lorella, who had had the good sense to walk instead of slide, moved past our carcasses and went to the closet where we had stored our wands a hundred years ago. She yanked it open and ripped open the tissue-lined boxes.

I accepted the wand she handed to me and sighed at its familiar weight.

"I hope we remember what to do!" Lorella wailed. She had never done well under pressure.

"It will come back to you," I said. "Like riding a horse."

"But I don't know how to ride a horse!"

~~~~~

A quarter of an hour later, Bastaba reached the castle walls. The storm came with her, hovering above the palace in a fever of growling clouds and lashing thunder.

She hadn't come alone. An army of gibbering goblins and a decidedly hungry-looking dragon were with her.

We had done our best to reinforce the spell barrier around the castle, we had barricaded as many windows and doors as we could, and waited.

We saw the blue ripple as Bastaba's more powerful spell caused a rip in our barrier, allowing her army to break down a courtyard wall and trample through the hedges.

Verity, Lorella, and I exchanged desperate looks from where we stood at the unbarred window beside the main doors, and raised our wands to fight for all we were worth.

But I was afraid we weren't good enough. Lorella was getting forgetful now that she had passed her thousandth birthday, Verity panicked during crucial moments, and as for me, I was full of such giddy lovesickness I could barely think straight.

My heart jumped in a flurry of fear as my gaze fell on the dark-clad figure that entered the courtyard behind her minions.

A hundred years was a mere blink in the life of a fairy, but the years had treated Bastaba rather shabbily. Her always-thin figure was as twisted as a dead tree branch while her shriveled skin looked like peeling bark. Wild eyes stared out of her gaunt face, and her long mouth was open in a snarl as she raised her wand in a swirl of dark magic.

One of the stone gargoyles lining the castle walls came to life with a shake of stone wings, swooping down at our window with bared fangs.

Verity let the thing have it with a blast from her wand and the
~~~~~

gargoyle shattered into rubble.

I stared at the gargoyle head that had landed at my feet — the thing that I had cleaned every single day for the last hundred years — smashed.

Fury exploded inside me. "So that's your game, is it?" I yelled to Bastaba. I waved my wand over the fountain.

The stone dragon above the little pool came to life with a snort that caused Bastaba to whirl toward it. It glared at Bastaba, squished up one side of his face and squinted one eye in concentration as it took aim, and then let forth a burst of water.

It was no mere squirt, it was a veritable geyser. I had a delightful view of Bastaba's petticoats as she was bowled over.

She struggled to rise, but the puddle of mud growing rapidly around her made it difficult to do so. She slipped and flailed through the mud, ending with the inevitable splat as she fell into the muck.

Verity, Lorella, and I laughed hysterically. We stopped laughing when Bastaba's dragon appeared over the hedge.

Bastaba peeled herself off the ground and cast us a look of triumph, along with a blast from her wand.

The castle's main door blew open, the spell that we had used to reinforce it disintegrating in a burst of light.

The dragon thrust its head into the doorway, followed by sinewy green shoulders. I stared in horror at the glittering eyes and flickering tongue and felt around frantically for the wand I had dropped.

I heard Bastaba berating the dragon to get a move on. It kept jerking and growling, as if someone was kicking its tail repeatedly.

The dragon opened its mouth and emitted a stream of fire that immediately incinerated the tapestries on the walls.

"Holy spell dust!" Verity screeched as a stream of fire blasted down the hall, sending us leaping into a side room to avoid being burned.

I crawled back toward the door, trembling with fear as I looked into the hall. The dragon had finally forced its way through the door. I raised my wand, trying frantically to recall my blasting spell.

Then the dragon's claws hit the floor we had just waxed earlier that day.

The dragon's legs crossed and uncrossed so rapidly it made my eyes hurt. The dragon huffed in alarm as it careened madly against first one wall and then the next, badly damaging the front hall and everything in it, but causing so much pandemonium the goblins that had been pressing in behind it at the door retreated back into the courtyard.

Verity and Lorella joined me in the hall, and we all raised our wands and sent the dragon blasting backward out the door.

It took out the doors, some of the wall, and an abundance of goblins in an explosion that rattled our bones. We immediately cast a patchwork spell toward the door to block Bastaba from entering and retreated into the inner hall.

"Well done, ladies," Lorella said, and we all wearily tapped our wands together in a show of camaraderie.

"Well done indeed!" a voice called from the window.

The three of us yelled and whirled around just as Mickle clambered over an open sill and tumbled into the room. He smiled and waved his wand by way of explanation. "Had to break my way in, sorry. Up you come, son." He reached over the sill and dragged up a singularly rumpled-looking young man covered in briars and bugs.

"Mickle!" I breathed. "You made it!"

Mickle stampeded past us with the confused-looking prince in tow. "That trick with the flying dragon sufficiently distracted the villains for me to sneak in! Well done, ladies!"

"Go, Mickle!" Verity cheered as they ran up the main stairs.

"And hurry!" Lorella urged.

"Come on, Prince!" he yelled, dragging the battered royal up the stairs.

"It's Roderick," the prince protested.

"We're very glad to meet you," Lorella called to him.

I used my wand to knit together the hole Mickle had made in the spell on the window and then ran to see how the barrier was holding up on the main hall.

"Ahh!" I screeched as goblins poured through the windows. I yanked open the door closest to me—the butler's pantry—and leaped over the sleeping dog that had occupied this particular doorway for a hundred years. Bonebag had fallen asleep in this spot and had never twitched a whisker since.

As I had hoped, the goblins rushed through the doorway without pause, tripped over Bonebag, and went flying.

I took the opportunity to use my wand, turning them to stone.

"What is taking them so long?" I cried to Lorella and Verity as I rejoined them. "He should have kissed her by now!"

"Go see!" Lorella yelled. "We'll hold them off here!"

As I labored to the top of the stairs, gasping for breath, I heard the battle coming from the end of the hall.

Mickle and Prince Roderick had been swarmed by a pack of stone gargoyles, and Mickle had lost his wand.

I raised my wand and sent lightning bolts into the mob, causing the gargoyles to fall to the ground, shattered.

"Come on!" I shouted to Mickle and Roderick, charging into Rosalina's room ahead of them.

The door banged shut behind me.

I whirled around. Bastaba was standing in front of the door, smiling.

Before I could move, she muttered a curse and my wand was jerked from my hand and flew into hers.

"No!" I shouted as a holding spell enveloped me.

Bastaba laughed in triumph.

I struggled frantically against the spell, but the more I pushed the more I could feel the spell tightening around my chest, robbing me of my breath.

"No!"

We had kept Rosalina safe for a hundred years and now, at the last hour, we had failed.

Bastaba brought her face close to mine and I stared into her hate-filled eyes.

"You've failed, you miserable little worm." She laughed. "You really thought you could keep me from my revenge? Everyone in this castle will die today. And you shall watch." She raised her arms.

And Mickle burst through the door.

"Kiss her, boy!" he roared, hurling the prince toward Rosalina's bed and then turning toward Bastaba with blazing eyes as she raised her wand.

"Stop!" I screamed.

The last thing I heard before the explosion was Mickle yelling, "I wish Bastaba and all her people to be turned into grasshoppers!"

~~~~~

The spell around me evaporated like a pricked bubble and I tumbled to my knees, gasping for breath and still blinking away the enchantment and the flash of the explosion.

My wand was lying on the ground beside a very large grasshopper.

As I watched, the grasshopper hopped frantically for the window and disappeared behind a dresser.

Beneath me, the entire castle seemed to tremble, down to its very foundation, like a stone giant shifting its muscles to stretch.

I knew what it meant. The spell was broken. The castle was waking up.

I looked first to Rosalina.

She was sitting up in bed, looking at the prince with surprise. The foolish expression that had been on her face a few minutes ago was gone. My heart expanded inside me with happiness as I stared at that sweet face and recognized the old Rosalina, the real princess, the little girl I had sworn to protect since she was born. She was back. Thanks to Mickle.

"Mickle?" I whispered, turning around.

He was on his knees, a little singed, but still alive — and still clutching the lamp that he had pulled from his doublet and brandished at Bastaba.
~~~~~

Mickle wiggled the lamp at me. "I'm a hundred years late, but I still brought Rosalina her genie lamp." He grinned at me. "So do I or do I not give the best presents?"

I laughed with joy and crawled toward him. "You do!" I said, throwing my arms around his neck.

Mickle hugged me tight. "I'm sorry for what I said before, Minty. I was wrong."

"We were both wrong," I murmured, reveling in the feeling of a silly grudge evaporating. More than one spell had been broken today.

We both stood up—a considerable process involving grunting, creaking knees, and clutching at one another.

Our groaning attracted the attention of Roderick and Rosalina at last, who appeared to be as entranced by one another as Mickle and I had been in each another.

At least one part of this had turned out to be easy.

"Mickle! Araminta! My dear old friends!" Rosalina swung herself off her bed and raced forward to wrap us in a hug. "I'm so glad to see you! Are you all right?"

"We're more than all right," Mickle assured her. "We're getting married. Aren't we, Minty?"

I smiled. "Of course! Someone has to keep you from making a mess of things."

Rosalina squealed and kissed me on the cheek. She turned to Mickle to shake his hand and then stopped. "I feel as if I saw you recently. Yes, in a funny-sort of dream. I was—" She paused and blushed prettily. "I think I thought you were someone else," she finished awkwardly.

"Ah well, we all have funny dreams now and then," Mickle said generously.

As he turned to the prince to apologize for chucking him in the bushes and stealing his horse—an apology that Roderick accepted good-naturedly—Rosalina whispered in my ear. "Araminta, I have the worst feeling that I was behaving a little stupidly a few minutes ago in my sleep."

She had, but that could happen when one had been under a curse for a hundred years.

I smiled into her worried eyes. After years of thinking of Rosalina as little more than a sleeping doll, I had forgotten just how much I had liked her.

"It's all right, Rosalina," I told her, touching the beautiful hair that I had given her. I smiled. "Everything is all right now."

The door flew open and the room was flooded with people. The king and queen raced through the door and flew to their daughter, pulling her into their arms. The prime minister and a bevy of ladies-in-waiting and knights stumbled in. Bonebag frisked between them, barking happily. At the end of the line, Verity and Lorella waltzed in, swinging their wands above their heads and looking supremely pleased with themselves.

As the reunion grew into an impromptu party, I leaned my head against Mickle's shoulder as we watched the king and queen take the hands of their daughter and her young prince.

New love was a beautiful thing.

My hand curled around Mickle's.

But old love was best.

END

SPINDLE
Hailey Huntington

Initializing recording…

Chills run across my arms as the holoscreen loads the files. It's not the first time I've watched this day, but every time I do, I get the morbid feeling of witnessing someone's death sentence.

Because in a way, I am. And it's mine.

13:18; 12.31.2241; New Dion Great Hall

The Great Hall of the New Dion settlement comes into view. It's filled with people milling about, all dressed in regulation uniforms. Between the gaps in the crowd, the 275-degree views of space are visible through the Great Hall's glass walls. Within a minute, the chatter has died down, and everyone has taken a seat. All eyes are fixed on the stage in the front of the room, where Chamberlain Jaxon steps in front of a podium.

"Fellow citizens of New Dion, welcome to today's Path Ceremony. It is with great pleasure that I announce that today's ceremony is for the daughter of our own First Captain Evann Laken and Lead Production Analyst Nova Laken. I'm sure that little Seren will follow in her parents' footsteps and achieve great things for this colony."

Applause fills the air as a couple walks toward the stage, a little girl between them. They're smiling, excited.

My parents had no idea what was coming next. And at four years old, I barely understood what was happening in the first place, much less the weight of everything.

The dad hoists his daughter into his arms as they step onto the stage. The little girl rests her head on his shoulder. The mother links her arm through her husband's. It's a charming picture.

Even though I can't see their faces, I know that everyone is looking at the girl—at me—the daughter of the colony's captain of the fleet and lead production analyst, the people who keep them safe and fed. Surely with DNA like that, I'd be a genius. I'd live up to Chamberlain Jaxon's words and do great things.

My stomach twists.

Chamberlain Jaxon nods his head toward the family and then looks out over the audience. "Will the Division leaders please come forward?"

Several men and women rise from their seats and join the others on the stage. A woman in a silver uniform steps up to the family first — Tegan Walters, head of Arts. "Seren has shown natural talents in singing and dancing. It would be an honor to mentor her and hone her natural gifts working in the Arts."

Bowing slightly at the waist, Tegan steps aside to let the next person step forward — Nicholai Preshvi, head of Resources. "Seren has shown her bright mind from an early age. It would be an honor to have her learn and serve New Dion in Resources." He smiles at Nova Laken, one of his top employees.

The ceremony goes on in a similar manner: the rest of the heads come forward, compliment young Seren Laken on a talent or skill she has, and offer her a path in their Division.

Right after the last man — Paul Kruse, head of Transport — finishes, the door to the Great Hall opens with a bang. Everyone turns to watch as a woman stalks down the aisle toward the front of the room. Her stare is fixed on the Lakens.

"Funny. I think I was somehow missed *when everyone was informed about today's ceremony." Her voice cuts through the room.*

Morrigan Ives. I shudder at the sight of her, even though I know it's just a hologram. I want to close my eyes, to turn off the recording. To pretend what happened in the past isn't real. But I need to watch what's next. I need it to give me the determination for what I'm about to do.

Morrigan stops in front of the family. "Little Seren. How precious. What a happy family you have, Evann." Malice drips from every word. Seren buries her head in her father's shoulder.

"What are you doing here, Morrigan? You're not a Division head." Nova's voice is steady, but she steps closer to Evann and grips his arm tighter. "You run a project. Those are individual activities."

"Chamberlain Jaxon," Morrigan turns toward the man, "forgive me if I'm wrong, but the Codes state that projects are allowed to invoke special recruitment privileges once a year, correct?"

"Umm. Yes, I think — "

Morrigan turns around. "Well then. It is the end of the year, and I haven't recruited anyone for my project. So, I now claim Seren Laken for Project SPINDLE."

Sleep Preservation Initiative, New Dion Legacy Effort. SPINDLE. A death without dying. Your body frozen in time while you sleep. If you wake up, it won't be to the world you left. *If* you wake at all.

Evann holds his child closer. "You don't need someone for SPINDLE. It's — "

"Nova." Morrigan crosses her arms. "You help manage production. You know that New Dion is predicted to run out of resources. We're looking at a crisis in the near future, are we not?"

Murmurs break out in the crowd.

Nova's face flushes. "That's not entirely true. We — "

"If New Dion faces a crisis, we need to be ready. My studies show sleep preservation to be our best chance. But before we can be certain that SPINDLE will be able to save our entire colony, I need a test subject. And that will be Seren."

I shut down the holoscreen, leaving me in the silence and darkness of my room. I have the arguments that come next memorized. I grew up with my parents telling me how they tried everything possible to get me out of SPINDLE. Could I get a medical exemption? Was there a loophole in the Codes? They even tried to cash in favors to get the Chamberlain or another Executive to illegally break Morrigan's claim on me.

Nothing worked. When project managers invoke special recruitment, there is no way out. You aren't given a choice. Morrigan declared that I'd enter SPINDLE when I turned sixteen.

I stand up from my bed and cross the room to my window. Stars fill the inky void outside. My gaze drops to the horizon of New Dion. In a few hours, the sun will rise, ushering in my sixteenth birthday.

This is our last chance.

With a smooth *whoosh*, the door slides up. I look over my shoulder at Dad. "It's time, Seren."

Grabbing the backpack at my feet, I sling it over my shoulders and follow him. Mom waits in the hallway. She presses a quick kiss to the top of my head.

I swallow, stuffing my emotions down. This is the only way. If we're successful, I'll still be able to see my parents. I'll be able to have a normal life.

I'll lose it all if SPINDLE takes me.

Leaving our apartment, we enter the Main Hub of New Dion. The planet's atmosphere isn't hospitable to life, so everything is enclosed, all connected in the Dome. The lights are turned off, shrouding everything in darkness. Only the starlight coming in from the Dome shows us where we are going.

We slink through the Hub like thieves, heading to the aircraft hangar. Mom holds my hand the entire time. I need her anchoring touch as much as she needs mine. Every tiptoed step seems to boom in the silence.

I look down at the thin tech band around my wrist displaying the time. It's taking us longer to sneak to the hangar than we'd planned. Blood rushes through my ears as my anxiety spikes.

After what feels like an eternity, we reach the hanger. Dad punches in his code, opening the door. Mom gives my hand a quick squeeze. I squeeze back, trying to ignore how much my palms are sweating.

Silently, we follow Dad through the hangar toward the mini-jets. My stomach flips. In a few minutes, I'll be blasting off into space toward another settlement. Alone.

Light suddenly floods the room. Instantly, we freeze. My gaze darts around wildly. My heart stops when I see Morrigan coming around a starship with the fleet Major following her. She clicks her tongue.

"A family outing to the hangar at dawn one last time? Strange choice, if you ask me. Unless there's more to it than that…" My blood burns as Morrigan taps her chin, pretending to think. "You're not trying to escape, are you? I wondered if something like this might happen. Not only is it bad form, but I think it's *illegal.* Major, Captain Laken doesn't happen to have any authorized flight plans for one of those mini-jets that he's standing by, does he?"

The Major's eyes are sorry as he looks at my dad. But compassion doesn't make him change the facts. "No."

Morrigan claps her hands together. "Well then. I think the Lakens might have to see the Executives for their suspicious actions." Two muscled men round the corner. They grab my parents' arms as Morrigan steps next to me. "Let's head outside, shall we?"

Despite the Major's presence, we all know that Morrigan is the one in charge right now. My legs shake as we walk back across the hangar, and I drag my steps. Every ounce of bravery and determination I felt is gone.

I swallow, my throat dry, when we reach the door.

"After you," Morrigan says.

I can't look at her. We step outside. The hangar doors close behind my parents and the thugs, shutting us back in the darkness. Morrigan taps her tech band, and two transport pods glide up. "Major, will you ride with Evann and Nova to the Executives' offices? Seren can ride with me in the smaller pod."

Desperately, I look to my parents. But they're silent, fire and fear warring in their shadowed expressions. A minute later, the thugs shove them into the larger pod. Mom still looks at me from the window. I blink, and the pod has zoomed away.

Morrigan grips my shoulder and I flinch. "Come along, Seren." The fake sweetness is gone from her tone. Wrapping my arms around myself, I enter the remaining pod.

The ride is short. I don't look up when we stop, but silently follow Morrigan inside the building. My panicked thoughts race. What do we do now?

A door glides open and I step in, expecting the Executives' chambers. But the faint pink and orange light coming in from the window illuminates sterile, steel tables and blank holoscreens.

Two thoughts hit me at once: I'm in a lab. And the sunrise caught me.

"Happy birthday, Seren," Morrigan says from behind.

Prick.

The needle burns my skin. Instantly, my head swims. As the ground rises to meet me, my parents' faces flash in my mind. And then everything's gone.

~~~~~

Documentation #34: The subject is stable. All vitals are normal.
Seren, baby. I'm so sorry…
~~~~~

The voices come and go continuously. Somewhere in the back of my mind, I know they should mean something. But I feel so heavy, and yet so light at the same time. Thoughts won't piece together. Everything is just out of reach.

So I drift through nothing.

Documentation #1437: Five years have passed. The subject shows no aging, even on a cellular level…

I'm endlessly falling. The world is darkness. Unending, unchanging darkness.

Documentation #2751: There appears to be no deterioration of the subject's mental facilities after ten years.

I don't know if you can hear me. But we are starting to have shortages. I thought we were making progress on convincing the Executives to wake you up, but now they're captivated by SPINDLE…

The voices are always there in the distance, so faint. Eventually, they start to sound different.

Documentation #10198: The subject has made it thirty years and continues to remain in perfect bodily health. Plans for restoring the subject's consciousness have begun.

The darkness deepens. The voices slip farther away.

Documentation #12102: Attempts to end the subject's sleep suspension have proven unsuccessful. As a result, the Executives have deemed Project SPINDLE unfit for public use.

Seren. We have to go. I'm sorry, baby. We love you…

Then there is just silence. I am alone in the void, falling deeper and deeper into myself.

~~~~~

"I think she's coming to!"

My brain feels like it's been stabbed.

"Pulse is steadily rising to normal levels. There's an increase in cerebral activity."

I'm going to be sick.

"Give her space, guys."

My eyes fly open to blinding light. Something's beeping. Terror spikes through me. Instinctively, I sit up. Nausea and pain blindside me. I can't breathe. I squeeze my eyes shut.

Steady hands rest on my shoulders.

"Easy! Take a deep breath. It's okay. Come on, breathe with me. In, out. In, out."

After a minute of forcing air into my lungs, my heartbeat finally slows. I dare to open my eyes again. A young man looks back at me, his eyes wide with concern.

"Are you okay? Does anything hurt?"
~~~~~

I ignore his words, taking in the room around us. I'm in a hospital bed, monitors hooked up to my body. Several more people stand by various machines. My parents aren't here.

Realization blinds me like a solar flare. I've woken up—but not in the world I know. Not with the people I know. They're gone.

Tears roll down my cheeks, silent at first before turning into heaving sobs. I can't control myself. Everything feels sluggish.

The man doesn't let go of my shoulders but lets me cry. It's like he can sense that I need it. Because the tears, the pain, as much as they hurt, pound the word *awake—alive*—into my mind.

Eventually, my sobs slow down. Between hiccups, I manage to ask, "How long?"

He understands the question. "Best we can tell from the stasis pod data, you were in a suspended sleep for a hundred years."

One hundred years. But when I look down at my hands, they don't look any older.

Someone else speaks up, a woman in front of a holoscreen. "We found you when exploring the abandoned New Dion settlement. Sleep preservation stopped being studied seventy years ago. We weren't sure if we'd be able to wake you up until Benji came up with KISS."

The man, Benji, blushes. "Kinetic Introduction System Series."

She shrugs. "We just abbreviate it to KISS."

Ignoring the acronym, Benji focuses on me. "Your body was essentially frozen. Only the barest amount of activity was happening to keep you alive. We slowly brought your body back up to speed."

My mind whirls, trying to process everything. I can't. Wasn't I just outside the hangar with Mom and Dad? But it's a hundred years later. They're dead, and I'm still sixteen.

The room spins.

Benji squeezes my shoulders, slowly easing me back against the hospital bed pillow. "Deep breaths. Your name is Seren, right?" I nod, though that only makes the vertigo worse. "We'll help you, Seren. Your body is still waking up. Why don't you rest—"

"No!" The cry is out before I realize it. I take a shuddering breath, gripping the sheets. "I don't want to sleep." Not ever again.

Understanding floods across Benji's face. "Okay. We'll just sit here, then."

The room falls into an orderly silence, as the other people work on their holoscreens and adjust the monitors. Benji sits in a chair next to the bed and doesn't leave me. I stare forward, blinking back tears.

When I first realized what being a part of SPINDLE meant, I was scared most of sleeping forever. Now I realize that waking up might be the hardest part.

I swallow. Thoughts spin around my mind, constantly whirling. The room eventually empties, except for Benji, and my brain starts to slow. One thought keeps looping around.

Life involves living. And that means being awake and facing reality. That's what my parents would want me to do if they were here now.

So maybe, for them, I can face this new reality. I can pick up my life, one hundred years later.

I'll face the fears. I'll be awake.

END

DREAM HOST
Pam Halter

Princess Zella reached out and touched the spindle end.

Ouch!

Everything went black.

~~~~~

Zella blinked a few times. Where was she? She sat up and looked around. All she could see was white fog. She waved her hand at the fog. It swirled around her wrist like a ghost snake.

"Hello?" she called.

Her voice fell flat. Strange.

After shaking the fog off her wrist, she stood. The floor — or ground — seemed solid when she slid her foot forward, so she took a tentative step. Then another. As she moved slowly forward, the fog started to dissipate. Shadowy shapes appeared and disappeared as she walked. Was she inside or outside?

Zella stepped into a clearing, a semi-circle of sorts, and could see wooden doors set in a brick wall, each with an engraved metal sign centered near the top. Black metal knockers sat under each sign. The signs read:

Dream Designer
Dream Mason
Dream Inventor
Dream Weaver
Dream Implementor
Dream Distributor
Dream Terminator

A larger door in the middle of the semi-circle had a gold-edged sign that read:

Dream Host Dragoon ~ No one enters without an appointment!

There was no knocker on that door.

"Where am I?" she asked, half expecting one of the doors to open. But they remained shut.

~~~~~

"How did this happen?" roared the Dream Host Dragoon.

All the dream hosts shuddered. The DHD was known for his bad temper. One of the hosts pointed to Dream Host Hal.

"She's *his* dream ward!"

Hal put up a hand. "How is this my fault?"

Everyone murmured. Hal shook his head.

"How is this my fault?" he asked again. "I've never seen a dream ward's spirit enter the dream realm, and I've been here for centuries."

The DHD cleared his throat. "Maybe it's not your fault, but you have the responsibility for your dream ward. Figure out a way to Get. Her. Out."

Hal got looks of anger, pity, puzzlement, and amusement from his fellow dream hosts. He wondered how any of them would handle this. He was the eldest. He had the most experience, and he had no idea where to even start.

~~~~

Zella walked the semi-circle of doors, touching each one lightly. As she came to the large door and lifted her hand to touch it, a small sound made her whirl around.

"I wouldn't do that," a strange looking creature said. "The Dragoon is in a bad mood today."

Zella stared at him. He had greenish-yellow skin, orange eyes, long, wild, reddish hair that stuck out all over his head, and a squat body with back legs resembling a dog's haunches. His arms were long and skinny with long, skinny fingers. No clothing that she could see unless it was the same color as his skin.

"Where am I? Who—what—are you?"

"I'm Hal. I'm your dream host."

"Dream what?"

Hal smiled. "I'm your dream host. I oversee all your dreams."

Zella frowned. "I don't understand."

"Here, let's leave this area. It's not safe for you right now." His long, spindly fingers grasped her arm.

"Let go!" Zella gasped.

"Please, Princess," Hal said. "You must come with me. I know you don't know me, but believe me when I say you're in danger here."

Zella glanced around. All the doors were still closed, but now a few of them had lights shimmering under them. The scent of lavender wafted from each one. A nervous sensation fluttered through her. She was being watched. "All right, let's go."

She started to follow him, but it felt like walking in thick mud. After she tripped twice, Hal reached back, grasped her hand and pulled her along.
~~~~

Time lost all meaning as they walked, Finally, Hal stopped at a small wooden door with an arched top. "I'm sorry, but you'll have to squat down to get through."

Zella started to protest. She was a princess! Princesses didn't squat. But a whispering sound caused her to glance behind her at the swirling mist. Did something just move? She shivered and bent down to crawl through the doorway.

"I'm going to need help," Hal said as he looked at a large hanging picture, if one could call it that. There was nothing on it but white paint. To the right, mounted on the wall, was a silver-handled mirror. Only it wasn't a mirror. There were no reflections in it.

A white painting. A mirror with no reflection. Zella took in a trembling breath and let it out as quietly as she could. She hugged herself as she sat on the floor. What kind of place had no furniture? Or windows? Or even other rooms? All she could see were small, square doors on every space of the walls. The room itself had no corners, just rounded sides. And it was made from stone, she guessed, but really, she had no idea.

Hal seemed to have forgotten she was there. He had grabbed a stone wand and was tapping on the white board, which now had several boxes drawn on it. Each box had very small lettering on them. Impossible for her to read from where she sat.

Tap!

"No, not him," Hal said.

Tap!

"No."

Tap!

"Maybe."

Tap!

"She hates me."

Tap!

"Can't depend on him."

Tap!

"Who? Who can help?"

Tap! Tap! Tap!

"Hmmmmm … they might know how to help. Yes." He grabbed the mirror and spoke strange, unrecognizable words into it. Then he turned to Zella. "You must stay here while I get help. Please. For your own safety."

Zella nodded.

~~~~~

Hal returned with three other dream hosts, Sar, Bek, and Cam. They stood with Hal at the white board, totally ignoring Zella after the initial introductions. They whispered to each other. It sounded a bit frantic. . She
~~~~~

wanted to ask them to include her, but when she moved forward to speak, Hal looked at her and shook his head. So, she sat and observed them.

They looked almost identical to Hal except for their hair color, which varied from black to dark purple to orange.

Maybe I'm dreaming, she thought. Then she chuckled at the irony. Hal shushed her and went back to whispering with the others. He traced his finger on the board, like following a trail.

I wonder how long I've been here. Zella stretched her cramped legs.

Hal turned to her. "I think we have a plan to get you out without being noticed."

Without being noticed? By what? "What does that mean, without being noticed?"

"We don't want the Nightmare Hosts to know you're here," Hal answered.

"Nightmare Hosts?"

The smaller DH, Cam, shivered.

Zella shivered, too. "That sounds bad."

"Worse than you can imagine," Sar said.

"We need to go quickly," Hal continued. "The longer you're here, well, I'm not sure what will happen. I've never known anyone's spirit to enter the dream realm before. I don't know what effect it will have besides getting the NHs' attention."

Hal pulled a sheet of parchment from under the white board. "This will help us navigate some places in the Dream Realm I'm not familiar with."

"Good idea," Bek said.

"Bek and Sar are coming with us," Hal told Zella. "Cam will stay behind and monitor Nightmare Host activity. If he notices anything amiss, he'll contact me through the DreamCom."

DreamCom? But before she could ask about that, she had another thought.

"What—what if we get caught by the Nightmare Hosts?"

"We can't worry about that right now," Hal said. "We need to get started." He turned to Cam. "You know what to do."

They slipped out the door. Hal and the group went to the left and Cam to the right. Zella felt not only out of place, but incredibly visible. She was easily twice as tall as the Dream Hosts. How could she possibly escape notice by the Nightmare Hosts?

They passed the semicircle of doors. Only the Dragoon's door had a light shining under it now. She wanted to ask if they should tell the DHD they were leaving, but Hal didn't even pause at the door, so she kept quiet and followed the group.

Past the doors, they entered what could have been called a forest, but the trees grew squat and short with dark brown trunks and fuzzy white leaves. Nothing like she had ever seen before. She brushed a finger over a leaf. Velvety.

Sar grabbed her hand. "Great. You've just changed someone's dream."

"I'm—sorry," Zella said. "I didn't know."

"Don't worry," Hal said. "I'll contact Cam and let him know. He'll find out whose dream ward this Linden Tree belongs to."

They moved past the forest and stopped by a stream. There were various sized rocks scattered on the beach, some big enough to hide behind.

Hal motioned Zella to come closer. "Everything in the dream realm is moved and changed by touch," he said. "It's the main way we control dreams. What we just came through controls dream segments. Every dream ward has their own Linden Tree. Each leaf on the branches is a different dream topic. And when a DH touches a leaf, the dream changes."

Zella frowned. "So, if I'm dreaming something that's continuous, none of the segments have been touched?"

Bek nodded. "Just the first one."

"And if your dreams are fragmented, your dream host is touching segment after segment," Sar added.

"How do you know what to do with the segments?" Zella asked.

Hal chuckled. "It depends on the mood of the DH, or sometimes we get orders from the DHD." He pointed to the stream. "This runnel is how we control the velocity of dreams."

"We use different size macadams to control the flow," Sar said, pointing to the rocks.

Zella shook her head in confusion. She had more questions, but they started to move forward again. This time they moved quickly from rock to rock, stopping in the shadow of large ones while Hal checked ahead. When they got to a narrow wooden bridge, they darted across it and onto a path leading into a field of tall grass that looked like wheat. As the wheat swayed in the breeze, each stalk changed color. Before Zella could ask, Bek whispered, "This controls the color of your dreams."

When they were several steps in and Zella couldn't see the stream anymore, they stopped. Hal pulled out the parchment map. He ran a finger over it. "We got through the first place we might have been spotted," he said. "And we'll have good camouflage here. But I'm worried about the Nukka Hounds."

"Where's here?" Zella asked. "And what are Nukka Hounds?"

"I can't explain everything," Hal said. "Nukka Hounds are like guard dogs for the Nightmare Hosts, okay? Come on! We need to keep moving."

Zella didn't want to get caught by the Nightmare Hosts, but she was so curious. "Couldn't you tell me a little more while we walk? I promise not to touch anything."

"No, it's too risky," Hal said. "We need to keep moving!"

As they started pushing quietly through the grass, Zella caught a movement from the corner of her right eye. She turned to look. A prickly feeling began in the back of her neck and spread across her shoulders.

"Keep walking," Bek whispered.

"I thought—" she started, then gasped. A dark image moved to her left.

Hal turned to her. "What is it?"

"I saw a shadow." Zella pointed. "There."

"Keep going!" Sar hissed.

They hurried through the tall grass and came out onto a dirt road with small white cottages along both sides.

"Stay in the middle of the road," Hal said. "And no talking now. At all."

Zella nodded, keeping close to her dream host. She looked from side to side at the cottages. She saw a curtain move in one. She shivered and determined to stop looking.

As they walked, she realized there were no natural sounds, which was as disturbing as too much noise. Nor were there any natural odors. She couldn't smell the dirt on the road or the flowers she saw blooming in some of the front yards.

Suddenly, Bek's panicked shriek rent the air. "Look out!"

Hal pulled Zella down and put his arms over her head. "Don't move!"

Zella's heart pounded as the ground trembled. She peeked through Hal's hand. A herd of giant hooved feet tramped past them on the right. It felt endless, but finally it moved past, and they all got up.

"That's why we stay in the middle," Sar said. "We never know what's going to come by."

"Whatever does come by always stays on the sides," Hal added.

They began walking again. *I must be dreaming,* Zella thought. *How can I wake up?*

At the end of the road, they turned left. Before them lay a sprawling land with huge towers situated in groups, which were separated by roads. Many of the towers were so tall, Zella couldn't see the tops.

Hal looked at the map again. "At the third tower we'll turn left again and circle around the entry to the NH tunnel. It will take longer, but I'd rather not move so close to the Nightmare Host lair."

"Where are we actually going?" Zella asked.

Hal glanced at the others who looked away. "The … the way out, of course."

"But if I'm in the dream realm, couldn't someone just wake me up?"

Bek put her hand on Zella's arm. "Only someone in the real world can do that."

"Well, that shouldn't take too long," Zella said. "One of my ladies-in-waiting will come soon with my breakfast. I've been here all night, I guess."

"Time doesn't work like that here," Hal said. "Let's go."

Zella followed Hal, but she now felt more frustrated than frightened. This was the stupidest dream she'd ever had. But it felt so *real*.

As they turned left at the third the tower, Zella felt her neck prickle again. She looked to the right. That road was darker. Shadowed. A cold breeze emanated from it.

It must be road to the Nightmare Hosts.

After going two blocks, they turned right . They had only gone past one tower when thunder crashed over their heads.

"Keep going!" Hal urged.

"Do we have to stay in the middle of the road here, too?" Zella asked.

"We should," Bek answered. "I've never seen anything come from the side or between the towers to the middle of the road before."

"Do you come here often?"

Sar shook his head. "No."

Zella gave a short laugh. "That's not very reassuring."

Thunder crashed again. They picked up their pace. Zella counted five towers. It felt like they were going toward the Nightmare Hosts' tunnel now. She reached out to touch Hal on the shoulder, then screamed. A small black spider crawled across her hand.

"Shhhhhhhhhhh!" the three Dream Hosts said.

Zella shook her hand. Another spider appeared. She shook her hand again. More spiders appeared. "Get them off!" she shrieked. "Get them off!"

Bek ran in small circles. "The Nightmare Hosts! They've found us!"

Spiders multiplied into the thousands. The road crawled with spiders. Zella frantically brushed spiders off her arms. Hal pulled a tube out of his bag and blew into it. The spiders leapt off Zella and skuttled to the sides of the road.

A low, long chuckling sounded all around them. Shadowy figures appeared on the sides of the towers. They growled as they approached the dream hosts.

" Zella! Come here with us!"

Zella heard Hal's desperate call, and she tried to let him know where she was, but her voice faltered. Fear was solid in her throat and threatened to stop her breathing. She walked in a daze toward the growling shadows.

The laughter grew louder. A mound of dirt sprang up in front of her, and fire ants swarmed out of the top.

Zella whimpered, turned, and ran. But like any other nightmare she ever had, her legs became iron weights, her movements slow and clumsy.

The ants drew closer.

The thunder grew louder.

As the swarm reached her, Zella cried out. The ants rushed up her legs. She stamped her feet, but it made no difference. More and more and more ants charged toward her. In seconds they were up to her shoulders.

Hands grabbed her arm and yanked her back. She fell hard on the ground.

The ants disappeared.

The darkness fell away.

"Get up," Hal shouted. "Get up! They're here! **Run!**"

Zella got up and ran.

She came to the edge of a cliff and skidded to a stop. Fierce barking sounded behind her. She whirled around and gasped. Gigantic dog creatures sprinted toward her, barking and howling. She didn't give it a second thought. She jumped.

She fell and fell and fell. For hours.

Splash!

Cold green water covered her head.

She struggled frantically, kicking her feet.

Slimy ropes wrapped around her ankles.

Down, down, down she went.

She screamed, bubbles bursting from her mouth.

The ropes fell away. She kicked furiously until her head broke the surface of the water.

"Can you swim?" Hal yelled. But before she could answer, he disappeared.

The water froze, encasing her in ice from the shoulders down. Numbing cold started in her feet and crept up her body.

"What do we have here?" a low, raspy voice asked.

Zella couldn't answer. Her voice was as frozen as her body.

A shape came into focus in front of her. It could have been a dream host, but it was larger and darker. And its eyes were a deep violet. The giant dog creatures lumbered behind it.

It snapped its fingers. Hal, Sar, and Bek fell from the sky and tumbled onto the ice.

"What do you Dream Hosts have?" it snarled at them.

Hal raised his head and glared at the dark shape. "It's nothing for you Nightmare Hosts to worry about."

Help! Help! Someone, help! Zella tried to move, but the ice held her tight.

The NH grinned. "Anything that comes to our tunnel is our business."

"We didn't come to your tunnel," Hal retorted.

"Close enough!" the NH roared. "Now, *what* do you have? What is it?"

Hal said nothing. Sar sniveled on the ice, but Bek squeaked out, "It's – it's – it's - a new dream program!"

The Nightmare Host poked Zella's forehead. "I don't think so." He turned and snorted at the three Dream Hosts. "Now, *who* would like to tell me *the truth*?"

"It's true!" Hal choked out.

The Nightmare Host roared.

Crash! Crash! Crash! Crash! Crash!

Five more Nightmare Hosts fell from the sky and landed on the ice. The ice cracked, but Zella still couldn't move.

"Yes, boss?" one asked.

"The Dream Hosts have something *new* they're trying," the boss NH sneered.

"Really?" a second NH asked.

The boss pointed at Zella.

They all approached her. *Wake up! Wake up!* she shrieked to herself.

After they poked her face and head a dozen times, the boss NH reached down and pulled her out of the ice by her neck.

Fire burned though her body as she kicked and struggled in his grasp. He gave a cruel laugh and dropped her. She scrambled backward and looked at Hal, who was holding the side of his head and speaking rapidly. Calling for help on the DreamCom, she hoped.

"Can you talk?" the boss NH asked her.

She nodded.

"Tell us then, what *are* you?"

Zella tried to speak, but only croaks came out of her throat. Fear was a living thing, a demon racing through her body. She shook as cold coursed through her again.

Another *crash* sounded behind her. She wept at the thought of more Nightmare Hosts, but then she heard the voice of the Dream Host Dragoon.

"What are you doing to my Dream Hosts, Rak?"

"Not a thing," the boss NH said. "Not a thing."

"He tried to snuff Hal's dream ward!" Bek cried.

"*Dream ward?*" Rak roared. "*How* did a dream ward get here?"

The DHD shook his head. "No idea, but we're trying to get her out. Why are you stopping us?"

"Oh, I don't want to stop you. I just wanted to know what was going on," Rak said. He didn't sound sincere to Zella.

The DHD apparently thought the same because he snorted. "You only want to be trouble. And now that you've caused some, why don't you go away and let us attend to *our* problem?"

The other NHs burst out laughing. Rak jabbed his thumb over his shoulder at them. "And deprive my troops of helping? Never!"

He clapped his hands and rubbed them together. "I've been watching you fumbling dream hosts from the time she showed up. Do you know what I discovered? She's in a *cursed sleep*. That means she belongs to *us*!"

Hal took a step forward, his hands clenched at his sides. "You *knew* she was here?"

"No!" Zella's voice broke through her swollen throat. "No!"

"*Yeeeeeessss!*" Rak's laughter actually sounded gleeful.

Hal crawled over to Aurora and sat in front of her. "She's *my* dream ward."

Rak smacked Hal, who went sliding across the ice. As he bent down to pick up Zella by the neck again, more Nightmare Hosts appeared, slamming onto the ice with mighty crashes. The Nukka Hounds snarled, baring their sharp teeth.

Rak looked deep into Zella's eyes. Cutting pain seared across her forehead. She cried out but was unable to close her eyes. She could only hang there and endure it.

"Wake up, wake up," she whimpered. "Someone, please, wake me up."

Rak guffawed. "There's no waking from a cursed sleep!" And he squeezed.

Her hands grabbed at his to no avail. Spiders and fire ants coursed down his arm and onto Zella's head. She screamed as they poured into her mouth, eyes, and ears.

~~~~~

Zella opened her eyes. A handsome prince pulled back from kissing her.

"Troy?"

He hugged her. "You're awake. Finally!"

She looked at him in wonder, and he kissed her again. "Darling, are you okay? You're trembling."

"I am now," she said. "But I had the strangest dream."

~~~~~

At the window, unseen to all, Hal smiled. All was right in the Dream Realm. He could now give the DHD a good report.

END

THE LOVELESS LIZARD
Stoney M. Setzer

I should have known something was up. Having been in law enforcement for all my adult life, I've learned how to tell when something is fishy—or so I thought. I guess I didn't suspect my own family of conspiring against me.

Cooking for her offspring was a big deal to Mom. Her love language, I suppose. Usually, Mom had me over for supper one night a week and did likewise with my sister Carla and niece Michelle. On the Sundays when I wasn't on duty, she would invite all of us to come over after church. So, when she said that she wanted us all over for supper on the same night this week, I didn't think too much about it. I didn't even think much about it when I saw an extra car in the driveway. I just figured Carla and Michelle had come in separate vehicles for whatever reason and that maybe one of them had gotten something new.

I entered Mom's house expecting to see three females, three generations of Carter women. Tonight, there was a fourth, and I knew right away that my family was up to something. Carla's mischievous smirk only confirmed my suspicions.

The kicker was that the fourth wasn't just anybody.

"Staci?" I said, hoping I was keeping some semblance of a poker face but doubting it seriously.

"Dane!" Dr. Staci Bridges, formerly Riley, sprang to her feet and rushed over to hug me. I'd be lying if I tried to say it didn't feel good—really good, too good. Like I didn't want to let go.

"What are you doing here? Last I heard you were working as a vet in Chattanooga."

"I was, until Dad got to where he couldn't take care of himself anymore. I had to put him in assisted living over at Magnolia Grove, so I moved out here so I could see about him. Just bought the Sardis County Animal Hospital, as a matter of fact." She looked me up and down. "And I hear you're the sheriff now?"

"Yeah, that's right." I was looking her over too, I'll admit it. She didn't look much different than she did the last time we saw each other, two years after graduation. Not that she necessarily looked twenty anymore, but she didn't look forty either. Not a tinge of gray in her reddish-brown hair, and if she had put on any weight at all since then, it was too negligible an amount to notice. If I hadn't known who she was, I might have guessed her to be thirty, maybe thirty-five at the most. "You're looking good."

"So are you."

I looked past Staci's shoulder at my family and knew that I had been set up. "So, are you and Brad...?"

Staci shook her head. "He passed away about three years ago. Car wreck." She looked down for a second before meeting my eyes again. "And your mom and sister tell me that you and Jennifer divorced..."

"I'm sure they did," I said, giving them the eye. "Well, the less said about her, the better."

She slapped my chest playfully with the back of her hand. "I could have told you that before you married her, Sherlock."

"Us too, but you see how much good that did," Mom volunteered. "Maybe he would have listened better to you, though."

We finally made our way to the dinner table, with me doing my best not to make too much eye contact with my scheming family. I wouldn't be able to avoid that for long, though. Staci had to leave to go see her dad before visiting hours were up. That left me in Mom's living room with the three of them.

"Okay, I'll bite," said Michelle. "Uncle Dane, what's with the two of you making goo-goo eyes at each other?"

Carla smirked. "Well, let's just say that back when your Uncle Dane and Dr. Staci were in high school, she was his...well, his *sort of*." She made big air quotes at the end of that.

"Ooh, really? His sort of?" Michelle giggled.

"As in, everyone else could tell that they liked each other, but they never could get themselves on the same page."

"But maybe they can now," Mom added, caring nothing for subtlety.

"We'll see, Mom. We'll see." I was trying to sound dismissive, but deep down I liked the idea more than I cared to let on.

"I have her phone number, if you're interested," Carla teased.

"Let's have it," I said, trying to play it cool even as the three of them snickered.

~~~~~

By the time I got home at 8:45 that night, I had my mind made up. What did I have to lose? I was going to call her. If it didn't work out, I wasn't any worse off than I was now. Still, my fingers shook more than I cared to admit as I dialed Staci's number.

"Hey, Dane," she said right away.

"How did you know it was me?" I asked, floored.

"Oh, Carla texted me your number already. She said she gave you mine, so I was hoping I'd hear from you tonight."
~~~~~

"Yeah, I just figured we could, you know, talk."

And talk we did, until well after midnight. Even after I hung up and went to bed, I had trouble sleeping, for my mind was filled with thoughts of her.

~~~~~

The next night, I couldn't wait to call her again. Somehow, I managed to make myself wait until 8:30, when she said she usually got home from helping her dad get ready for bed at the nursing home.

By 8:50, I was more than a little concerned. Four times I had tried to call Staci, and four times it had gone to voicemail. A million possibilities went through my mind, including one that I didn't care to contemplate but couldn't ignore—that maybe she decided she just didn't want to talk to me. Sleep eluded me again that night, but the thoughts that kept me awake were far less warm and pleasant than they had been the night before.

By the next morning, I had hatched a plan to hopefully see her and find out what was going on.

Sardis County isn't all that big, but we are big enough to have our own K-9 unit. First thing the next morning, I made my way over there and took a look at Nitro, our German shepherd.

"When's the last time he went to the vet?"

"Been about five months, sir," Deputy Annie Higgins replied.

"Hmm. Maybe I ought to run him by there today," I said, doing my best to sound casual. "You know, make sure he ain't getting heartworms or anything like that."

She raised an eyebrow at me. "Heartworms? But they checked him for..."

"Well, just to be sure. Nitro's a valuable part of the force, and it wouldn't hurt for Dr. Staci to just check..."

"Dr. Staci?" Higgins asked. A little smile tugged at one corner of her mouth. "Oh, you mean the new vet!"

"Uh, yeah," I replied, sensing that my little facade was like a sheet of glass.

"Well, then in that case, you probably should take him to see her. But instead of asking about the heartworms, I think I'd mention his flea medication instead. When she looks at his records, that might be more believable." That smile was getting bigger, big enough to wonder if she had been talking to Mom or Carla—or if I was just that bad at this.

~~~~~

As soon as I entered the Sardis County Animal Hospital, I could hear the commotion. If the noise had been the sounds of dogs barking, it would have been no surprise. Even if it had been normal conversation coming from somewhere past the reception area, it wouldn't have been too surprising. However, this was the human equivalent of barking, that being people yelling at each other. I could recognize Staci's voice as one of them.

"...not going to be bullied in my own clinic!"

"You haven't even tried, you quack!" a man barked back.

Deborah, the receptionist, was turned away from her desk, watching keenly as whatever scene unfolded beyond my view. At my side, Nitro tensed up noticeably, going on the alert.

"Hey! What's going on back there?" I asked.

Startled, Deborah almost jumped out of her seat. "Hang on, Sheriff, and I'll let you back there!" she exclaimed. "Room Four!" I realized she must have thought someone called for me, and I didn't correct her. She hit a button, and the door to the back of the clinic clicked. Wasting no time, I opened the door and made a beeline for Room Four.

Staci was standing on one side of a metal examination table, while a couple stood on the other. I recognized them right away as Tom and Haley Peterson. They were an incredibly easy pair to identify. He was the president of the bank and served on numerous boards of directors around Sardis County, rich and powerful and middle-aged. She was at least twenty years younger than him, maybe more, beautiful and spoiled rotten. Both of them were quite used to getting whatever they wanted.

They didn't seem to be getting their way right now, however. She was sobbing uncontrollably, and his face was as red as a tomato. Two cages sat on the examination table. One of them held a small dachshund, which seemed to be fast asleep. In the other cage was a huge lizard unlike anything I had ever seen before. Its coloring was black and purple, like a bruise, with eyes that gleamed a chalky white.

"Sheriff!" Staci exclaimed. She was startled, but I thought she looked relieved as well. Unless, of course, it was just my imagination. Second-guessing myself where she was concerned was a time-honored tradition.

"What's going on here?" I demanded in my most authoritative voice. "You could wake the dead with all this ruckus!"

Haley wailed loudly, and the look Tom gave me could have corroded steel. "Not loud enough, apparently!" he shouted, turning his glare to Staci.

"I told you, I'm going to try everything I can, but I can't guarantee anything," she said, exerting a herculean effort to retain her composure. "But you're not going to stand here and threaten me."

"What's going on?" I repeated, turning my attention to her. The idea of anyone threatening her didn't sit right with me, but of course I had to be careful not to let my personal feelings show.

"Apparently this lizard bit their dog, Beauty," Staci explained. "And ever since, the dog has been comatose. I'm trying to help her, even kept her here all night and stayed here myself trying to work with her." She gave me a little apologetic look, and I knew that at least I had an explanation for not getting her on the phone. "But as I told them, I'm not a herpetologist..."

"But that's not good enough!" Tom shouted. "I want answers!"

"So do I," Staci retorted. "That's why I stayed with her all night."

"We caught the lizard for her, Sheriff! Surely she ought to be able to do something with that, right? Shouldn't she be able to whip up some kind of antitoxin or something?"

"Again, I'm not a herpetologist," Staci repeated. "I have made a call to a research lab in Memphis, and they're supposed to be sending somebody out. But until they get here...Ouch!" She jerked her hand away from the table. Somehow the door of the lizard's cage had slid open, and it had slipped out and bitten her on the side.

"Staci!" I cried, hurrying to her side. "Are you okay?"

The look in her eyes told me that she was anything but. "Room...spinning..." she muttered, slurring her words. "Me...super sleepy..."

Staci sank like a rock. If I hadn't been right there to catch her, she would have gone all the way to the floor. Even with her slender frame, she was dead weight. All I could really do was guide her down safely as opposed to letting her just collapse on her own.

"Sheriff! Catch that thing!" Tom shouted. "It's getting away!"

The lizard was scurrying down the table leg. I knew that I needed to catch it, but I also needed to do it without letting it bite me. Nitro was barking his head off at it, and in response other dogs joined the chorus from other rooms. If Staci heard any of it, she gave no sign.

I looked around quickly, trying to find something to catch the lizard. Suddenly I realized my hat was my best option. Moving quickly, I grabbed it off my head and came down toward the floor, throwing it on top of the lizard just before he could run through the gap under the door.

"Quick, grab me something that I can slide under this!" I cried. I felt the lizard as he wrestled against the crown of my hat.

They fumbled around for what felt like a long time before one of them finally handed me a piece of printer paper. I slid it under my hat and hopefully under the lizard's feet.

"I'm about to flip this thing over, and then we need to get this lizard back in its cage. Hopefully it won't get out this time. Set that cage on its end and open the door!"

For a man used to barking out orders, Tom followed instructions quite well. Within a few seconds, we had transferred the lizard back into its cage and latched the door tightly. Tom flipped the cage over onto its other end, so that the door was at the bottom and blocked shut by the tabletop. Haley sank down into a seat and wept.

The commotion had no effect on either Beauty or Staci. With the lizard corralled, my attention fell back to the woman I cared for. In spite of the alarming circumstances, she appeared quite peaceful, as if she was merely taking a nap. The incongruity made the situation all the more jarring. I was by her side immediately.

"Staci? Can you hear me? Staci!"

One of the vet-techs had opened the door and gawked at the tableau with wide-eyed terror. "What's going on?"

"Call an ambulance, quick!" I replied. I guess I could have done it myself, but by now I was occupied with trying to do first aid on her. I knelt down beside her and elevated her feet. It didn't make much difference. Her breathing was normal and easy, but she showed no signs of reviving.

"This is absolutely insane," Tom lamented. "I've never seen anything like this in my life! How is this even possible?"

Haley wailed so loudly that I couldn't help but look at her. Her eyes met mine, and she wept so hard that her entire body convulsed.

"Sheriff, I have a confession to make," she stammered, her lip trembling violently.

As strange as this already was, I knew in the pit of my stomach that the weirdest was yet to come. "Yes, what is it?"

Her words were barely intelligible over her weeping. "The lizard...it's my fault! I did this!" She held her arms out in front of her, as if inviting handcuffs.

Sometimes I hate it when I'm right.

Tom gaped at her in disbelief. "What are you talking about, Haley?"

"I...I'm the one who brought the lizard into our house! It was supposed to bite Tom, not Beauty, and not the vet!"

Her husband swore. "Me! What kind of crazy..."

"Don't you see? I only married you for your money! You didn't think I actually loved you, did you?"

While Tom sputtered, I reached for my handcuffs, checking Staci to make sure that her breathing still appeared normal. Nitro was licking her face, trying in vain to awaken her. My thoughts toward Haley were turning dark, and I had to remind myself to try to keep my emotions out of it.

"But...but...I..."

"You didn't love me either, and you know it," Haley hissed. "This was all like a business transaction to you. I wanted out, but that stupid pre-nup you had me sign...this was the only way, and it didn't work! Not at all!"

Another expletive escaped Tom's lips. "You mean you were trying to *kill* me?"

"Yes, you idiot!" she screamed as I put the cuffs on her.

"I must have been an idiot," Tom said, "because I really did care for you."

~~~~~

Deputy Higgins had come by the animal hospital to gather Haley and Nitro, while I followed the ambulance carrying Staci to Bloom Memorial Hospital. I brought the lizard with me, hoping against hope that somebody could analyze its venom and make an anti-toxin. Somehow, I managed to call Mom and let her know what was going on. By the time I got to the hospital, she and Carla were already there. I couldn't say much at first, but I was thankful to have them there with me.

"We're going to move her to a private room," Dr. Navarro said after what felt like an eternity. "Still don't have any idea what is going on with her or how to help her, but we'll keep her comfortable while we run more tests."

"Have you been able to tell anything about the venom from that lizard bite?" I asked, wringing my hands.

Dr. Navarro shook his head. "We're working on it, but our resources here at Bloom are limited. We've rushed a sample to some contacts I have over in Memphis, but I can't promise anything. That lizard isn't like anything I've ever seen before."

"Same here."

"Crazy thing is, she doesn't appear to be in any kind of distress, like what you'd expect from venom. We just can't wake her up."

I nodded. After he left, I looked at my mother and sister. "Do you think one of you can stay here with her?"

"Yeah, but where are you going?" Mom asked.

"I want to question Haley Peterson. Maybe if I can figure out where she got that weird lizard, maybe it can help us find some answers." As I stood up, I took a long look at Staci and felt as if my heart was being ripped out. Why hadn't I told her how I felt before? What if I never got another shot?

"Are you going to be okay, Little Bro?" Carla asked me.

"Depends on whether we can help Staci or not." It was the most honest answer I could give her.

"Excuse me, Sheriff? I hope I'm not intruding."

I looked up to see a familiar figure, an old lady in a candy striper's uniform. She was short and stout, giving the illusion that she was as wide as she was tall. "Mrs. Dell," I greeted her, immediately going on the alert. She had a knack for being nearby when weird things went down in Sardis County.

"I'm not intruding, am I?" Mrs. Dell asked with a smile.

"Not if you can help me find some answers." I still didn't know all
~~~~~

there was to know about her, but I knew she knew more about the weirdness in Sardis County than anyone else. Before I knew it, I had filled her in on everything.

"Do you really want my advice, Sheriff?" she asked when I was done.

"Yes, ma'am."

"I don't know exactly what has happened to her, so I can't give you any exact solutions. What I do know is that the only hope you have is to be brave enough to face the unknown. Now, I'm afraid I'm needed elsewhere."

"Typical Mrs. Dell," Mom muttered as the older lady waddled away.

"What was that even supposed to mean?" Carla grumbled.

"Face the unknown," I said, rubbing my chin. "Well, I guess the only place I know to start is with the one who helped get us in this mess in the first place."

~~~~~

Haley sat across the table from me in the interrogation room. She wasn't weeping like before, but she was visibly devastated, as one might expect from someone who had just wrecked her own life by botching a murder attempt. Under the circumstances, I didn't have an ounce of sympathy for her. It was all I could do to keep a veneer of professional composure as I stared at her.

"It wasn't supposed to turn out this way, Sheriff. When I got that lizard, the plan was for it to bite Tom. Nobody else. I never thought it would backfire so badly…"

"You expected attempted murder to end well?" I asked. "That was your plan, to murder your husband?"

She shook her head sadly. "Not necessarily murder, because he wouldn't have actually died. The plan was for him to go to sleep and just not wake up. Just sort of stay unconscious."

"Like what's happened with Sta—I mean, Dr. Bridges and your dog."

"Yes, sir." She looked down at her lap. "The bite was just supposed to put him to sleep and keep him asleep indefinitely. So technically, it's not *really* attempted murder, right?" She looked up at me and batted her eyes. Clearly, she was accustomed to that helping her get her way with men.

Under the circumstances, it wasn't getting her anywhere with me. "I don't know what a judge and jury would say about that. But tell me where you got this lizard in the first place and how you could have been so sure what its bite would do."

"Would cooperating with you help me out?"

I hated making promises I couldn't keep, or didn't even really want to keep. Especially with somebody who was causing me as much grief as she was. Still, I knew that I had better play my cards right with this one.
~~~~~

"Again, I can't speak for a judge and jury, but I can tell you that your chances will probably be worse if you *don't* cooperate."

She nodded grimly and looked down again. "I bought it from Val Owens."

The name rang a bell immediately. Mom never told me very much about her, but from what I did know, there was bad blood between the two of them. I had found that out back when Michelle had been turned ugly by some weird mirror. Mom had been all set to accuse Val of it, since her daughter Angela had been one of Michelle's rivals in the local beauty pageants, only to find that Angela had been victimized herself. Even though Val turned out to be blameless in this case, I gathered enough to know that she was at least in some ways connected to all the strangeness that Sardis County was known for.

Maybe if she was really behind this, then maybe she knew how to awaken Staci. It was the only shot I had.

~~~~~

I prayed throughout the entire drive to Val's house out on Glyburn Road. My prayer wasn't anything that a theologian would be impressed with, but hopefully sincerity outweighed technique. I begged for protection over me, healing for Staci, and begged forgiveness for not having told her how I felt a long time ago. I prayed that Val would somehow provide me with the answers I needed. Most of all, I prayed for a miracle.

The Owens house and surrounding acreage was outside the city limits and well off the main road. This was the kind of place for people who didn't want to fool with a lot of visitors, but I couldn't have cared less at that point. Only one thing mattered right now.

Val Owens stepped out of the house as soon as I closed my car door.

"Hello, Sheriff," she said. "Ms. Lorraine didn't make the trip with you today?"

"Mom is visiting somebody at the hospital."

Her chuckle was devoid of mirth. "And if you saw fit to drive all the way out here, I'm guessing that you think I'm connected somehow."

Since she didn't beat around the bush, I figured I shouldn't either.

"I've got Haley Peterson in the jailhouse for attempted murder. Tried to have a venomous lizard bite Tom, and she says she got the critter from you."

"Tried? As in, didn't succeed?" Val shook her head.

"So you admit it, then?"

"I admit knowing that she hated Tom and that she wanted to be able to do what she pleased without him controlling her. I admit that I sold her a lizard. Neither of those things are strictly illegal, are they, Sheriff?"

"Never said they were."
~~~~~

"And once she left here with that lizard, what she did or tried to do with it was her responsibility. So it didn't bite Tom, then?"

"No, ma'am. It bit their dog, and then it bit the veterinarian. Right now, both of them are unconscious and so far can't be revived."

Val swore under her breath. "And then Haley pointed you in my direction."

"Like you said, there's nothing I can really charge you with." *Not that I don't hold you partially responsible,* I appended in my head. *Because I do. Staci wouldn't be in this mess if it wasn't for you.* "But if you have any knowledge of this lizard's venom that could help us, I urge you to share that."

She looked away from my gaze, suddenly consumed with the condition of her fingernails. "Problem is, Sheriff, my own knowledge of the Loveless Lizard is more limited than I care to admit."

"The Loveless Lizard?"

Val examined her nails under the glint of the sun. "That's their common name…if you want to use that word for something as uncommon as they are. Supposedly, they were used for incapacitation when one's love for another has grown cold, but they weren't quite willing to get blood on their hands. If you believe the old legends, of course."

"And apparently Haley did."

"Haley wanted out from under Tom's thumb badly enough to believe anything that gave her a ray of hope. As for myself, I wasn't sure how much I believed the legends until just now, but I certainly believed in Haley's money." Now she subjected the nails of her other hand to scrutiny.

I was just barely able to keep a lid on my frustration. "Do you know if there's a cure?"

"Beats me, Sheriff. Up until now I thought the Loveless Lizard was just a funny-colored critter with a legend, remember? For all I knew, I was just selling a discolored iguana to a gullible little bimbo with marital issues. Now, if that's all you wanted to ask me…"

To be totally honest, I can't even remember if I said another word before I got out of there. All I could think of was that the only hope I had of saving Staci had gone up in smoke.

~~~~~

Mom and Carla were still there with Staci, now joined by Michelle. To my family's credit, they didn't say a word when I walked back into Staci's hospital room. I'm pretty sure that I was wearing my emotions on my sleeve in spite of myself, and thankfully they gave me some space.

For what felt like forever, I just stood there and looked at her. She looked so gorgeous, so peaceful in spite of it all that it practically ripped my heart out of my chest.
~~~~~

"I don't know if you can hear me or not, but I'm sorry. I know I failed you."

No reaction from Staci. Just her closed eyes and soft, rhythmic breathing.

"And I guess I really blew my shot all those years ago. All the times I wanted to ask you out, but I was afraid you'd say no. Scared you'd give me some song and dance about not wanting to mess up the friendship or whatever. But now I wish I'd taken my chances. At least then I would have known. Heck, I should have said something when we were on the phone for three hours the other night, but even then I couldn't."

Vaguely I was aware of Mom and Carla and Michelle, but Staci was the only one that mattered right now. "It's so stupid. I've faced lawbreakers of every kind, and more weirdness than you can shake a stick at, and I don't blink an eye. But when it came to you, I was chicken. Too scared to admit that—that I loved you, and I'm starting to think that maybe I still do. I just wish I had told you when I had the chance."

I don't know what impulse came over me, but I leaned over and kissed Staci, right on the lips. I couldn't resist the urge, but I didn't hold it there long for fear of looking creepy. Slowly I pulled back…

…Just in time to see Staci's eyes flutter open. I had forgotten about that unique shade of green.

"Dane? Dane Carter?" she asked drowsily.

"Yeah, It's me. I just…I…"

Don't ask me what I had expected to happen next. All I can tell you is that I didn't expect Staci to throw her arms around me, pull me in, and kiss me back. Fervently. The kind with feeling behind it—*lots* of feeling. Shock paralyzed me for a moment, but not for long. Before I knew it, I was kissing her back, just as enthusiastically.

I'm not sure who snickered behind me—maybe Michelle, maybe Carla—but that was what interrupted the liplock.

Staci looked around her, her cheeks quickly going crimson. "Um, I'm not dreaming any more, am I?" she asked quietly.

I cleared my throat. "Um, no, but I was wondering if *I* might be." By now I was distinctly aware of the three of them struggling not to laugh out loud, with my sister probably doing the worst job of suppressing it.

Staci shook her head for a second. "Wait a minute…can somebody let me use their phone? I need to talk to the Petersons. It's important."

I raised an eyebrow. "You just woke up. Do you really need to talk to Tom right now?" I could tell her about Haley later.

She nodded emphatically. "It's really important, Dane. It's about their dog, Beauty. I think I know how to wake her up."

"Why?"

"Because while I was asleep, I had this dream…"

Carla cleared her throat. "Uh, yeah, Staci. We gathered that. If you don't mind sparing us the details…"

Staci shook her head. "No, besides that…uh, I mean, the answer for how to save Beauty came to me in another dream. Now is somebody going to let me use their phone or not?"

~~~~~

"Beauty's as right as rain now," Staci said as she examined Nitro. "Doesn't make much medical sense, but all she needed was a little love, and she woke right up."

"Hard to picture Tom giving that kind of love to a dog," I remarked.

"Well, he didn't, but I did. Apparently, there's some stuff in that situation that I missed, stuff I expect you to fill me in on later, but the bottom line is that he doesn't want anything that reminds him of Haley any more. So, he let me have the dog, just to be rid of her. She's mine now and as good as new."

"And that answer came to you in a dream?" I asked. "While you were sleeping?"

"That's when most folks do their dreaming, Sherlock," she laughed.

"Ha ha. But I meant *that* sleep."

"Yep. Those dreams were really clear, really vivid. I guess I saved her like you saved me." She coughed awkwardly and then busied herself with checking Nitro's heartbeat.

"Hey," I said, kneeling beside her and taking her hand. She turned to look at me, our faces mere inches apart. "I think we need to talk."

And we did—between kisses, that is.

END
~~~~~

A DOZEN FAILED RESCUERS
Laurie Lucking

I attempted to pry open my eyes, which seemed to have been glued shut with resin. *Why are they so dry?* As though they'd been closed for —

My pulse took off like a runaway carriage. *The curse.* I lay still, listening. No warm air tickled my face, no inquiries or muttered speculations broke the silence. I separated my eyelids enough to squint through.

No gentleman with pursed lips hovered awkwardly above me.

My breath released in a heavy sigh, but was it relief? Or deflation? No one had broken the curse. On the positive side, I wouldn't be swept away by some stranger eager to marry me as his true love. On the negative side…I'd been asleep for one hundred years.

I rubbed my forehead, slowly convincing my long-neglected muscles to ease me into a sitting position. *One hundred years.* What kind of changed world would I find out there? And everyone I'd ever known…gone.

My mother's rival-turned-sorceress had certainly gotten her revenge.

I swiped at the tears leaking from my swollen eyes. There would be time enough for processing—for mourning—later. Now that my body was no longer under the influence of an enchanted sleep, I'd be gone soon too if I didn't find some food and water.

Summoning what little courage my hazy mind could dredge up, I shifted my legs to dangle over the edge of the bed and recoiled when I kicked something floppy. At last my eyes opened to their full capacity as I peered over the mattress to discover what my feet had encountered.

A man. My stomach lurched as my breathing shallowed. His eyes were closed as though asleep, but his limbs were sprawled at an unnatural angle. Beside him, another man lay crumpled. And another next to him…

If only my eyes had stayed closed after all. Transferring my gaze to the ceiling, I attempted to rein in my stampeding thoughts. Dissolving into a fit of gagging and shrieking wouldn't do any of us any good.

I chanced a peek around the room. A dozen men, ranging from young to almost middle-aged, sprawled on the tasseled rug beside my bed. Each wore formal riding clothes, some with swords or daggers dangling from their belts, others with bejeweled crowns askew.

What happened here? Did all these princes arrive at once and get into a brawl? But every weapon remained in its sheath. I tugged my hair. Had they ingested some kind of poison? Or been attacked by—?

Oh, no.

I crawled to the far end of the mattress and slid off onto an exposed portion of the giant oval rug that covered most of the wooden floor. The nearest prince's head lolled to the side, with a line of drool gracing his royal chin. I leaned close with a cautious inhale. He didn't smell like death, only sweat and horses and preserved meat. I hovered my hand just above his lips. *Was that…? Yes!* A puff of air warmed my palm.

Not dead, then. Only asleep.

Relief warred with irritation as my shoulders sagged. *Does no one read the fine print of curses anymore?* The small script next to the asterisk clearly stated that while the prick on my finger would render me unconscious so I could be dragged away to this lonely tower, the curse-tainted air polluting the room would keep me insensible until I received my true love's first kiss. Or remained asleep for one hundred years.

Yet not one of these men wore a protective covering over his face or even a clothespin to plug his nose against the contamination. Little wonder my true love wasn't among this careless lot.

Well, nothing to be done about it now. They'd each have to wait out their hundred years of enchanted sleep just as I had. At least my long exposure had rendered me immune to the noxious stuff.

I rose to my feet, careful not to get tangled in my long skirt, then crossed to the door. *What awaits me out there?* Sunshine, fresh air, birdsong. Would the bramble forest look the same after all this time? Would there be a way out? And what of my parents' castle, if I could make it back to Akrele? Would the polished marble floors still gleam like—?

Tears threatened again, tightening my throat. It wasn't my parents' castle any longer. Assuming it was even still standing, it belonged to strangers. No one was likely to welcome me home, or even recognize me.

My hand stilled on the knob. Freedom lay beyond this door, beyond this toxin-blighted tower. *But…* I glanced back to the sleeping princes. Even if my true love didn't lie among them, they'd all come in attempts to save me from this fate. What if some of them still had living parents, siblings, or friends? Did they deserve to wake up to a world of strangers the way I had?

"I guess freedom can wait for another day." My voice sounded gruff from disuse, but at least it worked. Wrenching open the door, I peered down the winding staircase, then back at my horde of unsuccessful princes.

Suddenly, another hundred years of cursed sleep didn't sound so bad.

~~~~~

"Almost…there." At least the prince wouldn't hear my unladylike
~~~~~

grunts in his unconscious state. "Just a few…more…stairs."

My attempts at carrying the sturdy gentleman had proven fruitless, and a tumble down the stairway would've injured us both. So dragging it was. At least the sheets from my bed cushioned him from the sharp edge of each stair.

That was my hope, anyway.

Sweat streamed down my forehead as I pulled the prince's prone form out into the sunshine. *I've done it!* A few more tugs, just to be safe, and he would be free from the curse's influence. I attempted a deep breath amid my panting. The air felt cleaner already. Lighter, somehow. The sun's warmth on my face was pure heaven after —

"What're ye doin' to me, foul wretch!"

Shock froze me in place. Apparently, he'd woken up. And hailed from Umut, if his swashbuckling accent was any indication.

"Cursed princess, my bunions! Now I see, 'twas all a trap. What's yer game, lassie? Holdin' princes for ransom? Collectin' dragon bait? Ye won't fool me a second time!" He rose on wobbly legs, struggling to unsheathe his sword.

I backed away, my hands raised in a placating gesture. "I don't plan to harm you, good sir." My foggy brain had no intention of reminding me the proper way to address princes of every neighboring kingdom. "I am Princess Chryssa of Akrele. There's no trap, and I haven't seen any dragons. I apologize for the dragging, but it was the only way to get you out of the tower. Now you're free of the curse and welcome to return home."

His narrowed eyes swept the grassy clearing that surrounded the tower in every direction. "A likely story. What've ye done with my horse, if ye're so innocent?"

The horses. I frantically searched for any signs of life, or — my heart gave a palpable shudder — piles of bones. Spotting an assortment of broken lead lines, I released a sigh. Hopefully they'd all escaped.

I took another step away from the Umuthian prince, who regarded me with a snarl. He'd freed his sword, but it drooped in his hand as though the cursed sleep had left him little strength to wield it.

"I'm afraid I don't know where your horse has gone. You've likely been asleep here for some time under the influence of the curse that rests on this tower. It may have escaped the thicket and run off to live a happy life in the wild."

He huffed. "My prize stallion? In the wild? I don't believe it. Somethin' shady is afoot, and I aim to discover what's what." He flailed in an unsteady circle.

I squinted at the thorny bushes encircling the clearing. *There.* Severed branches indicated where the princes had entered and horses had hopefully exited. They were certainly long, long gone, but I summoned an enthusiastic façade. "It would be a shame to lose a prize stallion. But see there." I pointed to the coarse opening. "No doubt he headed in that direction. Perhaps if you hurry, you could still catch him."

He looked between me and the jagged path, clearly torn. "I'd best go after 'im, then. But don't ye think o' pursuit, ye hear? I'll have no more o' yer tricks." He gave his sword a feeble swing for good measure.

"I can assure you, you're safe from me. I hope you find your horse."

Muttering under his breath, he set out toward the path of broken branches. Hopefully he'd clear more of a trail for the rest of us to follow, if he could get his sword to be of any use.

Closing my eyes against the growing ache in my forehead, I gathered my dusty sheets.

One down, eleven to go.

~~~~~

My arms screamed in protest. How would I haul *five* more princes down the tower steps? The sunshine no longer felt like a blessing. It was making me sweat clean through my brocade bodice and heavy layers. And that fresh, clean air was just a tease when I'd have to turn around and head right back into the tower. At least the apples I'd found on a scraggly tree near the door had eased the dryness in my throat and emptiness of my stomach.

I paused and stretched my cramping fingers. In another tug or two, this prince would be outside of the tower, and awaken.

Adjusting my skirt, I felt for the dagger in my hidden pocket. Princes Two and Four had also drawn swords on me, and Prince Five likely would've if he'd had one, judging from the string of profanities he'd let loose.

I cringed. Some thanks I was getting for rescuing these hapless men. Prince Three had mercifully wandered off in a daze, but Six had studied my figure with interest before suggesting we return to the tower together.

Releasing a shudder, I glanced over the clearing again to ensure he wasn't lurking nearby.

I tightened my grip on the sheet and braced myself for the final heave. Thick, auburn curls surrounded Prince Seven's freckled face. How would he react to waking up in such an unconventional manner? Experience told me *not well*, but it couldn't be helped. Strengthening my resolve, I yanked the sheet out of the shadow of the tower.

Seven rolled his head from side to side, his face pinched in discomfort.

I planted my hands on my hips. "My apologies if I hurt you on the way down the tower steps, but it was the only way to save you from sleeping for one hundred years. No, I didn't put the curse on you, I wasn't
~~~~~

bait in a conspiracy, and I most certainly didn't steal your horse so there's no need to get violent." I'd given up on any attempts at civility several princes ago. "Please just proceed down the path, as it's been a long day and I have five princes yet to save." I pointed to the scraggly opening in the brambles, then backed toward the safety of the tower.

"Princess Chryssa?" The prince...*smiled.*

My mouth dropped open, my hand pausing on its way to my dagger. "Yes."

"Just as beautiful as I remembered." His cheeks turned an endearing shade of pink. "Did you say you saved me from that tower? By yourself?"

"Well, yes." Clearly my lengthy nap had done little for my vocabulary. "I figured there was no reason for the rest of you to sleep the full one hundred years if there was something I could do about it."

"That's right, you said there were more. May I help you remove them?" His gaze rose to the tower's full height. "If I recall, there were a great many stairs."

Eighty-two, not that I'd counted. "I—I suppose I would appreciate the help." I took a tentative step toward him. "But you're not angry? Or suspicious? Or planning to..." I detected no lewdness in his earnest eyes. "Never mind."

His forehead creased in a frown. "Why should I be angry or suspicious? You were more a victim of this curse than the rest of us. It's my own fault if I lingered too long without even..." He shook his head. "I knew based on the wording that I should've gotten out of there as quickly as possible. I can hardly blame you."

Finally, a man of reason. One who'd even read the entirety of the curse that had been filed in the Hall of Magic! My smile felt unfamiliar but pleasant. "You'd be surprised to hear how rare your sentiments are. But they are appreciated, and I would gladly welcome your help with the remaining princes."

His gaze stayed on my face a moment longer before he stood and patted his legs. "Uncomfortable predicament, isn't it? Sleeping for years in an ungainly heap?" He rolled his shoulders and stretched his fingers. "But I'm grateful to be in one piece, especially since my fellow princes sound like downright blackguards." He sauntered to my side with another warm smile. "Lead the way, Princess."

I paused in the doorframe, taking in his bristled jawline. Would the poisoned air put him back to sleep since he'd awoken before the full one hundred years? "Do you have a handkerchief or something to tie around your face? I'd hate for you to succumb to the curse all over again."

He pursed his lips. "Good thinking." He rummaged in his pockets and produced an oily cloth, likely used to clean his sword. "This'll have to do."

I stifled a giggle as he tied it around his nose and mouth. The resulting appearance of a bandit somehow didn't fit his formal attire and merry eyes. "Not the height of fashion, but hopefully it will help." I motioned him forward.

My leg muscles grumbled as I wound up the staircase yet again. Prince Seven's heavy footfalls behind me were a bit disconcerting, yet oddly comforting.

But he hardly deserves to be called Prince Seven when he's offered to help me…

"Pardon my rudeness. You know my name but I'm afraid I don't know yours." I tried to keep my voice steady despite my huffing breaths.

"Not at all. The fault is mine. Prince Hadrian of Seaghda, at your service." His words came out slightly muffled.

"It's a pleasure to meet you." I paused for a few pants before continuing. "I regret to admit I've been dragging each of you down on my bedsheet, but if you have a better solution, I'd be glad to hear it."

"Sounds like they deserved no better." He massaged the back of his head, likely where it'd struck each stair edge. "I may be able to carry them myself, depending on their size."

The last curve opened into what had been my bedchamber for the last hundred years. The gauzy curtains and luxurious comforter produced an eerie contrast to the crumpled men.

Hadrian took in the room with a critical eye. "None of them were your true love, then?"

"Apparently not. Though having met most of them, I can't say I'm disappointed. Or surprised. With the exception of you, of course. I mean — that is to say…" Heat seared my cheeks as I hazarded a glance toward him.

He kept his face down, scuffing his worn boots on a wooden plank. "You were stuck here for one hundred years. When I did nothing to —" He scratched where the cloth tugged at his ear. "You must be so disappointed."

I shrugged. "In a way. But marrying a stranger wouldn't have been easy either, even if the curse determined he was my true love." I scanned the remaining five sprawled princes. "I'm sorry you've been stuck here for so long, too."

He threaded his fingers together. "Not much of a loss, really. My parents had already passed away, and my paranoid older brother was eager to be rid of me in case I made some kind of bid for the throne." A hint of sadness laced his quiet chuckle. "He needn't have worried. I was much more interested in seeing the world and having adventures than running a country."

"I know what you mean. I didn't find the prospect of spending my life in a castle too inspiring, either." Sorrow pinched my chest. "But it is hard to accept that my entire family is long gone."

"I'm sorry for your loss." Hadrian placed a warm hand on my arm.

"Thank you." I leaned into his touch, starved for human interaction after being lifeless for so long. "I'm sorry for your loss, as well. Even despite your brother, you've lost a lot of time. I can't guess how long you were asleep."

He tilted his head. "It is strange to think about, but it also gives us a rare opportunity. How many people get to experience life in two eras? To see the changes over the course of many years without losing age or health? I'm curious to see what this new version of the world holds."

"What a delightful way to think of it." His optimism stirred an eagerness to explore in my own chest. I lost myself in his blue eyes, probably smiling like an idiot.

His gaze was soft until he blinked. "I'm not feeling sleepy yet, but we'd best attend to these fellows. Shall we try two at once? You take that one on your sheet, and I'll carry this one." He indicated the tall gentleman curled near the window.

"Yes, please. The less trips we have to make, the better."

"I guessed as much." He bent, grunting as he hefted the velvet-clad Prince Eight over his shoulder.

"Are you sure you can keep that up all the way down the stairs?" I adjusted the last corner of my sheet, then gripped the leather boots of the nearest prince.

"You wound me." He managed to shift a hand to the vicinity of his heart. "Have you so little faith in my might, Princess?"

I grinned at the dramatic creases at his temples. "Not at all, good sir. I merely wanted to express concern for your wellbeing. Your strength is clearly up to the task." A glance at his straining shoulder muscles beneath his crimson vest indicated the statement was likely true. Before the heat pulsing up my neck could appear on my face, I returned my attention to centering Prince Nine on my sheet. "And please, call me Chryssa."

"In that case, your concern is appreciated. Chryssa." He directed a shy wink my way before facing the door. "Shall we be off?"

"Indeed." I straightened, two corners of the sheet twisted around my fingers. "Though I'll let you lead this time."

He nodded, then began his descent.

The trek down didn't feel so long this time, despite my body's increasing weariness. I had company. I had *help*. My steps lightened as Hadrian whistled a jaunty tune, I suspected for my sake.

What a change this man was from the other princes. I could easily imagine going through life with his pleasant, laughing face at my side — just the kind of man I'd pictured as my true love.

I tightened my grip as my steps faltered. *Hadrian can't be my true love.* His kiss had failed to wake me, just like the others.

I resumed my descent, which felt like a trudge once more.

Oh, well. True love or not, I was still thankful for his aid.

We emerged into the afternoon light. At least, that was my guess based on the angle of the sun. Presumably *that* hadn't changed over the past hundred years.

"Careful." I attempted to project my wheezing voice to where Hadrian ducked under the doorway, Prince Eight still hoisted over his shoulders. "Once you get about five steps out of the tower, he'll start to wake."

"Good to know." His tone was cheerful, though strained. After clearing the doorframe, he crouched and eased the tow-haired prince to the ground.

I dragged Prince Nine alongside them. "Be warned, they haven't all taken this as well as you."

His brows assumed a quizzical tilt. "I assumed as much, based on your cynical greeting. The scoundrels." He shook his head, further tousling his bedraggled hair. "But rest assured, I won't let any harm come to you."

The thought of someone wanting to *protect* me when the others only blamed or leered… I grinned up at him as my heart awakened a little further from my lengthy sleep.

What must've been an answering smile lit the visible portions of his face. He swallowed, his gaze returning to the man slumped at his feet. "Shall we?"

I cleared my throat. When had I leaned so close to him?

"I suppose we'd better." I gathered the sheet into my fists and gave it a final yank. Perhaps a bit harder than necessary.

Hadrian grasped Prince Eight's boots and pulled until he was level with Prince Nine. Prince Eight grunted.

I tensed as my fingers fumbled for my dagger. Hadrian's hand rested near his sword hilt.

"What's this about?" Prince Eight sat up, his chiseled features darkening in a grimace. He recoiled at the sight of Prince Nine writhing at his side. "Knocking men out, dragging them who knows where. You have a lot to answer for." He made it to his feet and raised his fists in a protective stance.

At least this one didn't have a sword.

"Easy, man. There's no need to —"

Prince Eight railed on, indifferent to Hadrian's attempts to calm him. The greasy face cloth likely wasn't helping our cause. "Used the pretty girl to lure us in, no doubt. Wouldn't take us on in a fair fight, and now what?

You'll rob us? Hold us for ransom? Not if I have anything to say about it!" He looked to his groaning comrade, as though hoping Prince Nine would rally to his aid.

"Enough." Though barely raised in volume, Hadrian's voice radiated command. "This is Princess Chryssa of Akrele, and you *will* show her the proper respect. Though you may be too dense to remember, you came here in an attempt to save her from a sleeping curse and fell victim to it yourself. Now that the princess is awake, she took it upon herself to save us as well, for which we owe her unending gratitude. You may help us rescue the other princes or be on your way."

"Hmph." Prince Eight's narrowed eyes darted between us. "Princess Chryssa? Sounds familiar, but how do I know—"

"Princess?" Prince Nine cut him off, pausing in his flailing to stare at me. "How did I get here?" He'd tangled himself in the sheet, and the desperation in his eyes tugged at my sympathy.

Confusion, I could handle.

I knelt beside him, offering a hand to help him sit up. "I apologize I couldn't deliver you out of the tower in a more dignified manner. You were asleep up there," I pointed to the small rectangular window under the tower's pointed roof, "but I brought you out here so you'd wake up from the curse."

"Oh." He squinted, taking in the clearing. "I suppose my horse is gone?"

"I'm afraid so. But a path has been cleared, so it shouldn't be too difficult to find your way."

He nodded, his expression vague. "I see." Rising on shaky feet, he lifted a hand in a feeble wave. "Thank you." Jaw set, he wandered away from the cleared patch of brambles.

Jumping forward, I gently took his shoulders and steered him in the right direction. "Try that way."

He changed course with a mumbled assent.

Prince Eight regarded the exchange with pursed lips. "Letting us go, eh? In that case, I'll make sure he doesn't lose his bearing." With a wary glance toward Hadrian, he hurried after Nine.

My sigh came out half weariness, half amusement. "That's two more gone."

The sternness left Hadrian's face in an instant, replaced by concern. He crossed to my side, squeezing my shoulder as we watched them go. "You have my deepest sympathy you were given such a sorry lot of princes to attempt to rescue you. Small wonder you slept for the full hundred years."

"Most have been less than impressive, I'll admit. Imagine if one of them *had* awakened me?" A tremor rippled through me. "I appreciate your expert handling of Prince Eight. But poor Prince Nine seemed kind enough. Perhaps he's been asleep the longest."

"You numbered us?" Hadrian stepped in front of me, not bothering to hide the glint in his eyes.

I bit my lip, hoping to clamp down the warmth rising to my cheeks at my blunder. "It's not as though I knew all your names. And as you can see, precious few of you have bothered to make formal introductions."

His chuckle rumbled in a lower key than I would've expected. "A fair point." He gestured to the tower. "Shall we go fetch princes Ten and Eleven, then?"

"I suppose we'd better." I elbowed his side as I dashed for the stairs. "Prince Seven."

~~~~~

"Only...one...more."

Hadrian and I sat against the hard stone of the tower, resting in the shade after our latest slog down the stairs. This time he'd assumed an authoritative air from the start, sending Princes Ten and Eleven on their way before they had a chance to protest.

I nudged his arm. "If only I'd woken you first, it would've saved me a lot of trips."

"I would've been happy to help." He rolled his shoulders. "But I'll handle Prince Twelve, once I can feel my fingers again. You've earned a break." He glanced at me. "Unless you have belongings you'd like to bring along when you leave?"

My mouth opened and closed without a response. Was there anything I wanted to take from the tower? I pictured my gilded cage — a fancy bed, elaborate tapestries and rugs. Plenty of opulence, but nothing useful. "No, I don't think there's anything that would be worth lugging around. And I'm not sure I want any reminders." My voice thinned to a whisper.

"I can understand that." Hadrian rested his head against mine.

I wanted to melt against this strong, thoughtful man. To beg him to take me with him when we were done here.

But doubt dispersed the lovely daydream. *He's not your true love.*

With a resigned wince, I shifted. "Will you return to...Seaghda, did you say you were from?"

He shrugged. "I suppose I haven't thought that far ahead yet. There wouldn't be much left for me. I'm not sure how much time has passed, but I doubt anyone in my brother's family would welcome me back." He straightened the wrinkled white cuff of his sleeve. "I'd be happy to escort you to Akrele, if you'd allow me."

Akrele. My heart both pulled and sagged at the thought. "There's nothing left for me there, either." I wrapped my arms around my knees.
~~~~~

What would I do next? As eager as I was to get the last of the princes out of the tower, the gaping emptiness that stretched beyond made me want to cling to the certainty of my prison.

Hadrian patted his legs. "Well, let me set Prince Twelve to rights before we forget about him. It'll give us both a little time to consider what's to be done." His gaze rested on my face, full of—longing? Compassion?

I pasted on a fake smile. "Are you sure you don't want me to help?"

He shook his head. "Enjoy your well-deserved respite. Soon you'll be free of this tower forever." He reached as though wanting to take my hand, but instead turned away. "Prince Twelve and I will be out shortly."

My thoughts churned in his absence, hardly more restful than a march up and down the curving staircase. Where should I go? Did Hadrian truly want to travel with me? Did I want to travel with him? My heart sang *yes*, but my mind clamped it down. Just because he was the kindest of the twelve princes who'd happened upon my tower didn't mean I should tie my fate to his. Especially since I knew he wasn't my true love.

But does it matter?

I bounded to my feet, striding in the direction of the path widened by the already-departed princes. Their work was clumsy at best, but a slapdash trail of hewn and trampled branches extended deep into the thicket.

At least they'd helped a bit, in spite of themselves. The idea brought a smirk to my face.

"Chryssa?" Hadrian's voice held a note of panic.

"Over here." I waved, shading my eyes against the bright sun angled behind the tower.

He hefted Prince Twelve from his shoulders, tugged off his face covering, then hurried over. "You were...leaving?" His curious brow raise didn't mask the hurt in his expression.

"Not at all." Though of course it looked that way. *Brilliant move, Chryssa.* "I felt restless and wanted to see how well our friends had cleared the path."

"I see." The tightness in his jaw eased. "You're welcome to go, you know. Don't feel any obligation to stay with me. I realize we hardly know each other, and—"

"Excuse me, do you know what this place is?"

I started at the sudden appearance of Prince Twelve. He scratched his forehead, shoving aside a black curl.

"A cursed tower. But you're free now to be on your way." Hadrian gestured to the path. "Best of luck to you."

Prince Twelve's boots shuffled as he looked between the tower, us, and the brambles. "Ah. I thank you, good sir. Princess." He gave us a tentative bow, straightening the lopsided crown circling his head. "Good day." With a final nod, he marched ahead.

I swallowed a laugh and leaned toward Hadrian, keeping my voice at a whisper. "You're so much better at dealing with them than I was."

His grimace was half pained, half playful. "Only because so many of the surrounding kingdoms lack a proper respect for women. And my sword probably helped."

"Probably." I flinched at the sadness returning to his face. Sadness I'd put there. "Truly, Hadrian, I wasn't leaving. I wouldn't do that to you after all your help."

"You owe me nothing, Chryssa. It was the least I could do after you saved me from another goodness knows how many years asleep." He grasped the nearest branch like a walking stick. "I am happy to escort you—guard you—wherever you'd like to go. As long as you need me. But I don't want to force my company on you."

"Where do *you* want to go?"

"Anywhere with you." His warm gaze landed on me before he reddened and looked away. "But that foolishness aside, I'm not sure I want a set objective. I'd like to explore, see what the world holds." One shoulder lifted in a half-shrug. "I suppose that's imprudent, to have no plan."

"It sounds exciting." I arranged my rumpled skirt. "But would you really want to travel with me? Doesn't it…bother you?"

He blinked. "Doesn't what bother me?"

My mouth suddenly felt the full dryness of a day without water. "That I'm not your true love."

An unfamiliar spark lightened his eyes as he stepped closer. "What makes you say that?" Just as quickly, the light faded. "Ah, of course. Chryssa, there's something I should explain." He hung his head, kicking at the dirt. "I—I never kissed you."

"Oh." My mind tumbled with responses, questions, but none of them formed words on my lips. Had he not wanted to kiss me once he saw me? He didn't seem repulsed by me, but perhaps…

"I'm an idiot, I know." He rubbed his jawline. "To come all this way, only to fail in my one mission. But when I saw you, I just," he returned his gaze to me, equal parts embarrassed and pleading, "I could only stare. You are so beautiful."

Hope settled in my chest like morning dew. *Does he mean it?*

"Then after a minute I began to doubt myself. Who was I to kiss such a lovely princess? What if you didn't want to be kissed by me?" His breath huffed out in a snort. "Apparently, while I deliberated, the curse took me."

Confusion and hope tumbled through my mind like raging rapids.

He could be my true love. "But then how will we know?" The question slipped out before I could restrain it.

"Whether I'm your true love?" His posture gained confidence as he took my hands. "I suppose like anyone else—we spend time together, discover each other's faults, then see if we can still love each other in spite of them."

My stomach performed odd flip-flops at the sensation of his callused thumbs rubbing my palms. "I like the sound of that."

"Then shall we set out together? At first, at least? And as friends, of course, rather than... That is, I'd never expect—" He released one of my hands to pinch the back of his neck.

"Yes. Let's see what this new world has to offer. Together."

His wide smile turned his eyes into merry slits. "Where would you like to go?"

"Anywhere with you." My stomach gurgled as I accepted his offered arm. "But first let's find some food."

He placed a kiss on the back of my hand, his laugh spreading warmth across my fingers. "I like the sound of that."

END

OPERATION WAKE
Kathleen Bird

It's imperative that I remain focused and diligent on this mission no matter what else transpires.

That was the thought uppermost in his mind as he stood outside the classroom door with the faulty doorknob. It took a few good twists to get it to open properly, and when he finally entered the room, he was surprised to find he was not alone. Far be it from him to deprive other students of the opportunity to scope things out before class began, but he had anticipated a little more privacy, given he'd arrived fifteen minutes early to an 8 am lecture.

Armed with his thermos full of coffee and a stack of notebooks, he made his way to a seat near the back, which would provide the best vantage point for observation. The row in front of him was occupied by two girls, a blond and a brunette, who were talking quietly…or so they thought. Julius merely tapped what appeared to be a hearing aid but was actually an amplifier that allowed him to eavesdrop with ease.

"Are you sure I haven't seen you around before?" the brunette asked. "You seem really familiar."

"Um…well, I was online last semester," the blond said, "so, you wouldn't have seen me in class. But my boyfriend's band does play at a lot of the local coffee shops, so maybe you've seen me at one of those?"

The brunette looked thoughtful as she flipped through her notebook and found a clean page to begin taking notes for the day. "I'm not much of a coffee drinker. I like to sleep too much, you know?"

Her fellow classmate laughed and replied, "Honestly, I'm a tea drinker myself, so, I can't blame you. Hey, what about you?" she asked, turning to look over her shoulder at him.

Julius passed a quick hand over the amplifier to turn it off before replying to the unexpected question. "Oh, um…I'm team coffee, for sure. Need it for these early classes, am I right?" He fumbled with his thermos, barely catching it before it careened off the edge of the desk. Both girls were looking at him, and he felt captivated by the hazel eyes of the brunette that stared at him without recognition. His heart broke a little bit at the painful reminder of his current mission.

"My name's Annaliese," the blond said cheerfully. "And this is my brand-new friend…"

"Drema," his target said shyly. She nervously swept her hair behind her ear, and Julius felt his heart beating right out of his chest as he extended his hand to her. Gingerly, she shook his hand. He missed the warmth and strength that he'd been unconsciously expecting. It was difficult to keep the disappointment at bay and a smile on his face as other students finally began trickling into the room.

"Julius," he said softly, hoping and praying for a flicker of remembrance where there was none. The brunette merely nodded and released his hand without saying another word.

The blond prevented any further opportunities by saying, "Guess we'd better get ready to listen. Nice to meet you, Julius. Talk more after class?"

He nodded mutely and watched the two girls turn back around to face the front.

This is going to be harder than I thought for multiple reasons, he thought, as the professor began introducing himself and explaining the syllabus. Thus ensued an hour of pretending to care about art history, and from the looks of his fellow students he wasn't alone in that aspect.

Drema was yawning by the end of the class, and he smiled at the familiar gesture.

"Some things never change," Julius whispered with a chuckle. He pushed his glasses further up his nose before collecting his things and approaching Drema and her new friend.

"Would either of you ladies be free for breakfast in the cafeteria?" He tried to sound casual, but his heart danced in a staccato rhythm.

Annaliese eyed him suspiciously, glancing back and forth between him and his target with a meaningful look. "I've got to give my boyfriend a call before my next class, but didn't you say you were starving, Drema?"

The lovely brunette blushed and barely met his gaze to reply, "Yes, I...I'm a little hungry I suppose."

His heart soared, and his smile became genuine. "Excellent! Then let's be on our way."

They made their way out into the hallway, waving good-bye to the blond who'd already pulled out her cell phone. He was careful to observe Drema's mannerisms to be aware of any sign that she might flee. So far though, she was exhibiting the traditional markers of a shy, demure young woman: taking quick steps to keep up with his longer stride, holding her books close to her chest as she looked down at the floor, and every so often she tucked a stray piece of hair behind her ear. It was sweet and endearing, but strange to him at the same time.

The cafeteria was across the small campus, so they got to enjoy some of the fall foliage that presented itself in colorful leaves and cute sweaters worn by the other students. Julius took a deep breath of the crisp air, steadying himself in preparation for the difficult conversation that was to come.

But perhaps not today. Perhaps for today I can just be…Julius. He smiled, happy at the thought of preserving the peace for just a little while longer.

He opened the door to the cafeteria building and allowed his companion to enter first. She gave him a small smile before turning her attention to searching through her purse for her student ID card. They both scanned their cards at the front cash register, then took their place in the serving line and attempted to make their selections. While Drema remained fixated on the food options in front of her, he touched the amplifier in his ear one more time.

There weren't as many voices in the dining hall as one might expect, although the fact that college students tended to be night owls for the most part could be a contributing factor. But he still wanted to be as alert as possible, so he began to mentally sort through the conversations of other students in line and listen carefully for any threats.

"Do you know what you want, Julius?"

It took him a moment to refocus on the beautiful girl beside him, and he regretfully turned the amplifier off to better pay attention to her words. "I'll probably try a little of everything. Breakfast is the most important meal of the day, you know."

"I wouldn't know," she said with a soft laugh, "I'm usually still asleep. I only signed up for this morning's class because it was the only art history elective that fit in my schedule."

He raised a curious eyebrow before grabbed a tray and making his selections. The student worker who served him the eggs, bacon, and hashbrowns looked half-asleep himself. Drema opted for French toast with strawberries drizzled with chocolate sauce after another few moments of thought and a few grumbles to keep the line moving from the students behind them. *She used to be more decisive than this. I know they said she'd be different, but…I didn't expect her to be a completely different person.* He tried to comfort himself with the knowledge that deep down she hadn't truly changed. It was obvious even to a blind man that she still possessed the natural beauty and grace that he'd always admired. In fact, she was still the most beautiful woman he'd ever laid eyes on, and that made the warmth in his heart sing.

"Where should we sit?" Drema's voice interrupted his thoughts, and he chastised himself for his wandering mind.

"Why don't we head towards that window to the right?" The empty table he suggested would provide ample opportunity to observe the students coming into the cafeteria as well as exiting, plus he'd be able to notice any irregular movements going on in the courtyard. Drema sat with her back to the open archway, and he shook his head at such a foolish move, to leave herself exposed from behind. He tried not to stare as she began eating, and his brain raced through the most optimum conversation topics to achieve his goals. Once again, he was interrupted by her melodic voice with a question of her own.

"Is today your first day at this university as well?"

He nodded, chewing his own food carefully and slowly to allow for more thinking time.

"What's your major?"

His mind blanked. Somehow that topic had never occurred to him, a severe oversight on his part he now realized. "Oh, um…I'm undeclared," he said half-heartedly.

"Oh," Drema said puzzled, "Are you just taking a bunch of electives?"

"Sort of," he said once he'd swallowed again. The rubbery eggs were upsetting his stomach, so he pushed the remainder of them aside. "I'm just trying out different things I guess."

"That makes sense. So, what else are you taking?"

He blushed and shoved a rather large piece of bacon in his mouth to avoid answering. *She's going to be suspicious if I tell her since they're all the same as hers.* As he tried to come up with a way to change the subject, his eye caught an older student entering the room with a half-empty tray. Perhaps in his early thirties, the man in question was dressed oddly, as though he'd read stories about college students but had never been one himself. His outfit was a compilation of several stereotypes, including oversized sweatpants and a tight-fitting superhero t-shirt. But it was the sunglasses that he wore inside on a cloudy day that caught Julius' attention.

"Having trouble remembering? I have trouble keeping my schedule straight too. So many classes to keep track of," Drema said gently to fill the void of silence. He turned his attention back to her while keeping one eye on the stranger as he selected a seat at the table next to them.

Interesting, he thought as he tapped his fork on the side of his plate and picked up the dulled butter knife in his other hand.

"Yes, it's a lot to keep track of. But I was wondering, aren't you a little young to be attending university in the first place? What are you, fifteen?"

"Sixteen," the young woman protested. "I skipped a few grades in elementary. What about you? You don't look old enough to be in college either."

"Oh, um. I'm seventeen, but I'll be eighteen in a few months. Went to kindergarten early," he said without looking at her. The other student wasn't eating. He was pushing food around on his plate to appear busy, but he had yet to put a single bite in his mouth. Julius put his fork down and pushed his plate aside, but he kept hold of the knife for the moment.

"Are you all right? You seem rather distracted," Drema said

nervously. She'd abandoned her remaining food and was instead toying with the hair she'd pushed repeatedly behind her ear. It was cute in a way, but it definitely fell in the distracting category. Of course, that wasn't what she'd been referring to, but he couldn't tell her what was really going on in his mind as he continued to keep one eye trained on the out-of-place non-eating student.

"Um, yes, sorry. You're a little distracting…" He blinked twice and then felt the heat of a blush spread across his face. She was looking at him slightly horrified. He could've slapped himself for his stupidity. "No, wait. That…that wasn't what I meant."

"Maybe I should be going," she said hesitantly as she began to pile things onto her plate to discard. "I've got a class in an hour anyway."

"No!" he said frantically, reaching out to grab her wrist and hold her still at the table. The moment she'd moved to stand the operative posing as a student had begun to make his move. Now he stood half-seated with his tray in his hand, and a scowl firmly in place.

I've been made. This is why back-up plans were invented. He turned to say that he'd happily escort Drema to her next class, but the panicked expression on her face startled him. Her hazel eyes were like bright saucers that stood out among the pink that covered the rest of her face. He realized he was still holding her wrist.

"Oh!" He released her hand. "S-sorry, I just…there's not an explanation that's going to dig me out of this hole, is there?"

"Not really," she said as she rubbed her wrist. "Pardon me for saying so, but…you're acting really strange. Are you okay?"

"Um," he said slowly as his brain worked a mile a minute. The operative had given up on blending in and was now coming toward them with an evil grin on his face. Julius sighed internally. "Look, I can't explain right now, but we have to go."

He grabbed her wrist once more and tugged her toward the exit, ignoring her protests. Logic dictated the other operative wouldn't want to draw any more attention to himself, but he was speed walking to keep up with them. *I have to lose him. Too bad there's not more of a crowd right now. A proper distraction would be excellent right about now.* They wove through the entryway and back out onto the quad.

"Julius, what is going on? Can you let me go now?"

"No," he said fiercely. "I'm never going to let you go!"

Her struggling intensified to the point where he had to acknowledge her distress. He spun around to reprimand her, but her eyes were shining with tears and her lower lip was quivering.

I've bungled things again, haven't I? He retraced his words in his mind and found the root of the problem, which caused an external groan and an internal kick in the shin.

"Are you kidnapping me?" she whispered through her tears.

"No, of course not!" Julius looked up to see the enemy operative closing in on them with what appeared to be an innocuous pen in his hand. His trained eyes recognized the mini-stun gun aimed at them. If he couldn't take them quietly, then he'd be forced to use more imaginative measures. "You just have to trust me!"

"I don't even know you!" she shouted, and a few students stopped to stare at the exchange. He couldn't risk letting go of her now, as she'd be more likely to run, but he couldn't let her keep screaming and raising a fuss either.

Or can I? He smiled and leaned into his newly forming plan.

"I can't believe you don't remember me!"

She paused her struggling and gave him that wide-eyed stare. "What are you talking about?"

"We both went to that party a few weeks ago? It was at this fancy place near the capital, and you were wearing a red dress that should have been illegal. We danced and talked all night!" His continued shouting was attracting more of a crowd, and it appeared to have impeded the confidence of the approaching threat who'd now slowed to a stop in the second row of the growing audience. *Good, this is working exactly to plan.*

"You're lying!" she shouted, unknowingly playing her part to perfection. "None of that ever happened! I'd never met you before this morning!"

"Don't you remember? You told me about how your parents died, and you grew up with your aunt who lived out in the country. How passionate you are about chocolate and strawberries. You can't tell me you don't remember any of it?"

It was there. He was certain of it. For a moment, she remembered. He saw the recognition in her eyes before it clouded over again.

"I have literally no idea what you're talking about!"

"Well, maybe you'll remember this," he said smoothly as he pulled her in close to him and leaned in for a kiss. The crowd was whooping and hollering, and against his better judgment, he closed his eyes to lose himself in the moment.

She slapped him.

It was hard enough that his eyes snapped open, he released her hand, and fell to the ground. *She certainly hasn't lost any of that upper arm strength.* But before he could admire her further, she was running away from him amid the catcalls and jeers of the onlookers. Now he'd made himself an ungentlemanly rogue in her eyes, and all for nothing when he looked around and realized he'd lost track of their tail.

He reached up and tapped his amplifier, hoping to catch a whisper of a hint before running off blindly. Despite the importance of this mission, he seemed to be doing everything in his power to muck it up. At that moment, a soft chime from his watch signalled an incoming call from headquarters. He groaned as he dusted himself off and began jogging after Drema.

"The king and queen are longing for children," came a staticky voice from his earpiece.

"Their wish will soon be fulfilled," he muttered loud enough to be picked up on the microphone hidden in the watch itself, but not loud enough for anyone to wonder why he was quoting obscure lines from fairytales. Then again, probably not the strangest thing the average college student had heard.

"Please update, Agent Prince. Have you found the target?"

"Target is acquired but be informed that enemy operatives are also in pursuit."

"You must wake her before they catch up with her! This mission is of the utmost importance!"

"I'm well aware of that," he whispered sternly. "I have a personal stake in Operation Wake as well."

"Don't let your emotions get in the way of completing the mission, Agent Prince," the crackling voice reprimanded him in its sterile robotic tone. "Just wake the target."

"I'm aware of the mission," Julius said defensively as he peered behind a hedge to see if she'd found a place to hide. His amplifier was only picking up the miscellaneous chatter of co-eds going about their daily lives, and he was about to tap it off when a sinister voice finally broke through the haze.

"There you are, Agent Rose. We've been looking everywhere for you, you know. Why don't you come out of there and play?"

His heart was racing as his feet pounded the pavement, trying to get closer to that ominous voice. "I have to go, Headquarters. Prince out."

Coming around the corner of the brick building that housed the administration offices, he found the enemy operative approaching what appeared to be a disabled car. At least, it must be disabled because if Drema could have started it by now, surely she would have, right? She was sitting in the driver's seat, sobbing with her head buried in the steering wheel. And the approaching man had pulled out his stun gun.

She doesn't see him, Julius thought in a mad panic as he raced toward the man. The foolish operative wasn't watching his six, which made it easy to punch him in the face and send him crumbling to the ground. The stun gun skidded away. Julius grabbed it up and shoved it in his pocket.

Unfortunately, this had to take place immediately outside Drema's window, and to his great misfortune, she chose that moment to pay attention to her surroundings. Now, she was frantically pushing down all the manual locks in the car to prevent him from entering.

I can't do anything right today. He slowly approached her car with hands raised in surrender before tapping gently on the window.

"Can we talk? Please?"

She reached for the manual window control and cranked it enough to open just a crack. "Who are you?"

"I'm a friend, I promise."

"A friend who goes around kidnapping and punching people?"

"And attempting to kiss them, apparently," he muttered. Thankfully, she didn't seem to hear that comment. He cleared his throat and tried to change the subject. "Look, we need to get this car moving. Is it engine trouble?"

"No-no," she stuttered helplessly. "I just…didn't start it yet."

He stared at her blankly, completely at a loss for words. That was until the soft moaning of the man he'd knocked out brought him back to reality. He held out his hand and frantically motioned for her to open the door.

"Give me your keys!"

"I don't know you!"

"Yes, you do! You just don't remember, but at the moment you're in danger! Keys! Now!"

The impact of that statement was immediate. Drema stopped arguing, opened the car door, and passed him the keys while she climbed over the gearshift into the passenger seat. He slid in, jammed the key in the ignition and cranked it. The two of them barely had time to buckle their seatbelts before he was careening out of the parking lot and pulling onto the street. In their sleepy college town, there wouldn't be much traffic, even during morning rush hour, but he could head toward the interstate about twenty minutes away. Losing themselves on a crowded highway would be far more ideal than traveling on an isolated backroad. It was difficult to keep under the speed limit when his heart was racing as fast as a NASCAR driver. The hyperventilation of the young woman in the seat next to him wasn't helping.

"Can you, um, explain what you said back there?"

He sighed and gripped the steering wheel as he tried to organize his scattered thoughts. "It's quite complicated. Are you sure this is the best time to discuss it?" The countryside whizzed past them while he attempted to keep both eyes on the road instead of letting them wander to see her reaction to his words.

Her words were tinged with anger, and he pictured her crossing her arms in frustration. "I'm fairly certain we don't have anything better to talk about. Why don't you start with how you know me?"

"Um…" he drawled, allowing the car's bad suspension to distract the most panicking part of his brain. The uneven bouncing was slightly cathartic, and his unconscious mind settled down so the more rational part could begin speaking. "We used to work together," he muttered after a few tense moments.

"Not possible. I've never had a job outside of school," she asserted, and he smiled at the momentary strength he sensed in her words.

"Not one that you remember."

"You act like I've forgotten quite a lot, Julius."

The way she said his name, with anger lacing the edges of her words, brought back a plethora of his own memories. He struggled to regain his composure as they washed over him. Her smile. Her hair. Her touch. Her laughter. So many shared moments, seemingly lost forever.

"You have," he whispered as a tear trickled down his cheek against his will.

There was no time to discuss things further as they were suddenly rammed from behind by a Volkswagon Beetle in the most garish shade of orange. Their heads slammed forward, and the car skidded across the center lane before Julius could regain control. There were no other cars to see the ensuing battle, which was excellent in terms of minimalizing casualties, but he wasn't so sure he wanted to risk Drema's life to rid themselves of their attacker by playing bumper cars indefinitely.

She screamed as the Beetle hit them again, and he gripped the steering wheel until his knuckles turned white.

"Hold on!" he shouted as he slammed the accelerator to the floor. The car raced ahead, and he praised God for seatbelts.

They inched their way forward, but their stalker was determined and his pursuit was relentless. He continued to slam against their bumper. Julius finally risked a quick look at his unwilling passenger. Drema was bracing herself against the dashboard and whispering a prayer under her breath while she clenched her eyes shut.

That's a sure-fire way to break your arms should we crash, he thought absently, as he took the next turn too sharp and almost slid into the ditch. She opened her eyes.

"Watch the road!" she shouted.

"In case you haven't noticed, I'm doing the best I can, given the current circumstances!"

To punctuate his statement, the orange Beetle slammed into them once more. Her junker of a car increased its shaking exponentially. Julius took a deep breath as they approached a longer straightaway.

"Hold on, I'm trying a different strategy!" He pushed her car to the highest speed it could handle before swinging the steering wheel to the left so the car did a rapid U-turn into the opposing lane. He aimed directly for the oncoming car in a game of chicken and raced forward.

"Julius! What are you doing?"

"Don't worry! He needs you alive; he won't hit us!"

"Are you sure about that?" she screeched.

He didn't respond, instead focusing all his energy on maintaining control of the car as it approached its target. Just as he'd predicted, at the last moment the little orange monstrosity turned aside. He clearly didn't have control of his vehicle, as it ended up straight in the ditch.

"Woo hoo!" Drema whooped as she pumped her fist in the air. Her bright eyes brought joy to his weary heart, and he was relieved to see her tears dry for the moment. "So, this means you can drop me back off at campus now, right?"

He bit back a laugh at her optimism. "Hardly. These guys will just regroup and come after you again. It's best we put some distance between us."

She hmphed her disagreement and slumped down in her seat. They'd finally arrived at the interstate entrance, but that was no longer an option as they wouldn't be able to keep driving much further. The car was making some rather alarming noises at this point, so he continued to drive down the country road, looking for a barn or some other mostly deserted building where they could abandon it.

"You still haven't given me a reasonable explanation for why all this is happening," Drema said after they'd ridden in silence for a time. "Why are these people after me, Julius?"

His heart ached as she said his name once more. "They're after you because...because you're Agent Rose. A top-secret agent for the CIA. You've been a field agent since you were thirteen. We met about a year before that when you first entered the training program. You were a prodigy even then."

He wasn't sure what he was expecting in reaction to this announcement, but her lilting laughter was probably at the bottom of his list. "Julius, you can't expect me to believe that. What does that make you? My handler?"

"Your partner," he said tersely as he pulled the car into a roadside rest stop and shifted into park between two semi-trucks. "I am...I *was* your partner."

She was blushing now but still making attempts at humor. "What's your codename? Agent Beast?"

"Prince, actually," he muttered. "You used to give me a hard time about that. But I swear, I didn't choose it."

Her laughter hushed at the reminder of her lost memories. Julius wanted to say more, but she stopped him with her next words. "I'm going to use the bathroom. Why don't you check out the vending machines? I didn't get to finish my breakfast properly because of you, ya know."

"Oh, um, okay. Sure, I can do that."

She jumped out of the car, and he sat in the driver's seat watching her enter the small building while he pondered the next move. For now, their car was camouflaged in between the semis and other cars filling up the parking lot. Continuing to drive it was no longer an option as it was definitely giving up the ghost. *Should I try to hitch a ride? No, that would only place others in danger. Maybe we can just hoof it for a bit.* He finally unclipped his seatbelt and went inside to check out the aforementioned vending machines. Thankfully, he had enough cash and loose change in his pocket to pick up a couple bags of chips and two bottles of water.

"I can take these if you need to freshen up or something."

The soft voice startled him and made him spin around in a panic, but Drema's hesitant smile eased most of his nerves immediately.

"No, I'm fine. We'd better keep moving anyway." He offered her some refreshments, and she took her share silently. "I think it's best if we walk for a while. We won't get far, but we don't have a lot of other options right now."

"Gives us time to talk," she teased gently with a hopeful look on her face.

"Of course," Julius said with a half-hearted smile. He didn't want her to see how nervous he was to continue discussing her true identity.

They munched quietly as they started walking. If memory served, there was an abandoned barn just a little farther along the road that he had scouted as a potential hiding spot.

Perhaps we can cut through the ditch and avoid having to walk along the side of the highway. A quick glance at his companion's flip flops told him that whatever he could do to shorten their walk would be the best course of action. *It's not like I can blame her. She didn't expect to have to run for her life when she got dressed this morning.* He sighed in acknowledgment of how upside down her world must be right now.

"What's wrong?" she said brightly. The food and water seemed to have perked up her quite a bit and restored her energies.

"Nothing, just…pondering."

"Pondering what?"

He paused, considering the implications of telling her the whole truth, but decided to go for a half-truth instead. "Just impressed you're taking all of this so well, I suppose."

She laughed. A high pitch that sounded like a lilting song when it hit his ears. A sound he'd missed far more than he cared to admit. When she finally stopped laughing, he noticed that she had a few tears to wipe away.

"I'm not sure I'm dealing with it all that well. Still not sure I believe you, to be honest. But you did get one thing right."

"What was that?"

"I do love strawberries and chocolate."

He smiled, perhaps the first real smile of the day. Julius remembered, even if Drema didn't, all the times he'd surprised her with that particular treat. They walked on in companionable silence, and he wondered whether she wanted to talk more. Did she have any questions? His explanation had been thoroughly lacking. And she'd said she didn't believe him. The only way he knew how to convince her…well, that was an option he was trying to avoid if possible.

The property he'd remembered was in fact within a reasonable walking distance, and Drema didn't even complain about having to crawl through the wild prairie grass and the accompanying creatures that erupted from their disturbed nests. She abandoned her flip flops, opting to get her bare feet coated in mud instead as they waded through the puddles left from yesterday's rain. Their jeans were speckled with dirt and unknown substances by the time they arrived at the ramshackle old barn.

"This is where you want to hide out?" she said in disbelief. It was the first protest she'd made since letting him drive her car.

"Well, yes. It's discreet, abandoned, easy to defend if necessary, given that there's only one entrance…"

"It's leaning at like a forty-five-degree angle!"

"I don't think it's quite that bad," he said, tilting his head to one side as if to straighten the building in his mind.

"Julius, it's going to collapse on us."

"Well, hopefully, we won't have to wait here for long. I'll call in for backup once we're settled. I promise, we won't have to sleep here."

She nodded, although he could still see the uncertainty written across her wrinkled brow. But nevertheless, she took the hand he offered as he carefully entered the building, looking up and down for any unseen potential assailants.

"Shouldn't you pull your gun or something?"

"I don't have a gun."

"Don't all secret agents have a gun?"

"You don't," he said matter-of-factly.

"I don't currently remember being a secret agent."

"That is true," he admitted as he released her hand to step a few paces in front of her. It was true that most agents did carry a weapon of some sort, but he'd never believed in violence as a first line of defense when dealing with any situation. *And the old Drema always agreed with me. She would never suggest using a gun, even in self-defense. It's like the part of her I used to know is asleep somewhere deep inside her. I want her to wake up and remember…preferably on her own without any further interference on my part. But that's rather a pipe dream, I suppose.* He sighed again as he finished his inspection. "Looks clear."

"Makes sense," she said as she walked past him and headed toward a pile of furniture covered with an old sheet. "He probably totaled his car crashing into that ditch." She tugged at the sheet to free it and coughed due to the ensuing dust cloud.

Julius smiled at this small return of her observational skills. "I suppose you're right. I'm going to call for that backup now, so just don't leave the barn, promise?"

She waved in acknowledgement at him as she spread the sheet on the dusty ground and then began examining the items that had been covered by it. He took a few steps back toward the entrance so he could maintain his lookout position while he made his call.

Lifting his watch to his lips, he said, "The thorn hedge turned into flowers."

Nothing but a static crackling met his passphrase.

"Repeat: the thorn hedge turned into flowers."

Again, he heard nothing but static.

"Headquarters? Can you read me?"

Static, accompanied by a slight panic that sent a chill through his extremities.

"Headquarters? Please come in. This is Agent Prince requesting backup."

Not a single change in the crackling static, which made his heart sink right to his stomach. *We're on our own,* he thought worriedly. If Drema was back to her old self, things might be different, but given their current circumstances…

"So, how long before your spy buddies get here?"

He jumped at the sound of her voice and turned to see what she was up to. The pile of furniture was slowly rotting, so Drema had begun to pull out the more intact pieces, muttering to herself as she did so. This sight was much more familiar to him than the demure nature he'd observed thus far. His former partner had always preferred the hands-on approach to work, getting her hands dirty both metaphorically and physically. Seeing her in muddied bare feet as she pushed aside dusty, mildewed furniture brought a glimmer of hope to life.

"Perhaps you're still in there somewhere after all," he whispered as he joined her.

Her head bopped up to look at him as he approached, and he chuckled at the smudges of dirt across her face. Even her ponytail was starting to fall apart, leaving strands of brown hair sticking to her sweaty brow and neck.

I love you, Drema, his heart screamed while his lips remained silent. *I will always love you.* He thought his heart might burst from the depth of the emotions that were welling up within him.

"Julius?"

Shaking his head firmly, he pasted back on his serious face. "Yes?"

"The backup? When is it coming?"

"Oh, well, it's not. Something is wrong with my communicator," he said with a gesture at his watch. "All I'm getting is static."

"Signal jammer?" she said as she pulled a length of rope from an old hope chest.

Her sudden interest and aptitude on the subject threw him. *Did she notice the change too?* But a quick examination of her movements gave no hint that she'd suddenly recovered her memories. He cleared his throat.

"Um, it's a possibility. Which would mean that operative is closer to finding us than I'd anticipated."

"Then I suppose we have to be ready for him," Drema said thoughtfully as she began pushing a couch with only three legs.

"What precisely are you proposing?"

"I'm proposing that we, you know, build a trap or something to keep him here while we get away from the signal jammer. Then you can call in the cavalry, and I can get back to campus and explain to my professors why I missed the first day of three of my classes."

He was definitely getting some mixed messages at this point. Part of him could see the pieces of his partner's personality returning to the surface, but her amnesiac persona was still primarily in control. *Maybe she just needs a little nudge?* Nervously, he palmed the object he'd kept hidden in his pocket up until this point.

"Do you want to tell me how you think I ended up without my memories in the first place?" Her question was firm, like she was steeling herself for unwanted news, and she didn't look at him as she spoke. Instead, she continued to putter around with the various oddities she was collecting.

Before beginning his story, he reluctantly dropped the object back into his pocket and worked his way into the middle of the pile to join her. Granted, he had no idea what he was sorting or looking for. Drema had always had a mechanical gift about her that he'd never possessed. She handed him a broken mirror after scraping off some of the oxidized silver and motioned to a pile off to the left. He took the hint and deposited it as directed.

"Julius?"

"Yes?"

"Are you going to tell me or not?"

"Are you going to believe me?"

She paused before responding as she poked through a tin filled with dominoes. "I haven't decided yet. But the odds are more in your favor than they were a few hours ago."

He took a deep breath as he picked up an antique baby doll and tossed it into the pile he hoped was for trash. "It was on our last mission together. There was an organization that was putting together a new brainwashing technique involving a certain drug that would…um, well it would make someone susceptible to being retaught. Make them docile. Pliant. We'd gone undercover in a foreign embassy so we could find their hidden lab, but the local operative turned out to be a double agent. He sold us out."

"That's awful," she whispered. Her back was to him, but he thought he could hear some emotion in her voice. *Is that a good sign?*

"I don't blame him. The org's boss had taken his family hostage. It wasn't really his fault."

She didn't respond, so he took her silence as permission to continue.

"We thought we'd infiltrated the laboratory undetected, but it was a trap. They turned out to be waiting for us." The memories were flooding back into the forefront of his mind, and it was making it difficult to speak.

Things had gone to plan until they'd entered the laboratory. Agents Prince and Rose were typically known for their caution when they undertook their ops, but the sudden appearance of half a dozen goons just as they'd finished their infiltration had thrown them off. They knew the implications if this drug got into the wrong hands, and Drema had been desperate to destroy it before that happened. The enemy was closing in, and there were only a few seconds to act. There were only a few samples in the lab refrigerator, and she was certain if she could just get her hands on it…

He remembered the moment when Drema had reached for the drug. The glass box shattered and the needle inside pricked her finger when she tried to grab it. Normally, she would have been wearing thick gloves, but they'd been contaminated by acid as the two of them had avoided the various booby traps the organization had set up to stall them, and she had to abandon them. The drug had been designed with such potency that a single prick was all it had needed to do its dirty work.

There hadn't been any time. He heard Drema screaming his name over and over in a desperate attempt to cling to her memories before the drug stripped them away from her. The enemy operatives had held him back. He couldn't reach her when she collapsed unconscious on the floor. She'd remained unconscious until Headquarters had been able to rescue them a few hours later. Thankfully, the organization hadn't wanted to waste any more of their experimental drug on resetting his memories or he'd have forgotten Drema as well. He hadn't been allowed to see her again until Operation Wake had been put into action; Headquarters had decided it was better that he keep his distance until they'd discovered a solution…

"Julius?" That familiar voice broke through his wall as she reached out to touch his shoulder. She'd finished sorting the pile of rubbish, and now her hazel eyes were locked onto him intently. "What happened?"

"There was…an accident with the drug. You…" He let his words trail off before stating the obvious, that her memories had been obliterated. "We were eventually rescued, but it was too late," he finished lamely.

Drema didn't say anything. She just kept moving things about, replacing pieces of junk with different pieces of junk. He didn't know what to do, so he simply remained frozen as he awaited her response to the story.

I'm pretty certain I managed to mess this up too. Operation Wake is one big mess, and it's all my fault. I couldn't protect her then and I can't protect her now. His hand slipped back in his pocket, ready to tell her the rest of the story.

But before he could, Drema rushed at him and shoved him into a darkened horse stall. She landed on top of him and pressed a finger to his lips. Her breath was warm as she leaned down to whisper in his ear, "Someone's coming, Julius." The words meant nothing to him as all rational thought left his head.

"Julius, did you hear me?"

"Oh, yes, of course."

Her look of disbelief was comical, but he managed to suppress his laughter as he heard the crunch of heavy boots on the broken glass Drema had spread across the floor. Now he understood her words. The crunching seemed painfully loud in the stillness. Apparently, the enemy operative didn't appreciate it either.

"Agent Rose, let's stop playing this little game of cat and mouse. Or would you prefer I call you Drema?"

All the color drained from her face until she was white as a sheet. Her gaze drifted down to meet his as he looked up at her, still lying on the floor with her on top of him.

"I'm starting to believe you now, Julius," she whispered.

"And I presume you're here too, Agent Prince? Come to fail at rescuing your girlfriend once again?"

Now it was his turn for a sudden absence of color. Drema's eyes opened wide in surprise as she mouthed the word "girlfriend" in astonishment. He couldn't even muster an embarrassed smile before the operative continued taunting them.

"Don't think you're going to distract me with all this junk," he shouted. Something skidded across the ground when he kicked it.

"Forgive me for asking," Julius whispered fiercely. "But do you actually have a plan?"

"You're the spy!" she protested. "You're the one who's supposed to have a plan!"

"Well, you sure looked like you knew what you were doing with all that garbage earlier."

"Well," she said hesitantly. "I...I just need him to get a little closer."

"Closer to what?" He frowned when she put her finger back to his lips. She was kind of crushing his chest the way they were pressed together on the floor, but he didn't want to disturb her by asking her to move. They listened to the various clunking and crashing of the enemy moving through her pre-placed obstacles.

"Do you have a lighter?" she finally whispered.

"In my pocket. Why?"

She raised an eyebrow at him. "Do you smoke?"

"Of course not! It's just one of those useful things to have on hand. And I ask again, why?"

"Give it to me," she whispered as she held out her hand.

"You're going to have to get off of me first." He chuckled.

Her face turned as red as a sunset, and she scrambled off him in a rush. In her haste, she knocked over a pitchfork that had been resting against the wall. They both froze, and an eerie laugh echoed off the walls of the dilapidated barn.

"Come out, come out, wherever you are," the operative teased.

There was a clatter that sounded like dominoes falling, and Drema smacked Julius on the arm. "Give me your lighter! Now!"

He grabbed everything in his pocket and thrust it at her, which meant that along with the lighter she also found herself in possession of a Swiss army knife, the confiscated mini stun gun, two double A batteries, and a tube of lip balm. She dropped the rest of the items on the floor and rushed out of the stall, clicking the lighter on as she ran. Julius hopped up and was right behind her. When she burst into the visible space, the man in question was standing with his gun in hand on her sheet surrounded by toppled dominoes. It was also covered in the powdered oxidized silver...which burst into flames when she threw the lighter at them.

"Hard to shoot someone when you're trying to stomp out a fire," she said with a shrug. The man rolled across the floor in an attempt to put out the fire that had spread to his clothes. Julius wasn't going to give him a chance to resolve the issue and get back to trying to kidnap them. He pulled off his shoe and heaved it at the man, konking him in the head with enough force to knock him out for a few moments.

The two of them rushed over to the man and pulled him away from the fire. Julius stabbed the stun gun into the disabled man to ensure he stayed out long enough for them to deal with him. Then he looked at his former partner with a raise of his eyebrow. "Did you have a plan for putting that out?"

She gulped and started tugging at the unconscious man to pull him through the door. "Honestly? I didn't really think that part through. Probably best to get out of this barn filled with wooden flammable objects and who knows what other combustible items!"

There was no argument from him, instead he picked up the unconscious man and threw him over his shoulder with a grunt. Although Julius had surprisingly deceptive strength for his slight frame, it still took everything in him to break into a run as they rushed toward the tilted entrance. He heard the flames growing behind them, but he refused to look behind and see the extent of the damage.

Drema was huffing and puffing once they got sufficiently away from imminent danger. "Can you call 911? Hopefully it was a short-range jammer."

"Or it was in his pocket and was crushed during his attempt to stop, drop, and roll," Julius said as he lifted his watch to his lips once more. "The thorn hedge turned into flowers."

A brief crackle preceded the words, "And after he passed, they turned back into thorns. Greetings, Agent Prince. We were concerned we hadn't heard an update from you yet."

"Yes, there were some…complications on our end, Headquarters. Let's suffice it to say that we're in need of some emergency assistance at our current location, including fire suppression."

"Is the target in your possession?"

Julius glanced at the target, who was listening closely to the whole conversation. He uncomfortably cleared his throat before replying, "Um, yes. She is."

"And has she been awakened?"

The wide-eyed look on Drema's face told him he needed to get off this call and get explaining quickly. "Um, not just yet."

"Then best get to it!"

He could feel the angry gaze of the young woman next to him burning a hole in his back. "Yeah, um, Headquarters I'm going to need to call you back. Prince out."

The line clicked off, and he braced himself for the uncomfortable moment of facing Drema's quizzical expression.

"What did they mean by 'awakened'?"

He shoved his hands in his pockets and shuffled his feet, kicking at the smaller tufts of grass. "Well, it turns out the drug doesn't really *erase* your memories. It merely suppresses them, making that part of your mind go to sleep."

"Ah," she said knowingly. "So, your mission was to 'wake me up,' right? And how exactly where you supposed to do that? True love's kiss?"

His whole face felt like it was burning hotter than the barn behind them as he nodded. Her jaw dropped.

"Are you kidding?"

He sheepishly pulled out the tube of lip balm that he'd rescued from the barn floor, along with the stun gun, before their departure. "Headquarters created an antidote, infused it into this lip balm, and um…told me to kiss you."

"And they thought I'd just go along with this?" she said, hands on hips as he imagined the steam exploding from the top of her head.

"They thought I had the best shot," he mumbled. "Given our previous relationship."

She blushed as she suddenly remembered the enemy operative's words. "You really were my boyfriend?"

He nodded as he avoided her gaze. For a few moments, there was silence…other than the heavy breathing of the unconscious man on the ground and the crackling of the barn fire.

"Okay."

Julius' heart stopped at the sound of her voice. "Okay?"

"Okay," she whispered. "Let's find out if you're really telling the truth."

He smiled as he took a step closer to her. "Still don't believe me?"

She shrugged and returned the smile. "Better chance now than you did a few hours ago."

"I guess I'll have to take my chances," he said as doused his lips in antidote balm before pressing them gently to hers.

Then several things happened at once.

He felt his emotions overtaking him as memories of Drema filled him, and he pulled her closer to deepen the kiss. She didn't resist his touch, giving herself into the moment completely. Behind them, the barn exploded in a brilliant fireball, causing them to break the kiss and drop to the ground to cover themselves and the enemy operative.

"Julius?" she said shakily, touching her lips gently as though she could feel the same tingling electricity that he did after such a passionate moment.

He didn't know how to respond, so he simply looked at her, hoping beyond hope that those scientists had gotten this right.

Tears fell down her face as she threw herself into his arms. "My Julius! I remember! I remember everything!"

He crushed her in an embrace and bit back tears of his own. Another explosion rocked the countryside, and they both ducked once more, but he wouldn't let go of her.

"You're back," he whispered as her hazel eyes finally filled with the love and recognition he'd so been missing.

"I remember what you said that night," she said in a low voice filled with emotion. "I remember how we danced at the embassy, and you kept sneaking chocolate covered strawberries off the tray for me. How beautiful you told me I looked. I remember how we laughed and talked to kill time before the operation was a go. And…I remember…" She let the words trail off, so he finished the thought for her.

"It was the first time I told you I loved you, Drema."

She nodded and burst into tears. "And I didn't have the chance to respond before we had to go recover the drug. But Julius, I need you to know…"

"I know," he said softly as he pulled her into his arms once more. Her hair smelled like smoke, a familiar scent in their line of work, and he buried his face into the tangles to inhale it. Sirens were coming closer, so this moment would be over shortly. *But she's back. My Drema is awake once more.* He let his tears fall.

As the emergency vehicles pulled into the field, she pushed herself away to face him with her own tear-streaked face.

"I'll love you forever, Julius."

"Always and forever," he whispered as he leaned in for another kiss.

END

BEAUTY IN A BOX
Michelle L. Levigne

'Na had been abandoned. Granted, what pulled her two good friends away from the enchanted castle in her time of need were completely logical reasons, but still, she felt abandoned. Ambrose had had his birthday holiday cut short by King Ruprick, who needed him to deal with a palace full of disgruntled diplomats. Zella was off meeting the wizard Zerocs at some new invention called a café, where people looking for courtship went for hot drinks and conversation. 'Na entirely supported Zella snatching up this chance to find some romance in her life. It was just that the timing was somewhat … inconvenient.

She had a huge mess to clean up, after the devastation wreaked on the enchanted castle by Zerocs's patchwork monster. Yes, the housekeeping breezes were doing a wonderful job putting things back to rights, but so many errant spells had been released from wherever they had been frozen, tucked away from mischief, they interfered with the castle's self-repair magic. It needed supervision to work properly. Meaning 'Na.

And she had to do it before her parents returned from their latest quest to help the newlyweds, Prince Ruprick and Princess Phibbia.

If 'Na dared to use some magic spell from the library or a magical artifact from the many underground chambers to help her with the repairs, chances were iffy the magic would work entirely as expected. The enchanted castle was a tricky place to live, thanks to the sheer density of magic from magical objects crammed into the ever-expanding storage rooms and dungeons. It was essentially alive and aware, in many aspects. And because many magical artifacts brought to the castle were broken or seriously bent out of their natural function, the magic never quite worked out the way common sense said it should. Wishes unwisely spoken were often granted in unpredictable ways, and even carefully worded wishes rarely worked as expected.

Sometimes 'Na wondered if her parents spent so much time away from the castle, repairing broken magic or disciplining rebellious magic, because as much as they loved it, their home could be something of a perpetual headache.

~~~~~

'Na had spent the entire morning catching up on news throughout the many kingdoms touched by the enchanted forest, using the mirror
~~~~~

network. She knew her standard excuse for mirror-watching wouldn't stand up to scrutiny for much longer: anticipating the arrival of the next idiot prince in desperate need of something heroic to do. They had an appalling tendency to come to the enchanted forest to fight monsters who only wanted to spend their retirement in peace. Or worse, come rescue a damsel in distress.

Granted, there were still several hundred statues and other items who had formerly been princesses, princes, wannabe heroes, and damsels in distress filling the castle's corridors, gardens, and closets. Most had ended up there because the evil enchanters and wizards, witches, sorcerers, and jinn had so many prisoners, they were constantly tripping over them. The enchanted castle was a convenient place to get rid of clutter and make room for new prisoners and victims of evil temper tantrums.

Regular as clockwork, the right hero or heroine came along, sent by destiny and possessing the intelligence to ask for guidance, broke one of the many enchantments and freed their destined true love. Lord Zared was working on making it easier for rescuers to find the right subject of rescue, but enchanted prisoners still had a tendency to increase faster than curses broke. Still, they'd seen their fair share of happy couples riding off into the sunset.

'Na did her part, but she knew staying on the alert for the next hapless hero only worked so long as an excuse for not tending to that time-sensitive repair work.

"You're being silly, you know," Eyesallova the magic mirror said.

"Tell me something I don't know," she muttered.

Desperate messes called for desperate measures. 'Na took a deep breath and quickly phrased what she wanted to say.

"I wish—"

"Don't you dare!" Eyesallova shrieked. Her voice sounded like shattering crystals, shimmering and slicing through the air.

'Na headed out the door, determined to find some place where she could state her wish to call up magical help without being interrupted.

"You can't hide from me," the mirror called from the long panorama mirror in the ceiling that looked down on the central staircase. "If you try to finish that wish—"

"I won't, I won't!" 'Na lied. She fought the temptation to stick her tongue out.

Something thudded against the main castle doors. Sighing, she changed direction and hurried down the long corridor to the tower next to the gate. Caution said to call down from the tower, to determine if the visitor was a troublemaker or a potential hero, before opening the door.

Two visitors. A man and a girl maybe a year or two younger than 'Na. She sat side-saddle on her horse. He wore livery and stood in front of the door, his hand raised to pound again.

'Na's first impression of the girl was of a sparrow who had fallen into several dye pots. Her dress, the current in-fashion shade of lightning pink, was poufy and glittery, laced around a waist so narrow, 'Na wondered how she could breathe. Her eyebrows had been plucked into thin upward arches, so she looked permanently startled. Her eye, lip, and cheek paint was so rich and bright, it was clearly being held in place by magic. A ride through the enchanted forest should have been strenuous enough to make it all wear off. And her hair was a chilly shade of blonde that nature never intended, hanging in a straight curtain only achieved through magic.

"Welcome to the enchanted castle." 'Na managed not to laugh when the man-at-arms whirled around, startled and searching for the source of the voice. "Can I help you?"

"I come from King Wolfgang of Hafferzein," he stammered. "This is Princess Desdemona, his granddaughter. Lord Zared and Lady Ashlyn invited him to send her here for assistance." He held up a roll of parchment.

A housekeeping breeze yanked it from his hand and lifted it to the tower window. A shimmer of royal blue magic spread over the roll the moment 'Na touched it, verifying her parents had written and sealed the message.

They wanted her to take care of the granddaughter of their old friend and introduce her to Eyesallova, who would know how to help her. When a king was referred to as an "old friend" of Lord Zared, it meant at some point the two had switched places, thanks to a nasty take-my-place spell that had attached to Zared in his youth. Every time he had crossed a border into a new kingdom, he had changed to look, sound, and move like the current heir to the throne. His quest for magic to free him had eventually brought him to the enchanted castle. Ashlyn was reaching a point of desperation at that time, trapped in the double life of the brainless beauty and the beastly beauty. They had cured and freed each other, and the rest was history.

'Na opened the door for them. The man-at-arms announced he was to return to the king immediately. He unloaded Desdemona's leather trunks and rode away with rather more haste than 'Na thought the castle warranted, even with its quixotic reputation.

"I was slapped with a nasty breakage curse in school," Desdemona explained. "Makes me rather accident-prone. The sooner he gets away from me, the less chance it'll wear off on him. And please, call me Desi?"

'Na settled Desi in a room in the guest wing. Then she led her to the sun room to meet Eyesallova.

The massive gilt and curlicued frame of Eyesallova sat in the middle of the room, bathed in sunlight coming through the glass ceiling. The air sparkled and chimed in the language of magic mirrors. Eyesallova was obviously in conference with other mirrors in the network. The sound stopped just as 'Na signaled Desi to be quiet.

"I'm sorry," 'Na said. "Did we interrupt?"

"Just my daily gossip session," Eyesallova said. "Come in, come in. And who do we have visiting today?"

'Na made the introductions as they walked to the collection of chairs and benches gathered around the mirror. Desi moved in a daze, staring at the magic mirror. They sat down.

"Goodness, I know Desdemona quite well. Her grandmother's mirror, Spectrum, is an old friend. How is she? It's been ages since we've chatted."

"Spectrum?" Desi shook her head. "She's not—I mean, she's real—I didn't make her up?" She swallowed hard. "I didn't make you up? I know your voice."

"Sweetheart, when you used to stay with your grandparents, your grandmother would put Spectrum in bed with you and we'd tell you stories until you fell asleep."

"I remember." Tears welled up in the girl's eyes. "I thought—I thought I was just making it up. Everyone always tells me how silly I am, and how I let my imagination run away with me ..." She hid her face in her hands. She didn't weep, she didn't shake. She just sat there, breathing a little heavily.

"'Na, dear, why don't you go find some utterly decadent treat for the two of you, and let me and Desi get reacquainted, all right?"

Eyesallova could have asked the housekeeping breezes to fetch them something, so this was an excuse for some private talk. 'Na hurried away, glad to leave this in the mirror's metaphorical hands.

As soon as she left the room, the scroll tucked in her belt flashed. She should have known there was more to her parents' message, spelled to wait until she had delivered Desi to Eyesallova.

"What sort of help do you really need, you little dyed sparrow?" 'Na muttered as she found a place to sit and read. She would wager it had something to do with Desi hiding under hair color and makeup as thick as her thumb.

The story roused 'Na's sympathy and ire. Desi's father was a professional hero prince, working from the shadows to help hapless princes and farm boys with more honor than intelligence. Her mother was a victim of a sleeping spell tied into the phases of the moon. That left Desi in the hands of various servants and interfering nobles who insisted the heir to the throne needed to learn vital skills at a finishing school.

In the hands of the most influential girls and most critical instructors, Desi had changed her hair and eye color and underwent magi-cosmetic reconstruction on a regular basis. Even worse, the instructors, likely in the pay of enemy thrones, persuaded Desi that she didn't know anything, she would never understand anything, and she was in desperate need of others to tell her how to think.

Zared and Ashlyn recommended that Desi spend some time on the road with her father, to toughen her up and show her the real world. *Facing down ogres and a few hormonally-challenged dragons would normally be enough to terrify some common sense and balance back into anyone*, the letter said. *The problem is that she doesn't trust herself. She doesn't know what or who she is. Between you and Eyesallova, she should start to see clearly and use common sense again.*

~~~~~

After dinner, 'Na took Desi on a tour of the castle's lower regions, as suggested by Zared. This would begin toughening her up in preparation for going out on the road with her hero father. Desi had been rather rough-and-tumble when she was a child, according to Eyesallova. She had wanted to be just like her father, and had her own wooden sword and shield, rode her pony bareback, and swam like an otter. Until too many people clucked over how she was so not a proper princess, at such a high volume, she listened to them because she couldn't hear anyone or anything else. Not even common sense.

"She was so desperate to be a proper princess, she turned off her brain," Eyesallova had confided in 'Na. "Get her sweaty and grimy and out of breath. Shock treatment is a good start."

The girls wandered through shadowy rooms and down darkened hallways and opened doors that hadn't moved in years and protested loudly. The longer they explored, the less Desi startled at sounds coming out of the darkness, and the fewer times she trod on 'Na's heels in her efforts to stay close to the will-o-the-wisp that lit their way.

The castle seemed to be on the alert, muting Desi's breakage curse, and 'Na was grateful. The possibilities for disaster were incalculable, in some of the castle storage rooms. All Desi had to do was trip, knock some temperamental artifact into another, and start a cascade of quarreling, leading into destruction. 'Na had dreaded finding out just how strong that curse was. Then again, it might be imaginary. Too many princesses were trained to be accident-prone, to attract princes to rescue them. Such girls tended to trip over the one broken tile in the floor or prick their fingers on the only thorn in the entire garden or kiss the only poisoned frog in an entire pond full of frog princes. So far, Desi hadn't tripped or knocked over anything or woke some artifact in a bad mood.

Some of the magical items immured in the rooms did sigh and grumble in their sleep, but that was the normal reaction to movement and light disturbing the darkness and quiet. 'Na rather enjoyed the
~~~~~

exploration, despite the fear of bad reactions. Some rooms were new since the last time she had been down here. For every library room the castle added above ground, it added another underground, to deposit magical artifacts that had gone senile in their old age, or just bad-tempered and unreliable, or wonky. Such as an ever-replenishing water skin that had sprung leaks and needed to be stored sitting above a grating and pipe that fed into the castle moat.

"None of this magic works right?" Desi said, after two hours of wandering, 'Na had described enough stored magical artifacts that her throat was getting sore.

"Some do. Many just need to sit still and rest. They were broken by people who ignored the rules for magic, and the proper care of magical items." Something in the girl's tone, a little too carefully casual, caught 'Na's attention. "Why? Are you thinking of borrowing something?"

"I heard Grandfather asking your parents if they could just find me a couple charms that will fix whatever's wrong in my head, and make me happy with myself, just as I am." Desi shrugged, and didn't meet 'Na's eyes as she spoke.

"You know, they're all arrogant dolts at your school, don't you?"

That startled a sputter of laughter from Desi.

"Well, they are. Focusing on useless things. I'd rather be the hero than sit and wait for someone to come rescue me. That's all finishing schools do, turn you into the prize in a contest. And you're a bit of a dolt for letting them convince you that you aren't good enough for a top-ranked prince. A prince with a decent happily-ever-after won't be satisfied with the perfect outer wrapping and nothing more."

"Oh, really? Just how do you know?" Desi snapped, and even in the greeny-bluish pale light of the will-o-the-wisp, she flushed a nice shade of dark pink. "I don't see any princes laying siege to the castle to win your hand in marriage."

"That's because no prince worth his salt wants the possible curses that could stick to him if he makes a mistake here. And I know because half the books here have recorded all the trials and tribulations and testing of princes and kings, princesses and queens, poor-but-deserving heroines and heroes, and all the evil enchanters and lucky fools who have ever existed in our world. I grew up reading every book I could lay my hands on."

"Books?" Desi's eyes went glassy.

"Besides," 'Na said with a shrug and a sniff for punctuation, "princes aren't that wonderful."

"I wouldn't know." Her voice dropped to a whisper that had a little too much whine in it for 'Na's patience. "None will give me a second look."

"They will when they can see the real you again."

She studied the younger girl and wondered what sort of magic she needed to undo all the magical reconstruction done on her face and coloring and figure. What would it take to fix the damage done to her mind and self-image? Her parents always advocated using common sense and slapping some alertness into people, along with asking A'theosius to open their minds and hearts, before turning to magic to cure everything. Still, sometimes shortcuts were highly justified.

Castle, she thought, as loudly and firmly as she could, *find something simple to undo all this chopping and cutting. When she's back to normal outside, the inside might be more willing to listen.*

Considering all the magical artifacts crammed into the castle, it shouldn't be so hard finding something to suit the need. However, considering the number of magical artifacts, the search could take a long time.

She beckoned for Desi to follow her. "It's going to be a long night. How about I show you to your room before I get to work?"

"Doing what?"

"The answer is probably somewhere in the library. Either among all those history books I mentioned, or maybe the inventory." She muffled a sigh, and silently begged A'theosius that the library would cooperate and not try to hide the inventory of injured, retired, recalcitrant, warped, or outright wonky magical artifacts.

"Library? It'll take you all night to search it? It sounds ... huge." Desi finally lifted her gaze to meet 'Na's, and a flicker of eagerness lit them. "I'm not really tired. Could I help? I do love libraries."

Thank you, A'theosius ... there's more hope for her than I thought.

"Well, our library is very different from your ordinary library. First of all, many of the books are alive. Second ... remember not to make wishes within the walls of the castle. Especially in the library. They're not always granted the way you think they should be. If you're polite to the books, you'll be perfectly safe."

Desi got more dusty and rumpled rummaging through the shelves, climbing the ladders and getting down on the floor, than she had been in the tour of the underground corridors. She truly did love books, and her pleasure made the library's residents more cooperative, so none bit her when she picked them up. She wasn't one of those girls who needed to be constantly talking, and 'Na found her company and help comfortable. They worked until very late, searching catalogs and checking maps of the castle's many levels, above and below ground.

They had a list of possibilities as long as her arm, by the time they agreed to stop and get a few hours of sleep. Still, none of those possibilities seemed anywhere near right. 'Na escorted Desi to her room in the guest wing, then took a detour to the sun room. After all, Eyesallova never slept, and she could really use some advice.

"Silly girl," the magic mirror said with a chuckle, after 'Na had related a condensed report on all their work that evening.

"I knew it. I overlooked something." She started to crumple the list. Her head hurt, and she wished she had gone to bed and saved this depressing moment of truth for morning.

"It's right in front of your eyes, but I can see how you would overlook it. Thirtieth line down. You crossed it out."

"I did?" She un-crumpled the paper and spread it out. Her eyes kept trying to cross as she counted down. "But … that's the box of beauty. Desi put it on the list. Four times. I crossed it out each time. She still thinks if she's perfect on the outside, then all her problems are solved."

"Hardly. Just imagine how all those vicious girls will treat her when she goes back to school, more beautiful than them all." The mirror shuddered in her frame. "No, but the third time, the date of intake number assigned to the box is different. I can see how you mistook one for the other, because the numbers just appear to be transposed. It's the box of *inner* beauty. What makes it effective is that it's lined with magic mirrors."

"And that's good for Desi because …?"

"She'll be unable to leave the box until she sees her true self, sees all her good points, and wants to improve the areas where she falls short. Inside. In her mind and heart and soul."

"Oh." 'Na tried to wrap her mind around what this implied, but her head was throbbing and her eyes threatened to be permanently crossed. "Where is it?" She squinted at the list, but it didn't say in what level of the castle it was stored, forget about the storage room or shelf.

"That's the problem with truly useful bits of magic heavy on common sense. Besides being so rare, they tend to be forgotten, which makes them go invisible at the most inconvenient times."

"Oh … just lovely …" She rubbed at her eyes with the heels of her hands, too tired to even burst into tears. Which she rarely did anyway, but she was tired enough to wish she could do so, just to relieve the throbbing in her head.

"Go to sleep, dear. I'll rally the mirrors devoted to interior security and ask the breezes to start searching. We could have some clues by … well, dawn is just an hour or so away. Go to bed and say your prayers, and maybe we'll have some clues by lunchtime."

~~~~~

The housekeeping breezes woke 'Na just four hours later. They pushed her through the castle to the guest wing and slammed the door of Desi's room open, to reveal the princess was gone. Then, half-carrying her while they helped her get dressed, they hurried her to the sun room.
~~~~~

"She's already down in the fourth level," Eyesallova cried.

"What? Why?" 'Na ducked and got her hands up in time to catch the tankard of hot cider carried on a breeze, followed by a biscuit jammed with sausage and cheese.

"She woke up and decided not to wait for you to start hunting."

"Well, that isn't so bad. Most of what's in the fourth level is furniture. It's not like she can steal ..." 'Na decided to eat something and wake up her brain before she said anything even more foolish. There were good reasons *why* for every item stored away in the enchanted castle.

"She made a wish. To find the box of beauty."

'Na didn't know enough languages to adequately express the dread and nausea that surged through her. She gulped as much of the hot cider as she could without drowning, dropped the tankard, and ran for the nearest stairs to the lower levels of the castle.

Torches lit in front of her as she ran and died once she passed them. A light coming from a cross corridor far ahead meant she was catching up with Desi.

"Please, ignore her wish?" she said under her gasping breath, as she slowed. It wouldn't do to startle Desi, and any wonky magic she might have inadvertently awakened by this time. "The worst possible thing you can do is try to turn her into one of those useless princesses who can't do anything but look pretty and send idiot princes on dangerous quests."

Then she came to the intersection, turned right, and skidded to a halt as she saw the open door and the room directly in front of her.

Lanterns lit the domed ceiling, nearly two stories overhead. 'Na fought down a shudder. *Not* a good sign. An underground room, four levels down, should not be so spacious and tall. The things stored in this room were dangerously thick with magic, and something here was aware enough to influence the structure of the room.

"Thank you, castle," Desi called, just as 'Na caught sight of her. "I knew I needed another mirror, and there it is!"

She darted forward down a narrow aisle between piles of furniture. Beds and chests and dressers. On the bottom of the pile on the left side, turned upside down so its legs pointed up in the air, was a feasting table long enough for ten people on each side.

'Na had read of that particular table in one of the older inventory lists. It replenished the feast as quickly as the food was eaten. The problem was that those who ate from that table were never satisfied. They kept eating until they either fell asleep, or they burst their clothes. If they were particularly greedy and selfish, they burst their skins. The only way to stop the table from replenishing was to turn it upside down and keep it upside down.

This wasn't just a furniture storage room; this was a place where especially tricky, troublesome, bad-effects-outweighed-the-benefits magic was kept quiet and hopefully slept. And Desi was right that moment climbing a stack of chairs, holding onto a tapestry thick with dust that obscured its images. The frame of a tall mirror peeked out from the right side of the tapestry.

A mirror stored down here, instead of sitting upstairs in the sun room? This couldn't be good. Not in this room of tricky-dangerous magical artifacts.

Any moment now, that breakage curse and Desi's accident proneness were about to take over. That was just the way things worked in the enchanted castle. Especially when someone had been stupid enough to make a wish.

"Desi, please, climb down right now." 'Na stepped into the room, though she really didn't want to.

The stack of chairs wobbled, first to the left, then the right, then swung away from the wall. The princess yelped, flinging her arms up in the air. It swung to the right again, toward the wall and the tapestry. 'Na ran down the aisle, reaching for the other girl, wondering if she could catch her without both of them getting hurt.

The stack fell over. Desi snatched at the tapestry with both hands. Wailing, she dug her fingers into the thick cloth, dislodging decades of dust. With multiple *sproings* and *pings* and the shriek of metal being pulled out of stone, the tapestry came down from the wall, along with the rod that held it up and its brackets. Desi twisted around, landing on her belly on a chair, stopping her wail with a startled "Oop!" The tapestry cascaded down on top of her in a cloud of dust. Silence.

The mirror now revealed had a heavy ebony frame, as wide and tall as a man in armor. 'Na skidded to a stop as silver and blue sparkles swirled across the surface of the mirror.

"Huh? What? Who's there?" a heavy baritone voice called from the mirror. A mouth surrounded by a curly black beard and a pair of ebony eyes appeared in the surface.

"We're very sorry to have disturbed you." 'Na bowed to the mirror. Silently, she begged Desi to hold still, until she could be sure the mirror would be polite, if not friendly and cooperative.

"Disturbed me?" The eyes angled downward a little and the mouth pursed in what 'Na hoped was thoughtfulness. "No, rather, I think you've rescued me. How long have I been down here, trapped by that wretched tapestry of silence? It put me to sleep before I could send up the alarm. Ah, no, forget that question. Excuse me while I speak with the nexus." The mirror went blank.

'Na hoped that was a good sign. Then she studied the heap of tapestry burying Desi. Tapestry of silence? She had to get that horrid thing off her before it caused permanent damage. However, she knew better than to touch it with her bare hands.

"Castle? Help?"

Behind her, light flared extra bright out in the corridor. 'Na stepped out and yanked a freshly lit torch off the wall. She said a silent prayer, begging A'theosius that this was a time she could fully trust the castle. Yes, it had a tendency to play tricks, such as granting unwise wishes at odd angles to cause more trouble than the wishes solved, but it was helpful quite often as well. She called out to the housekeeping breezes, asking for water, just in case, then put the torch to the tapestry covering Desi.

It flared like dry cobwebs touched with flame. With a puff of sour-smelling smoke, the tapestry was gone, showering Desi and 'Na and the surrounding piles of furniture with multi-colored dust. Several large pitchers of water flew into the room on a breeze. Desi wasn't moving. 'Na took one pitcher and dumped water on her head. She gasped and sputtered and sat up.

The shape of her face shifted, the sharp, unnatural angles softening and rounding. Her eyes changed from what 'Na considered a rather creepy shade of violet to soft gray. The stark, icy blond of her hair washed out in a slimy-looking puddle, leaving behind a lovely, warm brown with streaks of chestnut. The painfully straight strands curled into delightful corkscrews.

"Restorative water. How clever! Thank you," she said, holding up the pitcher to let the breeze take it back. The pitcher bobbed in a curtsey and whisked out of the room.

"What happened?" Desi wiped at her face.

"You're more yourself, for one thing. Your breakage curse caught up with us." 'Na gestured at the wall where the tapestry had been, and her mouth fell open.

The mirror half-covered a heavy, iron-bound door. 'Na suspected the mirror had been put there to block the door, and the tapestry had been put there to silence the mirror and hide the door. And if anyone came investigating, put them to sleep as well.

"What's in there?" Desi asked, raking her dripping curls out of her face. "Hello, mirror? Can you help us?" she added, before 'Na could urge her to just get out of there before anything else happened.

"Hmm? Who? Oh, yes." The eyes and mouth reappeared in the right side of the mirror, and Eyesallova's signature swirl of peacock feathers appeared on the left side.

"It's all right, dear," Eyesallova said. "Dilatos is a good friend. I've wondered where he's been the last fifty years."

"Fifty years?" Desi squeaked.

"Indeed," Dilatos said. "Lovely to meet you, Lady Belladonna. Eyesallova was just filling me in on all the history I've missed. Yes, more than fifty years since that wretched prince wrapped me in that tapestry and brought me down here. Hmm, where's the tapestry? Don't touch it. It's rather dangerous."

"It's burned up," 'Na said.

The mirror burst out laughing, shaking enough to walk it away from the wall nearly an arm's length. That revealed the heavy iron latch of the door.

"Lovely. Oh, dear girl, I owe you a huge debt. How can I be of assistance?"

"What's behind the door?" Desi asked.

"Why do you ask?"

"I'm looking for the box of beauty. I made a wish, and a light led me down here and I was trying to look behind the tapestry, when ..." She blushed and raked wet curls out of her face again. "Is it behind that door?"

"I'm not sure."

"We really shouldn't be prying," 'Na said.

"There's a compulsion tightening around her," Dilatos said. "She'll get sick if she doesn't follow her wish to the very end. Sorry."

"Oh, wonderful," she groaned.

"How do we get the door open? Do you have a key?" Desi asked.

"Use the breakage curse I can see wrapped around you," the mirror said. "The compulsion is increasing its potency. Just press your hands on the door."

"Really?" A giggle bubbled out of her, then she stepped up and pressed both hands on the latch of the door. She gasped but didn't move away as streaks of rust spread out from her hands, like hoarfrost across a windowpane. All the iron bands of the door turned orange and fell to dust in the space of just a few breaths, then crumbled down. Desi stepped away, sputtering and waving the dust out of her face, while the planks of the door clattered to the floor. Lanterns came to life inside the small round room.

'Na only leaned forward enough to put her head into the room. She frowned at the oddly shaped pieces of furniture, mostly chairs and basins on stands, basins built into the feet of the chairs, all partially hidden under layers of dust or lavender sheets. The walls were covered in shelves full of small round rods and what looked like clips, and piles of combs and brushes, and other instruments she couldn't begin to describe, much less understand.

"What is this place?"

"It's a torture chamber." Desi shuddered.

"It's a beauty parlor," the mirror said, chuckling.

"Like I said, a torture chamber!"

"Beauty?" 'Na grinned, despite her sympathy for Desi's nauseated expression. She could guess that after all the princess had gone through at her school, yes, she would consider a room like this a torture chamber. "Would that box of beauty be in here?"

The sooner they could complete Desi's wish, the better. Compulsions were not comfortable. And she really did need to get the girl out of here before more artifacts woke up or she made another unwise wish.

"Hmm," the mirror rumbled. "That's what he was looking for, dragging that poor girl behind him, making all sorts of promises that anyone with one eye open could see he wasn't going to fulfill."

"Who?"

"Some wretched prince with big ambitions and too self-absorbed to understand true beauty. He wanted a kingdom, but the princess who came with the throne wasn't pretty enough for him. He brought her here, looking for the box, to improve her. Bah! The only improving she needed was to stand on her own two feet. He convinced the poor girl he was in love with her and she was in love with him, so she agreed to do anything for him."

"Do you know if they lived happily ever after, once she was beautiful?"

"No idea," Dilatos said. "I was trying to give him some advice, telling him everything I could see inside him, and inside her — that's what mirrors like me do, we give advice to help people find the real, the best version of themselves — when the ungrateful wretch wrapped me in that tapestry." He huffed. "Now you, dear, you've been going through some painful changes, but you're already much the better for them because you've had your eyes opened. That's why the water of restoration worked so well on you." He winked at Desi.

"Changes?" Desi's eyes opened wide, and she pressed her hands to her face. "Water?"

"Show her," 'Na said, and braced for the cry of dismay that she desperately prayed wouldn't come. The mirror's eyes and mouth and Eyesallova's peacock swirls vanished, and the surface turned silver.

"Oh!" Desi slowly smiled. "I'd forgotten what I look like."

"I think you look much better this way," 'Na said. "Even if you are sort of drippy."

That earned a giggle-snort from Desi.

"Is the box in here?"

"Is that it?" Desi darted into the room and yanked on a lavender cloth that draped something long, partially hidden under a table. Uncovered, it was a person-sized box, wrapped in chains. She let out a moan of dismay, then took a step back, her eyes narrowing. She looked at her hands, then the chains.

"I strongly recommend you get out of there before the magic traps you," Dilatos said. "Any moment now, you're going to sit in one of those chairs and let all those instruments of torture start to remake you."

Desi leaned down and press her hands on the chains. Rust spread out from her grasp.

"Did you hear him?" 'Na said. "Get out of there before you're trapped."

The first loop of chain shattered, spattering rust across the lid of the box and the floor. Two lengths of chain slithered and clattered and fell to pieces as they crashed to the stone floor. Links crumbled, sending up clouds of dust and rusty chunks of debris.

Blaring, off-key horns echoed through the room. 'Na went to her knees, hands clamped over her ears. Furniture rattled and pieces of beauty equipment bounced and slid and some cascaded over the sides of the tables and shelves.

Just when 'Na feared her ears would start bleeding, the sound stopped.

"That's not good," she said. "Mirror —"

"I would wager, someone set an alarm, so they would know when the box was opened." Dilatos shifted sideways to look in through the doorway. "Eyesallova suggests you wait until your parents return to the castle and they gather some strong defensive magics before — oh, dear."

The lid creaked open and up. It caught on the underside of the table standing over it. A thin, alabaster hand with a glossy, pearly manicure slipped over the side and gripped the edge of the box. Another hand reached up and pushed on the lid.

'Na had seen and read about enough prisoners released from magical containers, she knew the safest course of action to take. Even if the person inside that box turned out to be dangerous, she stood a better chance of surviving the encounter if she showed some compassion, or at the very least good manners. She darted into the room, braced to resist any spells trying to trap her, grabbed one end of the box and pulled it out into the open. Desi followed suit with the other end. In moments, the lid had opened all the way and fell back. A delicate yawn emerged and the two hands rose higher, revealing arms draped in thin, gossamer pink sleeves. A delicate-featured woman, with an amazing cascade of curly, pale golden hair that covered her like a blanket, sat up and blinked enormous lavender eyes with impossibly long, curled lashes.

"Oh, my," she breathed in a whispery voice like distant wind chimes. "Did I sleep too long?" She gasped and pressed her delicate hand to her lips. "What happened to my voice?" She looked down at herself and her eyes widened even more. "What happened to my hair? What happened —

to all of me?"

"Just how long have you been sleeping in there?" 'Na glanced at the piles of rust that used to be chains. Definite warning signs. What kind of trouble had just awakened?

"I don't know. Edward told me just a few nights was all I needed. He wanted our wedding to be perfect, and that included our wedding portraits and … oh, dear, why isn't he here?"

"Mirror? Do you think she's that princess you were talking about?"

Desi took over, showing more common sense than 'Na could muster with all the questions swirling through her head. She insisted on leading the princess, who said her name was Plicity, out and up into daylight. They took her to the guest room next to Desi's and got her settled with a long, scented bath, fresh clothes, and a hearty breakfast.

'Na asked the housekeeping breezes for assistance, and they brought Dilatos up to the sun room, where it would be easier to have a conference with him and Eyesallova. Eventually.

Plicity kept falling asleep. In the bath, then face-down in her stewed fruit, then sliding out of the chair in front of the dressing table while she tried to figure out what to do with her hair. It was a relief to give up and put her to bed, with Desi watching over her. 'Na headed to the sun room to hear what the mirrors had learned.

"Dreadful!" Eyesallova called out, the moment 'Na stepped into the sun room. "That horrid man has possessed that poor girl's kingdom for more than fifty years, all based on a lie!"

"What kingdom?"

"Drastenbourg."

"The schemer is Edward of Drastenbourg? Black Edward?" She thought she might be sick.

Black Edward had tried to trick her parents into betrothing her to his son just after she was born. He was highly offended that they refused to betroth a newborn to a boy who had a reputation for drowning puppies and kittens. He was constantly looking for reasons to lodge legal complaints in the courts of high magic against the enchanted castle. The last thing her parents needed was another unpleasant encounter with Drastenbourg. Then the rest of what Eyesallova and Dilatos had said came together into a somewhat sketchy, maybe even cracked picture in her head.

"Edward wanted Drastenbourg and promised to marry Plicity? Why did she want him?"

"Ordinarily, she had a good head on her shoulders. Until she fell for the flattery of that narcissistic, greedy, scheming …" The mirror's bearded mouth twisted in fury that had 'Na half-expecting to see fangs and maybe flames at any moment.

"So ... Plicity let Edward talk her into believing she needed a beauty treatment, they came here, he found the box of beauty, chained her inside, then found the tapestry to silence you, and ... how did he persuade her father to let him have the kingdom? Wasn't anyone suspicious?"

"I told you my girl had more common sense than twenty princesses and their counselors," Eyesallova muttered. "No, dear. Plicity's parents made some ridiculous bargains that came into effect when she was born and they vanished. They're probably still waiting for some hero to find and release them. Her counselors were magicked into supporting Edward. He returned to the kingdom claiming they had eloped and then she was kidnapped by a sorcerer. He just stepped in and took over. Had her declared dead and took the crown."

"But how do we kick him out, now that Plicity has awakened? Can we kick him out? She didn't marry him, did she? So he doesn't have a legal claim, does he?"

"We'll have to think on that," Dilatos said. "We'll need quite a few advocates. The twisty, sneaky kind, as well as the honorable kind. How's the poor girl doing?"

"Well, once she fully wakes up, I don't know how she'll feel when she finds out she's been sleeping more than fifty years, and that scoundrel lied and said she was dead."

Plicity slept through the afternoon and into the evening. That gave 'Na and the mirrors time to do more digging and research. 'Na found three books that spelled out the safeguards and problems of the box, and where to find the box of inner beauty. They still had to deal with Desi's problem, after all. The two boxes were so directly opposite each other, a repulsion spell kept the box of inner beauty as far away from the box of outer beauty as it could go in the castle. The housekeeping breezes went searching for it.

The news from the books was rather grim. Starting with the warning that beauty came with a price. A bond, created by a kiss, formed between the one who closed the lid and the one who slept. Any promises either side made were binding, with a curse on whoever broke one. While Plicity became more beautiful, outwardly, Edward drew on her knowledge of the kingdom. That explained how he had been able to take over the kingdom so easily. At the same time, Plicity knew everything Edward did to her kingdom while she slept.

What 'Na found rather chilling was the warning that the beauty that came from a prolonged sleep in the box generated an attraction nearly impossible for the opposite gender to resist. Meaning an unscrupulous woman could have power over any man who looked at her. If she was willing to sleep long enough.

"There seems to be more negatives than positives to all this," she commented.

Then the housekeeping breezes came to let them know Plicity had awakened, fully. Perhaps too much awake.

She remembered everything now, unclouded by whatever magic Edward had used to deceive her into thinking she loved him. She had had time during her long sleep to figure out what Edward had done to her, watching him live his life, while she was essentially frozen in time.

"What do we do? I don't much care about the throne for my own sake," Plicity said, when the five of them had been discussing the situation for more than an hour. The housekeeping breezes had kept the girls well supplied with comfort food. "But my kingdom and my people have suffered. And the scoundrels among the nobility have profited for too long."

Eyesallova had a suggestion. Plicity showed her common sense and dedication to duty when she didn't reject the idea outright, with attendant sounds of nausea.

Black Edward had seven grandsons. The youngest, Cadogan, was pure of heart, even though bullied by his brothers and cousins. This was according to Ripple, the palace's resident magic mirror. With the help of a Fae godmother, she had hidden, disguised as a lady's hand mirror. She had befriended Black Edward's many unfortunate brides, and had been passed on to his one daughter, the mother of Cadogan. Ripple had only good things to say about the young prince. That sentiment was mirrored by most of the citizens of Drastenbourg.

The simple solution, though 'Na couldn't see what was simple about it, was for Plicity to find Cadogan and marry him. They would then go on a quest to perform heroic deeds, prove themselves worthy of the throne, and find some magic to get his cousins and uncles out of the way. Without looking like rebels and usurpers. It was a family trait, after all.

"But what about Edward?" Plicity said. "He's not going to step down just because I've returned to the kingdom. He's more likely to have me arrested as an imposter."

"Hmm, yes, we need to deal with that," Eyesallova admitted.

"Is this, or is this not the enchanted castle?" Dilatos said, sounding slightly offended. "There should be something skulking about that we can use against him."

The housekeeping breezes showed up at that moment with the box of inner beauty. Before they could do anything with it, King Edward arrived, accompanied by fifty soldiers, his four sons and six of his seven grandsons.

"Attention, inhabitants of the castle," a herald shouted. "His majesty, King Edward, demands the release of Her Royal Highness Princess Plicity, rightful ruler of Drastenbourg."

The same magic that kept the gates locked tight, with a snapping shimmer of defensive magic, also brought the voices and faces of the invaders into the scrying cloud hanging in the center of the room where the five were conferring.

"That's not a good sign, is it?" Desi said. "We had to learn a lot of political maneuvering in school. Just in case some of us ended up as evil queens. Any time the enemy admits you have rights, he's planning on using them against you. Or at least for his benefit."

"You're very right," Plicity said. "How can we use that admission against him?"

Dilatos chuckled wickedly. "Worry not. Nasty creatures like him are so clever, they trip themselves up without any effort on your part."

"We have a plan," Eyesallova announced. "Trust us, dear. You need to go dress up to dazzle that nasty old schemer. All three of you."

While 'Na always trusted Eyesallova's guidance, she still grumbled. Mostly because she loathed the fancy, flouncy, heavily jeweled clothes she had to wear when her parents needed to impress high-ranking problems, rather than fling some nasty magic at them. She grumbled while the housekeeping breezes wound her hair with jewels and slathered makeup on her. Until a long sword glowing blue with magic floated into her bedroom, and the housekeeping breezes belted it around her hips.

This might just turn out to be fun.

She was sure of it when Dilatos outlined what they were going to do.

Plicity sat between 'Na and Desi, with Eyesallova behind them, on the dais in the rarely used throne room. The defensive magic only allowed King Edward to enter accompanied by his sons and the captain of the guard. When he stomped into the throne room, he triggered a spell attached to one of his many rings. 'Na saw the tiny flare of non-light as he flipped up the compartment hidden under the black gemstone, and the momentary haze that enclosed him. Then his wrinkled, sour expression melted into sorrow.

Edward staggered to the dais, dropped to his knees on the first step, and burst into sobs.

"My beauty! Words can't contain my joy at finding you at long last. How I have suffered all these years, wondering what happened to you." He stopped to sob and catch his breath. "You were so determined to make yourself breathtaking for our wedding. I was a fool to listen to you. I adored you just the way you were. Then, imagine my horror when I came to awaken you, and the box had vanished. Stolen away by the magic of this cursed, ensorcelled place.

"I searched for years. Heroes have lost their lives, trying to find you. Wizards have worn out their magic, seeking to find and release you and bring you back to me. I have suffered agonies, fearing the worst,

imagining you dead. But now, at long last, my dove, my utter delight ..."
He caught his breath, and a rapturous smile broke through his tears.

The sight of that magic-generated, false joy on his wrinkled, ugly old face, made 'Na fear she would lose her dinner.

"We can at last be married!" He spread his arms and puckered up.

Did he actually expect Plicity to throw herself into his arms?

A chill shot through 'Na when she remembered the need for a kiss to seal the magic of the box of beauty. Was Black Edward planning to put Plicity back in the box? Maybe reverse the draining this time around, so he could be young while she slept and faded, and maybe even died?

"No." 'Na stood and drew the sword. The sapphires and amethysts embedded in the hilt flashed. "Her Royal Highness Plicity, rightful queen of Drastenbourg —"

"Has no intention of marrying a wrinkled, ugly old prune," Eyesallova burst in, and leaned forward until she threatened to fall on top of the three girls.

"But we are in love, my dove, my darling!" Edward's voice cracked and fury sparked red in his eyes, battling with the spell that fought to keep up the mask of sorrow.

"I don't recognize you. Prove you are Edward," Plicity said.

"Prove?" The spell enveloping him died with a crackling sound. "I don't have to prove anything!"

"Yes, you do," 'Na said, and took two more steps forward.

"Who might you be, to tell me what to do?"

"I am Belladonna, daughter of the lord and lady of the enchanted castle." 'Na whispered the trigger words, activating the spell attached to the sword. She grew taller, and her dress changed into gleaming silvery-blue and amethyst armor. Her head came close to brushing the ceiling of the throne room, two stories overhead.

"You wanted me to marry *that*?" one of the princes shrieked. He blanched, then turned and ran. Followed by his brothers.

"Cowards! Weaklings! They all take after their mothers," Edward growled. He pointed a crooked, dirty finger at Plicity. "See here, we're betrothed, so you're going to live up to it."

"Marry a beautiful, young, resplendent princess to an ugly old prune like you?" Eyesallova's surface spun faster, streaks of red mixing into the blue and silver. "The least you could do is use a magic spell to make yourself young and handsome and strong, a face she'll enjoy looking at for the rest of her life. After all, she did that for you. And didn't she turn out splendidly?" she finished on a purr.

The magic of the box visibly struck Edward. Greed and lust lit up his face, so he was almost drooling.

"That seems only right," Desi said. "She deserves a handsome groom, even more than you deserved a beautiful bride."

"What do you expect me to do?" he whined. "Spend time in that wretched box that took her from me?"

"Why not?" 'Na had a hard time not laughing. Too bad all those chains had gone to rust. How were they going to keep him in that box? If they got him in that box. He had to go willingly, and close the lid himself, preferably without that wretched kiss. They had to prevent everything that would create and enforce the bond between him and Plicity.

Edward's scowl deepened. "Yes, of course, Plicity, my dove. But you must promise me you'll awaken me every morning and give me true love's kiss every night when you put me to sleep, until I am young and strong and worthy of you."

Clearly, he had read all the books warning about the box. What fool had woven the ridiculous concept of true love's kiss into so many magic spells?

"Behold, the box of beauty," Eyesallova announced.

The doors of the throne room burst open. The box of beauty hovered in mid-air, floating into the room, carried by the housekeeping breezes.

No. Wait.

That wasn't the same box Plicity had been sleeping in. This box was the right colors, but not the right shape. 'Na could swear she smelled … was that fresh paint?

The box settled on the floor in front of the dais. Edward was grinning like most despots did when they thought they had gotten the better of some too-good-to-be-true hero. He bowed to Plicity, stepped back, and walked over to the box. He bent to put his hand on the lid, then paused without opening it.

"My dove? I await your promise." His smile sharpened as he held out a hand to her. He clearly wasn't going to step in until she complied.

Maybe Eyesallova and Dilatos's plan wasn't going to work after all?

The breezes surged around the throne room, yanking curtains sideways. The lid of the box snapped upright, revealing the mirrors lining the interior. Edward shrieked as he was spun about and knocked off his feet. He toppled head-first into the box. The lid snapped shut, catching one leg at the calf. He kicked and shrieked and the lid rattled until another surge of breezes picked up the box and thumped it hard, so Edward went up in the air, spun around, and landed on his back, stretched out in the box. The lid snapped down hard, cutting off his shriek with a ponderous thud, like a dungeon door shutting.

"That is the box of *inner* beauty," Dilatos announced, with a rascally sort of rumbling chuckle. He stepped out from behind the curtains at the back of the dais.

"Shouldn't he have gotten in willingly, for it to work?" Desi said.

"Well," Eyesallova said, "he started out willing. We just helped him along before he could change his mind."

"That's enough to trap him?" 'Na said.

"He can't leave the box until he is a better man, inside and out. Even more important, and binding, he has to *want* to be a better man, to purify his mind and his heart," Dilatos said.

"That's going to be a very, very long beauty sleep," 'Na mused, as she contemplated reporting this development to her parents.

She and Desi and Plicity were silent as the housekeeping breezes picked up the box and carried it away.

"Now ... how do I set about finding Cadogan and rescuing my kingdom from his cousins and uncles?" Plicity mused. "I need a hero to be our guide, but a married one, so he won't expect me to marry him. That would certainly complicate things. Especially while I'm looking ..." She gestured at her face.

"Desi's father is a professional hero," Eyesallova said. "And I think it would be very good to have some father-daughter adventuring, like they used to do. Won't that be fun, Desi?"

"I think ... well ... Maybe could I take a nap, just a short one, in the box ... of beauty?" Desi finished on a whisper.

"Oh, you don't want to do that. Take it from me," Plicity said, wrapping an arm around Desi's shoulders. "Life is for living, not staring into a mirror that can't give you advice. Wouldn't it be much more fun to be a hero?"

Please, please, please, 'Na silently chanted, and caught herself just before she made the mistake of wishing. Although, the last wish made in the enchanted castle hadn't turned out ... too badly.

END

VILLAINS AND THORNS
Jessica Noelle

In my dreams, I'm a hero, saving the world. Then, I wake up, and reality comes crashing back in, threatening to drown me. I'll never be the hero. I'm the villain of this tale.

You might have heard it before, the tale of Sleeping Beauty and the wicked fairy who cursed her, angry over not getting invited to a party. What a petty motivation. Sadly, it's one I'm destined to fall into. I am that fairy who will curse Sleeping Beauty, who will ensnare a kingdom in thorns. It's inescapable and unavoidable. It's my destiny. There is no use trying to change it.

"Malia, you must focus." My mother's sharp words bite into my skin, a blade of ice driving itself into my heart. "You never focus. If you do not focus, you will be weak. Helpless. Do you want to be weak?"

"Sorry, Mama," I tell her, avoiding her cruel gaze. If she knew my dreams, I wouldn't get any food for three days. My stomach tightens at the thought, and I wring my fingers, not daring to meet her silver eyes, the one feature she and I both share. Mother's slender fingers yank my chin up. She inspects me, her features cool and collected, a deep contrast to the venom in her voice.

"You must practice your magic until you can cast a curse so tight that not even your wretched cousin can undo. That not even true love's kiss can awaken."

I nod, wishing my cousin could be here right now. Faye is my only friend, destined to keep my curse from killing Sleeping Beauty... but she's also my protector when she's here, shielding me from Mother. My father used to call us the sun and the moon—

"Malia!"

A slap stings my cheek, and I flinch, feeling the iron of my mother's rings burn into my skin. The physical pain will ebb I know, but the emotional pain...

"I'll do better, Mother." I choke the words out, sobs clogging my throat.

She nods, storming out of the room, her crimson dress billowing behind her like a pool of blood.

When she slams the door shut, the room brightens as if responding to her presence being gone. I swallow hard, gagging on my guilt. I don't want to curse a baby because her family doesn't invite me to a party. What did the baby ever do to me?

Still, nothing can change my fate. Others have tried before me, tried to break the fairytale cycle, but each one was driven mad, cursed, or worse—and still played their role to perfection, Mother says.

I rub my eyes, looking out the window to the ground three stories below, speckled with thorns formed by magic—*my* magic.

I suppose I should explain something about my magic. As a faerie, I can supposedly create, but I can also destroy, which is only what my magic seems to do. Take the trees, for example. Their leaves have gone, their trunks are withered, and their branches look like wizened fingers reaching for a sun that rarely shines. Today, I can only make out a single shaft of sunlight piercing through the tumultuous clouds, but that single ray is enough to hit me with a wave of bittersweet grief. Salty tears run down my face, but I still manage to smile at the light, remembering the last thing my father ever said to me before he died.

"Malia, see that sunlight? It's a reminder that there's always hope." He *pointed to the lone patch in the darkness, his other hand on the ground sending green tendrils of magic toward the brightness, causing a flower to sprout, unfurling its delicate petals.*

"But Papa," I snuggled closer to him, curling into the smell of him, of wind and rain and forest clinging to his jacket, "I'm the villain, and the good guys always win. How can there be hope for me?"

"There's always hope, Malia. You just have to fight for it."

"Mother says hope is a lie."

"Mother does not understand it. Those who have fear..." My father trailed off, stroking my head as he collected himself. "Those who have fear struggle to see hope, Malia. Besides, what if there is a reason for villains and heroes to coexist?"

"Huh?"

"Maybe the villains are there so the good guys can become good," my father clarified, his eyes crinkling as he smiled. "Without villains, there would be no heroes. Maybe that's why there are villains, to remind us that the light will always win. And not just to remind us that light wins, but to remind us that we have to fight for it. The villains are tests, opportunities for heroes and villains alike to see that."

I still don't understand what my father meant by those words, but I like to think that maybe he was saying that even though I'm destined to be a villain, I'm still a good person. Even if my magic only seems to cause pain. Even if my mother spends most days staring into a mirror, admiring herself and plotting how she will marry a powerful king and be the fairest of them all.

Yes, my mother is the Evil Queen, destined to try and fail to murder Snow White. She's a sorceress, but my father was a fairy. That's where I get my ability to fly, not that I know how. My father died before he could teach me, but sometimes, I wonder if his death wasn't accidental.

Sometimes, I think my mother murdered him...to marry the king whose messengers are even now approaching the gates of her estate.

I see the guards, clad in their sharp black uniforms, greet the messengers and take their horses. The guards bow low to the lead messenger, a man who must be no older than my seventeen years, and he enters the courtyard through the curved iron gates. My mother exits our home—not that it feels like home since Papa died—and welcomes the messenger. Even from here, I can see the wicked smile curling up her lips. Her plans are coming to fruition, and while she is filled with a wicked glee, I just want to run away.

Run away. The words echo in my head like they always do, but this time, I listen. My mother will be too busy with wedding preparations to notice I'm gone. I could do it—leave, never return...

I can't escape my tale, but I can escape my life, at least for a little while. I can escape the constant spellcasting, the magic that makes me burn every non-magical being I touch, the panic that threatens to overwhelm me when my mother walks into a room. I can escape it all. I can pretend I'm not destined to be a monster. I can pretend I'm a hero.

And so that's what I do.

~~~~~

A month passes, then two, and my mother still hasn't found me. She's sent her huntsmen, but I've dispatched them all with my magic, hating myself for doing it, but loving my new-found freedom too much to give it up. I won't be forced back into my mother's cage. Not now, not ever again.

Because my freedom means the world to me, the memories I've made and moments I've lived—trying cacao beans, weaving flower crowns, styling hair, baking—these moments have become my world, my galaxy.

I have a job now at the bakery, kneading bread and braiding it, watching it rise in the clay oven that is as big as I am. Vianca, the village in which I've found residence, is beautiful with its large grove of weeping willows, wildflowers, and shops of every shape and size. Even though the people struggle to make ends meet, they fight for one another, sharing as they are able. Vianca reminds me of my father...kind, gentle, hopeful. A place where hearts can be mended, where souls can heal.

Until I hear *it*. The dreaded news.

A royal baby has been born, and there is to be a christening. It is by invitation only. Twelve commoners receive invitations, and the herald announces in his nasally, pompous voice, "All faeries in the region are cordially invited to the princess's christening unless they have dark magic flowing through their veins and malicious intent beating in their hearts." A pretty phrasing to hide the truth: all faeries may come except the one who will harm the innocent princess. Everyone except *me*.

The herald continues, drawing me from my thoughts. "However, if a
~~~~~

dark faerie does come, know that through she has evaded capture thus far from both our illustrious kingdom of Veria and our esteemed neighboring kingdom of Kritos, she will be apprehended and face the punishment for her actions."

Two thoughts war in my mind: they've been seeking to capture me and I am the one not invited.

Why does my fate have to find me so soon? I don't want this for myself. I don't want to be a villain. My chest tightens, and I can barely breathe as the crowds close in. I shove my way through the throng, trying to escape, trying to find a way out, trying, trying, trying, trying, as my breathing comes out fast and shallow, as tears prick my eyes and fall down my cheeks.

I'm almost out of the horde of people when a girl catches me, her grasp steady. "Are you okay?"

I sniffle. "Fine." The response is automatic. *Don't show weakness. Don't show pain.*

I force my eyes up, eager to reassure the girl and slip away, and gasp. It's Faye.

The girl is Faye, my cousin and protector.

"Then why are you crying?" She gives me a grin, her golden eyes dancing.

"I'm trying to outrun fate," I confess. "I can't curse her, Faye. I won't."

"Then you won't." Faye hugs me tightly, and the tension leaves my body. "We'll prevent your story."

"How?" I pull away from her, panic making my magic writhe inside me.

"I'll take you to the christening as my guest, and then you get out of your story. No one will question it."

"Deal." I grin at Faye, hope sparking in my heart. There's a reason why she's my best friend and why my mother hates her so much. She has a heart of gold to match her eyes.

~~~~~

A week later, my feet ache, but I'm staring up at a grand palace, bile rising in my throat as I take in the castle and what lays outside it, connecting the two discordant images to the history my mother has taught me since before I could walk.

The kingdom of Veria hasn't lost a war in decades, but they constantly start them, eager to gain more power and wealth, and the castle reflects their wealth. Turrets sweep the crystalline sky, and each buttress is inlaid with gold. I've never seen so much wealth, and yet, people are starving on the streets. Children who are no more than skin and bones are begging, wounded soldiers are leaning against dirt walls as flies buzz
~~~~~

around their festering wounds, and mothers are stealing just to survive. It's appalling, and when Faye and I enter the palace itself, my disgust grows even more. Something I could have never foreseen.

Tables laden with food line the courtyard, piled high with more delicacies than any court could ever possibly dream of eating, no matter their size. Piles of gold ready to topple perch next to the baby's cradle, and the king is lounging in his throne. While his queen is beside him, he flirts with another lady of the court. He has everything men could dream of, yet he still lusts after more: more power, more wealth, more everything.

I can sense, even from here, his corrupt, dark heart sending its waves out to any faerie in the room. I'm dimly aware of Faye clutching my arm, of her fingers digging into my skin, but my mind is black with anger, my magic begging to be used. Maybe I don't curse the baby because I didn't get invited. Maybe I curse the princess because of this disgusting display of wealth while innocents suffer.

"Stay calm," Faye whispers, and I clench my jaw, barely dipping my head.

"Stay calm," she repeats, and I realize she is not talking to me. She's talking to *herself*. She repeats her words, her mantra, over and over, as the gift giving begins, each one more extravagant than the one before it.

What baby needs a gold loom? Or a diamond broach the size of an apple? Or a chocolate fountain? Then, the magical gifts start, each one shallower than the last, just like this wretched court. Who needs a good singing voice to rule well? Or the ability to cross-stitch? In my bones, I can feel my magic building up, my tale pushing against my very being, begging to be fulfilled. I have to stop this opulent wealth, this gluttony of power.

My anger and magic are dark harmony to Faye's melody, for I sense her magic building, buzzing against my arm. But it's *my* turn to do something, to protect someone the way she has protected me...even if that means breaking her trust and destroying our friendship.

I step forward, letting my magic snake around me. My simple blue dress changes into a deep forest green one in the style of the court, and then I speak, casting a spell that even Mother would be proud of, had she not heard the ending.

"The princess shall indeed have all these gifts, but for your pride, she shall also have a gift from me: before her sixteenth birthday is over, she will prick her finger on the spindle of a spinning wheel and fall into a deep sleep. In that sleep she shall forever remain, so long as pride and avarice rule the hearts of this kingdom. Only when she is ready to be a true and worthy ruler shall she wake. So I, Malia, have spoken, and so it shall happen."

The court descends into chaos, and I whirl to leave, pausing when I meet Faye's shocked gaze.

I'm sorry. The words are an unspoken song, a silent plea, but instead of anger, her face melts into a soft smile, her eyes filled with pride.

And I realize something as my cousin steps forward:

It's *her* turn to continue our fairytale, the story of Sleeping Beauty.

END

THE GIRL IN THE STARS
Angela R. Watts

"It's a lot of money, Ledger. We can't just pass on a job because you don't like women." Boone scoffed, tossing his cigarette butt into the trash across the control room of the *Lucky Lucy*. The spaceship was growing old in years and showed lots of wear and tear — like Boone.

"I like women," I said sharply. "What I don't like are *rich* women."

"Scared of 'em, are ya?" Boone smirked.

I threw my empty beer can at his head. Beer was a luxury in space, but being a mercenary had its perks, like luxurious items you stole from the wealthy. "*No.*"

"Then we take the deal. With dough like this, we can repair the ship and still have thousands left over. We could take it easy for a while, go off radar, just live a bit." That was Boone for you. He would risk his hide for fast cash, then spend it all on easy living, 'til it ran out, then he would drag me back to another job, so the cycle repeated.

"This isn't some smuggling op, Boone," I snapped. "This would be kidnapping."

"So? We've kidnapped. And we've killed. I think kidnapping some woman would be less weight on your conscience than murdering some big wigs —"

"That's not it." I cut him off. "Look." I pointed toward the control panels. On the holographic screen, the bounty information loomed. "Yeah, it's a lot of money for a bounty, but she's an Earth politician's *daughter*, for cripe's sake. Don't you think there's a reason she'd be in cryo sleep like this?"

"Ah, but she's only been in cryo for three years," Boone argued. "Besides, her dad died last year, and if my research has shown me anything, it's that her own mother put this bounty out. So there won't be any heavy duty security. We can bust into the ship and get goin' in an hour, tops. I'll bet on it."

"You lose every bet you've ever placed." I scowled, still staring at the panels. What kind of mother put a bounty out on her own kid? And a kid that was defenseless in cryo sleep, for God's sake.

Boone eyed me, then said slyly, "You know, if anything… We'd be saving her. Think about it. Her dad put her away like this, for whatever reason, and her mom wants her gone… We can get a bounty and then the girl would wake up, that's a pretty kind thing to do, isn't it?"

I gritted my teeth. "We don't have enough details." Maybe the girl was a psychopath and needed to be imprisoned, and they had only put her in cryo sleep to keep their reputation. Or maybe the girl had been suicidal and this was the next best thing that her parents allowed. Or maybe—

"C'mon, Ledger," Boone insisted. "We need the money, or we're outta business. I got first lead on this, and if we keep talking, word will get out and we'll miss our chance. The girl in the stars is ours for the taking."

"Don't say it like that." I scowled. But I forced myself to study the photo of the woman. Candi Azure. Short black hair, dark green eyes, short and slender. Twenty-two years old, though now, she'd be twenty-five. And she had missed three years of living.

The girl in the stars...

"Fine," I said. "Let's go."

Boone fired up the ship, but I couldn't help but wonder... Was I going to help this girl, or was I waking her only to thrust her into a hell worse than slumber?

~~~~~

The spaceship Candi slept on was large. Our lead had confirmed that forty guards lived on the ship, ensuring no harm came to Candi, but that was all about to change.

Boone kept our ship's invisibility shields up. They were a bit rustier than they used to be, but they did the trick, so long as we got close enough quickly, and the guards didn't look behind the ship. Our ship's radar scrambler, however, worked like a charm, and we wouldn't show up on their radar, even if they did see a strange flicker in space.

Everything went well.

Until it didn't.

My teleportation device landed me aboard the spaceship.

Right in the control room.

Smack dab center.

The soldiers in the control room jumped to their feet, and in a split second, every weapon in the room was aimed at me.

I was a faster draw.

And shot.

I hit two soldiers in the heads, with quick precision, and as their lasers blasted me, the strikes bounced off my protective shield. The shield in my suit held strong as I shot the remaining soldiers.

"Great going, Boone," I snapped into my ear comm. "You were supposed to drop me in the corridor outside the room!"

"I did."
~~~~~

"I'm in control!"

"Oh." Boone paused.

"That's across the ship!" I hissed.

"You have long legs. Get to runnin'," Boone ordered.

"You little—" I unsealed the control room door, poking my head into the corridor. Empty. I had to be grateful for the little things. "I get more than a fifty split."

"Sixty-forty."

"You aren't doing anything!"

"We're partners!"

Slipping into the hall, I hurried along, heading to the room where Candi slept: the west wing. The dimly lit corridor echoed my light footsteps.

Regardless of our usual bickering, something felt *wrong*.

Sure, there was only a small crew of soldiers aboard the ship to guard Candi.

Which was wrong enough. I mean, the situation reeked of corrupt politician parents just trying to hide their daughter away for some twisted cause. Which I didn't understand, but wanted to.

Anyway, the bad feeling in my gut. I never ignored it. Actually, I did a lot, but it was always right, and I always paid for ignoring it, so I ought to stop ignoring it.

The bad feeling said to stop and ask Boone why the guards hadn't noticed my arrival.

"Uh, weird." Boone's voice came through the comm.

"Where is everyone?" I whispered. "Don't they know I'm here? And don't they know I just sedated the whole pilot crew?"

"Well..."

"Boone."

"Uh, it looks like the rest of the crew is dead, Ledger."

"Dead?" My blood ran cold. "Like how dead?"

"Dead is dead."

"What do you mean, dead?" I insisted. "They were alive when we did the radar check. Four guards stationed outside the door in the west wing, and the pilot crew, so eight soldiers total—we saw that!"

"We did... But there's one person on the ship alive, and I just hacked into the security cams. The soldiers are dead—there's another bounty hunter aboard. I can't get a good look at his face." Boone paused.

"Another bounty hunter?" I quickened my pace. "Boone, you said we had first dibs on this job!"

"We did."

"Then how—"

The comm went dead.

Who killed the line?

Scowling, I rushed onward, down the corridors, and didn't slow till I reached the west wing.

Footsteps sounded that weren't my own.

I stopped around the corner. Waited.

The steps grew closer.

When the figure stepped around the corridor corner, I lifted my gun, leveling it at his head.

"Wait a second, moron," I snapped.

The figure froze. "*Moron?*" he snapped. He wore a loose-fitting outfit of black pants, a black shirt, a black coat, and a black helmet. The look was completed with black laser blasters strapped to his forearms.

He.

His voice sounded awfully feminine.

"What are you doing?" I demanded.

"Saving Candi," the man snipped.

"Well, back off. This is my job."

Saving? Why did he say saving?

"She's my family!" He pulled the trigger, and the bullet hit my shoulder. My suit deflected the bullet, but by then, the man had vanished.

I swore and ran after him. He headed toward the room—and if he reached the sleeping woman first...

"Wait!" I shouted. "Let's talk this out!" I needed the bounty. I couldn't slip up.

The man used an ID—how did he get a functioning ID? Off one of the guards?—and unsealed the door. I ran after him, but the door sealed in my face. I ran into the wall and swore.

"Hey!"

I yanked the ID I had snatched from the pilot. Shoved it on the keypad. The door unsealed.

"Hey, listen, I tried to be nice," I snarled, stepping into the room with my gun raised.

A woman stood over the cryotube, black helmet lowered, her brown hair in a tight bun. She wore black pants, a black jacket, black laser—wait.

"You?" I growled. "I thought you were a man!" I kept my gun trained on the woman, anger rising. "Back away from Candi!"

The woman turned her gun on me again. "A man?" She scowled. "Who are you? Don't take another step! I'll shoot!"

"Go ahead!" I snapped. "It can't pierce my suit."

She did but hit my helmet this time. The helmet deflected it, of course, but I didn't like her attitude.

"She's my cousin. You take another step, I'll find a way to kill you." The woman seethed.

I believed she meant it, but I laughed. "No one can kill me."

She fired again, the bullet hitting my gut. "Go away."

"No. This is my job."

"You won't get the bounty," the woman snipped. "Jennifer put the bounty on Candi's head, but she won't pay anyway for bringing her home."

"You don't know that," I said.

"I do. She's my aunt." The woman scoffed. "She'll kill the hunter that brings Candi in, and then she'll kill Candi."

Jennifer was the mom. I knew that much. "You don't have proof of that, so don't make dumb claims. Step back." Eyeing the woman in the cryotube, my gut twisted. She was thin, tall, and her short hair had streaks of gray throughout, despite her young age.

But what stung the most was how peaceful she looked.

The kind of peaceful that was fake.

The woman stood between me and the cryotube. "I'm taking Candi."

"I don't even know if you're her cousin," I said. "So this bounty is mine."

"If I gave proof, would you back off?"

Man, she was insistent.

I mentally added *stubborn women* to the list of women I disliked. "Fine," I agreed.

The woman pulled a tablet from her jacket pocket, but her gun never wavered from me. "Here." Lifting the tablet, she pulled up a holographic screen. It flickered with images—images of Candi and the woman, as children, then as young adults. The pictures matched their appearances.

Sighing, I mumbled, "So what do you have planned?" I couldn't let the job go.

And anyway, the woman had my interest. She had boarded a ship, taken out guards, and snuck past Boone and me. Not many could do that.

"I'm saving Candi." She gestured to my gun. "So get out."

"Wait, wait, wait," I said. "Just lemme hear ya out. I mean—"

"You want a bounty, and you won't get one, so go find another job." She raised one eyebrow, clearly ready to shoot me again.

"Look, my gut told me there was something more to this job, so... I can't just let it go." I holstered my gun. "See?" Lifting my hands, I tried to look innocent.

Not a skill I really had, but still.

The woman glared.

"I'm Ledger," I said.

"I am aware."

"Flattered to hear that." I grinned.

"Don't be."

"What's your name?"

"Tina," she said.

"Okay, Tina. Why is Candi in cryo sleep? Is she a criminal? Did Mom and Pop have to hide her tragic fate from the Earth's judging eyes?" I asked.

Tina's brown eyes narrowed. "Shut up."

"Fair."

"Jennifer and Paul had her put in cryo sleep because she was interfering with their lab work."

"Lab work," I repeated.

Tina turned. "Pull anything, and I shoot you."

"Gotcha." I watched as Tina typed on a giant contraption nearby. I figured that was the machine keeping the cryotube functioning. "So… What were they doing?"

"Classified."

"If it helps, I hate politicians," I said. "Your secrets are safe with me."

"Secrets safe with a bounty hunter." She huffed, typing away. "I've heard everything now."

I inched closer. "So?"

"So?"

"What lab stuff? Mutants?" I said it teasingly.

Tina nodded. "Basically."

"Oh." Eyeing Candi, I mumbled, "Oof."

"Yeah. Oof. What are you, five years old?" She huffed. "I'm overriding the machine to let her out." The machine beeped, then whirred. She stepped back.

Frowning, hand hovering over my holstered gun, I watched as the cryotube unsealed. The machine whirred and the door lifted sideways, almost like a big, white, shiny casket.

Candi lay still. Tina growled and stepped over to her. "Stay back," she told me.

"I didn't even move!" I glared.

Tina stroked Candi's hair gently. "It's time to wake up now, dear. C'mon."

I watched them, and to my surprise, Candi stirred. Her eyes opened. A smile tugged at her lips. "Tina," she said softly, her voice distant, small.

Tina hugged Candi tightly. "That's right," she said. "I've gotcha."

Just great. There went my bounty.

"Listen—" I started, but Tina turned, leveling her gun at me.

"I said leave," she snapped. "You got your proof, now get out."

"No," I said.

"Get out!" She started to step forward, but Candi sat upright, grabbing Tina's arm weakly.

"Wait," Candi said. "Tina…"

"He was going to turn you in," Tina snapped. "You want to go to Jennifer?"

Candi studied me for a moment. "If he was going to turn me… He would have."

Did she know who I was? I didn't have much of a name for myself before she went into cryo sleep, so how could she know who I was? "I need the bounty," I said.

Tina helped Candi stand. She wavered but jutted her chin at me. "You won't receive it by turning me in. You know that."

She was right.

I didn't trust politicians.

They didn't hold up their word to their followers; why would they keep a promise to a bounty hunter?

"I still need the cash," I said tightly. "And face it… If Tina got word about this, dozens of other bounty hunters will be crawling in this place in, what, ten minutes? Five? They'll sniff you out and the hunt will be on — they won't slow down till they have Candi. So I can help." Smirking, I puffed out my chest. "Come along, ladies. I'll protect ya."

Ideally, Boone would shoot any ship that got too close to us right now, but still.

I could handle this.

Tina scowled, opening her mouth to retort, but Candi whispered, "S-something's wrong."

I never liked hearing those words on a job. But I'd felt that way this entire mission. "What?"

Tina looked down at her cousin worriedly, but Candi gestured.

To me.

No, past me.

Jerking around, I pulled my gun and fired in a split second.

Thump.

The figure behind me hit the floor with a *thud*, his armor suit clinking slightly. On the right shoulder, a little red phoenix was embedded into the armor.

"Aw, c'mon." I growled. "Them? Now? Really?" If my comm was live, Boone would get an earful right now. The Phoenix crew hated me — why did Boone let them aboard?

Tina aimed her gun at me again. "You know them?"

"Who doesn't, lady?" I stepped into the corridor, but it was empty. "You two better c'mon."

"With you?" Tina scoffed.

"He wants to help…" Candi said softly.

"Grow up, Candi," Tina said. "Don't be naive. He wants to sell you to Jennifer."

Candi's piercing gaze locked with mine.

I shook my head, hissing, "If I wanted to do that, believe me, it'd be done. I can drug you both and go. But I'm not. Because I know a sham job when I take it, and I wanna see this one through. Get you both to safety." I didn't look away from Candi. Her eyes were intense, for such a small woman. Like she could see through me.

She nodded and squeezed Tina's arm. "I don't want you hurt," she whispered. "Please, let's trust him."

Trust me? The words made me cringe, but I went with it. "C'mon." Without waiting for Tina to argue again, I led them into the corridor.

The lights flickered on and off. Not good. I moved a bit faster, but Candi gasped and stumbled behind me. Tina caught her.

"She's been in cryo sleep," Tina muttered. "Her legs aren't used to this much…"

They had to be kidding me. I turned around. "We gotta run."

Candi jutted her chin, clearly angry at herself for being weak, but she mumbled, "I don't think I can. I'm sorry."

"Then hang on tight." Without asking permission, I grabbed Candi and tossed her over my shoulder. "Tina, keep close."

"Don't tell me what to do." She followed us down the hall and around the corner. With the power flicking on and off, I wondered if the Phoenix crew was scrambling signals, too. Had they disconnected my comm? But then, why had it taken them so long to get aboard the ship after they smashed the signals?

I tried my comm again. "C'mon…" If Boone was dead, I'd kill him.

Or something like that.

Not that anything could kill the jackal.

"I'm going as fast as I can!" Tina snipped.

"I'm trying to comm a friend."

"Huh?" both women asked in unison.

"Uh, call a friend, you know—"

Footsteps sounded down the hall. I growled, lifting my gun and firing as soon as the two Phoenix men came around the corner.

Candi covered her ears, then whispered, "Are they… dead?"

"Nah. I've been using sedatives, but I'll probably switch to real bullets soon." I kept going. "Lady, you got a big bounty on that pretty head of yours, so I'd suggest explaining a bit while we walk, 'cause Boone doesn't like strangers aboard *Lucky Lucy*."

"My… My parents put me in cryo sleep because I tried to save a few of the children," Candi said, voice small.

"That's vague." I led us down another hall.

"Their lab is government funded," Candi continued. She gripped me tightly, as if I might drop her as I ran. "Earth is still a wealthy planet—and it is fueled by slavery."

"Nothing new."

"It's wrong," she said weakly. "And when my parents brought children into the lab to be their test subjects... I couldn't watch it. I couldn't watch them make arsenal from children."

I paused. "Arsenal?"

"They turned people into monsters. They used their bodies for science. They..." She trailed off, and I realized she was crying. "They are monsters. And when I discovered it, I almost ended it... Almost... But..."

"It wasn't your fault," Tina spoke up. "You tried."

"I failed."

Sighing, I cut in. "So they whisked you into cryo sleep. I'll assume that means they're still doing all that creepy stuff on Earth?"

"Yes," Tina said, still keeping up with my pace. "But we'll end it. I have a plan. I just couldn't leave Candi here—and when the location was shared from Jennifer, I took the chance."

"You're both some ballsy women, that's for sure." I slowed at the end of the corridor. "Look, the Phoenix hate me, and they're tough, so—"

Tina rolled her eyes. "Get me to the control room and I'll teleport us out."

I stared. "You have a teleportation device on you?"

"No. I can access the ship's."

"But the power—"

"Just get us there," she said sharply. "I can get us out of here with their teleporter."

I led the way. A few Phoenix men got in the way, but we shot them down and moved along. By now, the Phoenix had to know we had Candi, and they would hunt us throughout the ship.

I didn't see a good shot of us teleporting offship with my teleporter. It wasn't meant to teleport more than one body at a time. We'd need more firepower, and our best bet would be to use the ship's teleporter, which was usually in control rooms.

Once we reached the control room, the power was shut off completely. I scowled. The Phoenix must have gained control. "Great. How are you—"

Tina hurried over to the lifeless control panels. She didn't acknowledge the sleeping men that I'd taken care of earlier. "Keep them away."

On cue, a few more Phoenix mercs scurried into the control room from the entrance, firing at me. I shot them down first—I hadn't built a reputation on nothing—and grinned. "Sure, why don't I just do that?"

Candi squirmed over my shoulder. "Put me down. I can help Tina."

"How?" But I dropped her to her feet. She staggered before going to Tina's side.

"Backup generator," they said in unison.

"If it's the same codes Paul used to use..." Tina ripped off a control panel, tossing the faux metal aside. "Ha!" She reached in and typed on a small keypad. The big machine beneath the panels beeped... And stirred to life.

"Who keeps a backup generator hidden in the control room?" I scowled.

"Smart people," Tina bit.

I took a warning step over. "Well, get the teleportation gig going and let's get out of here!"

Gasping, Candi grabbed my arm tightly, yanking me sideways. She didn't have much strength, but I moved with her instinctively. "Watch out!"

I quickly switched the setting to the gun as I raised it up, and then fired a few rounds of bullets into the man's suit. Their suits wouldn't have built-in energy deflectors like mine. But my suit wouldn't last long, either.

I watched the suited man's body hit the ground in the entryway. "Thanks, sleeping beauty," I said with a smirk.

"Candi," she corrected. Sour sport.

Tina glared up at me. "Back off." As she chastened me, she fired up the teleportation device, which stood to the far right of the little room. I hadn't even noticed when I came in here to sedate the pilot and soldiers.

Candi beamed. "You did it, Tina!" But she leaned against me, her thin arms holding tight to my right arm, like I was the only thing keeping her from collapsing. "Bravo!"

Then, outside the grand window overlooking space, the *Lucky Lucy* appeared. Boone had taken the invisibility shield down—that meant he was alive, at least, right?

"W-who is that?" Candi gaped at the ragged ship.

The sound of more gunfire in the corridors sounded. I recognized the different sound of the ammunition, mingled with sharp sounding ray guns, and I growled.

More bounty hunters had to be aboard.

The Phoenix guys didn't shoot to sedate. I didn't imagine the newcomers would, either.

"Friend." I scooped Candi into my arms. "C'mon. Tina, get us on that ship. Now."

Tina scrambled at the machine, kneeling, her back to the entryway. I held Candi and kept my gun trained on the door, growing uneasy. How many bounty hunters were here now? How had word gotten out? Not that it mattered now. All I needed to focus on now was how to keep Tina and

Candi alive.

Bleeding heart, and all, I guess, but I couldn't let them just face their doom alone.

Even if they were rude.

Men's voices came from the hall. More gunshots followed, ringing in the corridor.

"Done!" Tina jumped to her feet. "Get in! We're headed to your ship, ugly."

I slipped Candi into the large, glass-looking, closet-shaped device. It would be crammed, but we fit inside, and I put my back to the doorway.

Hell broke loose.

Phoenix men burst into the room. Their guns went off, and one bullet struck my back as the doors sealed shut behind me. My suit's energy shield was dying, and right on time, too. Shouts and curses filled my ears as the men lunged for the teleportation device, but in the next moment, we were gone.

Thud.

"Sorry!" Candi forced weakly.

Blinking, I glanced down, disoriented for a moment longer. Candi lay on top of me, and blinding lights poured over us. I winced. "You okay?"

She pushed herself up. "Y-you're shot," she said.

"It happens." I sat up, looking around. "The lounge..." Dirty laundry, empty beer cans, and other odds and ends littered the couches and table in the little, cozy room.

We had made it aboard *Lucky Lucy*. I didn't remember the overhead lights being so bright, though.

"Where's Boone?"

Tina sat up, rubbing her head. "Who?"

"Boone." Hauling myself to my feet, I looked back at the women. "Stay here. There are probably more bounty hunters outside the ship, we're not safe yet."

"Where are you going?" Candi stood, shaking. "You're shot!"

"And?"

"You could die!" Candi said, tugging my arm. "You need medical attention—"

"I need my dumb partner to get this ship moving, or we're all dead!" I pulled away. "Boone!" I shouted, but received no answer.

To my relief, however, the comm in my ear buzzed. Boone's voice followed.

"We're movin'. Pretty fast. I've lost 'em." A pause. "You're welcome."

"Then get the ship on auto and get down here," I snapped into the comm. "You gotta patch me up."

There was grumbling on the other end, followed by, "Fine."

I turned to the women, forcing a smile. "Welcome aboard the *Lucky Lucy*, ladies. Sorry for the mess."

~~~~~

"So... The politicians are making crazy mutants and war slaves... And you gals wanna stop it?" Boone asked, downing the rest of his beer and tossing the can. "Hmm."

"I... know it's a lot," Candi started, voice soft. "But we have to. There are too many innocent lives at risk to ignore this."

"Hard to believe they've managed to keep all this from the press for so long," Boone mused. "Not that I ever trusted a politician, but this takes slimy to a whole other level."

Tina rolled her eyes, shoving more food into her face. Boone had heated up frozen pizza for everyone after patching up my gunshot wound, which hadn't been severe, thanks to the suit, even if it had malfunctioned and let the bullet pierce it. Just my luck.

I sat stiffly beside Candi, who offered me another slice of pizza. I took it.

"We can do it," Candi repeated.

"We have to." Tina finished her slice. "Once you gentlemen drop us back off on my ship, we'll be on our way." She had taken us to Boone's ship so we'd be safe in numbers.

Boone hesitated.

I stared at my pizza slice. "Well... It sounds like a big job."

"It is. And?" Tina bristled.

Candi watched me with those intense, piercing eyes. I gulped. "I'm just saying... Maybe we could help."

Boone frowned at me.

Tina scoffed.

I continued tightly. "I mean, we're not monsters." I gave Boone a glare. "If children are being harmed... I can't walk away from that knowing I could've helped."

Boone rubbed his jaw, nodding slowly. "Same here."

"There's no bounty in this." Candi studied me, voice going soft. "I don't think we could pay you anything. And if we failed... We'd die... Jennifer is a wicked woman and has stopped at nothing to create her empire. We are going up against an impossible enemy... And I think we can do it... But at great cost..."

"I can't be talked outta jobs when my mind is made up, lady," I said.

"Who said we'd let you join us?" Tina demanded.

"Well, will you?" I looked between the women.

Candi looked at her lap, wiping at her eyes. "You both mean it?"

"We're good mercs," I said. "We can better the chances of success.
~~~~~

And anyway, it's worth a shot. The payment would be ruining Jennifer's empire — and hey, there's gotta be some money in that, too."

But for the first time in a long time, I didn't care about the money.

I wanted to help Candi.

I wanted to understand how she could sound so kind, and have such knowing eyes, even after all she had faced.

I wanted to help children, even when no one had ever helped me.

I wanted…

I wanted more than the *Lucky Lucy*.

I wanted more than the countless jobs.

I wanted a purpose.

And I thought I had found it, when I helped save Candi from cryo sleep.

Candi smiled at me. "We would be honored to work alongside you both."

Tina opened her mouth to argue but caught herself. Boone sighed.

"We'll have plenty to hash out later," he said. "And Ledger's right… Even if you don't want our help, we can't walk away from this, so we might as well combine our forces." He stood from the recliner, yawning. "I'm gonna get some sleep."

I watched him go. Tina slipped into the hall, too, mumbling goodnight. I eyed Candi.

"Thank you," I said. "I know this is a bit strange, but we won't let you down."

We couldn't. Innocent lives hung in the balance.

Candi reached over and squeezed my forearm gently. "I know. You have kind eyes, Ledger. I noticed them the moment I woke up." She chuckled. "Thank you."

"Huh?"

"For saving me," she said.

"Tina saved you." I frowned down at her.

She shook her head, tucking a strand of hair behind her ear. "You still saved us both… I know the bounty would have been wonderful… Still, you helped us."

I shrugged. "Don't mention it."

She glanced at me again. "You're very stubborn."

"So are you."

"Then I think we'll get along." She smiled softly, standing on shaky legs. "Goodnight, Ledger."

"Goodnight, sleeping beauty. Get lots of sleep. We'll need the rest before we conquer the Azure empire."

END

THE WEIGHT OF RAVEN FEATHERS
Meaghan Elizabeth Ward

Before

She woke with a ragged cry.

Her limbs felt like ice beneath a scratchy blanket. Each sharp inhale cut deep into her chest, and each exhale escaped with a whimper.

"Hush," crooned a gentle voice overhead. A warm hand cupped her cheek. "Hush, child. You are safe."

Safe? She didn't feel safe. Her head felt tight and packed with wool, as if she was waking from a nightmare into yet another dream. She didn't know this room. She didn't know this woman.

Over her thundering heartbeat, she heard the heavy shush of rain on a thatch roof, and beyond the rain, a raven screeched.

"Where—?" she croaked.

"Hush," said the woman again.

An arm wrapped around the girl's shoulders and eased her into a sitting position. A cup met her dry lips.

The woman's kind eyes softened further as the girl drank, but a troubled thumbnail crease remained between her brows, and her gaze drifted across the room. A pale-faced boy watched from the bedroom doorway.

The girl pushed the cup away.

"My son found you collapsed upon the moor and brought you here— to our home," the woman said. "Can you tell us what happened?"

"I... I don't know."

The creases on the woman's brow deepened. "What's your name, lass?"

"I... can't."

"It's all right if you tell us," the woman said.

"I don't remember." The girl started rocking, slowly at first then faster. Another whimper escaped. "I don't remember anything."

~~~~

Nine Years Later

In tales of old, it was foretold that to meet the glassy eye of a black-winged bird was to invite the cold touch of a curse until even the sight of raven feathers spelled trouble. Róisín was familiar with this kind of black
~~~~

luck. It followed her upon the moor, it found her on the banks of the burn, it chased her from the past, but as she stood in the cottage yard and the colors of the summer sunset blazed across her vision, she was sure she saw a flutter of white wings.

A strand of mud-brown hair feathered across her lips. She brushed it away with a smile as she leaned against the gate and blinked into the light. The balsamic scent of purple thyme lifted on the breeze, and the garden harebells whispered against the hem of her skirt.

On such a golden night, she could even believe the cold would not touch her.

"Are you sure you won't come with Ma and Pa and me now?" Oona had asked earlier.

"I'll walk over with Alasdair when he comes in from the pasture."

Oona scrunched her nose.

"What?" Róisín said, warily.

"Those handsome Allanach brothers will be at the gathering, but you'd rather wait here for my brother?" She threw Róisín a cheeky grin. "You look lovely tonight. I'm sure you'll take his breath away."

"Oona!"

There was no denying that Róisín had put on her good dress—the dusty pink one without patches—but tonight was a special occasion. The crofter families were gathering to celebrate the first harvest of the bere barley. It had been a good year, and the harvest celebration might be their last gathering before the weather turned bitter. And perhaps Róisín put more effort into her appearance tonight, but it really had nothing to do with Alasdair or how he'd once commented (while she wore this particular dress) that she looked lovely. Not a simple good or nice but *lovely*, and that certainly made her feel beautiful.

Oona's eyes sparked with mischief. "I've seen how you look at him, Róisín, and don't pretend you don't."

"I'm not sure what you mean," Róisín said, but her cheeks warmed. "He's like a brother to me."

"Are you so sure of that?" Oona said with a wicked grin. "Because I've seen how he looks at you in return, and it is not at all brotherly."

The very memory of Oona's words made a soft warmth bloom in Róisín's chest. The medallion she wore seemed to burn against her skin. She clutched at the shape of it beneath her neckline and drew in a slow breath.

Yes, it was easy to be content in the waiting.

The barn door rasped open, then shut. Sunlight caught on Alasdair's shoulders and in his hair. He must have snuck out of sight of the house to his quarters in the barn loft. He'd changed into his best clothes, too.

"You're late," she called, letting herself through the gate to meet him.

"I know," he said as he stopped before her. He smelled earthy like the moors, laced with the underlying lanolin scent of the sheep. It was not the most pleasant smell, but Róisín didn't mind it so much anymore. "You should have gone ahead without me."

"And given you the excuse not to join us at the gathering and abandon me entirely to the attention of the Allanach brothers?"

"Would that have been so bad?"

In truth, there was nothing *wrong* with the Allanach boys. They were handsome enough, but they were also desperate flirts in a croft that housed only two girls their own age.

They're not you, she wanted to say. Instead, she said, "Alasdair MacNair, are you going to escort me or not?"

He gestured grandly to the road. "Walk with me, Róisín?"

Warmth flooded her cheeks. "I thought you'd never ask," she said airily.

The road that led to the Allanachs' could barely be called a road at all. Instead, the wagon-rutted trail jounced across the flattest parts of the heath, linking the croft farmholds before jutting to meet the cliffside road, which led further still to the village of Callanway.

Róisín walked one wheel rut while Alasdair walked the other. The back of his hand brushed her fingers. Once. Then twice. His forefinger caught her little finger, and their hands hung for a long moment in the space between.

Not quite holding hands.

Not quite letting go, either.

She looked away with a smile.

Alasdair set an even slower pace. She loved these moments best: the long walks he stretched like a leisurely sunset, the space between here and there filled with just them. She was sure she could walk the road forever — past the gathering, past Callanway even — to the edge of the isle.

"I leave in the morning for the Callanway market," Alasdair said finally. "To sell the first of the barley and pick up some supplies."

A whingeing pain sparked behind her breastbone. She released a long, soft breath. "Oh?"

"It's a long road to travel alone."

"Is it?"

"You could come with me."

"Maybe next time," she said, perhaps too quickly.

The Allanachs' barn came into view as they rounded the base of the last hill. The dancing notes of Mr. Sutharlan's tin whistle and Oona's high, flirtatious laugh drifted to them.

Anxiety curled in Róisín's stomach. She imagined spending the night with her back to a corner, eating too much food, her cheeks aching with a painted-on smile. She took two more steps before she even realized Alasdair was no longer beside her.

When she turned back, he fixed her with a small grin. His eyes sparked with a look she knew all too well. "If you won't go with me tomorrow, then come with me now."

"What?"

"Let's not join the others."

"But… your parents are expecting us."

"Are you telling me you have a sudden penchant for crowds and gossip?"

"Not a whit! But more's the trouble when the gossip is about us. You know what Mrs. Sutharlan is like."

"Let's risk it. Just this once."

"You promised me a dance, remember?" She wasn't sure why she was bandying him. She couldn't even mask her relief at the idea.

"Och, I promised to save you from dancing with the Allanachs. That isn't the same thing." He held out a hand to her. "Come with me?"

Róisín recalled the bird at sunset and the brush of wings that might have been white. For a moment, she felt daring and a little bit wild—like a sprite courting both trouble and luck. Forget the rumors and doing what was expected, she *wanted* to go. And maybe, just once, that was acceptable.

She took his hand.

Alasdair laced his calloused fingers with hers. When he turned away from the trodden path, she skipped after him.

~~~~~

Róisín barely noticed the thistles snagging her skirt. Her hand was still captured in Alasdair's as if he had no intention of letting her go, and though she was breathless and flushed when they reached the peak of the nearby escarpment, she grinned widely.

The sun's dying rays bathed them in a fiery glow while the world fell away beneath them into shadow.

"There," Alasdair said, a little breathless himself. "Worth every bit of trouble, isn't it?"

"You and I have very different definitions of trouble."

"Aye, don't I know it."

In the year after she'd come to the MacNairs, Róisín became familiar with bitterness and resentment. She'd worn a name that didn't fit, but the one time she'd tried to run away from everything, Alasdair had stopped her. He'd abandoned his flock and followed her wordlessly across the fen until she was as lost as she felt inside. Then she'd gotten angry.

She turned on him and struck hard enough to give him a bloody nose. Then she'd started sobbing.

"Who am I?" she'd cried.
~~~~~

He'd shrugged and swiped at the blood slipping across his lips. "You're a MacNair."

"But I wasn't before."

"But you are now."

When they'd returned home, Alasdair took full blame for the scattered sheep and said nothing of her attempt to leave or why he came home bloody.

Róisín couldn't imagine leaving the MacNairs now. They'd given her their name and a place at their table. Alasdair moved into the barn loft so she could fill his space in the cottage, Oona shared her cot, and even though she'd long resented herself, they never did.

It still lingered though—that wool-packed hollowness she'd first felt nine years ago when she found herself in a stranger's home. She pushed it to the back of her awareness again and again, but it still made her feel like she was lost in a dreamscape waiting to wake.

Róisín watched the clouds fade from red to purple. Overhead, the stars woke abruptly. She met Alasdair's eye. He looked away like she'd caught him staring and gazed distantly into the horizon as the sun winked out of sight.

She had half a mind to nudge him in the ribs with her elbow like she used to do and ask what was on his mind, but they were alone, and they weren't children, and it felt wrong now.

Eventually, he straightened his shoulders and turned fully to face her. "There's something I've been wanting to ask you. Time and time again, I tell myself to wait just a little longer, but..."

He hesitated.

Don't say it, Róisín thought. *Don't.*

"It's been a good year. I find myself thinking of the future and of a stone cottage to call my own, and perhaps it wouldn't be anything fancy, but it could be a home. And I've been thinking too... about who I'd like to share it with."

"Alasdair."

"I can't imagine my life without you in it, Róisín. And I don't want to—imagine it, that is. I'm finally ready to admit it."

"Must you say these things now?"

"Is there a reason I shouldn't?"

Róisín trembled. She dragged her fingers from his before he could feel it and stepped away.

"Róisín?" Hurt colored his voice.

Anxiety punched deeper into Róisín's gut. If he asked her— officially—she'd have to say no. And she shouldn't tell him why.

She couldn't tell him.

"Róisín," he said again, calm and determined. His steadfast eyes settled on her. "You can lie to my family. You can even lie to yourself. But you never had to lie to me."

Her eyes darted from his caving shoulders to his unblinking gaze. "I don't know what you mean."

"Róisín..." His words dragged, slow and weighted. "We both know you remember."

White spots swam in Róisín's vision. She forgot to breathe. Words jumbled in her head and staggered past her lips. "I-I don't...remember."

Alasdair's mouth twitched. He took a long, hard breath.

She wished she could steady herself as easily.

"Maybe you didn't remember at first," he said, "but you do now, and you cannot deny it. I thought tonight might be different, but whenever I get close you pull away. I found you that day. I saw... and I never said a word to anyone. I see those memories tearing you apart now, and I-I love you too much to let you leave it unspoken, to let this secret we both know but pretend we don't continue to fester between us."

"I *don't* remember," Róisín muttered again, sharper.

"Zelia," he said.

Róisín's skin crawled with frost. "Don't. Don't call me that," she whispered. Her brows pinched so tight that a sharp pain stabbed behind her forehead.

A twisted, pained look mirrored in Alasdair's own eyes. "But that was your name once. Wasn't it?"

"Yes," she whimpered. "Once upon a misfortunate summer long ago..."

~~~~~

Before

Zelia wandered the hills behind her home. A crown of flowers was tangled in her hair, and a clump of wildflowers was clenched tight in her fist.

"Don't you think we should head home, Zelia?" said her best friend. Deirdre trailed behind her, weaving sprigs of heather into a crown for herself.

"Not yet," Zelia said. She was surprised her father's big friend, Lennox, hadn't already been sent to find her. She kept expecting to hear his heavy steps clipped by the metallic rattle of his dirk and short sword, but he never came.

"Do you think they've realized we're missing yet?"

"Definitely."

"Do you think we'll get in trouble?"

"Never."

It was a lazy, innocent, late afternoon—the kind of day where
~~~~~

anything felt possible, and everything was permissible when just the right amount of bottom lip made all forgiven. But just in case that wasn't enough this time, Zelia had a plan.

She set aside her bouquet and leaned over a cluster of extra sharp gorse. One of the last roses of summer nestled between the thorny branches, just out of reach.

"Zelia, don't," Deirdre cautioned.

But Zelia didn't listen. She rose on tiptoes and stretched farther.

She knew the wildflowers would make her mother smile, but the rose would give her mother that wistful look—the one where her smile touched her eyes and she no longer looked tired or worried or, most importantly, cross. If Zelia was lucky, maybe tonight after supper her mother would look at the pale petals and tell her again of Cymru—the lush, green homeland where she'd lived before marrying Zelia's father, and the garden of hedge roses she loved to get lost in as a lass.

"Zelia," said Deidre again.

"I just need this last one, then we can go home."

"Zelia!"

Zelia dropped back on her heels with a small huff and turned on her friend. "What?"

But Deirdre wasn't looking at her.

A boy had crested the hill behind them. He stood frozen, like he was so startled to find anyone in the hidden spaces skirting the moor that he couldn't be sure if they were human girls or long-forgotten fae. Then he stepped closer, picking a path through the coarse grass.

"We should go home," Deirdre said again, moving to Zelia's side.

"What for?"

"I don't want to be scolded by your *athair* for talking to strangers."

Zelia shrugged. Often, the village mistook her and Deirdre for each other. They shared the same dark shade of hair and the same dark eyes. But Zelia was nothing like Deirdre. The stranger had given her no reason to be afraid, so she wouldn't be. And her father didn't have to know. "It's just a boy, Deirdre."

Zelia was beginning to notice boys. How different they were from girls. Some with too-big ears and too-big teeth, some with too-loud voices and far too much dirt on their hands. Most were annoying. This boy looked less like one of the village boys, with their faded clothes and scabby elbows, and more like a hero from one of her father's stories.

"Ladies," he said in a cracking voice that didn't match his boyish face. "Allow me."

The brambles didn't even touch him as he reached around her, broke the rose stem, and twisted it free. He held it out to Zelia with a lopsided hero's grin.

"I've never seen you before," Zelia said.

The flower hung hesitantly between them. "I'm a passerby. Nothing more."

She pinched the flower carefully between her fingers. "You shouldn't wander the moor alone." The pale pink petals quivered. "It's not safe for strangers."

"I'm not alone," he said solemnly. His eyes glinted with something akin to confusion or sadness or both. "I should go. Beware the thorns, little princess."

"What? Oh." Her fingers found the flower crown in her hair. "Thank you."

He continued on to the next hill, deeper into untamed land. Now Zelia was left to stare.

No. *He* was not an annoying boy at all.

"Zelia, let's go home, please." Deirdre plucked at her sleeve, pulling her back toward home, and this time, she let her.

The bouquet lay forgotten in the dirt.

~~~~~

Zelia heard her parents calling for her even before the towering stone broch came into sight. Her father's deep voice carried over the hillocks. Her mother's followed, sharp and shrill.

"Zelia! Deirdre!" her mother cried when she saw them crest the last rise. She clenched her faded red skirt in a tight fist and ran to meet them. Her hands found Zelia's shoulders, then cupped her face. "Where did you go, lass? Where have you been?" Her fingers trembled against Zelia's chin. The pendant she always kept so carefully hidden beneath her neckline swung freely between them, winking in the light.

"Not here," her father said. His eyes skated over Zelia's head to the moor, then back to the tiny village on the shore, then to the broch that stood like a beacon in the burning light. "Not here," he said again. "Let's get inside. Quickly."

His hand tightened around Zelia's wrist. Her fingers curled in his grip, and she hissed at the prick of thorns. The forgotten rose fell from her hand. "*Athair. Athair*, wait—"

"Not here, Zelia," he said again. Harsher.

Zelia's bottom tip trembled, but this time, it wasn't an act. A droplet of blood welled on her forefinger as he towed her toward the broch.

The entrance lay off to the side, cut into the hill and shrouded by bog myrtle. A fresh, lemony scent drifted after Zelia as she stumbled through the short tunnel to the ground chambers. The cookfire had burned to ashes, casting the tower in night-dark shadow.

At that moment, Zelia realized something was very wrong.

Her parents weren't angry. They were scared. And the broch was too
~~~~~

quiet.

Deirdre's ma always tended the fire. If she were there, the tower would have been filled with the smoky scent of supper. Even stern-faced Lennox was missing, and the only time Zelia had seen him leave her father's side was when he'd been sent to bring her home from her wanderings.

"W-where's my ma?" Deirdre's cry shattered against the walls of the small space.

"She'll be back," Zelia's mother said, but the words rattled and shook. Still… Zelia's mother would never lie.

Her mother tugged Deirdre upstairs without another word, while Zelia's father crouched and met her eye.

"What's happening, *Athair*?"

"Zelia, you remember our nighttime tales?" he murmured.

She nodded. They were adventurous, heroic stories filled with noble princes, humongous dragons, and fierce princesses (who, coincidentally, were often locked in tower homes much like her own).

He smoothed the hair from her face. "Tonight, I need you to be brave like the girls in those stories."

"I don't understand."

The stairs creaked. Her mother swept back down the steps with a sobbing Deirdre tight at her side. Deirdre was in Zelia's good dress—the one even she was rarely allowed to wear. The collar lay crooked on her friend's hunched shoulders.

"Zelia," her father said again. "I need you to listen to me. Just this once. I need you to stay here until we get back."

"But where are you going?"

"Not far. We'll be back come morning."

"But… why is Deirdre going with you?"

"Deirdre is going to help us with a little game of pretend. But you need to stay in the tower. It's very important. Don't leave. Don't even go into the village. Do you understand, lass?"

No. She couldn't possibly understand, because her gentle father was staring at her with eyes like granite, and his fingers bit into her skin.

"Zelia?" He gave her a shake. "Do you understand?"

Zelia nodded.

Her father pushed to his feet and reached for his good coat.

Her mother knelt and brushed a shaky kiss against her forehead. "We'll be back soon, my love." She lifted the chain from around her neck and placed it around Zelia's, tucking the medallion carefully beneath her chemise.

Zelia had never seen her mother without the medallion. It was strange to see her throat bare. It was stranger still to feel its weight pulling at her own neck.

"Keep it safe for me?" her mother whispered.

Zelia nodded again, because that was what they wanted.

Her father returned, still shrugging on his coat. His fingers brushed her chin. "My brave lass," he said.

Zelia's eyelashes fluttered as she fought back unshed tears, and in the space of a blink, they were gone.

She heard Deirdre's small hiccuping breaths from the tunnel. The heavy door scraped open with a groan, then scudded shut.

Zelia slid to the ground and hugged her knees to her chest. Tight, pinched breaths rasped in her throat. A whimper escaped. The strangled sound echoed so loud in the stillness she thought for a moment that maybe she wasn't alone after all.

She crawled on hands and knees toward the tunnel and half stumbled to her feet, banging her shoulder twice against the heavy door before it cracked open. She sucked in a gasp of air.

Her eyes strained to see Deirdre and her parents on the path to the village through the tangled gaps among the bog myrtle branches. They weren't there. The sun sat low on the horizon, bathing everything in rust and gold. She shaded her eyes with an arm.

There! They'd just vanished between the cleft of two hills, heading deeper into the moors toward the far-off mountains.

Her pricked finger throbbed. She wanted to cry so hard and loud they heard, raced back, and told her they were sorry for ever thinking of leaving her.

Be brave like in the tales, her father had said.

She was brave. Braver than Deirdre, to be sure.

Stay here, her father had said.

But if there was one thing Zelia learned from his stories—full of danger yet happy endings—it was that she was not the kind of girl who sat in a tower needing rescuing.

And she could prove it.

Zelia swallowed her tears and stood tall as she slipped through the hidden door. Three ravens startled in the shrubs to her left. One pierced her with a long, dead-eyed stare. She jumped as their feathers slapped the air overhead. A black-winged heartbeat echoed in her chest as she turned her back on the tower and followed.

~~~~~

It wasn't until much later, when Zelia stumbled into an unfamiliar glen, that she realized she had not only lost her parents' trail, but she was lost herself.

Night had come swiftly. She spun in a tight circle, but everywhere looked the same. Colorless and empty.
~~~~~

She shook hard, both from cold and fear, imagining all kinds of twisted, storybook monsters prowling at the corners of her vision. Her mother didn't believe in the existence of sith that stole souls or banshees that foretold death, but Zelia did. Especially now, surrounded by darkness.

Tears slipped down her cheeks. She sniffled and swiped them away with her sleeve.

Princesses never cried.

Be brave, she told herself.

How long ago had twilight fallen? She'd already been stumbling around the uplands forever. Her legs were heavy and tired. Shouldn't there be light on the horizon?

Movement caught her eye. A stream nestled in the crook between her hill and the next. Moonlight embroidered the water in fast-moving stitches and knots.

Flowing water can lead you to the coast, and the coast will always lead you to a village, said her father's voice in her head.

She stumbled toward it, but when her boots hit the bank, she froze. The scratchy, mournful notes of a half-familiar folksong drifted in the air.

A frail washerwoman—a *bean-nighe*—knelt on the burnside. She had knobby elbows and hunched so low over the water that the curvature of her spine looked painful. Beside her lay a tight bundle of clothing.

She rocked forward and back as she scrubbed a garment in the shallows, then she stilled, and her humming stopped. The hem of her chemise fluttered in a stray breeze, ghostly in the moonlight, as she slowly cocked her head in Zelia's direction. The movement was so strange and birdlike that Zelia inhaled sharply and clutched her injured hand tightly to her chest.

Zelia didn't ask the woman why she was alone or washing clothes in water as bitterly cold as mountain runoff, and the woman didn't ask why Zelia was awake or wandering the moor or even if she was well—which she was not.

"Can you help me?" Zelia said softly.

The woman said nothing. Maybe her ears were as numb as her bone-white fingers. She slapped the garment against the rocks.

It was a skirt, just like the one Zelia's mother wore. It might have even been red, too.

"Please," Zelia pleaded. She clasped her hands before her. If there was a time to speak sweetly and innocently to her elders and ask forgiveness later, it was now. "Nana," she added. Because maybe speaking to the woman as if she were kin would earn her the answer she really wanted. "I-I cannot find my *màthair* and *athair*. My *màthair*… she wears a skirt just like that one. Have you seen them?"

"I have." The woman said in a scratchy half-whisper. She continued to scrub and did not look up. Silence stretched between them like the long moment before a thorough scold.

"Can... Can you tell me which way they went?" Zelia prodded. "P-please?"

The woman stilled again. Stringy hair curtained her face. Her bony, motionless hands created small eddies in the shallows.

"There is little magic left in this world, lass," she said in her rasping pebble voice," but what scraps there are can be found in the choosing. To let go. To move forward. In the seeking and believing. So I will give you this: one choice. Here. Now."

"I don't understand."

"Go home, lass."

"I don't know how to get home."

"Is that so?" The woman's words were barbed. The air between them tingled with spectral, otherworldly magic.

Zelia had made a mistake—a horrible mistake.

In her mind, the ghouls and banshees said to roam the night were hideous beings with too-long limbs and fangs. They were less human, more creature. But something about this *bean-nighe* was not fully human. Zelia could feel it in her bones.

Maybe, sometimes, monsters could look human.

"Please... Nana... Please." Zelia's breath rattled. She shivered hard in her boots like Deirdre would.

The creature's head lifted slowly. Her pale hand rose from the shallows, and a skeletal finger pointed, dripping beads of water.

It took Zelia a long, long moment to tear her eyes from the figure and find what she pointed to.

On the horizon, at the peak of the tallest hill, a ring of standing stones reached for the stars.

"Thank you," Zelia heard herself say.

"Don't..." rasped the frail figure. Her head bowed once more to her work. She set aside the skirt and reached for a coat, patched yet trimmed in silver... like Zelia's father's. "Don't thank me, lass."

~~~~~

Zelia's eyes darted continuously from the stones ahead to the shadows that seemed to chase her. The wind billowed her skirt, like she herself was a wraith or a woman in white.

Don't trust her, Zelia's head repeated. They were not her father's words, so she told herself they meant nothing as she continued to stumble over the heath and heather.

She'd heard of sacred, magical places like these standing stones. They glowed in the moonlight as if fae-touched. Beneath, a tunnel cut into the
~~~~~

hillside, and from within, a warm light beckoned.

She carved a quick path toward it. The opening was small. Her father, even her mother, would have had to bend double to enter, but it was just her size.

She almost called out for her parents then. But as she set foot into the mouth of the tunnel, she heard her mother sobbing.

She heard her father begging, "Please." Repeatedly.

Another man she did not recognize said, "I have conquered the Laird of Cymru. I won't rest until his every kith and kin is dead and forgotten."

"And what of your own kin, brother? What of our blood?" her father said. His voice broke. "Spare her. Spare them. For me. We'll sail beyond the ocean. You'll never see or hear of us again. I swear it. I swear—"

"Many things you have sworn to me, brother, and yet here we are again with whispers of rebellion between us. Your promises are lies."

"No—" Her mother's cry stretched into a shriek.

Zelia started running—not away, as her head told her to do, but toward her mother. She plunged down the tunnel and broke into the light.

The first thing she saw was her parents. Her mother lay on the ground in a puddle of red. Her father stood lock-kneed before the stranger, then he crumpled to his side and curled toward her mother. With one final heaving gasp, he stopped moving.

They looked like they were asleep. *Just asleep*, Zelia told herself, as blood spread in the dust around them.

A welling, tearing, fractured scream wrenched from Zelia's throat.

"Zelia!" Deirdre's frantic eyes found her from across the chambered cairn. She was trapped in a man's hold—no, not a man. A boy.

"What is this?" An armored guard snagged Zelia by the collar, cutting off her breath.

"Another one?" said the boy. Like he was surprised. Like he hadn't found them picking flowers earlier. Like he didn't already know.

He wasn't even looking at Zelia as he said it. His eyes were on the monstrous man standing over Zelia's parents, bloodied dirk in hand.

The man was watching Zelia.

Zelia bucked and twisted. Her collar pinched painfully around her throat as she drove her boot into her captor's shin. He grunted, and his hold loosened. Behind her, the boy cried out, "Ow! She bit me!"

Run, thought Zelia. To herself. To Deirdre. The word became a silent, monotonous ringing in her head. *Run, run, run.*

She caught the flash of dark hair and the blur of a familiar dress as the shape of a girl that could have been her barreled into the tunnel.

Zelia was a step and a half behind—a step and a half too slow.

An arm clamped around her chest and lifted her off her feet. "This is the one we want," purred the monster's voice in her ear. His blade wavered before Zelia's eyes.

"What of the decoy?" asked the guard.

"Go after her," he growled.

Zelia's heart pounded so hard that her chest ached.

This is a mistake, she thought. *A dream.*

She was going to wake up in the tower soon. Her parents would be there.

The rose—she would find the rose. Her mother would tell her of Cymru before her father could cut the story off with a sharp shake of his head.

All would be well again.

"*Athair*," said the boy. "Don't do this." His hooded gaze wavered to Zelia.

Zelia glimpsed again the boy who'd plucked the rose. The same look of confusion and pain painted his features now. "Please," he pleaded. He looked to his father again, then flinched.

"I'm not going to do anything." The man flipped the knife and offered the hilt to the boy. "You will."

The boy shook his head.

"You will," snarled his father.

The boy's pale hands closed around the handle. The point dropped toward the earth when his father released the blade. A droplet welled along the point and splattered at his feet.

Zelia was thrown forward. She rebounded against the curved earthen wall and slammed to the ground. Red soaked into her chemise. It stained her hands. Her breath shrieked in her throat as she twisted onto her back and scooted against the wall.

The boy hovered over her.

"Do it," his father said.

The boy pressed against her sternum, flattening her to the ground. His eyes met hers, steely and determined, pained and glistening.

"Do it!"

The boy's head ducked closer. His breath huffed against her face.

She heard the knife scrape along the ground.

"Don't...move."

The words were not in her head.

The boy pierced her with one final, hard glance as he tossed her onto her side to face the wall.

The blade dragged across her throat like cold fire. She felt the wet line drawn across her skin and waited for biting pain that never came.

Don't move.

Droplets soaked the collar of Zelia's chemise. A juddering sob rose in her throat. She swallowed hard and forced her body to slump.

Just a nightmare, she thought.

She was sleeping in the broch on the wool-stuffed mattress alongside her parents.

They were all sleeping.

The boy pushed away from her.

"Well done, son," his father said.

Hard footsteps clipped broken stone. Dead silence followed.

Still, Zelia didn't move.

Time shattered. Details came in jagged, dreamlike shards.

The cairn rushlights burned out.

She rose on numb feet and caught herself against the wall with a sticky hand.

She stumbled outside under a whirling, star-studded sky.

Gorse thorns burned her skin when she fell, and needle pain raked her body when she tried to move again, so she didn't.

She curled around herself in the briars, lost to a dark void that had chiseled a home deep within her chest.

That was where he found her.

"Crivvens… Can you hear me?" And then, "Hold on! I'm coming."

A scraggly boy with blonde hair shoved back gorse branches with his staff and waded into the thorns until he was by her side. He searched her for a wound that wasn't there.

She stared past him. A raven screeched. Its wings beat against the gray dawn.

The boy whispered something. Over and over. "You're safe."

Zelia remembered nothing more.

~~~~~

Nine Years Later

Róisín had always been safe with Alasdair, so for the first time, she let her darkness spill into words. Every detail—every thought—poured from her like fast-flowing water until she was left empty and shaking, and only bone-deep, shadow wounds remained.

"Deirdre." She whispered the name like a fragile wish.

"She might still be alive." Alasdair's fingers wove tightly with hers, tethering her back to the present. "Have you ever wondered?"

"You think I haven't? I've asked myself thousands of times—Did she get away? Is she alive? Is she safe?"

"I could help you find her. If you wanted."

She shook her head. "No. No, you don't understand."

"I want to understand," he whispered.

Róisín stared at their joined hands, but she was thinking of hedge roses and a land she knew only by a name whispered at night. "My
~~~~~

parents came to this isle for a reason. I think… I think my *máthair* bore the blood of someone important— important enough that someone dangerous wanted her dead. He wanted me dead, too. He wanted it enough that he was willing to kill anyone who stood in his way. What if that still makes me dangerous—to you, to your family?"

"Don't go there."

"How can you say that? Deirdre could be dead because of me!"

"You are Róisín MacNair, and nothing about your past changes that. You don't *have* to be Zelia. You have the rare chance to remake yourself, and no one has to be the wiser."

"I c-cannot forget."

"You never will. What happened was wrong in ways that words cannot make right. But you have every right to live—to let yourself be happy again."

"How?"

Alasdair eased closer still. He traced a slow hand along her cheek. She leaned into his touch and drew in a jagged breath.

"We'll take it one day at a time. One breath at a time, if we must."

We. Such a lovely, dangerous word.

Róisín wanted nothing more than to stay here forever with him. She wanted to tell him yes. Emphatically. Repeatedly.

But it wasn't fair to burden his future with her past.

Admitting her truths had left her teetering on a precipice she hadn't realized she'd been toeing. She didn't yet know which way she would fall. She only knew she couldn't drag him with her.

Her heart throbbed beneath her ribcage, and behind her heart, that nightmarish void still dwelled, hollow and echoing and so, so empty.

"I can't. I can't do this."

She stepped away and turned her back to him. When he called her name, she started to run, unmindful of the thistles.

~~~~~

Róisín kicked her dress into a dark corner, the hemline now riddled with burrs, and crawled into bed in the cottage's tiny corner room. When Alasdair's family returned from the gathering, she curled onto her side to face the wall.

"Are you awake?" Oona whispered as she slipped beneath the blankets.

Róisín kept her eyes closed and her breathing even.

Alasdair returned later still. Róisín heard the barn door squeal even from across the yard, then she bit her lip and cried silent tears into her pillow.

Sleep evaded her. She rubbed the lumps and cracks in the stone wall beneath her fingers, stared at the rafters strung with the feathery shapes
~~~~~

of drying heather, and counted the times Oona sighed in her sleep.

She finally rose with the songbirds, at some dark point in the morning, with the restless need to do something with her hands. She wrapped an arisaid sloppily over her chemise, belted it at her waist, and quietly let herself into the cottage yard.

Her head ached. Pain pressed behind her eyes as she knelt beside the garden along the fence and tore up weeds—at least she hoped they were all weeds—until her knees were damp, her fingers stiff, and pale blue light banded the horizon with the barest hint of morning.

Purple thyme lay in the dirt beside the weeds.

She plunged her fingers into the damp soil. A groan escaped between her teeth. "What am I doing?"

Which wasn't the right question to ask.

What am I going to do? That was the question that nagged her like a pebble in a shoe.

She rocked back on her heels and swiped away strands of hair with her arm. Droplets soaked her chemise sleeves when she brushed the harebell blossoms, and over the hills, a heavy mist roiled.

The clomp and clack of the horses in their harnesses came to her through the fog. She shoved to her feet as the wagon rumbled into sight. Alasdair rounded the team, murmuring soft words and running his hand over an arching neck as he checked the straps and trace line. His steps hitched when he spotted her.

Róisín grasped for the fence and sucked in a shallow breath as he left the horses and approached her.

Neither of them spoke. It was quite possibly the longest, most awkward moment of Róisín's life.

She was scared he would speak, yet terrified that he wouldn't—that he would turn away and leave, and that would be it somehow. Whatever *it* was. Her own words remained trapped in her throat.

"I'll be back in a few days," Alasdair finally said.

He'd told her that last night. Had he forgotten, or did he simply not know what else to say?

Róisín nodded.

I'm sorry. She almost said it aloud.

"Róisín." Alasdair's eyes narrowed like he was in pain, but then he pressed forward against the fence, and his hands found their way to hers. "I am with you. With you through the good times and the bad. With you through all the years within me. Zelia. Róisín." His breath caught. He squeezed her hands and met her eye. "When you are ready, I am with you until the end."

Tears choked Róisín's throat. She watched him turn away and climb into the wagon. He clucked to the team and disappeared into the mist.

Still, Róisín remained rooted, staring after him down the road so long her eyes began to sting.

Somewhere, a bird shrieked. Róisín clenched her eyes shut, afraid she'd see black luck in black feathers.

She was so tired of being afraid—so tired of being Zelia and Róisín. Both, yet neither.

You have a rare chance to remake yourself.

She wanted to remake herself. She should have told Alasdair that.

I'm sorry.

Thank you.

She should have told him a lot of things.

She remembered the *bean-nighe*'s words on that deadly night. *What scraps of magic there are can be found in the choosing.*

On the heels of that memory came another.

Once, a boy waded through thorns to rescue her. He didn't care whose blood ran in her veins. He would save her again if she was brave enough to let him.

"Róisín?" Oona blinked at her from the cottage doorway. "What are you doing out here so early?"

"What am I doing?" Róisín whispered again to the morning.

"What?"

"Oona, I have to…" Róisín pressed her frozen knuckles to her lips.

"Have to what?" Oona wrapped her arms around herself and stepped into the yard.

"I-I have to tell him."

"Oh," Oona said. Her eyes widened. "Ooooh."

Róisín clutched at the wayward folds of her arisaid and rocked on her feet. "I can catch him if I cross the heathlands," she said. "I have to try, don't I?"

"I'll say! Go, Róisín. Go!"

Róisín plunged down the rutted road with her heart in her throat. She darted off the path and bounded across the uneven ground of the hill leading up to the escarpment. She glimpsed the Allanach's barn through the rising, swirling mist—there, then gone.

Rays of sunlight pierced through the haze. Its warmth brushed her skin as she sprinted across a pasture. A flock of dun-faced sheep bleated and scattered as she arrowed through them.

The sharp scent of sheep and damp wool still clung to her nostrils when she stumbled onto the path once again. She gasped, lungs burning. Just ahead came the clatter and jounce of hooves and wagon wheels. She glimpsed a figure curled over the reins.

"Alasdair!" His name tore from her throat.

He reined in the team with a start and twisted on the bench seat.

She must have looked like a wild-eyed sprite, with her hair lashing her face and her chemise billowing around her calves.

"Róisín?" He tied off the team and jumped down as she staggered to meet him.

"What is it?" He caught her elbow in one hand and her shoulder in the other. "What has happened?"

Róisín shook her head. Her breath sawed in her throat. "I am with you, Alasdair." she clutched at his sleeve. "From now—now until the end… I am with you."

His fingers tightened on her forearm. "Are you sure?"

"Aye. I'm sure. I'm finally sure. I'm so sorry I—"

"Don't be."

Róisín reached for him. His arms wrapped tight around her, and his breath brushed warm and fast against her neck.

"Róisín." He pulled back suddenly. His cheeks were bright pink. "You shouldn't be out here. Not in your chemise. What if the Allanachs see? What would Mrs. Sutharlan say?"

Róisín rose on tiptoes and pushed her lips against his. "I don't care one whit about the Allanachs or the Sutharlans," she said when she dropped back onto her heels.

"You know… neither do I."

When Alasdair kissed her back, it was long and drawn out like a slow sunrise.

Róisín smiled against his mouth as warmth flooded her chest. It pooled into the empty, aching place within her—filling her with a shiver of hope, or happiness, or both—until she felt the darkness crack.

For the first time in nine years, something within her yawned and woke.

~~~~~

After

Róisín and Alasdair were married at the peak of the escarpment overlooking the moor the following spring. Only the crofter families bore witness, but to Róisín it was the best of nights, filled with starlight and reeling laughter and one particular hard-won dance accompanied by a slow tune from Mr. Sutharlan's tin whistle.

On a pleasant day not long after, when the last of the ewes had given birth and the final field been planted, Róisín found Alasdair waiting beyond the gate with the wagon hitched and supper already packed. She accepted his help onto the wagon seat without a word.

The road to Callanway was long indeed, stretched longer still by Róisín's anxious thoughts. The towering broch that crested the rise over the village was the first thing Róisín saw. Its stone walls were tangled in
~~~~~

climbing vines, and its base was choked with yellow gorse and budding bog myrtle. Róisín could feel the single black-eyed window watching her whenever she turned her back to it.

It was among the tartan fabrics and richly died wool at the market that Róisín crossed gazes with a woman with the same dark hair and haunted eyes as herself. A *bairn* cooed in the woman's arms. She bounced the child at her hip, but her eyes returned to Róisín, and they shared a smile that needed no words — one laced with pain and memory and relief.

"Have we met before?" the woman asked tentatively.

"Once. In a dream and nightmare. I'm Róisín."

"Róisín," she repeated as if tasting the sound of it.

They took tea together briefly, as stiff and polite as strangers, but Róisín smiled as she watched her old friend's gaze return, again and again, to the child she cradled.

When she and Alasdair finally turned homeward, a weight had lifted from her shoulders.

Before the year was out, Alasdair's dream of a small stone cottage was made real. The first morning Róisín woke in her new home, she found a white feather on the front stoop, and she smiled a little to herself as she closed the door.

Every once in a while, a flutter of wings beat outside her window, but Róisín didn't need to look.

END

BE CAREFUL WHAT YOU WISH FOR
Lindsi McIntyre

Glass shattered against the floor. The throng of maids who served the princess scurried away from her wrath in a flurry of black skirts and white aprons.

"You brain addled twit!" Aeliana pressed pale white fingers to the skin beneath her eyes, assessing the damage the fool had done. "I've told you a hundred times. You have to apply the potion gently or it will cause wrinkles." She picked up a nearby glass and aimed it at the offending maid.

"Aeliana!"

The girl turned to watch her mother enter the room with a baleful look, arm still extended for the throw that would have sent the glass crashing against the empty-headed woman's skull. The queen assessed the situation with an imperious look, then turned to the huddle of servants. "Leave us."

A series of quick bows and rushed footsteps left mother and daughter alone in the large sitting room. Aeliana turned back to her vanity. The potions weren't going to apply themselves and, *Clearly*, she thought, *I can't trust anyone else to do it properly.*

"Aeliana." Queen Liliana's voice was tinged with exasperation. Aeliana rolled her eyes. "This is getting quite out of hand. A lady, a *princess*, does not shriek at her ladies' maids—"

"I did *not* shriek."

"Trust me, my dear, what I just heard was a shriek."

Aeliana scoffed.

Queen Liliana sighed, the soft exhale carrying with it a thousand words of recrimination. Aeliana was above them all. Her mother would never understand. The queen just *accepted* the wrinkles that had slowly taken over her once beautiful face. It was as if she *wanted* to grow old and ugly.

Aeliana shivered. *Not I!* She applied the soft cream with gentle taps to her skin.

Her mother's soft, *wrinkled* hand settled on top of Aeliana's shoulder. "Sweetheart, my sunshine. This obsession you have with youth and beauty is unhealthy. The outside of a person is just a shell. The heart is what truly matters."

For a moment, the old nickname, spoken so often to her when she was a child, cut through the haze of panic the thought of aging produced in Aeliana. In childhood she was free from the fear of getting old. Free to laugh without worrying about the lines it would make around her mouth. Free to run in the sun without wearing a hat to protect her skin. Free to —

But that was all in the past. Her mother's face, ravaged by age, now staring imploringly at her through the looking glass's reflection proved Aeliana right. Time was her enemy. And it was winning.

With a shrug, she dislodged her mother's hand. "That's nice, Mother. Now if you'll excuse me, I need to finish getting ready. I am going riding again today."

For a moment, it seemed as if Queen Liliana would refuse to leave. Eventually, however, the woman sighed one last time, and left her daughter to her own devices.

~~~~~

With a firm tug on the reins, Aeliana kept her mount squarely on the path. The skittish creature attempted to run off at every leaf's rustle and twig's snap within earshot. Tulip was normally the most easily managed horse in the stables. But as soon as they'd entered The Forest, she'd been jumping at shadows and fighting to turn back. Even the more rigorously trained mounts ridden by Aeliana's guardsmen fought against the command to walk the enchanted path deeper among the dark trees.

As if they sensed some great danger hidden just out of sight.

"You're certain this is the way?" Aeliana asked.

Sir Archibald, head of her guard, shot her a glance then returned his attention to keeping his horse in line. "Yes, Your Highness. We're almost upon the place."

"And you're certain *this* one will be able to fulfill my wish?"

"Certain? No. But Malevolent, as the thing likes to be called, is considered one of the most powerful fairies in the kingdom. If she lacks the power to grant your wish, there won't be another who can."

Aeliana sat back in her saddle, not feeling particularly comforted by the man's gruff words. The trail, if it could be called that, ended at the base of two large, black trees. The hunks of living wood rose into the sky and seemed to disappear into a swath of black branches above, going on forever and ever. Surely as old now as they had been from the beginning and never to be anything less than ancient.

Beyond the formidable sentries, light poured into a small clearing where a tiny cottage perched amongst a field of wildflowers. The air felt alive as Aeliana passed beyond the trees, alive and watchful, as if waiting for something. The party crushed flowers underfoot as they made their way to the door of the cottage.

Sir Archibald dismounted and then assisted Aeliana out of her saddle.
~~~~~

"*This* is the home of a powerful fairy?" she asked.

"That's what our sources claimed…" The knight looked skeptical. He stepped up to the door and pounded his fist against the flimsy barricade. "Open up. In the name of the king."

"The king, you say."

Aeliana jumped, her gasp mixing with the startled sounds of her men. The voice sounded as if it came from all around them.

"In that case." The door swung open. "Come in. Come in."

Aeliana could only stare. Instead of a tiny cottage, the door opened up on a large foyer made of grey stone. Windows, overlooking a landscape far different than the forest at their back, lit the space with sunlight. Tapestries spun from thread that shimmered like gold hung from the walls. And a massive staircase rose up from the floor and vanished beyond view of the door.

There was certainly powerful magic at work here. A spark of excitement lit within Aeliana's breast. Powerful magic was just what she needed. She and Sir Archibald peered past the doorframe, studying the strange phenomenon. They exchanged a look. His said they should turn back. Hers urged him on. She gave a nod, the kind that carried a command. His face tightened in displeasure, unhappy to have lost the exchange, but he dutifully stepped inside with a cautious examination of the area. Aeliana followed with a confidence bordering on childlike giddiness.

The rest of her guard dismounted, ready to join them. But as soon as Aeliana crossed the threshold, the door slammed shut behind her with a deafening *thud* that echoed through the foyer. A terrified spin brought her up against a wall of grey rock.

The door was gone.

A sound that could only be described as the flutter of a thousand wings pulled Aeliana's gaze away from the wall and back to the stairs. There, a woman had appeared, resplendent in black silks and gold jewelry. The green stone sitting atop the staff she held glowed with an ethereal light. The air shimmered with raw energy. Surely *this* was a true fairy. Not like those other flimsy things Aeliana had dealt with in the past.

The woman's blood-red lips stretched into a cat-like smile. "And what brings such illustrious guests to my humble abode this fine summer's day?"

Sir Archibald drew his sword. "Return the door, witch—"

"Enough!" Aeliana stepped forward and silenced the brute with a scathing glance before he could ruin everything. "Put your sword away. Now!"

The knight did as he was told, looking none too happy about the order.

Aeliana turned back to the fairy woman standing regally on the steps above them and decided a bit of deference might earn her favor. "I've come to seek a boon, Lady Malevolent."

"Oh." The single syllable sent a chill up Aeliana's spine. "And what will happen to me if I refuse to grant this boon? Will I be branded with iron rods, locked away from the sun and have my wings ripped off?"

Aeliana blinked up at the woman. *How does she know about that?*

An icy edge tinged Malevolent's smile. "Oh, yes. I am quite familiar with the past dealings you've had with my kind, Your *Highness*."

The woman threw open her arms and the air shimmered as a wave of power rolled off her body. Aeliana flinched as the magic struck her like a physical blow. "You've been quite busy for such a little thing. Sending your men through our forest and stealing away any fairy unlucky enough to cross your path. And for what? What world-shattering wishes did you hope to have granted? What life-altering woes did you hope to assuage?"

Sir Archibald moved to draw his sword again, but this time the weapon would not come out of its sheath.

"Golden curls. Lips red as a rose. Eyes that would never lose their lustrous shine." Malevolent's smile grew and her face was transformed into a cruel mask, no less beautiful but ten times as threatening. "*Vanity*. You tormented my kind for the sake of your simple vanity."

And then, just as quickly, the power faded, leaving the two humans staggering in its wake. "But," said Malevolent into the shocked silence, "far be it from me to keep a *princess* from achieving her heart's truest desire. After all," she gave a mocking bow. "I am but a humble servant of every human king that deigns to claim dominion over the random chunks of dirt that take their fancy at any given time." With a flurry of silk, she turned away and began to climb the stairs. "Follow me. What you seek lies just above. In the tower."

Trembling, Aeliana could only blink at the woman moving so elegantly up the steps.

After mounting a few stairs, the fairy stopped, turned back and said, "Aren't you coming? You've gone through all this trouble. I'd have thought you'd want to finally see the end to your journey."

Pulling in a fortifying breath, Aeliana approached the base of the staircase.

Sir Archibald grabbed her arm. "My lady. I beg you. Let us plead for the door to be returned and flee this place. This one is different than the others. Her help will come at a steep cost."

Aeliana yanked her arm from his grasp. "I care *not* what it costs. You should know that by now." With a twirl she turned and started up after Malevolent. The knight's heavy booted steps followed behind, but Aeliana didn't look back. This was what she'd been waiting for.

The stairs twisted to the left in a deceptively gentle spiral around a thick stone pillar. The incline was far steeper than it seemed and before long, Aeliana was short of breath. Light from the windows faded further away with each step she took. Soon, it was replaced entirely by the green glow of Malevolent's staff guiding her up.

And up.

And up.

Finally, they reached a black door that looked as if it had been wrought from the wood of the very trees that had stood watch at the edge of the clearing where they'd first spotted the cottage. The fairy waited for Aeliana at the top step. When the princess reached the landing, the woman waved her hand with a rustle of her black silk sleeve. The door swung open with an eerie creak.

Green light poured off Malevolent's staff into the room, illuminating an ancient spinner's wheel and chair. Both were covered in cobwebs and dust, the only things held within the grey walls.

"There. Your prize, princess."

"Where?" Aeliana asked, thoroughly confused by the sight of such an everyday and disused item in such a wondrous place.

"There." Malevolent nodded at the spinning wheel. "Prick your finger upon the needle and you'll be young and beautiful forever. That *is* what you wanted, isn't it?"

The sharp point of the needle sparkled temptingly in Malevolent's light. Aeliana exchanged a glance with Archibald, but the man's look of disapproval was no help. She squared her shoulders.

"Yes. That is what I wanted. What I *want*."

She heard Archibald shift uncomfortably behind her as she passed Malevolent and entered the room. The two watched the young princess approach the spinning wheel with chin high. She stopped just short of the needle. It looked sharp. Malicious. For the first time, a true spark of fear settled into Aeliana's breast. With a scowl, she shot a look back at the fairy. "Keep in mind, creature. If you plan evil this day and harm should befall me at your hand, my knight will not hesitate to turn on you in kind. You wouldn't even find the time to regret your deceptions."

The witch's smile never faltered. "But of course," she simpered. "One would expect nothing less from such a...*devoted* servant of the crown. And we all know he is quite proficient in harming my kind."

With a nod she hoped conveyed power, Aeliana faced the needle. Fingers trembling in the sickly, green-lit air, she stretched out her hand to the sharp point. The edge sliced through the skin of her first finger. Pain radiated from even that brief impact. She pulled back with a hiss and moved to place the finger in her mouth, when the room began to spin.

"Wha—what's happen—"Aeliana stumbled and fell into the dust-covered chair beside the spinning wheel. "I—I can't—" Her muscles refused to move. Bleary eyes struggled to focus on the door. Words would not form.

Sir Archibald drew his sword. But before he could use it on the magical being who grinned wickedly beside him, a puff of smoke engulfed his body with a hiss. When it cleared away, he was gone, leaving Aeliana alone.

Panic, raw and brutal, flooded her being as Malevolent approached. The black form flickered in and out of sight, as Aeliana's eyelids grew heavier.

"And now, my dear."

Sleep as heavy as death pulled Aeliana into its dark embrace. Malevolent's voice echoed from some far-off place through the dark of her mind.

"What I promised. Youth and beauty that will never fade. Pity no one will ever see it."

Aeliana didn't understand the fairy's words. So she dismissed them. Some part of her fought against the sleep trying to claim her. She dismissed that too. She could worry about it when she woke up. She was just so very *tired*...

~~~~~

By the time Sir Archibald had found his way back to the palace from the empty field Malevolent's magic had dropped him in, Aeliana had already fallen into her eternal sleep. After his report of their journey and an unpleasant accounting of their previously hidden interactions with fairies, the king and queen launched a rescue mission to bring their daughter home, but neither the cottage nor the tower where the girl was last seen were ever found.

Days passed. Then months. Then years.

Decades and centuries were not far behind.

Kingdoms rose and fell, but Aeliana's tower still stands.

Malevolent did indeed fulfill the princess's wish.

Aeliana remains young and beautiful, sitting on the spinning wheel's chair. And will remain young and beautiful. Covered in cobwebs and dust.

Forevermore.

END
~~~~~

FIGHT THE GOOD FIGHT, DREAM THE GOOD DREAM
Michelle Houston

They say dreams are a gateway to other worlds.
They are right.

However, these other worlds are not kind or welcoming. Rather, they are inhabited by beings that are hungry and grasping.

Though your dreams are not real, they do hint at a hidden reality. When a monster is about to get you or you are running from something menacing that you cannot see, there really is a shadowy form of a creature trying to reach into our world, clawing and feeding through your dreams to try to find a way in.

However, a few individuals have the power to move through gateways into other people's dreams and banish the monsters within.

I am one of the few.
I am Au'WelGwynFain.

I am a protector. I am the reason the claws never quite reach you, the reason you wake up before your plummeting body hits the ground.

Those I do not reach in time die in their sleep. I mourn each and every one.

I spend my life asleep, dreaming, prowling the pathways of dreams and the gates that open into other worlds while my body lies still on a stone platform.

I will never have a husband's embrace or the growth of a child within my womb. I will never again feel the rain on my face or hear the blackbird call in the dawn.

It is worth the sacrifice.
My actions matter.

My history with the Au'Wel began when I was young.

Like all children, I had been taught by my parents about the AllTruth, and the evil one who seeks to destroy through lies and nightmares. But unlike most of my playmates, I had good control of my dreams, which meant I didn't suffer from nightmares but could create new things in them instead. I remember the first time I managed to hover an inch above the ground in my dreams. I was so excited, thinking that yes, I could actually fly! Or the dream where something was chasing me and I decided I had had enough, so I made a door and left the monster behind. Or the one in which I decided our colors were too boring and I would start seeing ultraviolet and radio waves as well.

This brought me to the Au'Wel's attention.

It was the night after my color experiment that Au'WelMyaFain found me. She appeared first as a beautiful snowy white bird, whose softness and warmth drew me in. She then changed into an equally lovely older woman, with creamy chestnut skin, wavy brown hair and sparkling green eyes beneath lush black lashes. In my dream, we had a lovely tea under a purple sky served by grey, fluffy bunnies and raucous bluebirds in a tiny castle made of moss and mushrooms. The drink tasted of honey, oranges, and sunshine, while the teacakes were crumbly bites of cinnamon. She told me wonderful stories of adventures within mountains or on top of raging rivers, of rescues through castles and swamps, and of tenderly shepherding the helpless past black, raking monsters. She told me I had been gifted a powerful dreamsense by the Creator, and that I could be one of these guardians.

Then she took me hunting with her.

That night she destroyed a vampire, a balrog, and a maelstrom threatening a ship. She pushed energy into a handful of other people, propelling them out of their dreamworld and away from the monsters. She showed me the campsites in the snowy peaks on the opposite side of my physical world that a seasoned adventurer was dreaming about and a herd of unicorns dancing to lilting fairy music in a young girl's mind.

The excitement, the sights, and the strong sense of protecting the helpless was enough to hook me. I begged to be her assistant.

So I started, learning first the tenets of her order within the safety of my dreams.

She taught me to sense the evil that hid in dreams, that became the monsters and the fears that we contain: "There is an enemy of all humanity, who has set as his mission to destroy the beloved creations of the AllTruth."

She taught me to protect those being attacked, to stand between the evil and the helpless: "The Au'Wel fight against the power of the enemy, to be a bulwark for the needy, to be a shelter for the hopeless, to be a light for those blinded by the dark lies, to be a shearing edge to cleave the attacks of the enemy."

She taught me to look not to my own strength, but to the strength of the One who gave me these abilities: "The Au'Wel look to the AllTruth for hope to fight against hopelessness, strength to fight against weakness, love to fight against despondency, and truth to fight against deception."

She taught me to duel, on land, in water, and in the air. She taught me to shape-shift within dreams, to create weapons and traps from a thought, to avoid the barbs and pits that the enemy slings.

She taught me to take a bit of energy upon leaving a dream; maybe a cookie from a party, or a leaf from a forest, or a fish from a sea. Not too much, but enough to sustain myself so that my mind and body would live.

She taught me that truth is usually revealed in dreams, as the hidden thoughts are released and allowed to scream their defiance against the lies people tell themselves or others. But the enemy tries to twist those truths into monstrous lies upon which to feed.

She taught me that despite any preferences, it was my job to protect both the innocent and the guilty. She said that no matter what was revealed in the dream, we still didn't know all and judgment was not in our domain. Our enemy was the evil from elsewhere.

In the safety of my own dreams I honed my perception of truth and lies until
I was ready to battle.

The first time she brought me to another dreamworld after I became her apprentice was in my second year of training. She had to wrap me in gauzy layers of her own dream energy to whisk me out of my world into another's.

I stared around at the colorful landscape, so different from my own dreams, in awe. The green, evenly cut grass waved in the breeze, little yellow and pink flowers shyly peeking above the surface like kittens exploring for the first time. Birdsong filtered through the air from unknown sources as orange butterflies and red ladybugs flitted from flower to flower.

But as I watched, the grass started to stiffen and glitter. The flowers got bigger and sparkled in the light. Even the insects started reflecting the sunlight, throwing darts of color into my eyes.

Everything was now made of glass. The grass growing just off the path we were on, the flowers stretching up toward the crystal blue sky, the insects zipping around. All colored glass.

A blue dragonfly landed on a nearby flower. I crouched down, amazed at the intricate detail of its lacy wings and jeweled black eyes that stared back at me.

A laughing human voice focused my mind on my task here. I straightened, watching a group of young adults sipping from crystal cups inside a nearby glass cottage. The dreamer was instantly recognizable by the solid presence she emitted in the fairy-like landscape.

She seemed happy, at ease, chatting with her friends in a loud voice as even more insects joined the dance in the sky. I scanned the visible area, the edges of the dream fading from cut glass to formless grey. I saw nothing threatening.

I glanced back at Au'WelMyaFain.

"Well?" she asked. I couldn't glean any hints from the sound of her voice.

I looked around again, but nothing had changed in the happy scene except the cottage now looked more like an apartment building. "It looks safe, but..."

"Mmmm..." was her non-committal reply. I was on my own for this analysis.

"But it feels like something is gathering, something building." I turned to her. "Am I wrong?"

MyaFain grimaced. "No, you sense the truth here weakening. This is a recurring nightmare, a lie she constantly battles that allows the enemy to come in." She nodded in the distance, into the grey. "It will start soon."

I stared in the direction she indicated but saw no form taking place.

Instead, a deep, bell-like tone rang out across the landscape. I could see the air bending beneath its onslaught. The glass insects broke, pummeling to the ground and punching holes in the flowers. Silence followed, the group in the apartment having disappeared, leaving the lone dreamer frozen with dread on her face.

Another tone rang out. Cracks appeared in the walls. The flower stems broke, causing the petals to crash into the grass.

A large shape appeared from the edge of the dream. It was simultaneously made of sharp edges and hazy outlines. It lifted a gigantic leg and brought a foot slamming down into the ground.

Another tone pierced the air. The walls shattered. The dreamer screamed, "No!" She picked up one of the larger pieces of glass and held it up as a barrier to the monster. "You can't destroy it!"

MyaFain's soft voice cut through the chaos. "She has built her security on her own accomplishments and popularity. She fears it breaking, fears she will have nothing left. The enemy uses the fears and lies to weaken her, feeling off her energy."

The monster now had at least four legs, each one bringing the ringing tones that broke the glass as it strode forward. The shapeless body sported no head, but three tentacles started to form, reaching out to grab pieces of the dream and consume them.

MyaFain placed a hand on my shoulder, turning me to look in her eyes. They were dark with pain but also with determination. "I want you to handle this."

"Right." I turned back to the monster and willed a walled trap around it.

Nothing happened.

My shock must have shown on my face. MyaFain gently reminded me, "This is not your dream; you cannot change the dreamscape. However, neither are you a part of it."

"Right," I repeated, this time willing my twin swords into existence.

Faith and Fire blazed into solidity in my hands. Without taking my eyes off the monster, I leaped over the broken remnants of the flowers, remembering to wrap thick-soled shoes around my feet just before I landed. I charged the beast, swinging at its grasping dark tentacles. I cleaved the first one off as it was picking up a broken flower. It withered into nothingness. The second one evaded my strike, pulling a couple of dragonflies along and stuffing them into the body.

I charged closer, jumping over the third tentacle as it swiped at my legs.

I saw more tentacles emerge from the body. Though I had stopped the monster from heading closer to the dreamer, it was still sucking energy from her mind. Chopping off pieces was not going to work.

I willed a shield around me, repeating what I had been taught: "The Beginning, the AllTruth, created all peoples and made them his beloved. He continually pursues and protects them with his Au'Wel." I rolled under another tentacle, hacked at a stump, and tore into the body, Fire and Faith blazing bright. Pieces of darkness boiled away from me, the monster dissolving under my attack.

As the air cleared, MyaFain strode up to me. A small smile played across her face. "Good job." She motioned to the woman, still rigid but without the dread on her face. "You destroyed the nightmare."

The dream was starting to fade. The jewel colors were muting into pastels and the grey edges were creeping closer. I looked up at the Au'Wel. "Should we go?"

MyaFain nodded and wrapped me up again.

"On to the next dream," I heard her say as we passed through the gateway. I smiled. I couldn't wait.

~~~~~

We continued my training for over three years, each night starting as she visited my dreams and took me to defend others.

The night she showed me how to travel a gateway will never leave my mind.

Gateways are invisible to most dreamers. They exist on a deeper level of sleep, hidden from our conscious minds.

Have you ever woken up from a dream only to still be dreaming? I had to do the opposite. I had to go to sleep in my dream, then fall into a deeper trance that would let me see the reality underneath the dreamcloth.
~~~~~

For me, gateways look like sturdy wooden doors with thick iron padlocks. I thought I had to open the door and undo the locks to get through.

I struggled. I tried to make a key, but they all broke in the padlock. I tried to cut the lock off, but it stood firm. I tried to take the hinges off, but the door stubbornly refused to yield even without support. I even tried to make myself small enough to clamber through the crack under the door, but the space shrunk even as I approached it.

Au'WelMyaFain patiently waited through each attempt, then pointed out my mistake. I was too focused on myself and my plans. Only by loving others would I be able to get out of myself and into their dreams, to protect them from the lies and despair of the evil ones.

So I tried, and tried, and tried again. I thought about the dreamers I had seen in my training so far, needing hope to fill the gaping holes created by the monsters in their lives. I thought about the joy I felt when I destroyed one of the lies plaguing them, or the warmth that came from laughing and playing with them. But still the door barred my way.

I finally gave up on myself and focused on the truths I had been taught while I wearily leaned against the rough wood barrier:

"The AllTruth loves us."

"The AllTruth gives us strength, hope, love."

"The Au'Wel give up their lives so that the beloved of the AllTruth can enjoy lives as his creation and glorify him."

And the door wavered, allowing me to waft through it to emerge on the other side, where I could access other dreamers.

It was sacrificial love that could
smash down the obstacles keeping people apart.

She trained me for five long years, teaching me while I slept.

My family worried that I was sleeping too much and eating too little. More than once I came across my burly father, weary from a day moving bricks at the factory, running his red-brown hand through his greying hair as he wondered how to comfort my crying mother. I did my best to reassure them, tried to eat one more bite at dinner, but in the end, I couldn't give them the answers they were seeking. I couldn't tell them of my new adventure.

For the Au'Wels must remain secret. We are vulnerable to physical damage to our bodies while we mentally battle in the dreamscape.

I could only reassure them of my love.

At last MyaFain declared me ready to become a full Au'Wel, and we planned my strategy to remain hidden.

Au'WelMyaFain had warned me about starting out. Some people, with loyal servants, can take them along to tend to the house so that everything looks normal. These are the people you hear about who are infamous recluses.

But most people are like me and must make it alone.

She told me the cautionary tale of an Au'Wel who slept at the top of a stone tower, near a window. Somehow a man found out about her and climbed up to "rescue" her. Poor Rapunzel was never able to join the Au'Wel sleep again.

So we must hide to protect our bodies. Some hide in plain sight, in hospital beds as coma patients. Some hide deep in forests or high in mountains or down in caves.

As my country was lacking in caves and mountains, but sprouted plenty of dense forests, the decision was easy for me. Au'WelMyaFain helped me identify from dreams a crumbling building being consumed by the forest, abandoned after the owner died.

When I turned eighteen, I left my crowded thatched home and my loving parents and siblings to become a full Au'Wel. I visit them often in their dreams.

I traveled for days on foot, fighting through forests, avoiding roads and sleeping in trees for safety. I missed the building the first time I passed it, the grey rock walls coated with leaves and moss blending in perfectly with the surroundings.

The inside was as covered with debris as the outside. Animal nests, bones, blown leaves littered every room. But several rooms were still sturdy, including the kitchen with a wonderfully large stone table.

I moved in, cleaned it from top to bottom, and started sealing up the whole structure. MyaFain worked some dream miracles and had people deliver supplies to a nearby town that I picked up.

I mixed my own mortar, placed my own stones. The windows were secured first, followed by the doors. It was my wish to have no way for any creature to get in, whether they be human or bug.

I filled the cisterns in the kitchen, then took one last bath in the dark. I settled down on the stone table in the middle of the room for my long sleep, cushioned and covered by blankets. Au'WelMyaFain then handed over her duties to others for five days as she guided me into the sleep we Au'Wel need; a sleep that lets us ignore our bodies; a sleep that lets us roam constantly through dreamgates.

It was hard work, but pure joy when I at last slipped into my place among the Au'Wel.

I was ready for
what I was made to do.

My first fight was easy. The dreamer was being chased by a shadow monster, its long, dark extensions reaching out to tap strength from the runner, making them stumble and allowing the beast to get closer and closer. My swords cut through it, drawing its attention from the dreamer and allowing them to escape. At first it tried to steal from me as well, but my blades were too sharp. Then it turned into a screaming multi-headed hydra with wicked teeth and searing breath. But I conjured up a net and trapped it tight. Its last attempt to conquer me was to take the form of a cute, sad-eyed puppy dog. But I could see the formless evil behind the facade and destroyed it.

My second battle was much harder. A duke was being stalked by his wife, whom he had killed years earlier. I loathed what I felt in his mind, but I reminded myself that our battle was not against the sins of humanity, but against the monsters who would rip humanity's mind to shreds and feed on the remains. Still, it was hard to strike the form of a pretty blond girl with green eyes and rosy cheeks. What saved me was the occasional glimpses of the evil within that would appear as a sardonic twist of a smile or a malicious glint in the eyes. I cut down the monster with my swords.

~~~~~

I have been battling for uncounted years now. Though sometimes hard, I love this life. Dreams are a playground where I can dance in the air, fly through the water, and perch on the rainbow. I have attended numerous feasts, ranging from a simple mother's porridge with sweet steam wafting into my nose to a king's banquet with roasted boar and candied fruit that melts on my tongue. In the dreams I am the ultimate confidant, the best friend, the shoulder supporting a hundred tears.

My life as a Au'Wel was one long, interesting dream, until the waking world abruptly intruded.

I was fighting a boss in a factory, one that had been terrorizing a dreamer with threats of reprisals and layoffs, when I felt a strange tug on my head. I ignored it, sweeping my swords around to cut off the path of the boss to the dreamer, forcing it back toward the edges of the dream. I called up a huge wind, blowing the boss off the dreamscape. The tug came again, this time accompanied with the feeling that someone was touching my hair.

It was creepy. I looked around for the new threat.

And I woke up.

I Woke Up!

To a face right above me, with lips touching mine.

I screamed as I sat bolt upright, banging my forehead hard into the face. Dim light danced into the room from the hallway.

I rolled off the table, wrenched open a kitchen drawer, and grabbed the first two items I found. I flipped back around to see my enemy.
~~~~~

It was a young man, probably nobility from the red and purple satin tunic and the gold band around his head. Blood was leaking from under the band where my forehead had shoved it into his face. He was holding his hands to his face and grumbling in pain.

"Get out!" I made my voice as loud and threatening as I could. "Leave!"

The man lowered his hands and stared at me as if I was crazy. I stared back.

"It's okay. I am here to help you." His voice cracked low and rough. He stalked around the table, his hand leaving a smear of blood on the edge.

I scooted back and raised my weapons. I was surprised to see I had grabbed a butcher's knife and a small icepick.

"I don't need your help. Leave now!" I spat out the words. What would it take to get him out of here?

"I'm sure you think so, but I can help you. I'll take you to the palace. Maybe get you some cake to eat? A pretty dress to wear?" He smirked and edged forward some more.

I was getting frantic. I had to get back to the Au'Wel now! Already I might have missed some real monsters and lost some innocent lives. I had to get rid of this person.

"If you don't leave now, I'll have to hurt you," I threatened. I moved sideways to keep the table between us.

His mouth turned down. "Now stop that. You are being childish. Put that knife down. We are going to the castle and I will take care of you."

He lunged around the table, grabbing the wrist of my knife hand and pulling me toward him. I brought the ice pick around and shoved it up under his ribs. He gasped in shock, letting go of me and stumbling backward. I ran to the other side of the table.

He stared down at his shirt, a rivulet of red spreading through it. He glared at me.

"You beast!" Anger infused his face, filling his voice with hate. I flinched.

"Fine, stay here! Obviously, no one wants you!" He coughed and red spattered from his lips. He staggered out the door and I heard his steps go outside. I collapsed against the wall, trembling. The weapons fell from my hands.

I had never attacked a real human before, only monsters disguised as people. And I couldn't pretend he had been a monster. The fact was that I had hurt someone the AllTruth had made.

A sob wracked from my lips.

I'm not sure how long I stayed there until I felt calm again. I knew I needed to get back to the dreamfight, but I also knew I couldn't do so with my heart beating wildly. Eventually I got up and went to the hallway. The door had been hacked open, a large gaping hole piercing the safety of my home.

I peered outside but didn't see the prince.

My mind felt foggy. I wanted to sleep.

I shoved a massive half-rotted wardrobe from the hallway in front of the door. It mostly blocked up the space and might keep out the more dangerous animals.

Desperately trying to put the unpleasantness of the day out of my mind, I laid back on the table, closed my eyes, and started the Au'Wel trance. My breathing slowed, my pulse calmed. I felt my mind start to drift into sleep.

And was jolted awake when the house creaked. My heart beat fast.

I blew out my breath in desperation. I had to ignore this. I had to get back into my dreams.

I started again, fixing my mind on the truth I had been taught. Again, my mind started to drift off into sleep as my body completely relaxed.

My stomach growled. My mind jerked awake again.

Hopeless, I sat up. Maybe if I waited until night I could get to sleep.

In the meantime, my body, which had lived solely on dream energy for an unknown amount of time, was wanting care. It craved food and water.

Sighing, I got up and drank a large glass of water, purposefully avoiding looking at the corner where the ice pick lay. I then used the bathroom. The experience felt strange. I had not been a slave to my body for ages.

Food would be a bigger problem, since there was none in the house.

I wondered if I could find any outside.

I scrounged up some coins and left the house, carefully picking my way around the perimeter, trying to avoid the wall of thorns that pushed close to the house. About halfway around I found the hole the man had hacked in the vegetation and followed it out, pushing aside the barbs digging into my flesh with as much care as I used to push aside our slobbering dog my mom sent to wake me up.

Once outside the brambles I looked around, a bit lost. Every direction was the same, a wall of green, spindly trees stuffed between dense copses of dark bushes, shaded by towering trees. I couldn't remember which way was the closest village. My mind still felt stuffed with regret and loss.

A shuffling noise came from the left. I cautiously pushed through some trees and bushes to find a riderless horse grazing from the leafy tips of some shrubs. The saddle blanket was the same red and purple color of the clothes of the man who had attacked me. I shrank further into the trees, not wanting to be found.

But no one approached the horse. I waited for what seemed like hours, wondering when the trap would be sprung. Sweat dripped down my face.

Still, the only movement was from the horse, which by this point had moved past me, meandering along as it looked for the tastiest plants.

I followed the path the horse had made and found it nibbling around a small stream. I approached it cautiously, but no one jumped out to grab me. The horse was friendly, nosing me and snuffling my dress for treats before turning back to the grass growing at the stream's edge.

I followed the path backward to where I first saw the horse, worry starting to worm through my mind. Once there, I started searching.

It took me another hour before I found the body of the royal. He lay on a patch of rocky ground, his head twisted at an odd angle. In the end I don't know what killed him: my attack, the fall, or the rocks his head must have impacted. I cried.

I went back to the horse and took off all its tack, hoping it could care for itself now. Then I retrieved a shovel from my house and dug in the soft soil by the stream. It took me the rest of the day, but I eventually buried his body and saddle.

Standing by the grave I started to cry again.

"I'm sorry."

Snot ran out of my nose. I snuffled, then closed my eyes. I trembled, despite the heat and the exertion.

My mind kept circling back to the moment he grabbed me. What could I have done differently? Did I act in truth and love, or in lies and hate?

I slowly shuffled back to the house, carrying the food I had found in the saddlebags, completely exhausted and ready to escape back to my dreams. I shoved the wardrobe back in place over the door and felt my way into the dark kitchen.

I slid down the wall until I hit the hard floor, then slowly forced myself to eat the bread and sausage, despite the rancid taste in my mouth. Another visit to the bathroom, and I laid down to sleep, bundling the blankets around me as a shield.

This time I was able to easily slip into my dreams. I cried in relief at the familiar appearance of the blue grass and mushroom trees, the fluffy grey bunnies greeting me with yaps and yips.

I could see my gateway, its solid wooden block a dark presence against the blue field of silky grass, but I before I could approach it, I sensed a dark force building behind me. I whipped around to see a wispy, shadowy monster stalking me, reaching out hungry tentacles. I created my swords and swung into it, knowing I would need peace before I could join the Au'Wel.

All night long monsters came at me in guises that preyed on my fears. Some called out that I was failing the innocent, others took the shape of the prince I had inadvertently killed, a few pretended to shake me awake again. All of them kept me from my gateway, kept me from jumping into other dreams, kept me from sleeping peacefully.

Their sneering syllables of failure ran through my head all night.

In despair
I screamed against my incompetence.

I woke up the next morning, staring at the bleak, dimly lit ceiling. I wondered how many innocents were dying right now, needing the help of an Au'Wel.

Is it possible to cry for days? It felt like I did.

I tried everything I could think of to avoid my monsters and sleep deeply.

I found lavender surviving among the brambles and used it to make a tea and a pillow. But I slept fitfully, constantly battling shadowy princes all night.

I tried to work myself into exhaustion, repairing the damage the royal had created and cleaning everything again. All that did was leave me sore the next morning after enduring multiple monsters waking me from dream to dream.

I tried to meditate on the truths of our order, repeating them again and again in increasing discouragement. The truths kept being drowned out by the whispers:

"You killed him."

"Murderer."

"It's all your fault."

"You are too messed up to help others."

Nothing worked to get me past the monstrous princes and into an Au'Wel sleep.

The other Au'Wel visited me in my dreams when they had time. They sympathized but had no real advice. The fears and lies I was battling were in my own head.

I traveled to a village thinking I would buy some sleeping draughts. I wandered down the dirt streets, avoiding piles of horse and dog dung while peering into windows to see what was being sold. The fresh bread, wooden carved bowls and utensils, nails and plows did not interest me. But the sight of skeins of dyed yarn, with the old proprietress hunched over a spinning wheel in the back of the store, brought me to a stuttering halt.

I knew her. From her dreams. I knew that pale pink shawl covering her shoulders, a gift from her loving late husband. I knew the canisters of dye that she kept in the back to color the wool brought in by her doting son. And I knew the peace she had after successfully battling fears for many years. Her nightmares were few and weak.

I hesitantly entered the store, weaving between shelves of colorful yarn and finished garments. The spinning wheel stopped. She straightened up with a creak and a smile, her silver hair framing her wrinkled face.

"How can I help you?" Her voice was just like in her dreams, rich and warm.

I smiled hesitantly back. "I...I was wondering if I could talk to you."

She frowned and shuffled forward. "I have paid all my taxes. And I already told the guardsmen I know nothing about Prince Charmant. What do you want to ask?"

Guilt and fear warred with hope. I mixed my worry with courage and told her the truth. All of it.

Afterward she stared at me, shocked, her hands rubbing together in mindless agitation. "That is quite a tale. And yet you do seem familiar, in a dreamlike way."

She hustled me over to the stool by the spinning wheel, handing me a cloth for my tears and a cup of water to calm my breath. Then she sat down and started spinning again. She smiled at me. "I think better when my hands are busy."

We both sat there, lost in our thoughts against the background whirl of the wool turning into yarn.

"You know, when my husband first died, I had all sorts of horrible thoughts running through my head. Of what I might have done differently while he was alive, of how we were going to survive on the farm without his help, of how I was going to survive without him." She sniffed. "It took me years to realize those were all lies. I was not perfect, but I did my best toward him while he was alive. And he knew it. I still miss him, but I also find joy and love all around me." She looked at me, her hands feeding brown, shapeless wool into the growing plump strand, her foot pumping the pedal. "From what you have said, you did your best too. Not perfect, but your best. You have to trust the AllTruth to work through that."

She stopped the spinning wheel, nodding to me. "That spindle is full. Can you take it off and replace it with one of the empty ones over there?"

I removed the yarn-covered spindle, my mind turning over what she had said as I walked over to the shelves. Though I knew the enemy lied, their accusations had felt like truth. But she was right. I had done my best. I was not a murderer, I was not messed up. Whether the AllTruth chose to make me an Au'Wel again or not, I could still try to help his people.

I grabbed an empty spindle without thought and shoved it on the spinning apparatus. A sharp pain pierced my hand. I gasped, jerking my hand back to see a long splinter hanging from it, blood starting to well up out of the gash.

The proprietress jumped up, all apologies, and bandaged my hand. But the sight of red seeping through the cloth gave me an idea.

When a child, my brother had slipped and gashed his leg open on a rock. A surgeon had visited to sew him up and mentioned he would sleep a lot due to his blood loss. I wondered if something similar, along with the truths I had just realized, would help me get into the Au'Wel sleep.

I left the shop, unwilling to wait another moment to try my idea. I hurried home through the hot afternoon air, pushing through the bushes, past the stream until I got to my hidden house. In the cool dim light of the kitchen I found a knife and some cloth. I climbed onto the table, took a deep breath, and stabbed my arm.

Pain bloomed in my limb and blood welled out, dripping onto the cloth.

I watched, feeling more and more woozy as I lost more and more blood. Finally, I wrapped my arm tightly in a bandage and laid down. My head was spinning.

I closed my eyes and started the Au'Wel trance again, reciting their truths. My mind drifted into sleep.

My dreamscape was large, as usual, filled with grey trees, purple brooks, fluffy bunnies and silky grass. It felt idyllic until the monsters formed, their black shapes each mimicking the prince.

"You killed me."

I looked straight at the monster and smiled, slinging the truth at it instead of my swords. "No, I was defending myself."

"You are messed up," another one spewed at me.

I strode past it, confident in my answer. "True, but no more than when the AllTruth chose me before. No matter what, I will continue defending his people from you."

I thought about the people needing an Au'Wel. I wondered if my arm was still bleeding.

I reached my dreamgate, a solid barrier against my hopes.

I took a deep breath and tried to slip through.

Nothing.

Despair tried to well up, but I refused to allow it. Despair was the opposite of what I had been taught. Instead, I focused on truth and hope and love, especially the truth that the AllTruth had chosen me, the love I felt for the people I had met, the hope I had in the AllTruth's purpose for my life, and finally the truth that the evil could not control me. I felt my mind slipping further into peace.

I pressed against the gate again and its soft edges filtered through my being.

I was through. I was on the other side.

I let out a shout of thanksgiving, of joy, of undiluted excitement.

I created Faith and Fire and jumped into the nearest dream, running straight toward the nightmare looming over a young boy. My head continued to spin as I sliced through the monster, turning it into shreds of shadowy mist that faded away as the boy's dream turned bright and cheerful.

I laughed out loud.

I didn't know what the future held. My body might still be bleeding, dying right now. Another man might find me and wake me again.

But for this moment, I was doing what I was created for. I was protecting the helpless, defending the defenseless, loving the unreachable. I was an Au'Wel.

I was finally free to sleep again.

END

FROZEN BEAUTY
Christy Eberling

December 1923
Lauralee

"You're too far behind in your rent; no more extensions." Harold O'Clery waved a red eviction notice in the air, then set it on the scratched coffee table.

Lauralee Merrywater stepped closer to the living room door and peeked in. She saw her father, Bill, rub his bad hip as he stood facing their landlord, his frown deepening. He looked down at the eviction notice, then at a framed picture of Lauralee's sister beside it, before focusing on his landlord again.

"Mr. O'Clery, I am a widower. My youngest daughter, Amelia, has a rare heart condition that's left me with expensive medical bills. She's in the hospital again right now, but she comes home in two weeks." He cleared his throat. "Would you consider letting me do physical labor in lieu of rent, after I finish in the coal mine each day, so my family won't be evicted? I can do maintenance at your rental properties, or at the business building you told me you bought last year. I'd even mow lawns or shovel snow." His voice cracked. "Anything, sir. I will do anything to help my family."

Mr. O'Clery straightened his gray tie and heaved in a breath, making his paunch more pronounced. "Say nothin', tell nobody about what I am about to say. Not until the newspapers have had an opportunity to interview and photograph me." He lowered his voice. "I am conducting an experiment."

"What kind of experiment?"

"The kind I'll forgive your debt for, me lad, in return for your compliance. You can volunteer to be a part o' something huge." Beefy hands spread wide apart in the air. "Once you have signed the contract, you will no longer owe me another penny. I am a man o' me word, of that ye can be sure."

"I'm listening."

"I call me history making experiment The Freeze." The landlord talked with his hands gesticulating in the air. "You will be the first person to live one hundred years, lad, and I will be remembered in history as the man who made it possible. I will freeze you a week from now, December

23, 1923, with me secret elixir to keep you alive. Your body will be put into a thick, clear, glass box and frozen. Your bodily functions will slow, and you'll enter a deep sleep until you thaw in the year 2023." Mr. O'Clery rubbed his hands together. "All of this will take place in me state-o'-the-art facility, with nursing staff to attend to you around the clock."

Lauralee watched her dad pinch the bridge of his nose. "Please understand my circumstances. I'd be unable to support my family if I was sleeping in a block of ice."

"Tis a shame," Mr. O'Clery said, sliding his arms into his overcoat. "I'm sure the homeless shelter will be happy to house a father, his teenaged daughter, and a child with a heart condition. Unfortunately, the shelters are full." He glanced outside. "Tis fierce windy outside, I suggest you reconsider me offer."

Lauralee stepped into the living room. "I'll volunteer to be frozen if you will forgive my father's debts, and let my family live here rent free for at least ten more years, until my sister becomes a legal adult."

Both men shook their heads.

"Absolutely not—"

"Are you for real? Yer a child."

"Enough!" Lauralee interrupted them. "I turn eighteen in two days. As an adult, I can legally enter into an agreement with Mr. O'Clery."

Bill limped over to Lauralee, favoring his hip, and put his hand on her shoulder. "Please don't do this. Even if you lived through the experiment, all your family and friends will be long gone by the time you're awake again."

"You're in pain, Father, there's no way you could handle more labor. I've already tried unsuccessfully to find housekeeping work." Lauralee lowered her voice to a whisper. "This experiment is our last option."

"You could die."

"I know."

"There has to be another way."

Lauralee shook her head. "I wish there was. Please let me do this for Amelia."

Bill frowned. After a long pause, he nodded.

"Come 'ere 'til we have a lookatcha," Mr. O'Clery said.

Lauralee stepped forward. Her hands worried the white pearl necklace she wore. It was the last remnant she had of her mother, something she'd never part with. Then she smoothed the material of her faded blue dress.

"It's a grand idea," Mr. O'Clery said. "I'll have me assistant bring the contract to your home for you to sign, in precisely two days." He picked up his briefcase and went to the door. "Report to the O'Clery Laboratory, on Route 40, right here in Gurnsey County, Ohio, at 1 pm on December

23. I've arranged for a photographer to be there to commemorate the occasion. Be sure to wear something pretty for photographs, Lauralee. A frozen woman will draw even more attention to me experiment."

He reached for the door handle, paused, then turned back. "You and I will pose together facing the camera first. Then you'll sit in a chair, and the photographer will move his equipment closer, to focus on your arm, when I inject the elixir. The photos will be used in newspapers, maybe even history books!"

"It'll be the bees' knees," Lauralee said, her flat voice indicating otherwise.

Frigid air blew in when Mr. O'Clery left. Lauralee shivered.

She dreaded having to say goodbye to sweet Amelia. Still, she went to get her coat. She'd spend as much time as she could with her little sister until she had to be frozen.

<div align="center">~~~~~</div>

April 2024
John

John Sullivan led his therapy dog, Theo, toward a centrally located nurse's station at Gurnsey County Hospital. A young girl, holding a doll, seemed to appear from out of nowhere and stepped into his way.

"Mister, can I pat your dog?"

John smiled when Theo's tail wagged excitedly. "Theo loves kids."

Tucking her babydoll under her arm, the girl rubbed her hand over the dog's black fur. "I bet Theo will like Sleeping Beauty."

"Who?"

"Come on." She ran and disappeared into a door two rooms down.

John motioned for Theo to follow the child.

By the time he reached the room, she was perched on a chair, rifling through a backpack. The occupant was a woman, sleeping with an IV in her arm.

Realizing the girl was probably supposed to be there, John released a sigh.

A harried looking woman hurried in. "There you are, Emmerson. Don't run off like that ever again. I've been looking for you, sweetie."

"I came back." Tears welled in Emmerson's eyes. "I went looking for my lost book so I could read it to Sleeping Beauty, but I never found it."

"I'll buy you another one soon."

Theo nudged Emmerson's hand. The girl nuzzled him and quickly forgot her tears.

"I'm Emmerson's mother, Nola. Have you brought the therapy dog to see Lauralee?"

John glanced at the woman in the hospital bed. Raven hair framed a heart-shaped face. Her mouth was pursed in a bow, as if waiting for a kiss. "She's beautiful."

"That's why Emmerson calls her Sleeping Beauty, and why she likes to read that story to her."

"I'm John Sullivan." He held out his hand. "I bring Theo in sometimes to visit patients, usually children and elderly. Do you volunteer here?"

Nola shook his hand. She glanced over at the girl and dog playing, then sat on a neutral-colored couch by the window. She pointed toward the sleeping young woman. "Lauralee Merrywater is my great-great aunt, or something like that. I've lost track of how we're related."

John's eyebrows raised. "Your family must have had children very young; she doesn't look over eighteen."

Nola laughed. "It isn't like that. Lauralee has been alive, frozen by some kind of freaky science experiment, for the last one hundred years. The story has been passed down through generations of my family. My great-grandmother Amelia made her daughter and granddaughter promise to always be there for Lauralee." She bit her lip. "Sadly, all of them have passed away. Now I continue the tradition of visiting my relative." She shook her head. "According to the legend, Lauralee was supposed to wake up four months ago. The facility she'd been staying in closed, from lack of funding, so she was moved to the hospital."

Had he accidentally visited the psychiatric ward? Was this woman living in a different reality? The story seemed unbelievable. John cleared his throat. "I really need to take Theo to visit patients." He left the hospital faster than he ever had before.

~~~~~

John went home and searched the internet for anything he could find about Lauralee Merrywater. Clicking from one story to the next, he learned that Nola's story was true. Lauralee was known as Frozen Beauty in the old papers, but John liked Emmerson's nickname, Sleeping Beauty, better.

He began to visit Lauralee regularly, sometimes with Theo and sometimes without. He told her about how he became a dog trainer and chuckled as he shared funny antics the dogs had done. Over the course of weeks, he even told Lauralee about the wrenching loss of his wife.

"Do you think she can hear you?" Nola asked, when she came in for one of her weekly visits.

"I hope so."

"The roses are pretty. Are they from you?"

John shifted from one leg to another beside Lauralee's bed and glanced over at Nola. "Where's Emmerson today?"

"She's at a friend's house." She rested her hand on John's arm. "You
~~~~~

don't have to talk about your feelings for Lauralee. I know sometimes people just feel drawn to others. It doesn't have to make sense." She smiled and removed her hand. "The flowers smell wonderful. I'm sure Lauralee appreciates them on some level."

John nodded and reached over to take Lauralee's hand into his own. "I want her to know she's not alone."

"She can have this, when she wakes, too." Nola took off a pearl necklace she wore, and set it on the bedside table, beside the vase of roses. "It was passed down, from woman to woman, in our family. But it belongs to Lauralee."

John nodded to Nola, then used his free hand to remove a stray hair from Lauralee's face. "You have family and gifts waiting here for you. I'm here too. Please wake up."

The sound of her soft breathing was her only response.

~~~~~

Lauralee

Lauralee was unable to move, couldn't even make a sound. She was trapped in her own body! What was going on?

Help! she cried out in her mind several times. But nobody heard.

She guessed the clinical visits she received were from doctors and nurses. They always said as little as possible, checked her vitals and left to see their next patient. Their footsteps, though muted, moved as if they were on a mission.

Sometimes a woman brought a little girl in to see her. The woman, Nola, usually only spoke to her daughter. Did she not think Lauralee could hear her? But the child, Emmerson, would always read a story. It didn't matter that she was obviously messing up several words, the girl's sweet voice entertained Lauralee.

It was John, the man who'd been frequently visiting, who'd kept her sane. She felt butterflies in her tummy whenever she heard his distinct footsteps or smelled his woodsy cologne.

He was the only person to provide her with skin-to-skin contact. Doctors and nurses had something over their hands, something she heard them take off after every time they touched her. Not John. He interlaced his fingers with hers, sending warmth, and a tingling sensation, spiraling through her. She liked that. A lot. *If only she could give his fingers a little squeeze or hold his hand in return!*

The sweet perfume of the flowers he brought lifted her spirits! Roses reminded her of her mother, outside gardening, before she was taken by sickness.

When John told the story about how his wife had died, years ago, Lauralee's heart ached for him. She wanted to comfort him, to let him
~~~~~

know she understood because she, too, had lost someone close to her.

John admitted to Lauralee that he hadn't been willing to share his feelings with another person, or to let himself feel for another woman…until now.

Nola and Emmerson came to visit while John was there again. Nola's shoes squeaked as she crossed the room, and the couch cushions made a crinkly noise when she sat.

"I brought my favorite book to read." Emmerson said. "Once upon a time…" Pages rustled as the girl chose the next page she wanted.

"Then Sleeping Beauty woke up from…" Emmerson raised her voice dramatically as she paraphrased, probably looking at the pictures. "A magic kiss."

Lauralee felt the tender touch of a man's lips on hers. Her heart began to beat double time and the butterflies took flight again in her stomach. That, along with John's woodsy scent, made her so happy that she made a sound deep in her throat.

"Lauralee?" John asked, his voice incredulous. "Are you waking up or am I dreaming?" He took hold of her hand.

"I heard it, too. Wait here, I'll get the nurse," Nola said. Sneakers squeaked across the floor.

A nurse came in and checked Lauralee's vitals.

Lauralee groaned.

"She really is responding. This is wonderful! I'll call her doctor."

Don't speak as if I am not here. Though Lauralee tried to form the words, they would not come. Not yet.

"She woke from a kiss, just like in the story." Emmerson sounded like she was jumping up and down.

"This is one story that I want to end happily," John said.

Lauralee squeezed his hand

~~~~~

John

"I just wish she'd open her eyes," John said to Nola in the hospital cafeteria. "It's like she's changed her mind and doesn't want to wake."

"It's only been two days since she started to wake up." Nola stabbed her salad with a fork. "Remember what the doctor said. It's going to take time. Plus, she's going to need therapy to learn how to do basic things, like walk again."

John finished the last of his coffee. "I need to let her know she won't have to go through all the scary changes of entering a new world by herself."

The next time John went to visit Lauralee, he had a small cardboard box filled with items. From then on, every day he introduced something
~~~~~

new from the box to her. He believed that she heard him and was soaking everything in.

"This has a lot of potential to access information, and to socialize," John said as he explained a cell phone. "But it also has been used negatively, like when people text and drive, or when parents devote too much time to their device and not their children."

John set the phone down. "Lauralee, I'm trying to prepare you for this century. It's completely different than what you're used to. But you're not alone. I will help you every step of the way."

Lauralee's lashes fluttered.

"Lauralee?"

Her eyes opened.

"Welcome to the twenty-first century, sweetheart." John took her hand in his.

"I...I..."

John reached for a glass of water. "Take a sip of this." He held the glass to her lips until she took in a tiny bit of water.

Lauralee tried again. "I heard...you...Thank you for—"

"You don't need to thank me." John cleared his throat. "It sounds crazy, but I'm falling in love with you, Lauralee."

Lauralee smiled. "Me...too. With you."

"She's awake." Emmerson bounded into the room with Nola following. "Good morning, Sleeping Beauty."

"Her name is Lauralee." Nola said. "She's a real person, not a character in a book."

John smiled. "She can write about her story someday if she wants to."

Emmerson jumped up and down. "I hope I can be in the story." She looked at Lauralee. "How will your fairy tale end?"

Lauralee licked her lips and her eyes met John's. "Happily ever after."

END

THE DREAMWALKER'S ROSE
Kaitlyn Emery

The darkness is so heavy, I can feel it pressing in on my chest. My eyelids feel weighted as I try to force them open, willing my mind to push through the fog that seems settled in it. The surface beneath me is cold, like a block of ice cut from a frozen lake.

Consciousness swirls around me before everything clears as I open my eyes and gasp for air, flying into a seated position. Thankfully, I'm not lying on an icy block, but I'm not in my warm bed, either.

The scent of decaying wood fills my nostrils. The world around me is dark, and my lungs burn from the frigid air. Slowly my eyes begin to adjust to the low lighting, and I realize I'm lying beneath a mass of tangled brambles, the moonlight above barely filtering through their knotted chaos. I've never seen vines like this, thick as tree trunks, with thorns as long as my hunting knife back home.

Back home!

Panic seizes me as the awareness of my situation hits. I'm the crown prince, alone in an unknown location, exposed to the elements. The last thing I remember was being safely in my bed at the castle, tucked beneath the velvety comfort of Prussian silk. Fear, lodged in the back of my throat like I've swallowed a giant rock, blocks my airways.

I've been abducted. It's the only explanation. Plenty of people would want to destabilize the Moore Kingdom by kidnapping the crown prince, son of King Fallon.

I need to stay calm and remember all my training. Someone must have drugged me at the party last night so I wouldn't wake up before they deposited me here, wherever here is.

I also need to find shelter and triangulate my position. I stand up, slowly testing my limbs. Nothing seems broken.

My poor mother! When she realizes her only child has been taken, she will be distraught. The thought of my mother helps ground me, and my lungs release their spasm.

There are no sounds of water or civilization to help me determine my location, just eerie silence. As my eyes adjust, I notice through the warring vines there is a large structure not far off. My best bet for shelter would be within those walls and, based off the apparent size of the structure, it would be an excellent vantage point to determine my whereabouts.

I gingerly climb through the thorns and branches seemingly reaching out to grab me, aware my movements must be methodical if I hope not to flay open my skin. The stone structure ahead is mostly obscured beneath flora vengeful enough to flourish unchecked in the inhospitable environment.

The vines seem to close in tighter the closer I get to what appears to be a castle entrance. Gingerly, I hoist myself up on a vine that closely resembles a tree trunk and try to duck my way through the barrier. I drop down from my perch and pain sears my shoulder as a razor-sharp thorn flays open my skin. The wound burns, but it appears to just be a flesh wound. I'll live, so long as I avoid any more run-ins with those anxious-to-impale assailants. Plus, I'm now at the entrance of the castle.

Once I enter, the air tastes stale, almost like I've been sealed inside a crypt. Beside the door I notice a barrel full of torches. Taking the flint and steel conveniently placed on a table beside them, I light a flame, illuminating a way through the suffocating blackness.

Cobwebs drip from pillars like draperies, and the meager light of my torch leaves the vaulted ceilings in shadow. An eerie glow appears near the door at the far end of the room, and then seems to vanish just as quickly as it came. It happens so fast I'm not sure if I imagine it or not. Holding on to my only weapon and source of light like my life depends on it, I slowly walk further into the castle. The halls seem lifeless, which makes sense with the lack of care to the outside of this place. But oddly, the inside of the castle is filled with everything I would find in my own, just covered in a layer of dust and slumber.

"Darrian?"

I whirl around at the sound of my name, the wind knocked out of me as I see what can only be the ghost of my fiancée. Memories flood my mind as I look into those eyes, large and innocent like a doe but the color of a fresh leaf. I remember riding at the head of the funeral procession beside her father, King Briar. Everyone was draped in black mourning as they tossed white roses at the golden coffin that paraded through the streets of the Gilded Kingdom. The weeping still rang in my ears, mixed with the endless condolences that did nothing for my heart that day.

Yet there she is, curls spilling down her back and shoulders like a golden waterfall, lips reminiscent of the pink roses for which she was named, staring at me in equal disbelief.

"Rosette?" My feet catch up to my brain and I rush toward her, dropping the torch on the stone and meeting her embrace with desperate need. I hope this is real, but even if there is just some hallucinogen in my system, it doesn't matter in this moment.

As our lips connect, something feels off. They are not as I remember. No warmth. No connection. I can't feel the fullness of her bottom lip, or the caress of her nose against mine. She almost doesn't feel real. Tears pour down her face as she clings to my neck, but she feels weightless, almost spectral.

"Why do you look so real, yet feel like a dream?" she asks, her cold hands cupping my face as she looks up at me.

I don't know, but I don't care. I haven't held her in what seems like a lifetime. I pull her close, kissing away trails of tears and burying my face in her hair. I long for the scent of her hair. "I never thought I'd see you again."

"I wish this were real," she whispers into my neck. "And that you could stay."

The shock of seeing her is wearing off, and in its place a flood of questions remain. I pull back to look at her.

"It's not really you, is it?" she asks, her lip quivering as she uses the heel of her hand to wipe back her tears.

"I—I don't understand. We… we thought you were dead."

"Is that what my father told you?"

"That's what the Gilded Kingdom told everyone. I was there when you were buried."

Rosette looks down at my chest, her long lashes hiding her gaze from me as she mindlessly picks at a loose thread along my collar. "My father, still up to the same old tricks."

"Rosette?"

She looks up at me, her eyes sad yet determined. "I can't leave, Darrian, so I might as well be dead. Please don't forget me when you leave here. Always remember that I was the first girl you loved."

"Leave here? I'm not leaving without you, Rosette. Where is here? Where are we? And how did we get here?"

An icy finger of dread trails down my spine, and my senses tingle with the feeling we are not alone. I feel the presence, lurking just beyond the shadows.

Rosette clutches my shirt, drawing my lips close to her own. "You must go. Go and don't ever come back." Her lips lock with mine, and for a moment, I feel a tingle of warmth pierce my skin just before an invisible force throws me backward to the ground, parting me from the woman I love.

With snake-like reflexes, a hand grabs the neck of my shirt, her long nails digging into the fabric, and my captor turns me and brings my face within inches of hers. Confused, I look into a pair of emerald green eyes that mirror my fiancée's, yet hold a dark edge I had never seen in Rosette's.

This woman's cheekbones are like the edge of a blade, her hair as black as night. She is beautiful and terrifying at the same time, and I recognize her instantly as a Fae. But not just any kind of Fae. I can feel powerful changeling magic crackling in her grip.

"What sorcery is this?" she hisses, spittle flecking my face.

"Please, don't hurt him, Mother. I beg you!" Rosette cries.

"Mother?" I choke through the feeling of someone clamping invisible hands around my neck. Why would she call this woman mother? I knew Rosette's mother. She was the Queen of the Gilded Kingdom, wife of King—

"Quiet, little sprout," the Fae chides, her eyes never leaving my face. "What magic brought you here, boy? Who is empowering you?"

"Please, I don't know what you're talking about. Just let her go, let me take her home—"

"She is home, and she is safe. Now begone. Tell King Briar I'm not to be trifled with. The next errand boy he sends, I will not be so kind."

With a flick of her wrist, a green vapor engulfs me, and the world goes dark.

~~~~~

With an uneasy feeling of having done this before, I was flung forward into a seated position, having been flat on my back, gasping for air. But this time, there was no icy feeling or lack of recognition. I was in my bed, surrounded by the luxuries and comfort to which I was accustomed. But alone, longing for the woman who had vanished from me a year ago.

It had all been a dream. A strangely realistic dream, but still just a dream. She invaded my mind every waking moment, sustaining my affections with every memory of our shared past. Now she was invading my dreams, too. I flopped back on my bed and a burning sensation crossed my right shoulder. I reached back to investigate the source of the pain and warm, sticky, half-dried blood covered my fingers. A gash was sliced across my flesh, and I instantly remembered my dream.

If this was real, then Rosette was alive.

"Guards! Call the White Mage! Call for Cornelius!"

~~~~~

"It's called dream-walking, and it's a very rare gift," Cornelius said with a pleased smile as he inspected my shoulder.

"This is an extremely serious matter," my mother said, worry lines forming between her delicate brows as she glanced over at my silent father. "What can we do to prevent this situation from happening again? Our son was injured in this dream world."

"I'm fine, Mother, really," I tried to console her.

My godfather tried to school his features to a more serious nature for my mother's sake. "Of course, my queen. You are quite right."

I turned my attention from my mother back to Cornelius. "So, you're saying it felt so real because it was actually Rosette?"

"Of a sort," Cornelius replied, as he stepped back to the table spread with his healing supplies, and started crushing herbs between his mortar and pestle, preparing a poultice for my injury. "The world you were in is very real, but you yourself were just a spectral version in it."

"Then how do you explain the injury?" my mother asked, placing her hand on my non-injured shoulder.

"Because Dreamwalker powers are fluid and can change based on their mental state. When Prince Darrian first entered the dream, he believed it to be real. Thus, the world around him solidified and became more formed, able to reach his physical body. But the moment he saw the princess, he began to doubt the reality and his physical form began to fade from that place. It's quite complicated, and we really should explore this more fully. At the appropriate time, of course," Cornelius quickly added to satisfy my mother. "But if we teach young Darrian how to harness this gift—"

"No." My father's voice cut through the discussion like a knife in a cheese wheel.

"No?" I reiterated, positive I had heard him incorrectly from his chair in the corner of the room where he sat, brooding.

"Correct. Whatever this is, it's dangerous. You're lucky all you received was a scratch, and that the Changeling chose restraint. As my son and heir to the Moore Kingdom, I forbid any more of this— this..."

"Dream-walking," Cornelius offered.

"Yes, exactly."

I looked to Cornelius, my godfather, most trusted of my father's advisors, hoping he would say something. Cornelius was himself a Fae, one who had saved my father's life. Their friendship had led to ending the war on magic within our kingdom when my father came to power. He had freed the Fae folk from the fear they had lived with of detection and annihilation. And at his side had always been my godfather, Cornelius the High Fae of the Moore, White Mage.

I locked eyes with Cornelius, begging him to intervene, to make my father hear reason that he would never hear from me, his son. After a moment more of my silent entreaty, Cornelius sighed and gave in.

"Fallon, the boy can't just shut it off. If he doesn't understand his gift—"

"His gift?" My father rose to his feet, frustration furrowing his brow. "How is this a gift, Cornelius? My son was injured. Threatened by a powerful woman. Left vulnerable. No guards to protect him."

"My king, that is why he must understand this power. He must learn how to use it—"

"How did he get it in the first place, Cornelius?" my mother interrupted, trying to diffuse my father's growing irritation. "Neither Fallon, nor I, have any Fae blood."

"True, but magic of this nature can occur through an intimate connection to the source."

"You mean a connection like Briar's daughter," my father replied.

"Rosette?" my mother asked. "King Briar and Queen Clarissa are clearly not of Fae-born."

"She called the Changeling her mother," I replied, playing over the conversation in my dream-walking. "And oddly, Rosette did look like the Fae, in a way."

"But Clarissa," my mother interjected, only to be cut off by my father's voice.

"There were rumors once, long ago, of an affair when we were younger. I don't think anyone ever believed them because of Briar's vocal disdain for the Fae, but I also found the insistence on a closed casket for the princess of the Gilded kingdom to be out of character at the time of her funeral. Seems Briar has a lot to explain if he wants to remain in the good graces of the Moore Kingdom. We will summon Briar to the castle. I told that fool someday his bigotry would be his undoing. Let's hope he doesn't drag the rest of us with him."

King Briar and my father had never mixed well. My father was a fair and just ruler of all his people, Fae and human alike. King Briar, however, resented other beings who could have more power than himself. He tolerated my father as a means to an end, an alliance to secure the safety of his much smaller kingdom. My father tolerated Briar because of my love for his daughter Rosette.

"Do you have any idea where I was, Cornelius?" I asked as the Fae finished wrapping my arm and my father left to send messengers to the Gilded Kingdom.

"From everything you told me, I would wager the princess is being kept in the Rose Kingdom."

His answer surprised me. "I thought the Rose Kingdom no longer existed."

"Not in the sense that it did when it was the birthplace of my people. But yes, the ruins of the Fae kingdom remain."

"So… if I wanted to see her again, to find out what information I could—"

"Darrian." My mother spoke softly, her hand touching my arm. "Promise me you won't do anything rash. You are my only child…"

I saw the plea in my mother's eyes. "I promise not to be rash, Mother. But I wouldn't be your son if I didn't try to fight for my love."

I could see the resignation settling in her features. "Is it safe, Cornelius? For him to go back?"

The Fae shrugged. "I could try to cast a protective spell to help tether his body to our world and minimize the physical risk, but dream-walking is a fluid experience. It is ever changing."

"But how do I go back?" I pressed. I should care more about the safety and risk of this new-found skill, but all I could think about was seeing Rosette again.

"Oh, you won't have a problem getting back. Fix your thoughts on Rosette, catalog every detail of her that you can think of, until she almost takes physical form in your mind. Think of the Rose Kingdom. The way it smells, the way it looks. The feeling in the air."

I listened with bated breath, soaking in every word, longing to return to the dreamworld that could temporarily reunite me with the woman I loved.

~~~~~

My soul burned to be near her—my heart yearned for the sound of her voice. And if I was ever going to hold the real her in my arms again, I had to get answers. Answers I hoped Rosette could give me.

As I closed my eyes and sank into my pillow, I embraced the memories flooding my brain like a tidal wave. I'd loved Rosette since our early days in school together. The different kingdoms, to unite and bring peace after the Rose War, decided to create an academy for certain months of the year where their children could receive instruction and education together.

My father headed up the unity effort, which placed my mother at the center of all the kingdom gossip. Rumor said Queen Clarissa was not fond of children, including her own. Some whispered that the mere sound of Rosette's voice would send the queen into a fit of rage.

My mother, who had always wanted another child, hated the idea of Rosette locked away in the highest towers of the castle with only her maid to keep her company, in an effort to avoid upsetting the queen. She reached out to the Gilded Queen while I was still a child and offered for Rosette to stay with us one summer. My mother was so tactful, making the excuse to Queen Clarissa that our kingdom was a shorter distance from the academy and a summer spent in the fresh air of the Moore Kingdom would be good for Rosette. But after that first summer, Rosette never did spend another with her parents.

Mother used to joke that Rosette's intimacy with our household had ruined the meek and mild child she used to be. The truth was, Rosette blossomed under the love of my family, changing her from a timid, frightened child into a force to be reckoned with. My mother saw Rosette as the daughter she could not have, and my father enjoyed the girl's quick wit and diplomatic brain that flourished in an environment where her voice was encouraged.
~~~~~

Rosette and I were inseparable. The other royals teased us about our attachment before there ever was one. Rosette was my best mate, my first pick in every school-related activity, from capture the crest to debate.

I remember the first time she kissed me. My surprise, but also the fire that awoke inside me. And for several years that fire grew until it consumed my entire being. And then King Briar announced that his daughter, the princess of the Gilded Kingdom, had come of age to make an alliance through marriage, and my whole world became threatened.

My lungs felt heavy, just like they did all those years ago when I heard the news. My eyelids opened, to find myself transported back to the Rose Kingdom, a spectral version of myself.

This time, I felt surer of my surroundings. As I picked myself off the ground, I remembered the warning the Fae Changeling had given me. I could not be found out this time, so I skulked through the castle like an assassin sent to murder a king.

Harnessed with the knowledge that this reality was still only a dream, I moved quickly through my surroundings, less consumed with safety and scenery.

The moment I saw Rosette, all caution fled my brain. She stood across the hall, looking down at me from a flight of stairs. Golden warmth radiated from her like sunlight, and the sight of her made my breath catch. Desire blossomed in my chest like a rosebud in spring.

In this place of darkness, she was the light.

"Darrian," she whispered as she descended the stairs, grasping my hand in her own and ushering me deeper into the castle. "I told you not to come back!"

The smell of fresh rain wafted off her hair. Oh, how I missed that scent. I knew I should be paying attention to the twists and turns she was taking me down, but all I could focus on was the feeling of her hand in mine. It had been over a year since I had felt that, even if it wasn't quite real.

Finally, she stopped, pushing me under an archway shrouded in secrecy.

"You shouldn't have come again," she said, but her hands reaching to tangle in my hair and pulling me closer contradicted her words.

"I was always terrible at following directions." I smiled, placing my arms around her waist.

Her soft smile was so familiar, even after all this time. "I'm glad you haven't changed much, then."

Our hearts beat against one another's chest in sync as we enjoyed the small moment of normality.

But I didn't have the luxury of time or normalcy. "First question. Are you okay?"

Rosette nodded.

"Good. But I don't understand how you got here. I want to bring you home, Rosette. Talk to me, tell me what is going on."

She shook her head. "I can't go back, Darrian."

"Why not? Is it the Changeling? Has she spelled you?"

Rosette drew back, leaving my arms. "No, don't say that! She would never hurt me!"

The vehemence of her statement was jarring. The fire in her eyes made me remember I wasn't talking to a damsel in distress. I was talking to the woman whose capability had won my heart.

"Then tell me," I encouraged her. "Let me understand."

Rosette's jaw grew firmer as she straightened her back "You can ask my father."

"I don't care what your father has to say, Rosette. We both know if I don't have some information to use as a truth stone against him, he will continue to lie through his teeth, as he has already done. He told us you were dead, Rosette. With a funeral and everything. Clearly, he has no interest in the truth."

Her eyes grew soft, misting over. "I'm so sorry... I wish you hadn't had to suffer that pain..."

"It will pale over time if I can be with you again. For real, not like this," I said, gesturing to my not fully formed figure.

A long silence filled the space between us as Rosette worried her lower lip between her teeth. It was an adorable childhood habit that had carried over into adulthood.

Finally, she spoke. "You know the stories, after the Rose Wars?"

"Of course, they were told to our fathers by our grandfathers."

"Turns out our grandfathers lied."

Having had no relationship with my grandfather and hearing the stories of the tension between my father and grandfather, it was easy for me to put aside what I knew and listen to her with an open mind. "How do you know?"

Rosette looked at her hands. "I've learned a lot in the past year, and I can see things... see the past. Please, Darrian, you must believe me."

I didn't know what she meant, but I took her hand in mine, reassuring her. "I do believe you. So tell me the truth. Help me see what happened."

"It happens that the king of the Rose Kingdom had a daughter, a powerful Fae among her people. When her father's kingdom fell, she was a young girl, displaced and alone, the remainder of her bloodline killed in the massacre that had followed the destruction of her father's throne. With all the pain and loneliness building within her and fueling her powers, the Fae princess enacted a curse upon her oppressors. The lines of kings would be broken, that they might feel the same emptiness she felt, their hope for a future taken from them."

Rosette paused, as if to ensure I was still listening, before continuing. "Her curse stole the life-force from the wombs of all humans who would join themselves to the sons of the kings who has stolen her homeland and destroyed her people. The Moore king's son was among those cursed, as was the son of the Gilded Kingdom."

My father and King Briar had been babes when the Rose Wars were fought. Consequently, they were the last children born to their fathers' households. "But that would mean my mother and yours were cursed. They would have been unable to have any children."

"Correct. And while Queen Clarissa never did conceive a child, your mother was given a gift. The gift of Fae magic."

The pieces to the puzzle slowly began to fall into place in my mind. "My godfather."

Rosette nodded. "Cornelius believed the generational curse to be wrong. Your father was not the man his father was. He was better. Kinder. Just. He fought for the Fae people, and under his reign, after the overthrow of your grandfather, peace was seen in the Moore Kingdom. So the High Fae did what he could. He could not undo the powerful magic of the Rose King's daughter, but he could provide a temporary relief. Enough to give the king and queen a chance at one child, but only one. And to them a son was born. Fair, just, kind. A champion of all. A true king to one day sit upon his father's throne."

She reached out and brushed my hair away from my temple, her eyes having grown soft through her tale. I grasped her hand in mine. Much as I wanted to hold on to this moment of purity, I needed to know the rest of the story. I needed the rest of the pieces to the puzzle that could bring her home. "And your father?"

Anger seethed in her gaze. "My father's curse remained intact. So he chose to use his powers of charm and seduce a girl, sad and alone, and manipulated her into believing that he cared for her. He preyed upon her desire for a family, her loneliness, and intended to enact his own revenge against the Rose princess.

"She conceived a child during her time with the Gilded Prince. Half human, half Fae. She resembled her human side, but had features that took after her Fae mother, giving her a bewitching look that the prince believed would bring suitors flocking to his kingdom. The not-yet king devised an even more despicable revenge that would benefit him far more. If he could not have a male heir, he would gain one through an arranged marriage of his child. The infant was ripped from her mother's arms, and raised by another who resented her husband's indiscretion. The child grew up, never knowing that she was a pawn in a much bigger game, the daughter of King Briar and Princess Rose."

I have never been an admirer of my future father-in-law, but even this heinous an act seemed beyond him. But looking into the eyes of my princess, known throughout the kingdoms for her otherworldly beauty, recognizing the resemblance between her and the woman I had met previously, and so many other little things that clicked into place in my mind, I knew her story was true.

"Your mother was the King of Roses' daughter. The Fae who cursed our bloodlines."

"Yes, but she was grieving, Darrian. She was a child, and she reacted in the only way that made sense in her grief." Rosette's eyes begged me to understand.

"I know, Rosette. And I will not judge her pain. Who knows but I might have done the same had I lost everything I loved. But you can't stay here. Let me talk to her. Surely now, all these years later, she can see reason—"

"Rosette, where are you, child?" a voice called from down the hall.

Her eyes grew large. "You must go, Darrian! She thinks you mean to take me back to my father."

She sealed her words with a kiss, before yellow sparks of magic began to tingle across my skin beneath the fingers that cupped my face.

"What are you doing?" I asked, shocked to see the woman I thought I knew so well producing golden orbs, like a hundred little fireflies, from her fingertips.

"I'm sending you home, where you're safe."

"No, don't! Let me talk to her. Let me prove that I am not a threat—"

Golden starbursts filled my vision, and I felt like my very soul had connected with an invisible force.

I was back in my bed, alone, far away from the Rose Kingdom.

~~~~~

Sitting in the council room across from Briar with my father and godfather beside me, I tried to remind myself I had made promises I would keep my emotions in check, but I couldn't take any more of Briar's lies.

"How dare you raise your voice to me, boy?" Briar roared as he paced the floor of the council room.

"Where exactly have you kept the Rose King's daughter all these years?" I demanded.

"I don't answer to you, boy. I am a king! And I am growing tired of these accusations."

"But you will answer to me, Briar." My father's thunderous voice rose over us, calming me somehow. "We are on equal footing, at best."
~~~~~

"At best?" Briar spat the words with disgust.

"You and I both know my kingdom has superior resources in every way. That's why you agreed to the union of our children, despite your hatred of me. You wanted a piece of this kingdom, and guaranteed protection should someone choose to oppose you. We both know if you could have gotten a better offer you would have rejected Darrian, despite your daughter's love for him."

Briar narrowed his eyes at my father but did not deny his words.

"The crown prince asked where you kept the Fae King's daughter all those years," Cornelius pressed.

Briar's nose twitched, trying to suppress a snarl. "Remove this filthy creature from our midst and I will confide in you, Fallon."

My father's eyes narrowed, and his voice resembled the edge of a blade as it pierced the room. "You are not a guest in my home, Briar. And you will give the Moore King's Royal Advisor the respect his title demands. In my eyes, he is not only your equal, but superior."

Briar bristled, but sighed, admitting defeat beneath the accusatory gazes of the three of us facing him at the table. "Wretched girl. My own flesh and blood! She betrays me for that creature."

"Her mother," I corrected.

"She is no friend to you, boy. She cursed us to begin with."

"As a child, pained by the crimes of our fathers," my father reminded him.

"The Rose Princess, what did you do with her after the birth of Princess Rosette?" Cornelius pressed. I knew, though his loyalty to my father would never waiver, that his own roots begged for answers to his people's history.

"I tracked down a sorcerer strong enough to hold her prisoner and sent her away to a solitary tower where he could keep her and minimize her threat," Briar spat.

"Then how did she escape?" my father questioned.

"I guess, over time, she continued to grow stronger, eventually defeating the sorcerer and stealing my child from my home about a year ago."

I was disgusted. "You mean *her* child? The one you stole first?"

"Rosette has lived a life of comfort, without want or need. You act as if I banished her to that tower."

I opened my mouth, but my father's voice carried over me. "You willfully choose not to acknowledge the trauma you wreaked in the lives of everyone in this situation, Briar. Our fathers are the reason we are in this mess to begin with. Their hatred and bigotry led to a young girl lost and alone in agony. And instead of having compassion for the suffering of others, you chose to compound that grief further and destroy what was left of her life. I have always told you your inability to see beyond your hatred would lead to your undoing and it has! And you've taken my family along with you. No more!"

My father rose to his feet. "Our ties to the Gilded Kingdom are over. May your legacy collapse and fall around you. May your people seek refuge in other kingdoms and flee the sinking ship that is your birthright."

"How dare you?" Briar roared. "And what of Rosette? If you cut ties—"

"As far as I am concerned, Rosette has always been more a part of our family than yours."

Briar rose. "I have a clear conscience. I did what was best for my kingdom. Can you say the same?"

"With absolute certainty," my father replied. No hesitation. I felt pride watching him. He had always been both a great king and a great father, and at times I probably took that for granted.

"Then we are at an impasse." The Gilded King rose. "But when that witch casts her curses on your kingdom, don't come crawling to me for help!"

I watched as Briar stalked out of the room, his guards following behind him.

My father finally broke the silence. "Cornelius, do you think you could protect my son from your natural sovereign?"

Cornelius hesitated. "To an extent, my king. Her skills are far superior to any I have encountered. As we saw with the line of kings curse, I was not able to undo what she had done, merely hold it at bay for a short time."

My father nodded, shifting his eyes to me. "A great wrong has been committed, my son, in the name of humanity. Not only against the woman you love, but her kin. As a king, I seek reconciliation with the Rose Kingdom. As a father, I desire your heart restored. My head tells me to send you with your godfather as a delegate, but my heart fears losing my son. So, I remove myself from the equation. This decision must be yours. I know I cannot stand in the way of who you are as a man, a lover, and a future king."

While the different parts that made up my father were warring within him, within myself there was complete peace. "With your blessing, Father, I would like to take a small delegation, accompanied by Cornelius, and travel to the Rose Kingdom."

"And what will you do, once you are there?"

"I intend to speak to the rightful queen of the Rose Kingdom and request her daughter's hand in marriage."

~~~~~

Had my godfather not been a Fae himself, born in the Rose Kingdom
~~~~~

during the Rose War, I don't think I would have ever found the wasteland that I had traveled to in my dreams.

The ruinous structure we approached, encircled by barbs and brambles, looked devoid of life, but I could imagine the grandeur of this place at the center of the kingdom, in the days before the senseless war. The Rose Kingdom once was the height of society and fashion before the destruction. Now no roses grew among the untamed vines, just thorns and despair.

Reality's harsh lens did not reflect kindly on the violated realm.

The journey had been long, but here we were. So close to a reunion with the woman I loved, yet still so far away. How would the uncrowned queen handle our presence? Would she see me not as the men of the past who had wronged her, but as myself?

Above the stone towers covered in vines, a dragon with scales as black as an obsidian stone circled in the sky.

"That's her, isn't it?" I asked my godfather.

Cornelius nodded. "What power," he mused, admiring her impressive display of shapeshifting. "But remember, Darrian. Though you may pity her past, life has made her dangerous and unpredictable." He eyed the winged beast as she began her descent. "Battling a sorcerer for freedom over a decade has made her unmatched in strength. And every dragon has its treasure. I have a feeling this dragon would kill to keep hers from being stolen again."

The earth shook as the dragon touched down, barring the entrance to the former palace of the Rose Kingdom. Her eyes flickered like wildfire, and green vapor wafted from her nostrils, pooling on the ground at her taloned feet. She let out a blood-curdling roar, throwing her head back and flapping her wings, as if to challenge us.

I took a step forward. "We come unarmed, rightful queen of the Rose Kingdom, and have left our men down the trail as a sign of good faith."

Another thunderous roar spewed fire from her belly. Cornelius jumped in front of me, producing a shield of raw energy and deflecting the flames so they did not harm us.

"Stop!" Amidst the green magic rolling off the dragon's black scales and the smoke rising from the fire-singed ground, Rosette emerged, placing her hand on the dark scaled beast, and stroking her. Tears gleamed on her face. "Please, Mother. Don't hurt them."

Rosette's tears seemed to distress the creature, who turned to nuzzle her child. Within the space of one breath, the dragon shape-shifted into a woman, her arms circling protectively around Rosette.

"My child, I told you to stay within the castle. It isn't safe!"

"Mother, please, let go of the past. Let me show you what the future looks like." Rosette gazed across the small field separating us.

This time, I took a step forward and cleared my throat. "May we approach, rightful queen of the Rose Kingdom?"

The Changeling looked into the entreating eyes of her daughter for what felt like forever before addressing me. "You may approach, but I am warning you. I will not think before destroying you should you foolishly try something."

Without hesitation, I approached, my godfather following close behind. I kept my eyes locked with Rosette's the entire way, her coaxing smile encouraging every step forward. When I was near enough, she stretched out her hand to me. Her mother tensed like a cobra about to strike.

"It's all right, Mother," Rosette soothed, her fingers lacing with mine slowly. "Mother, I know the pain you have endured at the hands of mankind has been despicable. But I promise, the world is filled with potential, if we are all willing to set aside our differences."

I tried to listen to her words as all my senses seemed to misfire. I could finally feel her. The warmth, the familiarity. The tingling of my skin.

But I had to stay focused. If I didn't want to lose that feeling again, I needed to act. "Your highness, this war cannot continue. For your people, or mine."

"Might I remind you, boy," her words jabbed, "that it was your kind that started this war. Your kind that feared my people and sought war with a peaceful nation to pillage our lands and cripple us."

I nodded, feeling the weight of her words. "I know, your highness —"

"I am no ruler, boy. Just a mother intent on keeping her child safe from the greed of man."

I felt the pain in every word she spoke.

"Respectfully, your highness, you are both. The natural-born ruler of the Rose Kingdom, rightful queen of the Fae. And you are also mother to the woman I love."

Rosette's mother looked at me intently for a moment, visibly unsure how to respond to my declaration.

"Mother," Rosette interjected, pulling me closer. "Please, let me show you glimpses, so that you might see what I see."

Her mother hesitated but gave a barely visible and reluctant nod.

Rosette smiled, turning her attention back to me. "Darrian, do you trust me?"

"With everything that I am."

She smiled, tears glimmering in the corners of her eyes. She released my hand, and raised her own hand to side of my face as golden energy began to collect within her palm. "Do you still trust me?"

I saw Cornelius take a tense step forward. His job was to protect me, but I did not fear the Fae side of the woman I loved. I held up my other hand to silently stop him. "I learned a long time ago to trust your instincts."

"Then let me take us on a journey," Rosette said, holding out her free hand to her mother.

"Where are we going?" I was positive I was ready for anything.

Golden magic sparked from the tips of her fingers as she placed her other hand against the side of my head. "Down memory lane."

Everything went black.

I had felt this feeling before. Darkness so heavy my chest felt like it was caving in. Weighted eyelids. A fog filled my consciousness and swirled around me. I was lying on my back when I came to, and I flew up to a seated position, the world spectral and fuzzy.

Rosette offered me a hand up. "Are you ready?"

Cornelius was gone, the only thing in focus now being Rosette and her mother, both standing beside me.

"Where are we?"

"In your memories," Rosette answered, as if it were no more casual than an afternoon promenade.

"Do her powers disturb you, boy?" Rosette's mother asked, her arched brow intimidating.

"Quite the contrary, they intrigue me, your highness."

"Shhh." Rosette laced her fingers with mine and pulled at my arm. "This is the moment I fell in love with you."

Confused, I followed her gaze to the hazy portal that opened, displaying a scene before us, almost like a play.

As I watched, the scene in front of us grew familiar. I had somehow been transported back to the royal academy, with our tutor at the front of the classroom.

And there we were, younger versions of Rosette and me, seated in the chairs amongst the other royals.

Prince Bastian pulled Rosette's long, blond braids.

"Ouch!" the past version of her cried, her hand flying to the back of her head. "That hurt, Bastian!"

"Boo hoo, go cry about it, you big baby."

The heel of my younger self connected with Bastian's shin under our desk.

"What the heck was that for, Darrian?" Bastian cried, drawing the attention of the tutor.

"Boo hoo, Bastian," I said. "What are you going to do, go cry about it?"

The tutor called all three of us up to the front of the classroom, where I gave a tongue lashing to Bastian and the tutor threatened to send a messenger to my father about my unruly behavior in his class.

"Go right ahead. My father doesn't believe in people getting away with bullying. He'll tell me 'good job, son.'"

The memory faded as a new one emerged. Now we were looking down over the shrubbery maze at my father's castle, the exact place where Rosette finally agreed to marry me.

A much thinner, teenage version of me was chasing a merry and flush-cheeked Rosette. The spectral girl rushed by with the apple she had stolen from me behind her back.

I caught up to her, breathless as she leaned back against the shrubbery wall, looking up at me.

"You stole my apple."

"Did I?" she asked and took another bite of the fruit of pursuit.

The past version of me smiled down at her, leaning in closer. "Now I must steal something from you."

"It's not stealing if it's given freely," Rosette replied as she moved to kiss me first.

As our lips parted, I sighed, resting my forehead against hers. "Marry me, Rosette."

"Darrian, we've been over this. My father hates yours and his quest for equality among Fae and humans. You know he won't say yes."

"I know your father has been shopping you around to suitors to fill his coffers with your bride price and looking for an alliance that will strengthen his kingdom. I can offer him more of what he wants than any of the others he keeps trying to force on you."

It wasn't the first time we had had this conversation.

Rosette bit her lower lip, as she always did when she was thinking. "What if he says no?"

"Then I'll persuade him. I can be persuasive and charming!" I flashed her a grin that, in hindsight, looked incredibly ridiculous.

"Oh, don't I know it!" She laughed, entwining her arms around my neck, the half-eaten apple still in her hand. "Do you promise to love me till death and always fight for those who cannot fight for themselves?"

"I will love you beyond the grave, regardless, Rosette. But I promise to always fight for what is fair and just, if you promise to always be the one by my side, no matter how small the battle."

Her smile, brighter than the sun, reached from ear to ear. "I promise to always do battle alongside you, but also to be your queen. The one who comforts you when the crown grows heavy, and the one who ensures power never corrupts you."

"Wait, did you just accept my proposal, finally, after all this time?"

"No, I was promising the other crown prince, you adorable fool!"

The false reality around me shifted, jarring me back to reality, and I stared at the woman with whom I had just relived those beautiful memories. Rosette gave me a kiss on the cheek.

"Thank you, for the beautiful life we have lived together."

Her Fae mother stared at me. If Rosette hadn't been there, offering me strength with her very presence, I might have tried to crawl under a rock to escape her gaze.

"Your highness, please, may I confer with you?"

Rosette's mother seemed to consider my request. "The Fae, who is he? A servant?"

I glanced over at Cornelius who had managed to draw closer. "He is the King of the Moore Kingdom's royal advisor, and my godfather." I motioned for Cornelius to join us.

"And how do you justify this level of intimacy with the king after the atrocities done to our people by the Moore Kingdom?" The Fae princess addressed Cornelius.

"I make no justifications for the wrongs committed by the Moore Kingdom during the Rose War. But I also do not judge the children of wicked kings based on their fathers' actions, but rather their own."

"Do I detect a level of judgment in your words, Fae-born?"

For a moment, I thought I heard an ounce of admiration in the woman's voice.

Cornelius held her gaze. "When I was a young boy, the king's son witnessed my use of magic. I was an emaciated urchin and the prince, instead of turning me in to his father, brought me into their home as his companion, never uttering a word of my secret. I followed him into battle when he decided to free the Fae people, and I saved his life as he had saved mine from his father's wrath as a boy. Under his rule, our people have flourished, and his treatment of the Fae folk have spread to surrounding kingdoms. For these reasons and more, I would lay down my life for the Moore King and his heir."

"I cursed the son of the Moore Kingdom for his father's cruelty. How did his queen come to bear this heir?"

"I did not think it right to end the line and legacy of a good king because of the cruelty of his father. King Fallon proved many times over that when given the chance, he did not become his father."

"So you countered my curse." The Rose princess turned her attention back to me. "For the sake of my daughter I am willing to listen to you, boy, but do not waste my time flattering me with empty words. I have heard enough meaningless talk from powerful men to last me a lifetime."

I took a deep breathe. "Princess Rose, rightful queen of the Rose Kingdom, on behalf of the people of the Moores, I have come to ask you for your daughter's hand in marriage. To form an alliance of the strongest bond between your people and my own, and together rebuild and reclaim the birthright of Fae kind."

She seemed stunned for a moment, as if struggling to process my words. "What of your ties to the Gilded Kingdom?"

"Severed," I replied confidently.

"So then, your betrothal to my daughter has been nullified?"

The words stung. I knew the reality was our betrothal had been dissolved the moment we cut ties with her father, but the truth still hurt. "Yes."

Princess Rose nodded, deep in contemplation. Everyone present seemed to hold their breath, waiting for her next words.

"You don't fear me, boy? Or what my powers, or that of my daughter, could do to your kingdom?"

I held Rosette's mother's gaze. "I fear the evils of man and corruption, not Fae power, Princess."

A smile spread across the Fae Princess's face, soft with a hint of warmth, reminiscent of Rosette's own smile. In that moment, I could see a strong resemblance between the two of them.

"Then you have my blessing, Prince of the Moore Kingdom. Should she choose to bind herself to you."

It took me a second to register her words. I had spent so much time preparing myself for rejection, that I hadn't figured out what I would do if my offer was accepted.

Fumbling over my words, with none of the charm of my previous proposal, I took the hand of Rosette. "My love, will you bind yourself to me once more?"

"I will, I really will!" she cried, throwing herself into my arms. This time, I could feel the entirety of her warmth and embrace, no longer a dream between us.

END

THE REAL PRINCE
Deborah Cullins Smith

This story takes place within the timeline of **Habitations of Violence,** *from* **Moonlight and Claws.**

Wind whipped a light snowfall inside the rustic ranch house, and Mina Harker pulled her shawl around her shoulders with a shiver. Henry Tunstall's ranch hands labored with a huge bundle, which they dragged across the wooden floor of the dining hall.

"Doc! Billy! What in the world are you doing?" Mina asked, trying to hide her smile. She had just been lamenting the lack of Christmas décor, and from the sweet smell of pine, she had a feeling the bundle they now hauled might be boughs for hanging around the hearth. Henry Tunstall, Mina's friend from London, brought up the rear of the party and he clapped his hands together heartily as he burst into the room, red-faced and cheery.

"Set it up there in the corner, boys," he instructed. His ranch manager and right-hand-man, Dick Brewer followed close behind him with an armload of short pieces of lumber and a bag of nails.

The young men scurried around, cutting ropes and pulling away the canvas to reveal a five-foot-tall pine tree, its spindly branches dropping needles copiously as it was held up for Mina's inspection. She clapped her hands and laughed with delight.

"You actually went out and found a Christmas tree?" she exclaimed.

"Billy found it," Henry stated, clapping the lad on the shoulder. "He insisted that we go out and chop it down immediately, just for our Miss Mina." He winked in her direction, eyes twinkling merrily. Henry insisted that her presence on his ranch had been a rare and wonderful gift. They'd had their share of problems in Lincoln County with the competition, Mr. Lawrence Murphy and James Dolan, who owned the mercantile, the bank, and most of the rest of the commerce in this area of New Mexico Territory. But Mina had definitely had a refining influence on his rag-tag family of misfits and outcasts. It was one thing for a gentleman like Henry Tunstall to believe in them, but when a lady like Mina Harker believed in them, that was something to live up to.

Billy's cheeks flushed a dusky pink. "Found it on my last night out runnin'," he mumbled. "I jus' figured it would make a pretty Christmas tree for us, Miss Mina. Like you was talkin' about last week. You think we can fix it up? Maybe not as fancy as a London tree, but something like it?"

"Of course we can, Billy." She smiled at him. Of all the boys, Mina felt the most akin to Billy Bonney. The boy was a loose cannon and as wild a child as ever wore boot leather. But they had discovered the secret he harbored during the past summer.

Billy was a werewolf.

For a few days out of every month, the moon afflicted Billy, turning him into a wolf. It was a condition the Native Americans called shapeshifting, and they considered it an honor that the animal bestowed on certain men. Now that the boys were aware of his condition, they all accepted Billy just as he was. Gradually, they had stopped fearing him, and they found that once in a while, his "gift" proved useful in unexpected ways. This time, his nightly excursions had led him to the rare pine tree in the New Mexico landscape.

Dick knelt by the base of the tree and hammered the pieces of wood into a makeshift stand that anchored the tree on four sides.

"Hold 'er steady, Fred," Dick grumbled from under the scraggly branches.

Whip-thin Fred leaned into the effort. "Tryin', Dick. It's heavier than it looks."

Jim French laughed boisterously, his dark complexion ruddy from the winter chill. "Let me help, *amigo*." He reached in and steadied the slender trunk between Fred and Robert Widemann. Robert was the serious one, a somber lad with wideset dark eyes. Dick continued to hammer, requesting now and then that the boys turn the tree just a bit as he laid in another brace to anchor the stand.

When they could finally release it and it didn't rock or sway precariously, they whooped for joy. As they maneuvered it into the corner, discussions began in earnest about decorations.

"Let's talk about this over dinner," Mina said. "I was afraid I would burn it all, just trying to keep it warm until you got home. But this surprise was well worth the wait."

Doc Scurlock and Charlie Bowdrie nudged each other in the ribs.

"Told ya' she'd like it."

"She's lit up like a firefly in June, ain't she?"

They washed up quickly to remove the tree sap from their hands and hurried to the long dinner table. Mina's dinners were always events to remember. They all took turns with the cooking, but Mina's meals were favorites. Tonight, Mina treated them to a lovely pork roast wrapped in bacon and seasoned lightly with rosemary and thyme. She also served potatoes and green beans on the side, and fluffy golden biscuits.

Not as good as Mrs. Hardman's, but they'll do, she thought with a smile.

"A penny for those thoughts, Mina?" Henry asked softly, a question in his gentle brown eyes.

"Oh, I was just thinking about our housekeeper, Mrs. Hardman," she said, embarrassed to be caught with her emotions showing so plainly.

"I remember her," he said. "Such a lovely woman. Betsy always thought highly of her."

Betsy was once Mina's housemaid, until a vampire took her life. Henry had never recovered from the loss. He had proposed to Betsy and had tried in vain to save her life after she had been bitten. Many blood transfusions later, Betsy was still vulnerable to the call of the master who had enslaved her, and just when they had thought they were victorious, he struck again and took Betsy's life. Heartbroken Henry had left London for the New World, and his ventures had brought him — ironically — right into the midst of another vampiric nest. Mina only hoped she could stave off another disaster.

Decorating the Christmas tree with these motherless boys definitely fell into that category. They needed to find joy in the moment. Disaster had a way of finding them, whether they wanted it to or not. For now, Mina enjoyed their enthusiasm.

After saying grace, the boys filled their plates with heaping mounds of meat and vegetables and began offering up suggestions for decorations.

Dick waved a fully laden fork a bit as he spoke. "I seem to recall my momma stringin' popcorn and cranberries on a thread, then winding it around the tree. That was real pretty, all white and red against a green tree." He shoved the forkful of pork roast into his mouth and sighed with pleasure. Gulping down the well-chewed bite, he dug into his plate again. "Don't know what you used to spice up this roast, ma'am, but it sure is tasty."

"Thank you, Dick. I'm glad you are enjoying it. I have a few surprises up my sleeves," Mina said, smiling brightly. "But all ideas are welcome, and we'll all share in making up the decorations."

"Maybe we could invite some of the neighbors in for a Christmas Eve shindig?" Charlie asked hopefully.

"Like maybe the McSweens? And maybe they'll bring that little Mexican girl along, the one that helps Missus McSween with her laundry?" Doc elbowed him in the ribs.

Charlie blushed deep red. "She ain't my girl or nothin'. Fact is, I think George Coe is sorta' sweet on her. But we could invite them out too."

"You never know, Charlie." Dick chuckled. "She might just like sawed-off little runts of the litter like you."

"Aw, cut it out, Dick," Charlie mumbled as he slouched in his seat, but Mina could see his smile. The rest of the boys hooted and hollered, and the room rang with their laughter.

~~~~~

Christmas Eve brought in a sprinkling of snowflakes and crisp winter air. Mina breathed deeply as she stepped out on the porch to greet their guests. The dining hall would be packed, but it would be a party to remember. John Chisum and his niece, Sally, had already arrived, with Sally contributing several plates of cookies and some fruit-filled breads that made Mina's mouth water in anticipation. Together, they had finished ladling up meatballs in a thick, savory gravy, and laying out some mushroom caps stuffed with breading and cheese. The boys had eyed the latter with skeptical eyes, but after sampling a few she cut up for them to taste, they were all too eager for the party to begin so they could have more. She'd also made up pork pies, stacked high on a large platter, and little cherry pies at the other end of the table with the desserts. Dick had used the soup pot and mixed up a punch bowl that made Mina's head swim just to smell it, until Henry made them dilute it significantly.

Alex and Susan McSween arrived with pies and mincemeat tartlets, and at last the long table groaned under the weight of the feast. They did indeed bring little Maria with them, and close behind came the Coe cousins with their banjo and fiddle. Added to Dick's guitar and Billy's harmonica, they had a regular orchestra for their holiday music, much to Mina's delight.

Maria curtseyed shyly when introduced to Mina, then clung to George's arm as he proudly introduced her to the Chisums and the rest of the boys. Charlie sat glumly in the corner watching their progress around the room. Maria was a delicate girl with long dark hair that curled around her plump face. Her smile lit up the room, and Mina could see why Charlie—and obviously George Coe as well—were thoroughly smitten with her.

Mina slipped into the chair beside Charlie and said softly, "George does play the fiddle, does he not?"

"Yes'm."

"And one cannot play the fiddle and dance at the same time, can he?"

"No'm."

"Then perhaps someone else can claim a dance or two while the fiddler fiddles..." She left her sentence dangling while watching him from the corner of her eye.

She smothered her grin the moment that thought truly registered with Charlie. He sat up straighter in his chair, adjusted his collar and cuffs, and yanked on his jacket. "Well, ma'am, I suppose that *someone* could do just that very thing." His smile was as wide as a Cheshire cat's.

Mina chuckled softly. "Happy Christmas, Charlie." She rose and returned to her duties as hostess.

Everyone was amazed by the Christmas tree, festooned by cranberry
~~~~~

and popcorn streamers the boys had made, and big red bows and little fabric angels Mina had hand-sewn from quilt scraps gleaned from Susan McSween's scrap bag. Mina had also bought a few oranges from the store, poked them with whole cloves, and hung them by yarn from the branches. Not only were they bright splashes of color, but they gave off a sharply spiced aroma. Billy had picked up small balls of tumbleweeds and woven some bright bits of yarn through them for ornaments. Chavez, one of their part-time cowboys, had dropped in and eyed the tree thoughtfully. He was one of Billy's closest friends and it was his Apache heritage that had been so useful at the point when Billy was bitten by the wolf. Chavez had explained what was happening to the boy, and how to deal with the changes he was experiencing. Mina was only beginning to discover the depths of this quiet young man's knowledge, but she sensed a great warrior beneath his reserved veneer. Chavez used some string and twigs to make a few small trinkets he called 'dreamcatchers' which he also contributed to the tree's décor. They looked like tiny round spiderwebs scattered on the branches.

"I must remember to do this myself next year," exclaimed Susan, as she fingered one of the oranges. "What a marvelous idea."

Dick counted off, then began to strum his guitar as he skillfully fingered the strings. The music set feet to tapping and the few women in the room were much in demand by the overwhelming number of young men who wanted their turn for a dance. George grew more and more unhappy as he watched "his" girl twirled around the room by the other boys, but most often by Charlie. The party was too good, and the food too comforting for hard feelings though, and everyone enjoyed themselves.

Henry twirled Mina around the room, spinning her back into his arms as she laughed with the sheer joy of the moment.

"Look what you've done here, Mina. What a difference you've made on this ranch. How can I ever thank you?"

"Henry, you took me in, remember?" she said. "I'm grateful for a roof over my head in this wild country!"

"No, you could have stayed in London, my dear." He shook his head. "You came here to help me with Murphy and Dolan at the behest of my parents. While I don't exactly feel it was necessary, I will always be grateful to you for your presence and your influence in my household."

Mina blinked back tears. "Thank you, Henry. Happy Christmas, my friend."

When the boys took a break to grab some refreshments, and the ladies sat for the first time in a couple of hours, Mina, Sally, and Susan gravitated to a corner while George took Maria's hand in his once again and tried to steer her away from Charlie.

Sally giggled. "Poor George. I thought he was going to have a fit of apoplexy every time Charlie asked Maria to dance."

"All's fair in love and war. Isn't that the saying?" Mina said with a little laugh. "Charlie has been smitten for a long time."

"Well, he may have been smitten, Mina, but he hasn't done anything to let Maria know his feelings. Until George began to court her, that is." Susan's lips pressed into a hard line, but her eyes showed more sympathy for Charlie than her words implied.

"You mean George is really serious about Maria?" Mina asked.

"He's already asked her to marry him," Susan whispered. "But Maria hasn't said yes yet. I think she's a little timid around George's cousin. Frank can be a little frightening until you get to know him."

Mina glanced over at the bearded man, lean of frame, craggy and weathered. Yes, she could see how Maria might find Frank Coe intimidating. "But you think she will say yes to George?"

"It's a good match for her, Mina," Susan said, patting her arm sympathetically. "George owns the Coe ranch, so Maria would have a stable home. Frank helps him run it, but George bought it himself. What can Charlie offer her? A place in the bunkhouse? That's no life for a newlywed. I'm sure Henry would try to do something for them, but can he really afford to build houses for each of the boys if they decide to find wives? And Charlie would still be just a ranch hand."

Mina bit her lip. She was only thinking of Charlie's broken heart, but Susan was thinking ahead to Maria's future, as well she should. Life in the territories of the United States was difficult enough for women. Maria would need every advantage she could come up with.

"I shouldn't have encouraged Charlie to pursue her so heartily tonight," she whispered. "I had no idea that things had gone so far with George Coe. I really didn't."

Susan sighed as the men headed back to their instruments. "I think we're in for another round of dancing. Really, Mina. The next dance, you need to invite more women."

"I don't know more women in Lincoln County." She laughed.

"I'll introduce you to some at the next church sewing circle." Susan groaned. "I can't keep up with all these young boys. And Alex wants a few dances himself."

They danced, then partook of refreshments, then danced again, until the clock began to chime out the midnight hour. The boys slowed down the music, and they all sang Christmas carols like *Silent Night* and *God Rest Ye Merry Gentlemen*.

When the time came to depart, Mina, Henry, and the boys stood on the porch and waved farewell to all their guests in the cold, wintry night.

"That was the best Christmas party I ever been to," said Doc softly.

"That was the only Christmas party I ever had." Billy's voice was oddly incredulous as he said that, as if he'd just realized what he'd been missing all his life.

Charlie just sighed and looked up at the moon, a dreamy love-struck look on his face.

"Well, it was a dandy party, and one we'll have to repeat every year," Henry pronounced.

"Hear! Hear!" Mina chimed in. "To the annual Tunstall Christmas Party!"

But even as she said the words, foreboding filled her heart. Was this just the devil trying to ruin a beautiful evening, she wondered, or did it mean that some truly dark times were waiting just around the corner?

~~~~~

Mina and Henry rode into Lincoln a few days after Christmas. Henry and Alex needed to discuss business affairs, and Mina took every opportunity to visit with Susan. The dark-haired little lady was outspokenly candid, and Mina found within her a kindred spirit. They left the wagon at home and rode horseback this time, and Mina enjoyed the wind in her face as they galloped across the miles. By the time they slowed their horses to a walk at the edge of town, she felt rejuvenated by the combination of the brisk winter breeze and the rare warmth of the sun. It had been the perfect morning for a gallop across the desert.

"That was wonderful, Henry," she murmured.

"Yes," he said, frowning as they passed the Murphy & Dolan Mercantile and Bank. "Too bad we had to be coming into this viper's nest, isn't it?"

Mina spotted a dim shadow in the doorway, thin and indistinct. James Dolan. She still hadn't met him, but she strongly suspected that he would turn out to be the vampire in their midst. He didn't come out in the sunlight—or hadn't yet, that she'd seen. And he appeared to be avoiding an outright introduction, which she found odd, considering his partner, Lawrence Murphy had made a point of introducing himself to her as soon as she came to town. Mina suspected these men had intercepted all her telegrams to Henry and had been well-informed of her arrival. Something about this shadowy figure raised her hackles, and had since her first day in Lincoln.

Soon, Mr. Dolan, you and I are going to have to meet face to face, she thought grimly, wishing she had Sister Joan Phillippe's sword strapped around her waist. Of course, she was armed with a couple silver daggers and a small pistol loaded with silver bullets. But that sword was her favorite weapon when she had to deal with vampires. Too often they were able to dodge bullets, and daggers allowed them too close in proximity. The sword was deadly accurate and kept them at a comfortable distance while she safely dispatched them. Well, perhaps *more* safely. Dealing with
~~~~~

a vampire could never be considered 'safe'.

They dismounted at the McSween house and tied their houses to the hitching post. Alex came to the door.

"Don't leave them out front today, Henry," he said, his face creased in a frown. "Take them around to the barn. I think it might be safer."

Mina and Henry shared a startled gaze, then Henry nodded and did as he was bid. Alex ushered Mina into the cozy parlor and took her coat and scarf. Susan greeted her with a swift hug, her eyes reflecting her husband's pinched worry.

"I prayed you would come," Susan whispered.

Mina was bursting with curiosity, but she chatted about the ride over, the weather, the Christmas party, the boys, anything mundane, until Henry had dealt with the horses and joined them in the parlor.

"Mina, I think we need your wisdom." Susan paused and looked up at Alex for reassurance. He nodded for her to proceed.

"You see, it's Maria."

Mina felt cold inside.

"The day after the party she was supposed to come here, but she didn't show up. The next day, she appeared..." Susan hesitated. "But she was...different. She seemed listless, so unlike her usual happy self. I asked if she was all right, but she acted almost like she didn't hear me. Then she became weak and almost keeled over while she was washing some dishes. I guided her to a chair and tried to give her some tea, but she turned away from it. It was her favorite tea!"

"Did she stay here?" Mina asked.

"No, she went home," Alex said. "But later that night, George Coe showed up here with Maria in his arms. She was unconscious. He said he had come to see her and her father had thrown her out of the house. Said she was cursed, the pawn of the devil or something like that. He said the old man was raving in Spanish, and he could only catch about half of what the man was saying, but he was clearly scared of his own daughter. George was angry at the old man, but he was also scared for Maria. He said he couldn't take her home with him or her reputation would be ruined. Besides, he felt she needed a doctor's care here in town. He begged us to help. Even said he'd pay all her doctor bills himself."

"So, she's here now?"

"Yes," Susan said. "We have her upstairs. Will you look at her?"

"You know what I'm going to find, don't you?"

Alex and Susan glanced at one another before turning back to Mina. "Yes, we do."

"She has the marks on her throat?"

They nodded.

"Has she gone out at night? Tried to leave?"

Alex shook his head. "You don't understand, Mina. Maria can't leave. She can't move. She has fallen asleep, and we can't wake her up."

~~~~~

Mina stared down at the lovely girl on the bed. Her dark hair was neatly brushed and braided and framed a face that had gone from a healthy glowing light brown to deathly pale. The holes in her neck over her carotid artery glared at Mina. The girl lay perfectly still except for the soft rise and fall of her chest, which proved some portion of her still lived. Mina felt her wrist for a pulse, as Professor Van Helsing had taught her. Weak, but there.

"Don't leave us, Maria," Mina whispered. "We'll find a way to bring you back."

"Doc Walter has been to see her already, but I'll get him back over here if you want to talk to him." Susan's voice was low and she watched as Mina examined the girl.

"I do," Mina said. "Did he have an opinion?"

Alex left to fetch the doctor.

"He's baffled," Susan stated. "We told him you might have some ideas though."

Mina smirked. "How did he take that? A woman telling him how to treat a patient! Most doctors of my acquaintance are not open to suggestions."

Susan squeezed her shoulder. "He wants to help, Mina. He's a crusty old country doctor, but he's faced with something beyond his understanding. If you've seen something like this in London, he'll listen. We more or less hinted that you'd seen similar cases in the church hospital you were connected with. We did a little name-dropping with the Order of the Sisters of the Maid working out of White Chapel. He hadn't heard of them, but it sounded impressive."

Mina glanced up sharply at Susan and saw the twinkle in her gaze. The women shared a moment of soft giggles before turning their attention back to their patient.

"I bet it did," Mina murmured. "Well, let's see if he can keep an open mind. This is one case history he'll never forget."

They heard the front door open and close, then footsteps on the staircase. Doc Walter was a gray-haired, stooped man. Behind his gruff exterior, Mina sensed a kind heart, and she instinctively liked and trusted him from the start. She listened intently as he rattled off his findings on his initial exam, but smothered a smile as she realized that he was testing her knowledge with this clinical rundown as well. He was determining if the McSweens had overstated her credentials in hospital work. To her credit, she followed his summary fairly well, having been coached and trained by the great Van Helsing in the treatment of vampire victims.
~~~~~

"Tell me, Dr. Walter, have you had any other cases of sudden death in this area over the past several months? Even the last few years. Cases where you've seen similar blood loss without catastrophic injury? Weakness, then death within days?"

Dr. Walter frowned. She saw the denial hover on his lips, then instances danced in his eyes. Doubt flickered. His gaze sharpened. He looked down at the girl on the bed, then back at Mina.

"All right, young lady," he said brusquely. "You have my attention. Tell me your story."

"Perhaps over tea in the parlor," Susan suggested.

"No, I think not," Dr. Walter said emphatically. "I want to remain right here in this room with the patient. If Mrs. Harker needs to show me anything to back up her diagnosis with this patient, I don't want to have to traipse up and down those steps."

"Then I'll bring the tea up here," Susan said. "I've heard the story, so go ahead without me. I'll be back shortly." She disappeared from the room with a smile.

Mina spent hours with the doctor, relating everything, from her own experience with Dracula and Van Helsing's work to keep her from that final change, to her training with Father Gregory, and their battle for Henry's beloved Betsy, then the death of her own husband at the hands of the vampire Frederick Von Bardenburg.

"I've seen victories and I've seen losses, Dr. Walter," she said simply. "I will admit I have never seen one fall asleep like this. They usually thrash around, and they fight to leave their beds when the one who bit them 'calls' to them. It's almost always a call to their death eventually, but the draining is either a gradual process or it's done all at once."

"Then if she wakes up, will she become one of these … vampire creatures?" he asked.

"Only if he convinced her to drink his blood as well."

Dr. Walter grimaced. "Revolting thought."

"Yes, but they are very seductive and powerful. At the time, everything they suggest makes the utmost sense. Maria comes from a very religious background, though," she continued thoughtfully. "I strongly suspect she was attacked, set upon, and it was a deliberate stab at both George Coe and Charlie Bowdrie, who are in love with her. Both men are connected to Henry by allegiance. This was a way to hurt them. I doubt she was enticed. I think it was simple brutality, but they took too much at once and left her far too weak to continue functioning."

"I'm not saying I believe all this, Mrs. Harker," the old man sighed. "It's all just a little bit too much like a dime novel for my taste. But if I were to accept that what you say is true, what would you suggest I do for this poor girl? Because I have no clue."

"The first thing I would suggest is blood transfusions. Have you done them before?"

"I've seen them done, but it's not something we do out here much. I patch 'em up and send them on their way. I suppose I could try it in a pinch." He looked at Maria uncertainly.

"I've assisted Professor Van Helsing with hundreds of them," Mina assured him. "I would be honored to assist you, if you would allow me. Diseases of the blood is a specialty of the professor's, and he worked with me at the hospital in White Chapel. We used blood transfusions as the first treatment for most of our patients who came in with bites like these." She pointed to Maria's neck.

Dr. Walter nodded. "Tell me what you need."

Mina smiled grimly. "Actually, I have most of the proper equipment with me, Doctor. You see, I came prepared. I'll have to ride back out to the ranch for my kit, but I can be back in a couple of hours."

Henry stepped forward. "Maybe you should bring some of the boys back with you, Mina." He swallowed hard. "I remember how many men it took to give transfusions to my Betsy when…" His voice broke off. Mina patted his arm. She knew this had to be bringing back horribly painful memories—memories Henry had left London, left England, to escape.

"I will, Henry," she said.

"Won't you and Alex do?" Dr. Walter asked.

"No," Mina said. "Not nearly enough." She turned to Susan and Alex. "And we might be here for a few days. I'm sorry to burden you."

"No!" Alex protested. "You can stay. As many as necessary. Just help this girl, Miss Mina. We'll manage."

"I'll put on some stew," Susan said.

"Plenty of red meat, Susan," Mina said, stopping her abruptly.

Susan's jaw dropped for a moment, then she nodded. "A beef roast then." She hurried from the room.

Henry turned to Alex. "We should ask John Chisum if he can spare us some beef. If you're going to be feeding several of us for a few days, you may need some provisions of meat. And Mina is right. The men will need the red meat to replenish their own blood and give them strength back."

Alex started to protest, but Henry cut him off. "He's a partner in this too. He won't want to be left out and you know it. Besides, he has more than enough cattle and will be least hurt by the slaughter of one."

Alex nodded. Henry took Mina by the arm and they headed for the stairs. "I'll help you saddle your horse. Make sure one of the boys goes to Chisum with this news. I'll write out a message for you to send."

"I'll send Billy," she said. When she saw surprise in Henry's face, she added, "We can't risk using his blood. We don't know what part of the wolf might be passed to Maria. I don't want to take that chance any more than I can give her my own blood. This way, Billy will have a job to do. You know he'll need that. Then I'm going to send him out to fetch George Coe too."

"I'm here, ma'am," said a soft voice from the parlor. Mina turned and found George standing by the fireplace, twisting his hat in his callused hands.

Mina smiled at him warmly and crossed the room to take his rough hand in her own. "I'm glad you're here, George. Can you stay?"

"Yes, ma'am. Long as Maria needs me. Is she doin' any better?"

"No, George, I'm afraid not. But we're going to be working on that. You're going to have to trust me."

George searched her face for a moment, his gaze seeking something in her to trust, something to believe in. Evidently he found it, because he nodded and gripped her hand firmly.

"Yes, ma'am."

~~~~~

Mina returned several hours later, her saddlebags packed with the instruments Van Helsing had given her before she left London, hoping she would never need them. Jim, Charlie, and Chavez accompanied her. The others wanted to come too, but somebody had to take care of the ranch. Dick kept Doc, Billy, and Robert behind for the moment. At all costs, Dick had to keep the ranch running in Henry's absence. Billy was dispatched to Chisum with Henry's message, and Mina knew they would have his ranch hands if needed as well. But how much blood would it take to wake Maria up? Was that all it would take? This sleep was so unnatural, she wasn't sure they would be able to bring Maria out of it at all.

As she and the boys rode into Lincoln, Lawrence Murphy strode into the street to greet her, his hat in his hands. She reined in her horse, irritated to be waylaid by this snake of a man. His hair was oiled back, and his eyes shone with a malicious delight that told her he knew more about the situation than he should.

"Well, well, well, Mrs. Harker!" His voice seemed jovial, but carried a bite to it that hadn't been in her initial encounter with him last summer. "Tired of life on the ranch? Ready to move into civilization now?" He laughed, but it rang false to her ears, and she bristled.

"I'm busy, Mr. Murphy," she said brusquely. "I apologize, but I don't have time to waste, bandying words in the street today."

"Well, you're not the only visitor coming to our fair town. I have friends in Europe too, you know. And I've got someone coming who's just dying to meet you." He laughed again, but his eyes were hard as rocks. Mina stiffened in the saddle. She felt the boys reacting to his veiled threats too. Only Chavez remained calm.
~~~~~

God bless Chavez, she thought. *If only we could all be that stoic in the face of this beast.*

"Well, for today, I have pressing business. Please step aside, Mr. Murphy." Mina kept her voice low and even, but ice chilled her tone as she nudged her horse forward.

"Oh, sure, sure, Mrs. Harker," Murphy said, sweeping his hat back up on his head. "But you're going to just love my friend. He's a real prince of a fellow." He laughed. "Yeah, a real prince. Might be just what you need, you know." His laughter followed her down the street.

"What's he laughin' 'bout, Miss Mina?" whispered Fred. "I don't see nothin' so funny."

"Neither do I, Fred," she murmured, frowning. *There's a private joke in there somewhere. I only hope I can figure it out – before it lands on my head.*

"He's up to something evil," Chavez muttered, pulling up closely on her other side. "And whatever it is, he knows exactly why we are here."

"I believe you're right, my friend," she said softly. "Which is why we must be on our guard every minute."

The boys all nodded, their eyes fixed firmly on the McSween house before them. They would not give Lawrence G. Murphy the satisfaction of a backward glance.

~~~~~

For the next three days, Mina and Doc Walter worked tirelessly to save Maria. They started with George, Chavez, Fred, and Charlie. After Maria had received transfusions from all four men, they waited to see what effect the treatment would have. But other than a slightly better pulse rate, nothing happened. Maria did not wake up.

George wasn't happy to see Charlie at first, but as Maria's condition remained serious, he became less concerned with petty jealousy. In fact, the two men found comfort in each other as they watched and waited for her to improve. Mina dove into her Bible, hoping for some word that would provide inspiration.

And she rarely left Maria's room.

Something about Lawrence Murphy's words bothered her. He was hinting, but what did he mean? She knew he had to have invited a vampire to New Mexico; that much was certain.

"How is she?" Henry's voice jolted her so much, she dropped her Bible. "Oh, my dear Mina. I'm so sorry. I didn't mean to startle you so."

She reached down to retrieve her Bible, her heart hammering. She hadn't realized just how tightly she was wound.

"I really must get some rest. You shouldn't have been able to sneak up on me like that."

"Mina, I didn't sneak up, my dear. I walked up the stairs normally. You were completely lost in thought." He laid a gentle hand on her
~~~~~

shoulder and squeezed. "But you do need to rest. Why don't you go catch a nap? I'll stay with Maria. I know what to watch for, and I'll be sure to sound the alarm if she stirs."

"I don't know if I can sleep, Henry," Mina confessed. "I feel so… agitated. Something is coming. I don't know how to put it into words, but I feel something in the air."

"Well, if it will ease your mind at all, Billy is downstairs. He said he felt something very similar to what you just described, so he's guarding the house. I think you can relax for at least a couple of hours."

Susan entered the room in time to hear Henry's words, a steaming cup in her hand. "Henry is absolutely right, Mina. You need to rest. You've been up for days now. Drink this and come lay down in our room."

"If I drink tea, I'll be wide awake," Mina protested.

"It's chamomile tea," Susan replied, "so no, you won't. It will help you rest. Come now. I insist. We'll all be especially vigilant while you get some sleep. You'll think better once you've rested."

Mina surrendered, drank her tea, and allowed Susan to tuck her into their soft down-filled bed. She was asleep in minutes.

"Once upon a time, there was a king and queen in a far away land, and they wanted a child so very much."

"Is this the story of Sleeping Beauty, Papa?" Mina asked. "That's my favorite story."

"I know it is, my dear. Do you want to tell it to me tonight?" Her father's smile was gentle. "You must know it very well by now."

"No, you tell it, Papa," she begged.

"Very well," he said, tucking the blankets around her small body. The words of the story swirled indistinctly into a foggy mist. Mina strained to hear the story, to see her child-self and her father through the mist, but it was fading.

The rattle of a stagecoach and the hoof beats of horses jangled into her dream. The stranger from London stepped down from the coach, his top hat dusty, and sunlight glinting off his tinted sunglasses. The vampire. Mina tried to lunge at him, but he stepped toward Murphy and they both turned to laugh at her.

Mist swirled around them and Mina fell into blissful darkness.

~~~~~

Mina bolted straight up in bed, her eyes searching the deepening shadows. The sun dipped to the edge of the horizon, and she could barely make out a rim of light from the window.

"I've slept for hours," she murmured, brushing her hair away from her face. She slipped from the covers and stopped long enough to smooth the bed linens, thankful for the comfort of the McSweens' bed for the much-needed rest. The aroma of roasting beef wafted up the stairwell to her, and her stomach rumbled. "First things first," she told herself sharply. She headed for the guest room to check on Maria. George sat beside Maria,
~~~~~

his head bowed and his hands folded. Charlie stood watch by the window, leaning on his rifle. His gaze roved the street restlessly, searching the shadows. Henry sat in a wing-back chair, calmly reading Mina's Bible. He looked up when she entered the room and smiled warmly.

"You look much better," he observed.

"Thank you." She grinned at him. "Don't look so smug, Henry Tunstall. You could do with a nice long rest too."

He chuckled, but they both sobered when they gazed at the silent figure on the bed.

"No change?" Mina asked.

"None." Henry sighed. "Should we consider another round of transfusions yet?"

She thought for a moment. "You and Alex gave blood yesterday, the boys two days before that. If she doesn't stir by tomorrow, we might need to try again tomorrow," she said, biting her lip. "Her color is good, and her pulse has been better." She stepped up beside George and took Maria's delicate little wrist between her thumb and forefinger. She nodded. "Much stronger. I don't know that more blood is what she needs. The problem is I don't know what else to do. I've never seen anyone react this way before."

Fred burst into the room. "Miss Mina! I think you better come downstairs."

Henry was on his feet and moving, as Mina headed for the door. "What is it, Fred?" she asked.

"Billy's been out scoutin' in town, and he's back with some news. The stage arrived while you was sleepin' and some strangers got off. Billy's been tryin' to find out more about 'em. He wants to talk to you right away."

Mina's dream tickled at the back of her mind, but she pushed it away. Time enough to try to interpret dreams later. For now, she wanted facts.

Billy paced in front of the fireplace in the parlor, his face puckered in a frown. It cleared only a little when he saw Mina and Henry enter the room.

"What's happened, Billy?" Mina asked. "Tell me everything."

"Well, Miss Mina, I seen two men step out of the stage and Murphy was right there to greet 'em like they was long-lost kin. He was really bowin' and scrapin' too."

"What did they look like?" she asked.

Billy's face scrunched up. "Well'm, one was tall and real dandy-like. Wore a top hat, but not wore out like mine. His is all shiny and new. And he had this fancy scarf around his neck, and these funny little tinted glasses."

Mina felt her knees give way. *No, it can't be! It can't be the vampire from*

London! They had never learned his name, but he had followed Mina, hounded her steps like a scent dog. He had killed practically on her doorstep. What would he be doing here?

"Miss Mina?" Billy was kneeling in front of her, and Mina discovered she was sitting on the sofa. She shook her head as though to clear her thoughts.

"Go on, Billy," she ordered, taking a shaky breath. "What else?"

"Well, this other fella', he looked like he might be the big boss of the two of 'em. He wore a real fancy suit with one of them cravats and a shiny doo-dad holdin' it in place, like a diamond or something. Murphy swept off his hat and practically bowed to the guy! Right in the street. I managed to get fairly close to them by sidling around behind the bank, and I heard the top hat guy call the other one 'your majesty'. That mean he's a king or something?"

"He's a real prince of a fellow," Mina whispered. "Murphy wasn't kidding! He was hinting. But why? Why show his hand to me? Lord, show me what I'm missing."

"That ain't all, ma'am," Billy said, drawing her attention back to his story. "There was this other guy who rode in on the box with the driver. I didn't even notice him at first. He sort o' slipped off while Murphy was kowtowing to these two fellers. So I headed over to the hotel to check up on him. I heard him tell ol' Bob Gibbs that his name was John Smith, but he hesitated over the last name. Ma'am, he was lying."

"Are you sure, Billy?" Mina asked, frowning at the young man.

"The wolf knows when someone lies, Miss Mina. He was lying." Billy almost spat the last word.

Mina patted his arm. "I believe you. Tell me what he looked like."

"I couldn't get a good look, ma'am. He seemed to know I was there. I had to keep ducking out of sight. But he was sort of medium build, and he talked with an accent, but not like you and Mr. Tunstall do. More southern-like. He had tinted glasses, but I don't think he was a vampire." Billy's expression grew confused.

"Why not?" Mina asked.

"He smelled… different," Billy said. "Sort of sickly. I can't explain it, but I think he might be human. You think he's in the process of turnin'?"

Mina considered that. "Maybe. We'll watch for him. We'll watch them all." She stood and turned as they heard Susan announce that supper was ready. "They're up to something. I just don't know —" Mina staggered as her dream hit her full force. Henry caught her arm.

"Mina, what is it?"

"I dreamed… I remembered… No, it can't be—"

Henry held her arms and spoke softly. "Just tell us, Mina, and we'll help you sort it out."

Susan and Alex entered the parlor and froze.

"I dreamed of my father. I was a little girl and he was telling me a bedtime story, my favorite one." Mina took a ragged breath and stared into Henry's deep brown eyes. "It was the story of Sleeping Beauty." She heard Susan's sharp gasp and felt Henry's grip tighten. "When we came into town and Murphy stopped us in the street," she swallowed hard, "he said that he had a guest coming from Europe. That he was a real prince of a fellow. Just what we might need. And he laughed. We couldn't figure out what was so funny."

Henry's face went white. "Dear Lord."

Alex murmured, "A prince to awaken a sleeping beauty? No, it can't be! You can't be serious!"

"But he won't just wake her up," Billy said. "He'll kill her, won't he? Ain't that what he means to do?"

"He may intend that, Billy," Henry said, "but we're not going to let him get away with it. Not this time."

Mina looked up to see the smoldering anger in Henry's gaze. *He's remembering Betsy*, she thought. *Not again, Lord. Please, not again.*

~~~~~

Dinner was subdued, each of them deep in their own thoughts. Billy ate little, then slipped out to patrol around the house. Mina excused herself and stepped out for some fresh air too. Hearing footsteps around the corner behind the store, she headed in that direction, expecting to find Billy. A shadow loomed to her left and reached for her arm. She smelled the scent of death, giving her only seconds to reach for the knife up her sleeve.

"Someone wants to see you—" The voice cut off as the figure disappeared in a puff of ash. The hand on her arm disappeared, and a silver blade dropped to the ground at her feet. Another figure cursed and grabbed her from behind, but she was ready with her own blade this time. She stabbed backward and heard another curse, as she whirled away from the arm that had jerked away in pain. When she slashed across the throat of the man behind her, he vanished in a rain of ash. Another figure darted from the doorway of the mercantile just as a gray wolf charged down the alley. Another dagger flew from the opposite alley, catching the attacker in the eye. The vampire shrieked and tore the blade away. Mina lunged forward and plunged her own blade into his chest and he, too, turned to ash.

A familiar voice rose from the shadows a few feet away. "Why is it, Miss Mina Harker, that I always seem to meet you in dark alleys in such distressing company?" The southern inflection was unmistakable. She had heard that voice before in an alley in Denver on her way to Lincoln, and they had fought off vampires together that night too.
~~~~~

"Doc? Doc Holliday?"

A wet, hacking cough spilled into the night air, then the voice responded as the figure emerged from the shadows. "Why, none other, Miss Mina. It's good to see you looking so well."

The wolf skidded to a halt, and Mina stepped forward. "No, Billy! No! He's a friend." She looked up. The moon shone bright and full. *Of all nights...* She heard a whimper. "It's all right. We'll see you in the morning."

"You do keep the most interesting company, Miss Mina," Doc said with a sardonic grin.

"Come with me, Doc," she said. "We've got a very strange situation, and it's obviously not going to be safe out here tonight."

"I gather someone wants to talk to you that you'd rather not meet with."

"That's understating it, Doc. I don't want to attend that meeting without my sword and a lot of holy water in my hands. And I don't intend to take prisoners."

"Indeed!" He smirked. "That much is obvious." He looked around at the ash swirling at their feet, mixing with the melted snow, and raised his eyebrows in that sardonic way so characteristic of Doc Holliday. "Sounds like my kind of party."

They slipped back to the house, where Mina introduced Doc to Alex and Susan, as well as Fred and Charlie, who were still sitting at the dinner table. Susan offered Doc a plate, which he graciously accepted. While he regaled them with the tale of his meeting with Mina in Denver, she went upstairs to Maria's room where Henry and George were still holding vigil.

"Where's Chavez?" Mina asked, realizing he was the one person unaccounted for.

"Keeping an eye out for Billy, I believe," Henry said. "Full moon." He nodded toward the window.

"Yes, I know. I had to call Billy off just a bit ago. But I didn't see Chavez."

Henry frowned. "Did you have a problem? Mina, you've really got to stop running off on your own."

She chuckled. "Well, it was worth it in more ways than one. We have an ally that I didn't count on." She filled them in on her meeting with Doc Holliday.

"*The* Doc Holliday is *here*?" George's eyes were as big as silver dollars. "Holy smokes!"

"The disturbing part of this is the fact that someone was sent to fetch me for a meeting tonight—with or without my consent." Mina paced. "I was well equipped to handle the situation, but Doc dealt with the first vampire before I even had a blade out. His appearance was welcome, under the circumstances. But I'm wondering if God has another purpose for bringing him here. Perhaps he can help us with Maria."

"Ain't he a doctor? Could he help?" George asked.

"Actually, he's a dentist," Mina said apologetically, watching the man's face fall. "I rather doubt he'll be of much medical help. But if we could awaken Maria, maybe Doc could get her out of Lincoln and away from danger."

Henry pondered this thoughtfully. "I've been reading your Bible, Mina. I hope you don't mind." She shook her head. "I found these verses in the Song of Solomon and I've been thinking about them. 'I adjure you, O daughters of Jerusalem, by the gazelles or by the hinds of the field, that you will not arouse or awaken my love until she pleases. Listen! My beloved! Behold He is coming, climbing on the mountains, leaping on the hills!'"

"What's that mean, Mr. Tunstall?" George asked, scratching his head.

"Well, George, the Song of Solomon was a love story, written to God's people, expressing His love for His people much like the love of a groom for his bride. I suppose I was struck by the phrase 'awaken' in this case because of Maria's deep sleep. But this next verse says that the One who loves her is coming, in spite of all obstacles."

"But I'm the one who loves her, Mr. Tunstall," George insisted, tears welling up in the corners of his eyes.

"Yes, I realize that, George," Henry said gently. "But as much as you love her, God loves her even more. As He loves us all. Do you see? He wants to save Maria from destruction just as much as you do. More even, because He wants to save not only her body, but also her soul."

"So Murphy and his friends want us to believe that they can awaken her, that they have the answers to helping her," Mina said slowly. "But it's all a lie. They'll only bring her death and destruction. Redemption from the Lord is the way to awaken Maria, and the only way to save her life. But *how*?"

"You mentioned holy water, Miss Mina," Doc Holliday said from the doorway. They turned to see him leaning against the frame. "Have you tried that? Anointing with holy water? I am hardly a religious man, but I was raised by a very saintly mother."

"Holy smokes," George whispered.

Mina's smile slowly widened. "You may not be a religious man, Doc, but I do believe you have been sent to us for this very moment." She introduced Henry and George to Doc then turned to rifle in her bags for a vial of holy water. Bending over the sleeping girl, she anointed Maria with the fluid and prayed silently for a few moments. Then aloud, she prayed, "The prince of darkness seeks to claim her for his own, but we believe Maria's soul belongs to You. So, Lord, we ask You to be the Prince Who awakens Maria. Be the Prince Who saves her from the evil in this town. We entrust her life into Your hands. For You are the Prince of Peace, and our Redeemer. Awaken and arise, Maria, in the name of our Lord Jesus Christ."

They waited and nothing happened.

Mina looked at Henry, then Doc. She'd rarely felt so helpless.

Henry stared at George Coe, his shoulders slumped in defeat, his big, callused hands tenderly cradling Maria's little hands. "Mina, I think this may be up to George instead of you."

George's head shot up. "Mr. Tunstall, I ain't no prince! I can't wake Maria up like in no fairy tale, or even like in the Bible."

"No, George, but you love Maria," Henry explained. "I think perhaps you're going to have to give her up to God and ask the Lord to take care of her until this battle is fought and won. But that's a hard thing I'm saying, George. Can you do it? Can you give Maria up to God, not knowing if He'll ever bring her back into your life again? There are no guarantees, you know. Can you love her enough to let her go if it means restoring her to health?"

George's Adam's apple bobbed up and down, and a tear streaked down his cheek. He didn't answer right away, but bowed his head for several minutes, just holding her hand in his. When he finally looked up again, he nodded. "I'm ready."

"You'll have to say the prayer, George," Mina said, "but we'll be right here with you. Just speak from your heart. There are no set words to say. Just tell God you're giving Maria to Him and trusting Him to take care of her, whatever He chooses to do."

George nodded. He took a shuddering breath. "God, You know I ain't much on praying, but I love Maria. I love her more than I ever loved anyone before in my life. If giving her to You will save her life, then that's what I'm willin' to do. Will You please save her life and her soul and keep her away from them folks that want to hurt her? Even if I never get her back again, I want her to live and be happy and safe. Will You please wake her up and get her away from here? Mr. Tunstall says You love her more than I do. If that's so, then I reckon You can take better care of her than I can. And I'll trust You to do that. Be her real Prince, Lord. Amen."

They waited, almost holding their breaths collectively. Maria took a deep breath and sighed. She turned her head on the pillow and moaned softly. A moment passed, then slowly, slowly, her eyes opened and she smiled up at George, who burst into tears. Mina slumped as the tension melted from her body, and Henry came up beside her to press one arm around her shoulders tightly. She leaned her head against his shoulder. They'd won!

Now to get Maria out of Lincoln.

She looked over at Doc and saw him raise his hip flask in her direction in a silent toast. Still drinking. But God bless him! *If God can use the jawbone of an ass, He can still use Doc Holliday*, she thought ruefully.

~~~~~

"Where could you take her?" George asked.

Maria wolfed down another bite of Susan's roast. Though her bites were dainty, she was on her second plate and her color steadily improved. She could tell them nothing of the attack or the days after it. She remembered nothing after the Christmas party.

"A mercy," Susan murmured to Mina.

Doc opened his mouth to answer, then frowned. "Perhaps it's better if you don't know where we're going. You can't be forced to tell what you don't know, George Coe."

George's chin jutted out belligerently, but Henry laid a hand on his arm.

"He's right, George," Henry added.

"George, you don't realize what you're up against," Mina added. "These creatures can be very coercive. If they ever got hold of you, they could force you to divulge details that you would never mean to tell them. You might not even remember later what you'd told them. Maria will be safer the less any of us know. Doc and I will manage to keep in touch. Once this is all over, we can see about meeting up again."

George and Maria gazed into each other's eyes and finally nodded their assent to the plan.

"The sun will be up in about an hour," Alex observed. "Do you want to wait until sunset tonight?"

"I think we should go now, before they have time to regroup. They don't even realize Maria is awake yet. I'd like to get her away from here before they know we're gone." Doc's eyes were alert as he watched from behind Susan's drawn curtains.

Maria hugged them each in turn, lingering the longest with George. She was moving slowly and a bit shakily but appeared to be regaining her strength. Doc turned to Chavez, who had returned about an hour after Maria's awakening. While they were dealing with the three vampires in the alley, Chavez had taken out two more waiting behind the bank. By the time he had caught up to Billy, Doc and Mina had returned to the house.

"Can you get my horse from the town stable without getting caught?"

"I can." He nodded tersely.

He slipped out silently. When he returned a bit later, he told them flatly that the enemy had two less foot soldiers. Obviously stationed at the stables in case they tried to depart.

"Thank you, son," Doc said with a smile. "I'm sure that will be most
~~~~~

helpful as we leave town."

"You can say thank you to a certain gray wolf, if you see him," Chavez said with a straight face. "His name is Billy."

"You don't say?" Doc said, his eyebrows raised as he glanced at Mina. "A wolf named Billy? How … interesting."

Mina smothered a grin. "He's going to be very annoyed at not getting to meet you, Doc. He's a great admirer of yours."

"You do meet the most fascinating people, Mina Harker. How do you do it?"

"You're one to talk, Doc," she said, giving him a swift kiss on the cheek. "I don't know how you managed to show up when you did. But I owe you."

"You never know, Miss Mina. One day, I may just call on you to collect." Doc Holliday swept up his hat.

"What about your gear at the hotel, Doc?" Alex asked. "We can hold it here and you can let us know where to send it, but I'm not sure Bob Gibbs will let me have your valise without your consent."

"There is nothing in my valise that I need, Mr. McSween. As Miss Mina can tell you, I travel light." With a quicksilver smile, Doc whisked a dark cloak around Maria's shoulders and they disappeared into the night.

As the hoof beats faded, they heard a wolf howl mournfully.

"Billy is not happy," Chavez murmured.

END

MEET THE AUTHORS

Kathleen Bird is the author of the *Adven Trilogy*, a Christian fantasy series, and the *Isles of Miadhra*, a series of steampunk fairytale retellings. You can also find her writings included in anthologies such as *Tales from the Tower*, *Finding God in Anime: Vol. 2*, *Wither & Bloom*, *Cadence Writing Fantasy Anthology: Vol. 1*, and *Hope Amid the Darkness*. She loves traveling and seeing new places, which give her inspiration for her writing; but when she and her husband are not traveling the world, they live in Des Moines, IA. Be sure to check out her website (*www.adventrilogy.wordpress.com*) and her Instagram (*@birdsthewords*) for more information about her books and where to find them.

Rosemarie DiCristo isn't sure which came first—her love of reading, or her love of writing. She just knows she's been telling stories forever, trying to create for others just a touch of the magic and delight she's gotten from the books, movies, tv shows, and plays she's loved. She's published dozens of stories for children and teens (alas, most of the magazines, like *Pockets* and *Encounter*, no longer exist). More recently she's published flash fiction in *Havok* and now, this story in *Perchance to Dream*. She's currently polishing a middle-grade mystery involving shelter dogs, counterfeit Rolexes, menacing villains, and bickering tween brothers whose six-foot-five bodyguard is a pacifist and coward.

Christy Eberling lives in Ohio with her husband and their spoiled Rottie-poo (also sometimes called a Rottle). Her son, and two bonus kids, are adults now. When not writing, Christy works as a substitute teacher. She enjoys fishing, boating, motorcycle rides with family and friends, couples-country-line-dancing, and taking her dog on walks or to Flyball. Her bachelor's degree, and associate degree, are both from Kent State University. She's a member of the Great Lakes Fiction Writers. Christy invites readers to like and follow her reader page, Christy's Creative Companions, on Facebook. She loves to hear from readers and can be reached by email at *christyeberling4@gmail.com*.

Kaitlyn Emery started her career at a young age, winning a multi-district school writing project in the wake of 9/11 to help kids cope with the state of the world around them. Her writing journey was based in the harsh truth that reality was darker than fiction. That theme would become an anthem in her life, following her into adulthood where she channeled her talents to give a voice to the hurting and voiceless, focusing on broken characters people could identify with and often incorporating her love of fantasy to accomplish that goal. Kaitlyn has been featured in various magazines, flash fiction for Havok Publishing, and had stories published in several anthologies including *Rebirth, Sensational, Prismatic, Casting Call, Animal Kingdom, When Your Beauty is the Beast, Tales from the Tower, Moonlight and Claws, Who's The Monster, The Depths We'll Go To, The Heights We'll Fly To, Aphotic Love, Fool's Honor, Sharper Than Thorns, Wither and Bloom, Masquerade*, and *A Sky of Tragic Moons* releasing Spring 2023. For more information, you can visit her website at *Kaitlyn-Emery.com* or follow her on Instagram under *@kaitlyn_scribbling* where she is addicted to getting the perfect bookstagram aesthetic!

Beka Gremikova writes folkloric fantasy from her little nook in the Ottawa Valley, Ontario, Canada. When she's not trekking across the globe, she plays video games, dabbles in art, or curls up in a cozy corner with a mystery novel. Her work can be found in various anthologies — including *Tales From the Tower, Equinox & Solstice, Fantasea*, and *Tide & Scale* — and her indie debut, *The Other Cinderella*, is now available in ebook and paperback from Amazon. Her first full-length book, a collection of fantasy and sci-fi tales currently codenamed Project Dragon, will release with SnowRidge Press in Fall 2023. To keep up with all her writing mayhem, you can sign up for her newsletter at *bekagremikova.com*, follow her on Instagram *@beka.gremikova*, or join her reader group, "Beka's Books," on Facebook.

Pam Halter is a children's book author and editor. Her picture book series, *Willoughby and Friends* (Fruitbearer Publishing,) have won Purple Dragonfly awards and a Realm Award. Her YA fantasy, *Fairyeater* (Love2ReadLove2Write Publishing), also won a Purple Dragonfly. Her short stories appear in several anthologies, including the *Whitstead* books and *Realmscapes*, as well as Ye Olde Dragon Books. Pam lives in South Jersey where she enjoys writing, gardening, cooking, quilting and playing the piano. She enjoys walking on long country roads where she finds fairy homes, emerging dragons, and trees eating wood gnomes, but she's never encountered her Dream Host. She's not sure she wants to. Learn more about her at *www.pamhalter.com*

Michelle Houston loves creating new worlds and civilizations and occasionally getting them on paper. She is a Christian, wife, mother, teacher, and scientist, who strives to connect young adults with the wonders found around us. She spends her free time reading everything in sight, going outside as much as possible (to the relief of the dust bunnies inside), trying new recipes and of course, writing. Her previous works can be found in the anthologies *Moonlight and Claws*, *Tales from the Tower*, and *Adventuring Together: A Flash Fiction Anthology Season Three*.

Hailey Huntington loves adventures, and she's always ready for another one—whether it's discovering Narnia, traveling across Middle Earth, hiking a mountain in Iceland, or simply going on a walk with her family. Aside from adventures, Hailey also loves board games, music, ice cream, laughter, witty characters, fantasy, emojis, and Jesus—though not in that order. She's had numerous flash fiction stories published, and her work can also be found in select anthologies, such as *Casting Call* and *Animal Kingdom* by Havok Publishing and *Wither and Bloom* by Twenty Hills Publishing.

On the road to publication, **Michelle Levigne** fell into fandom in college and has stories in various SF and fantasy universes' fanzines. She has a bunch of useless degrees in theater, English, film/communication, and writing. Even worse, she has dozens of books and novellas with multiple small presses, in science fiction and fantasy, YA, suspense, women's fiction, and sub-genres of romance. Her training includes the Institute for Children's Literature; proofreading at an advertising agency; and working at a community newspaper. She is a tea snob and freelance edits for a living. (*MichelleLevigne@gmail.com* for info/rates), but only enough to give her time to write. Her crimes against the literary world include co-managing editor at Mt. Zion Ridge Press, launching Ye Olde Dragon Books, and the storytelling podcast, Ye Olde Dragon's Library. Be afraid… be very afraid. Despite that, please visit her websites: *Mlevigne.com* and *YeOldeDragonBooks.com*.

Laurie Lucking loves books, music, and spending time with her family in beautiful Minnesota. A recovering attorney, she now spends her days chasing her active one-year-old, answering hundreds of questions for her preschooler, and struggling through her sons' math homework (plus a little cooking and cleaning when absolutely necessary). When she finds a spare moment, she writes young adult romantic fantasy inspired by fairy tales. Laurie's novels *Common* and *Traitor* were finalists in the Carol Awards and winners of the Excellence in Editing Award. Her short stories have been published in *Deep Magic* e-zine, *Brio* magazine, and a number of anthologies. She enjoys connecting with readers through her website, *www.laurielucking.com*, and in the Facebook group she co-founded, Faith and Fairy Tales.

Jessica Noelle is a writer, reader, dreamer, and believer who believes that faith, hope, and a good story are some of the most powerful things there are; she loves Jesus, playing with her dog, and spending times with her family and friends. . . but she also loves large cups of piping hot tea and geeking out over books, Marvel, and more! You can find more of her work in Havok Publishing's *Animal Kingdom Anthology*, on Havok's website, and in Owl Hollow Press's *Change the World : All-Teen Anthology*. You can also find her gushing about her favorite things on her Instagram (@jessicanoellewrites) or on her website (*https://jessicanoellewrites.com*).

Stoney M. Setzer lives south of Atlanta, GA. He has a beautiful wife, three wonderful children, and one crazy dog, and he is also a diehard Atlanta Braves fan. He has written a trilogy of novels about small-town amateur sleuth Wesley Winter (*Dead of Winter*, *Valley of the Shadow*, and *Day of Reckoning*). He has also written a short story anthology *Zero Hour*, featuring Twilight Zone-like stories with Christian themes. Mr. Setzer is currently completing a novel featuring the fictional community of Sardis County, Tennessee, which is also the setting for his story in this anthology and has also figured into his previous contributions to the Ye Olde Dragons anthology. He hopes to have this novel completed and released later in 2023. Learn more at *www.tinniepress.blogspot.com* or on Facebook @stoneymsetzerofficial.

Deborah Cullins Smith has been writing stories ever since she could hold a pencil, but she came to her actual career in writing rather late in life. In 2019, she published the trilogy, *The Last of the Long-Haired Hippies*, in a rapid-release timed for the 50th anniversary of Woodstock, which she covered in great detail in the second volume. CWG Press released *Shroud of Darkness*, *The Birth of the Storm*, and *Victoria's War* over a four-month period, a culmination of almost twenty years in development. Ms. Cullins Smith's first Mina Harker adventure, *Mina: Warrior in the Shadows* won the 2022 Realm Award for Horror Novel. Her next novel will continue the saga of Billy the Kid, which she began in the anthology *Moonlight and Claws* with the story *Habitations of Violence*, and continued in *Who's the Monster?* with the story *Phillippe*. Her love of historical research makes these books challenging, as she is devoted to maintaining as much historical accuracy as possible while sliding things sideways to suggest that a few characters might be more than we gave them credit for! (No disrespect intended.)

Allison Tebo is a writer committed to creating magical stories full of larger-than-life characters, a dash of grit, and plenty of laughs. She is the author of the *Tales of Ambia*, a series of romantic comedy retellings of fairy tales, and Realm Makers Reader's Choice finalist *The Goblin and the Dancer*. Her short stories have been published in *Splickety*, *Spark*, *Saddlebag Dispatches*, *Inklings Press*, *Rogue Blades Entertainment*, *Pole to Pole Publishing*, and *Editing Mee*. You can follow her on Instagram *@allisonteboauthor.com* or visit her at *www.allisonteboauthor.com*: she loves making new friends!

Meaghan Elizabeth Ward is an author and freelance illustrator with a passion for storytelling. She mainly writes high fantasy with low magic and loves drawing inspiration from world-wide cultures and myths. A companion story to *The Weight of Raven Feathers* can be found in the *Tales from the Tower* Anthology. Her flash fiction can also be read on Havok Publishing's website and in two of their anthologies: *Stories that Sing* and *Casting Call*. When not writing or reading, Meaghan can be found drawing her story-worlds, creating fanart, and daydreaming of what would happen if she stumbled into a fantasy world. You can find her on Instagram *@meaghaneward*.

Angela R. Watts is the bestselling and award-nominated author of The Infidel Books and the Remnant Trilogy. She's been writing stories since she was little, and has over 24 works in print, ranging from gritty adult novels to clean children's fiction. Some of her other titles include *A Solstice of Fire and Light*, *Winter of the Bees*, and *Where Giants Fall* (a fantasy anthology). Angela is a Christian, freelance editor (she's also a lead editor at Story-weavers Publishing), article writer for magazines and publishers, founder of Speculative Fiction Society, and artist. She lives in Tennessee with her family and many pets. You can get in touch with Angela and follow the journey on social media (*@angelarwattsauthor*) or subscribe to her newsletter at *angelarwatts.com*